FRIENDS ROMANCE

Can a man come between friends?

□ **A TASTE OF HONEY**

by DeWanna Pace   0-515-12387-0

□ **WHERE THE HEART IS**

by Sheridon Smythe   0-515-12412-5

□ **LONG WAY HOME**

by Wendy Corsi Staub   0-515-12440-0

All books $5.99

Bedazzled

CHRISTINE HOLDEN

JOVE BOOKS, NEW YORK

MAGICAL LOVE is a trademark of Penguin Putnam Inc.

BEDAZZLED

A Jove Book / published by arrangement with
the author

PRINTING HISTORY
Jove edition / March 2000

All rights reserved.
Copyright © 2000 by Leslie-Christine Megahey and
Shirley Holden-Ferdinand.
Cover illustration by Lisa Falkenstern.
This book may not be reproduced in whole or in part,
by mimeograph or any other means, without permission.
For information address: The Berkley Publishing Group,
a division of Penguin Putnam Inc.,
375 Hudson Street, New York, New York 10014.

The Penguin Putnam Inc. World Wide Web site address is
http://www.penguinputnam.com

ISBN: 0-515-12774-4

A JOVE BOOK®
Jove Books are published by The Berkley Publishing Group,
a division of Penguin Putnam Inc.,
375 Hudson Street, New York, New York 10014.
JOVE and the "J" design
are trademarks belonging to Penguin Putnam Inc.

PRINTED IN THE UNITED STATES OF AMERICA

10 9 8 7 6 5 4 3 2 1

Acknowledgments and Thanks

It always amazes us how many special people in our lives continue to support and encourage us. With them behind us, we find it much easier to exist in what can sometimes be a solitary life as we move forward in a business we love.

First and foremost, we thank God for His blessings. Without Him, we wouldn't be here.

We also thank Judith Palais, who took a chance with us. You've helped to make our dreams come true.

To Albert Aubry, for his generous gift that allowed us to finally realize our Web site.

To Top, our dear cousin, who showed his support by lending assistance when our world seemed upside-down.

To Eddie Boettner, for his willingness to offer ready advice and generous encouragement. Thanks, too, for sharing your contacts. And words cannot express our gratitude for the Canadian trip. You're in a class by yourself!

To C. J. Charbonnet, for your kind and encouraging words this past year, and always remembering us at holidays.

To Valencia Gaither Robinson, Star Mary Kay Consultant, who knows her business, and her own hero, David. Thanks for understanding our crazy schedules.

To Marcella Badie, for dragging us away one afternoon for a much-needed break, wonderful conversation, good food, and fine wine. Thank you.

To Aunt Naomi and Uncle Louis, for your prayers, encouragement, and love. We love you, too.

To Aunt Rose and our beloved neighbor, Esther Sykes, simply because we love you.

To brothers and uncles: Louis, Donald, Michael, Blaise, and Craig, for laughter and joy through the years.

To our friends at Bally's Casino Lakeshore Resort, Norbert

A. Simmons; Lorenzo D. Creighton; Terry Thompson; Pauline Deffes; Bianca Williams; Monique Fleury; Mia Caldwell; Joe Gaimo; Lamar Crowe; and everyone else we've unintentionally omitted. Thanks for always taking care of us. And thanks especially for the champagne!

To my friends at the HRI Group, Edward B. Boettner, for his continued generosity and support of our career; J. D. Roscoe, for her willingness to always lend a hand; Barbara Files; Pres Kabacoff; Andrew Fields; Sydney Barthelemy; Tony Herle; Suzette Pittman; Richard Hosey; Selim Berkol; Lawanda Thompson; Hal Fairbanks; Alex Dipp; Wayne Clement, Sr. and Jr.; Miles Thomas; Tara Hernandez; Robin Cancienne; Pamela Fischer; Shelley Crone; and Sylvia Pizzalato. It's always a pleasure seeing you all.

To fellow writers and a backbone of support, the Southern Louisiana Chapter of the Romance Writers of America. Thank you all! A special thanks to Rexanne Becnel and Hailey North for taking time out of your busy schedules to lead my discussion at Barnes & Noble when I was in the hospital. And to Steve Harris, who helps to keep me laughing, in the darkest of time, with his E-mails!

And last, but certainly not least, to Zoey, forever the light of our lives.

Thanks one and all. We love you.

Bedazzled

One

 (decorative flourish)

"Hey, Ashley! Wait up!"

Readjusting the package that contained her recently bought antique bowl, Ashley Douglas turned toward the sound of the call. Her older brother, Zachery, stood on the median at the intersection of Carrollton Avenue and Bienville Street, waiting for the onslaught of cars to cease or the stoplight to momentarily halt the flow of traffic. She glared at the brown bag in her hands, an attestation to her weakness for spending, and waited until Zach crossed the street to where she stood.

When he reached her, Ashley displayed her brightest smile, hoping he wouldn't comment on what she held. "Zach, fancy meeting you here!" she gushed brightly.

"I could say the same about you, Ash." Zach's mocha-colored eyes focused narrowly on the sign hanging from the eaves outside of the antique shop. "What are you doing in this part of town?"

Her smile felt pasted on her face. "I could ask you the same thing."

Guilt. That's what she was feeling. But Zach understood

her, almost better than anyone else. He'd taken up for her against their parents countless times. Seven years ago, he'd consoled her after she'd made a fool of herself over his best friend, Jordan Bennett, and declared her undying love for Jordan. Her only consolation was that she had been sixteen and had truly thought herself madly in love with the handsome, good cooking Jordan.

Memories of Jordan made the same pull she'd felt when she saw the bowl inside the shop tug at her insides once again. Her grip tightened on the bag. Bright sunshine added extra degrees to the hot, humid day. Maybe the heat exacerbated the light, giddy feeling stealing into her, but she doubted it. She was a New Orleanian, born and bred. Even if s e didn't like the summer temperatures, she was used to them. She frowned at her bundle.

"What gives, Ashley?" Zach asked sternly.

Ashley tore her gaze from the bag, catching a small glimpse of tarnished silver. "I'm searching for a piece for Mr. Russell to place on the table in the foyer of his home."

Folding his arms, Zach inclined his blond head toward her bag. "I'm sure your boss will be happy because it looks like you've found it."

"Oh, this?" Ashley laughed weakly, the guilt she'd felt moments ago deepening at Zach's sardonic tone. "Um . . . well . . . um, no. I-I really haven't found it. I've scoured Magazine and Royal Streets, and all the other antique shops in between."

"Two questions, Ashley. First, what exactly are you looking for, for Mr. Russell? Second—and this is the million-dollar question—what's in the package, and who's it for?"

Ashley exhaled a long-suffering sigh. She really hated the fact that her brother was witness to her lapse in judgment. After weeks of using her money wisely, she'd once again given in to her urge to buy, and she knew part of

Zach's interrogation stemmed from his disappointment. Pretending indifference, she sniffed. "Zach, you said two questions. I believe you asked three. To answer your first question, I don't know what I'm looking for. When I find it, however, I'll know."

"In the meantime, you're scouring and buying . . . for yourself."

"No," she snapped, his resigned tone rankling her. "No, Zach. I promise you I haven't been buying. This is the first thing I've bought in nearly a month."

"Ash, you promised me before."

"And I've tried to keep my promise, Zach. B-but this bowl kinda *drew* me to it. Look at it." In a rush of excitement, she pulled the old bowl from the plain, brown bag.

Horrified embarrassment washed through her. Seeing it in the light of day made her better understand Zach's disappointment. It was a heavy dish, but nearly black with tarnish, and the stand attached to it appeared to be crooked.

"A new toy, Ashley?"

She closed her eyes at the sound of the husky, snide comment drifting over her shoulder. It couldn't be! Not Jordan Bennett, with his unthinkable frugality and condescension toward her as the out of reach, older man. Her heart pounding furiously, Ashley whirled to face him. The bowl slipped from her fingers and clattered to the ground. Zach's disapproval floated to the back of her mind, and she stared at the tall man before her. Her day was going from bad to worse.

Not only hadn't she found anything for Mr. Russell's foyer, but she'd spent nearly a hundred bucks on an ugly old bowl. If things hadn't turned completely disastrous when Zach spotted her, they certainly had now.

"Jordan?"

It had been nearly four years since she'd last seen him, and this was quite an inauspicious meeting. She always imagined that she'd be in a little slinky dress, her hair bouncing with body, and her nails well manicured when this moment finally came. Of course, in her fantasies, Jordan gazed at her with longing, instead of the annoyed amusement gleaming in his blue-gray eyes. Dressed in baggy denim overalls and a white T-shirt, her hair in a ponytail, she no doubt reminded Jordan of the kid he remembered, instead of the woman she now was.

"Hello, Ash." He leaned down and pecked her on the cheek. "It's been a long time, but I see you haven't changed."

He thought she hadn't changed? That wasn't good. In many ways she *had* changed—except where money was concerned. Yet she was trying harder than anyone gave her credit for, something Jordan would never admit, even if he *had* been around these past years.

Jordan stooped down and picked up her bowl. Frowning in concentration, he studied it for long moments, then raised his gaze to her.

A spark of electricity generated between them. Desire warmed Jordan's eyes, turning them the color of storm clouds. Ashley's breath caught in her throat. What had changed between them in the few minutes since he'd walked up? Smiling tentatively at him, she reached for her bowl. Their fingertips brushed and fire flared within her, an uncontrollable inferno that thrilled and amazed her.

She placed the bowl in her bag. Almost instantly the customary scowl spread over Jordan's features. After their apparently mutual awareness of each other just now, it shocked her.

Still, she threw her arms around Jordan's neck in a fierce hug. "Hi, Jordan," she said, her breathless tone in direct contrast to the neutrality she would've liked to get across. Jordan Bennett had been only a schoolgirl's crush. She had dreams to fulfill and goals to attain. Most importantly, she wanted to prove to herself and her family that she wasn't the reckless spendthrift everyone thought her to be. Jordan included. "It's been a while."

"It has, hasn't it? But it seems we keep meeting after one of your binges. As I recall the last time I saw you, you had a bagful of newly purchased CDs, and you said you'd overspent." He glanced at Zach, dismissing the conversation with Ashley. "About ready to roll? Fawn and her friend are probably waiting for us. You need us to drop you off someplace, Ashley?" he asked, without missing a beat, the sunlight adding lustre to his dark brown hair.

"No," Ashley said softly, unwilling to admit how much his cavalier attitude hurt, not exactly liking what he'd remembered about their last encounter. He was acting as if he hadn't gazed at her with such intensity earlier. "I'll be fine."

Zach placed a gentle hand on her shoulder. "Are you sure?"

Her brother's tone indicated his concern. She refused to let him glimpse her full upset. It would only create friction between him and Jordan. She waved them away.

"Yeah, yeah. You guys go ahead. Wouldn't want to keep you from your hot dates."

"Ashley, it's been great seeing you." Jordan placed another quick kiss on her cheek. "I moved back to New Orleans two weeks ago. Maybe we can go out and have a drink soon. I'll meet you at the car, Zach."

Jordan hurried toward the corner, where he waited for the light to change to red. Without a backward glance, he crossed the street to where Zach's SUV was parked, near China Imperial Restaurant.

"Are you sure you don't want a ride?"

"Positive, Zachery. But please don't tell Mom and Dad."

Zach's eyes narrowed. "Tell them what? If you're referring to the money you wasted on that hideous creation, they already know what a spendthrift you are. That's why they cut off your allowance, remember?"

How could she have forgotten? She didn't fault her parents, however. They believed their tough love approach was the first step to Ashley becoming a responsible, productive adult, after growing up in wealth and luxury as the youngest member of the family. When her father, Murray, lost his company in a corporate takeover and almost lost the shirts off all of their backs, Ashley continued on as though nothing had happened.

At seventeen, she should have been old enough to understand their need to tighten purse strings. It wasn't so much that she was selfish and mean-spirited, as that she was supremely confident her father would recover. Which he did. Murray, Zach, and her mother, Glynis, all learned from the experience. She didn't, and her family feared she never would, unless drastic measures were taken. So when she turned twenty-one, her father cut off her allowance.

Zach, who was nine years older than she—and a year older than Jordan—thought that was *too* drastic, but in this instance he couldn't sway their parents in her favor. Becoming miserly proved harder than she expected, and Ashley finally realized that she might have a problem.

"I truly have tried to change. I'm telling you it's just that the bowl . . . well . . . it *called* to me to buy it."

Zach laughed. "That's a new one, Ashley, but not very original. What did you say about the other things you bought? They had your name written all over them?"

"Guilty," Ashley said with a giggle. "I'm sorry I let you down. Give me another chance to prove to you and Mom and Dad that I really am trying."

"I know you are, little sister. But I thought you only assisted in some area of hotel buying. Why is Russell asking you to shop for his home?"

Tempering her annoyance that Zach refused to recognize

how much Jim Russell valued her, she shifted her weight. As Mr. Russell's executive assistant, her job consisted of much more than purchasing items for the hotel. But her success at her job held little interest for her family. They took nothing she did seriously, so it wouldn't do any good for her to explain this to Zach for the umpteenth time. "Mr. Russell thinks I have good taste. He's right, of course."

"Of course." Zach chuckled. "But does his wife agree?"

"Totally concurs. And she insisted I get a bonus for my troubles."

"Which you've probably blown already, on your bowl."

Ashley bit down on her lip. Zach was right about most things.

The continuous honking of a horn drew their attention across the street. Jordan was leaning inside the open car window, one hand on the horn. The other he was using to gesture for Zach to get a move on.

"Go, Zach. Jordan's having a fit over there. Don't worry about me. I truly don't mind riding the bus. In fact, I like it."

"All right, Ash." Embracing her, Zach planted a kiss on the top of her head. "Take care."

"You, too. Tell Jordan I'll call him soon and take him up on his offer."

"Give up, Ashley," Zach warned. "You're not his type. He was only being polite when he offered to buy you a drink."

"We'll always be friends. I have everything under control where Jordan is concerned."

Zach looked at her a long moment, before sighing his resignation. "Okay," he said as he walked away from her.

Ashley watched as Zach made it to his Land Cruiser. She lingered until they drove off, then walked to the bus stop, uncertainty and guilt weighing heavily upon her.

Jordan was still the most handsome man she'd ever seen,

with his perfectly sculptured tall frame and dark, good looks. For a moment today, magic pulsed between them, but just as quickly evaporated. That moment made Ashley realize that love potions, enchanted elixirs, and mystical spells were only fairy tales—despite how much she wanted to believe in them.

Jordan reclined back in the comfortable, leather passenger seat of Zach's big Land Cruiser, still reeling from the strange feeling that had stolen into him when he'd picked up Ashley's bowl. He'd felt a strange pull toward *Ashley,* of all people.

It wasn't that she wasn't cute, because she was. But she was young and inexperienced—and his best friend's baby sister. She also took the phrase "shop 'til you drop" literally, while he was frugal at best and stingy at worst. His father, Coleman, had been killed when he was five years old. Two years later, Jordan's mother, Karen, his older sister, Tracie, and himself, were evicted from their home when his mother couldn't make the rent. The Douglases had saved them from living on the streets.

Murray Douglas and Coleman had been golfing buddies, and their wives became fast friends, so Glynis insisted Karen move into the mansion for as long as she needed. Coleman's investments failed miserably, and he'd used the insurance money intended for the family to pay off his debts. Instead of recouping the family wealth and restoring the big policies, he'd suffered a premature death in a car accident and left the family penniless.

After Coleman's death, they stayed with the Douglases an entire year. In that time, Zach and Jordan became inseparable and forged a lifetime friendship.

Jordan doubted Ashley knew any of this, since she hadn't been born yet. While he understood the need for and value of money perfectly, Ashley never got the concept. Perhaps it was because she had been handed whatever she wanted from everyone—himself included—from the time she was born. But he had to admit she was quite good-hearted. She would just as quickly buy a wardrobe for a friend as she would for herself. Yet he couldn't see himself married to a woman who couldn't understand his cautious ways, and the reasons for them.

In short, they were no good for each other.

But today, just for a moment, he'd seen her as a passionate woman, to whom he could become deeply attracted if he wasn't careful. Her long, brownish-blond hair and expressive hazel eyes were attractive features on her tall, model-like frame.

Zach pulled the car to a stop in the parking lot at Uptown Square. "Fawn and Marie should be in the lobby."

"How long have you been dating Fawn?"

"Only a couple of weeks. It's nothing serious. We're just friends hanging out, as it would be when and if you and my sister go out. I haven't even introduced her to Ashley or Mom and Dad yet."

Jordan sighed. "No wonder Ashley shot daggers at me. If looks could kill, I'd be laid out by now."

"I saw that look, too, and I'm sorry about that. I thought Ashley was past her infatuation with you. I'll talk to her again."

"Don't. I wouldn't want her to suffer any undue embarrassment. If anyone talks to her, let it be me."

"Sure thing, dude. Just go easy. Remember, she's still young."

Opening the door and slamming it closed, Jordan shook his head. It annoyed him that Zach sounded like an overprotective big brother with *him*. Jordan had been Ashley's friend for years. There was no need for Zach to take that approach with him. "She's twenty-three," he said over his shoulder, starting toward the huge European-styled shopping center, where the cinema was located. "Not exactly a baby."

With a few long strides Zach caught up quickly to Jordan. "Yeah, but she's never had a boyfriend. She's put off every man who's ever been interested in her, for one reason or another. I wouldn't want you to take her out and put ideas in her head, then walk out on her."

"First of all, Zachery, I wouldn't do such a thing. I consider Ashley a friend. Second, I think your fear stems more from the fact that I'll take her out and possibly take things farther than I should."

"That, too," Zach admitted. They reached the brick building that encased the wrought-iron staircase. "Ashley's always been mad for you, and with just a little encouragement on your part, you two could end up in a compromising situation, with you regretting it afterward."

He wouldn't comment on Zach's last statement. Given Zach's current frame of mind, any statements about taking matters too far with Ashley might cause a brawl. Jordan hoped that Zach's attitude would change if Ashley and he ever explored an intimate relationship, however.

"What brought this conversation on?"

"I saw the look you gave her. She's quite a pretty kid and can be very persuasive when she wants to be. I've run roughshod for her with Mom and Dad more than once when I swore I wouldn't. I've also bailed her out countless times when I agreed with my parents and told Ashley she was on her own. Now that I'm in the company business, Dad has warned me if he finds out I'm helping Ashley, he'll demote me and even kick me out of the company."

Jordan released an amazed whistle. "Whoa, man! That's kinda harsh, don't you think?"

"Sure. But deep down, I think Dad is on to both Ashley and me. For my sister's part, she does try. It's just that it's going to take an act of sorcery to break her of her habit.

Just as no matter how much *you* try to place yourself above her to stay out of her reach, you have a soft spot for Ashley."

"True," Jordan conceded. He halted on the second level and stared at Zach. Remembering the currents that sizzled between him and Ashley earlier made his heart pound. Now that he was thinking logically, however, he knew that Ashley wasn't his type. She was an attractive young lady with whom he shared a friendly affection. "I do have a soft spot for her, but I can never cross that line between friendship and an affair. Nor would I, even if that was an option. I wouldn't want to jeopardize our friendship," he finished, testing Zach's reaction.

"You're right. I think Ashley needs someone closer to her age, who shares her interests. You two have nothing in common. Ashley likes to spend money. You're a fanatical saver. You love to cook—so much so that you've made it your career. Ashley can't boil an egg. A relationship between the two of you is a disaster waiting to happen."

Zach's pronouncement sounded like an omen. Disappointed by his friend's present attitude, but believing he'd change his mind if there would ever be a romantic involvement between Ashley and him, Jordan dropped the subject.

In silence they proceeded up the last flight of stairs and quickly made it to the glass-enclosed theater, where people were queued up waiting to buy their tickets. The scent of hot popcorn, along with indistinguishable chatter, filtered in the cool air, a welcome relief from the summer heat.

"There they are."

Zach waved at two women, both dressed casually in jeans and blouses. Smiling in their direction, the women returned Zach's wave.

"Which one's which?" Jordan whispered as they neared them. "They both have black hair."

"Fawn is the one with dark brown eyes. Marie's eyes are blue."

Fawn was also the one who threw her arms around Zach's neck and planted a huge kiss on his lips. "Hey, darlin'! We thought you'd forgotten us. I couldn't wait for Marie to meet you. I told her how we've spent almost every moment you've had away from the company together and in each other's arms. Now that you guys are here, we're gonna run to the little girl's room, then come back for the introductions and such."

Pulling himself out of Fawn's hold, Zach watched as the women hurried away, then he gave Jordan an abashed look, his cheeks slightly red.

Clearing his throat, Jordan scratched his chin. "Just friends hanging out, huh?"

"Hey, listen—"

"Don't worry, Zach. You didn't have to downplay your involvement with Fawn to make your point. I got your message where Ashley is concerned. If it'll make you feel better, I won't even take her out for the drink I—"

"Are you out of your mind? Ashley would murder me if she ever thought I stopped you from taking her out. Maybe I was out of line for pretending Fawn and I are not as serious as we are, to warn you away from Ashley, but I'm just trying to do what's best for the both of you."

"I know, and I promise you have nothing to worry about on my part. I don't know what happened to me earlier. It was a momentary awareness that Ashley certainly isn't a little girl any longer. But I know for a fact it would require the casting of a love spell for that feeling to come into me again. Ashley is safe with me. She's like the little sister I never had, and nothing more. So stop worrying and let's enjoy the rest of our evening."

Sure in his knowledge that whatever had passed between Ashley and him earlier would never happen again, Jordan patted Zach's back and smiled at Marie, just as the women reached them again.

Two

After making several stops to purchase necessary household items and riding four different buses, Ashley finally reached her immaculately kept, sparsely furnished apartment later that evening.

Setting her bags on the floor, she flicked on the light switch and wearily stretched her neck from side to side.

This had been one of those days that she *hated* buses. Usually she simply disliked them, but she'd never confess her sentiments to Zach. He'd helped her out enough, and she wouldn't put it past him to buy her a car, which she couldn't have. Zach was the senior vice president in the family's oil and gas distribution company, and she wouldn't want him to lose his position. He loved to wheel and deal, and Dad might very well can him if he discovered Zach had assisted her.

Donated furniture that she vowed to replace one day dominated her apartment. The sofa Aunt Stella gave her was sturdy and clean, but old. Not antique, just *old* and faded. It sat in front of the sofa table Zach found for her at one of those moving-out-of-town sales. Practically new and traditionally styled, the table put the sofa to shame.

Picking up her shopping bags, she went into her compact kitchen and placed the packages next to the sink on the only counter she had. Then she went and got her bowl from the floor, discovering an additional bag in the process. Knowing it was the new brand of shampoo she'd bought, she took both bags to the sofa and sat down.

She inspected her bowl, hoping to discover something that supported her claim of being drawn to it. In the brightness of the ceiling light, however, she found nothing she hadn't seen as she stood outside the shop on Carrollton Avenue. She turned it over. The scratched bottom and crooked stand only added to her annoyance. Setting it down on the sofa table behind her with a thud, she grabbed the other bag and yanked out her shampoo.

She hoped *this* had been a wise purchase. Her hair and the heat had never mixed, and the limpness of her tresses disgusted her. She'd had a very busy day, and the heat and humidity assured a bad hair day from the very beginning. No matter how she started in the morning, by evening her hair looked like wet noodles. No wonder Jordan had changed his tune so abruptly.

With a heavy sigh, she threw the bottle of shampoo in the bowl. After she rested a few minutes she'd treat herself to a long, hot shower and try out her new shampoo.

Leaning back on the couch, she closed her eyes. Jordan had moved back to New Orleans. The impact of that wasn't lost to her. She *still* had it bad for him, only now she wasn't jailbait. The only thing that stood in her way at present was Jordan himself. A huge stumbling block indeed, she thought wryly. Yet there was hope. She'd seen it in his eyes. Something had happened between them for a few seconds; Ashley had only to discover what that was to make it happen again.

The tapping noise on her door broke her reverie. She

knew who it was before she answered the knock. She didn't need any additional aggravation tonight. Frowning, she stomped to the door, pulled it opened, and then, without saying anything, trounced back to her seat and sat down.

"Is that any way to greet your neighbor and landlord, Ash?"

"What do you want, Harry?" Ashley glared at him. "It had better not be to pressure me for a date. My answer is still no. You have a harem at your apartment, and I won't be added to that revolving door."

Actually Harry Roberts was a pretty nice fellow, but she'd never been able to warm up to him. He just wasn't . . . he wasn't . . . Jordan. At twenty-nine, besides being the owner of the triplex she lived in, he *was* a philanderer.

"My visit has nothing to do with your continual refusal of my invitation." Harry handed her several envelopes. "I was being neighborly and bringing your mail to you."

Shuffling through the pile and throwing all but one of the windowed envelopes in her bowl, Ashley heaved a sigh. "Shoot! I forgot about my Entergy bill." She tore open the envelope, her gaze widening when she saw the charges for the month. "This is nearly a hundred bucks! I'm not home often enough to have a utility bill this high!"

"How could you have forgotten that your gas and electricity needed to be paid? Don't worry about it, though. If you need an extension on your rent, just let me know."

How indeed? The small figure left in her bank account popped into her mind. This type of crucial mistake was becoming less frequent for her, but, with her limited budget, she couldn't even afford *one*. She thought about calling Zach and begging for his help, but she quickly decided against it. Her brother had been disappointed enough earlier today. This time she'd have to suffer the consequences and face her responsibilities alone. Which is all her parents asked of her anyway.

"Thanks, Harry, but I've got that covered." Problems of her own doing weighing her down, she pulled herself off the couch and gestured toward the kitchen. "May I offer you a glass of something cool?"

"Some other time, sweetheart. I've got to run."

Giving him a knowing look, Ashley shook her head. "Let me guess. A hot date?"

Harry started for the door. "I have to keep myself amused in some manner until you make up your damned mind to go out with me. I'll talk to you in the morning. See you later, Ash."

"Bye, Harry," Ashley said, laughing. "Have fun."

"Always."

Left alone and out of sorts, Ashley gazed around not quite sure what to do with herself. Maybe she should accept Harry's invitation to go out with him. What harm could there be in an innocent date? At least she wouldn't be alone dreaming of a man who might never be hers and obsessing over her bills. Fearing she would let something slip about the bowl, she didn't even dare call her parents.

Her gaze fell on the bowl again. It *was* beautiful, but she couldn't imagine what was so special about it that had made her want to buy it. Deciding she'd possibly appreciate it more after it was cleaned, she set to work doing just that.

When she finished, the bowl glowed like no silver she'd ever seen before. Intricate designs of encrusted bells, butterflies, bows, and flowers made it an exquisitely interesting piece of work. Even the stand that she could have sworn was crooked now looked erect and brand-new.

Suddenly quite pleased with herself for buying the bowl, she stared at it for long moments. Love and romance crystallized in her thoughts, competing with images of Jordan Bennett. Feelings of intense longing and unsated passion coursed through her—strange feelings that somehow added a new dimension to her already overactive imagination where Jordan was concerned.

Tidying up the mess she'd made in the kitchen, her thoughts wandered to where she should place the shiny bowl in her living room. Such a lovely object needed to be seen and admired. Her sofa table was the perfect place, not only because of its newness, but it was the only other piece of furniture in the room besides her sofa.

Placing the envelopes back inside the bowl for the time being, she then concentrated on centering it. When she had positioned it perfectly, she nodded in satisfaction, then went to the bathroom and finally started the water in the shower. After shedding her clothes, she remembered the shampoo she'd left next to the bowl and hurriedly retrieved it.

Warm, relaxing water streamed over her hair and skin, soothing away her tiredness. For several minutes she stood under the flow of the shower before she took her shampoo and poured it over her hair.

The potent fragrance heightened her senses, made her feel alive and vital. Massaging her hair and scalp, she generated a fluffy lather, then rinsed the shampoo out again. She glided her fingers through her hair, amazed at how good it felt. Usually she hurried through her shower, but tonight she spent extra time under the spray of water, shampooing her hair a second time.

Finally finished and more relaxed than she'd been in a while, she stepped out of the shower and wrapped a towel around her head to absorb the moisture, then used another towel to dry her skin. Fatigue stole into her all at once, and she crawled into bed, devoid of clothes, the towel still wrapped like a turban on her head.

When Ashley awakened the next morning, the first thing she noticed was the towel partially covering her eyes. She was annoyed with herself for falling asleep without combing her hair. It would be a tangled mess, and the short time she had to herself in the morning would be wasted trying to comb it.

Very aggravated with herself, she pulled the towel off her head and slipped out of bed. Still nude, she went into the kitchen to start the coffee, absently threading her hand through her hair. It glided through like a hot knife through butter. Pausing, she slid her other hand through the silky strands.

Making a beeline for the mirror in the bathroom, Ashley gasped. Long, blond waves cascaded over her shoulders, and ringlets dripped from her forehead. Her gasp became a squeak. Her mouth dry, she glanced behind herself to make sure *her* image gleamed from the mirror and not someone else's.

Seeing that she was indeed alone, she touched her hair again. "Oh, I'm beautiful," she managed.

Her one flaw had always been her hair. It was very long, extremely straight, and quite unruly. Secretly she'd always wished for curly or wavy hair, and at last she'd found a shampoo that worked to her advantage.

Ashley halted her thoughts. "This is ridiculous! No shampoo can make anyone's hair look freshly permed, without it *being* freshly permed!" The bowl slipped into her mind, and she glared at her image. "So what about it? It's just an ordinary silver dish."

Grabbing her bathrobe hanging on the door hook, she slipped it on. She rushed into the hallway and stopped, peeking in the living room toward the table where the bowl sat. Narrowing her eyes at the thing, she burst out laughing.

"Get a grip, girl. It's just a bowl. The five-dollar bottle of shampoo was well worth the money. I'm going to have to buy a couple of cases to stockpile. Once the public finds out about its properties, dealers won't be able to keep the stuff on the shelf."

She glided to the kitchen and fixed herself toast and coffee before getting ready for work. When she was completely dressed, her tennis shoes on and the heels she would put on when she got to work in her bag, she remembered her Entergy bill. She'd figure out a way to pay it at work. With that thought, she went to the bowl and grabbed the letters . . . and stopped in her tracks when the envelope that had contained the Entergy bill last night fell to the ground. Glimpsing a dollar bill inside, she picked it up and released a short scream when she pulled out a crisp *hundred*-dollar bill.

"Oh, my God!" Her eyes wide, she drew in short breaths. She focused her gaze on the bowl. "Impossible!" Rushing to her telephone, she speed-dialed Zach's number. One ring, two, three. "Come on, Zachery. Answer!" Four, five—

"Yes, Ashley? You know, I started not to pick up when I saw your number pop up on my Caller I.D.—"

"Zach, tell me you were over here after I went to sleep last night and left a hundred-dollar bill—"

"Slow down, Ash, and take deep breaths."

Drawing in a hearty breath, she started over, striving for calm. But it wasn't easy. She'd lived in the apartment for seventeen months and had never had an inkling of it being haunted. Either Zach left the money, or an apparition had. If it was the latter, she'd be moving out shortly.

"I went to sleep early last night and I slept like a rock. I wouldn't have heard anything, I was so tired." Afraid to repeat her question, she swallowed deeply. "D-did you come over late last night and leave money for me? One crisp hundred-dollar bill to be exact."

"Hell, no! I was otherwise engaged last night. If you recall, Jordan and I had a double date—"

"Yes, I remember perfectly," Ashley interrupted crossly, not wanting to think what type of activity Jordan might have been engaged in.

"Why would you think I stopped by your place?"

Unsure of what to say, she released a weak laugh. If Zach thought someone had been in her apartment, other than himself or their parents, she'd be out of there by nightfall. Yet even though she was struggling to find her own way, she liked the independence her own place afforded her. Other than being evicted, which she wouldn't allow to happen, or finding out the place really was haunted, she didn't want to leave.

"Ashley, talk to me," Zach ordered in his best imitation of their father.

She hated that tone from either of them, but knew when she heard it that she had little choice but to comply. "I, uh, I found a hundred-dollar bill on the floor of my living room," she lied. "It must have fallen out of my purse when I was leaving yesterday, and I didn't realize it."

Cringing at how much more irresponsible that made her seem than she actually was, she waited for the explosion. It was an easy excuse to fall back on, because no matter how much she tried to do better, her family really didn't expect her to succeed. They *hoped* she would, but didn't anticipate it.

"How could you not miss a hundred dollars, Ashley?" Zach snapped. "When are you going to learn that money doesn't grow from the ground, and grow up!"

Since she wasn't up to an argument this morning, she decided it best to hang up. It had been a mistake to call anyway. Deep inside, she'd known that Zach had nothing to do with her good fortune. "I gotta go, Zach. I'll talk to you later."

"Ashley—"

Before he said anything more, she hung up. His anger had been expected, but her reaction to it wasn't. As an innocent bystander this time, it upset her to realize how easily Zach thought the worst of her.

Still, her brother's opinion of her wasn't the pressing

issue at the moment. She had to discover how she'd come into the money.

Marching to the bowl, she noticed the other unopened envelopes laying there. She grabbed the envelope containing her credit card bill and tore it open. As expected, she found only the statement and return envelope, along with a few advertisements and special offers. When she opened the other two credit card statements, as well as the telephone bill she'd received yesterday, she found the same thing.

The piercing ringing of the telephone drew her attention away from the bowl. Dropping the bills back into the bowl, she rushed to the phone and grabbed it. "Hullo?"

"Ashley, if you don't tell me what's going on, I'm calling Mom and Dad and then I'm coming over there."

Ashley groaned. "I appreciate your concern, Zach, but I'm fine. I told you what happened."

"You don't keep money long enough to just casually drop it on your living room floor and not miss it during the course of the day. I'll see you in a few."

"Zach!" But only silence greeted her. "Shoot!" She was out of there before *he* got there!

Deciding not to question her good fortune further, she'd pay her Entergy bill, enjoy her luxurious hair, and ponder the strange events thoroughly when she returned home.

Three

Later that morning, Ashley sat behind the desk in her office, engaged in a phone conversation. A knock sounded on her opened door, and she looked up.

Jim Russell, her boss, stood there, smiling broadly. She beckoned him inside with a wave.

"I know, Wood, but we've already received three bids for the refurbishing, and no one meets our time limits. Mr. Russell doesn't care if they drop the price. His answer is no! The job is to be completed in fifteen months tops. Tell your boss that. Call us when you have the answer," she said in closing, and hung up.

"Good morning, Mr. Russell," Ashley said brightly, uncomfortable with her boss' openmouthed gawking. He was a friendly man and happily married, but he was looking at her as if he'd never seen her before. "How can I help you? I just got through talking to Wood about the Blackwell bid—"

"I trust you've handled everything."

Pleased at the compliment, Ashley straightened in her seat. Jim Russell trusted her opinion on a lot of issues, and she never failed to live up to his expectations—or her own; for that matter, at least where the hotel was concerned.

Several months ago, when she'd suggested to Mr. Russell that he seriously consider a makeover for the hotel, he had readily agreed. The huge hotel, owned by him and his family, had begun to lose money over the past year. Every idea to save it was welcomed. Knowing her own family wanted to divert their money once again, she'd suggested to Mr. Russell that he offer to sell her father a small amount of stock in order to pay for the refurbishment. Although it was Zach who finally convinced Murray to buy, the deal was made, and Mr. Russell gave Ashley the phenomenal task of handling certain aspects of the hotel's overhaul.

She couldn't have been happier, but securing a contractor was only the start. A chef was still needed, as well as new furnishings . . .

"What the hell have you done to yourself?" he gushed, his green eyes wide. "You look terrific!"

Ashley flipped her hair back with a shake of her head. "Thanks, sir. So nice of you to notice."

"It's the hair, huh?" he said in astonishment. "Geez, the things that can be done with fake hair these days are amazing. That wig almost looks like your natural hair."

"Thanks again, Mr. Russell," Ashley managed weakly. "You're very observant." Why tell him the truth and have him pulling on her hair to see if it was real?

Shaking his head, he looked at her hair again and laughed. "Unbelievable! *Unbelievable!* That wig really is something. Not that your own hair isn't nice, of course."

"Of course."

He patted his own bald crown. "I might have to find something for myself. Think I could?"

"Sure," Ashley said with a laugh. "But I doubt you'll run across the product I'm using."

"I might can talk you into telling me your secret."

"Perhaps." She looked at him in question.

"What?"

"I suppose you're here about the piece you asked me to find for your foyer?"

Mr. Russell frowned. "What piece?"

"Mr. Russell," Ashley began, exasperated, "didn't you ask me to find an appropriate ornament for the table in your hallway?"

"Oh, that!" He waved in dismissal. "Forget it, Ashley. Our housekeeper picked up a wood sculpture on the Gulf Coast this past weekend. She has a daughter there, you know? She saw it in one of those shops along the beach. It's a fertility god. Beautiful. Simply beautiful."

Tempted to ask for a rub on it to insure easy conception if Jordan ever saw her as a romantic interest, Ashley squirmed in her seat. "I see."

"Don't feel bad. We still need you. Barbara and I are taking a short vacation and would like to leave our Yorkie with you."

Ashley rubbed her temples. "Your dog?"

"Yeah. Little Hades is less trouble than a baby."

"Hades?" Less trouble than a baby? Yeah, right, and she and Jordan were engaged to be married. In agitation, she picked up a pen and tapped it on the desk. "I can't, Mr. Russell. I-I mean I just bought a brand-new bowl and—"

"Oh, that's no problem. Just keep the seat down and close the bathroom door."

What a flake. I can't believe I'm having this conversation. Nor could she believe that her bowl had come to mind to use as an excuse to turn Mr. Russell down. "I'm sorry, Mr. Russell, but I *really* can't, although little Hades sounds like an absolutely perfect doggie."

"No problem, Ashley. I understand. You young people live in the fast lane today. Hades likes the housekeeper anyway. The only time he snaps at her is when she cooks chicken liver for him." He stroked his beardless chin. "Let's see. There was something else I came in here for." He snapped his fingers. "Oh, yeah! We just hired a new chef this morning. He comes highly recommended."

"Great!" That was one to-do she'd happily scratch off her list. The nationwide search for a new head chef had been a pain in the rear end. Human Resources had taken over a couple of months ago, promising to deliver a cook within twelve weeks. Ashley was impressed because there were still nearly five weeks left to their allotted time. "What's his name?"

"Julian Brantley? Er, Justin Benton? I forget. Just glanced over his résumé a few minutes ago and only remember that his initials are J. B."

Laying the pen down and rising slowly from her seat, Ashley folded her arms across her chest. Her heart beat so hard her blouse almost rose and fell with the rhythm. It was pure coincidence, but somehow she already knew the answer. "Could it be Jordan Bennett?"

"Yes, that's it! Jordan Bennett! I'll have to remember that," he mumbled. "Do you know him?"

"Yes, very well. Our families have associated since way before I was born." And as long as she remembered, the thought of him had caused butterflies to flutter in her stomach. "He's a wonderful cook. Always loved being in the kitchen."

"Good. He can report to the restaurant manager, Petersen, who'll in turn report to you, and you can keep me informed."

"W-well, um, th-that s-sounds good." She wasn't so sure Jordan would enjoy knowing how closely they'd be working together, but she'd keep her worries to herself and deal with that problem when and if it arose.

"It's wonderful. In the meantime, I have a business meeting to attend, so why don't you go and welcome, uh, J. B.

aboard? He's here now getting acquainted with the restaurant staff."

Panic set in. She definitely wasn't ready to face Jordan right now. He might notice her out-of-control emotions. "Isn't there something else I can do for you right now? I still have some phone calls to make."

"Save them for later. Nothing's pressing at the moment."

"Wonderful. I'm off to the kitchen." And she brushed past him.

Although she could have taken a service elevator that opened directly into the kitchen, she went the circuitous route—down the dully decorated guest elevator, past the outdated registration and concierge desks, until she reached the entrance of the restaurant.

She needed to get used to the fact that she'd see Jordan every day. Every day! As well as she already knew him, in her wildest dreams she didn't think she'd be in such a position to get to know him better.

Walking fully into the restaurant, she found she didn't have to go all the way into the kitchen. Jordan was sitting at one of the tables, holding court with Curtis and Arthur, two of his helpers, whom she knew well.

At first sight of him, Ashley drew in a breath. He should be arrested for being so good-looking. Even in the muted light, his rich, dark brown hair gleamed, a perfect contrast to the white of his chef's jacket. As she drew closer to him, she noticed his stubbled chin and jaw, and a thrill shot through her. Glancing up, he gave her a cursory glance, then went on talking.

Ashley stopped at his table. "Hello, Jordan."

Looking at her a second time, his mouth flew open. "Ashley?"

"Ashley?" two additional male voices chorused.

"Oh, come on, you guys, you know it's me."

Jordan stood from his seat, while Arthur and Curtis

looked at her as if she'd grown two noses, instead of having wavy, honey-blond hair.

"Er, hi. You look great." Jordan frowned at her, then looked over her shoulder, as if searching for someone who had accompanied her. "What are you doing here?"

Lord, he doesn't know! Fingering her newly styled hair, she smiled tremulously. "I work here, Jordan. Have for the past three years. Didn't Zach tell you? I would think in the two weeks you've been back in the city, he would have mentioned something about me."

He met her level look, his blue-gray eyes seeming to penetrate right to the core of her.

"You work here?" he asked, genuinely surprised. "In what capacity?"

"I . . . well . . . I'm assistant to the general manager." She chuckled softly, uncomfortable now. It wouldn't be long before he put two and two together. "I hope you don't mind."

"Certainly not," he said with a laugh, exposing straight, white teeth in an absolutely perfect, sculpted mouth. The shock of her new appearance hadn't faded from his countenance, and his gaze continued to devour her. "Sweetheart, you look great. With your changed hair, it seems like it's been months since I've seen you, instead of hours. I always thought you were attractive, but that style is breathtaking. You're simply beautiful."

At least *he* didn't think she was wearing a wig. Besides, he was actually complimenting her. That alone was worth every penny she'd spent on the shampoo . . . and the bowl.

She didn't believe in magic, and still wasn't fully convinced that the bowl had first yielded a tonic for her limp hair and then money to pay a bill. Yet she couldn't think of any other explanation. She rejected the idea of her house being haunted.

"When I saw you yesterday, you'd just bought some kind

of old bowl for yourself. Have you thrown it away yet?"

"Antique," Ashley corrected. "Not *old*, please."

"Antique? Of course. Why in blazes would I call it *old*?"

"Maybe it's because you're being just a tiny bit sarcastic?" Ashley asked without rancor. Although he *was* being sarcastic, he was also joking with her, so she took no offense. "Anyway, I polished it, and it looks brand-new."

"Really? That I'd love to see. As for Zach mentioning you to me, about the only thing he said about you is that you were fine. He kept me so busy going from one place to the other, reacquainting myself with my old friends and making new ones, I really had no chance to delve into your life."

For a moment, they both fell silent, at a loss for words. It sounded as if Zach had kept Jordan purposely busy to stay away from her. That didn't bode well for any relationship Ashley hoped to start with Jordan. Suddenly the powerful shampoo fragrance floated between them, an irresistible scent that made her giddy with anticipation. Her premature concerns about Zach's objections drifted to the back of her mind. Jordan's eyes darkened, and she knew that he wasn't unaffected either. While she was more than willing to succumb to whatever was going on, his resistance came through in the stiffening of his shoulders.

Jordan only tolerated her for friendship's sake. She imagined him with a bevy of female acquaintances; he didn't need her. But since yesterday afternoon, she'd centered her hopes on the impossible—having him for her very own.

"All right, you're on!" Ashley blurted.

"On?"

"Yeah. You said you wanted to see the bowl. Let me know when you have some time to spare, and I'll invite you over to see it."

Even though she was appalled at her forwardness, first in turning down Mr. Russell's request to dog-sit and now with Jordan, an idea had formed in her mind. It almost seemed as if that shampoo had changed not only her hair color and style, but her psyche as well. She felt overly sensitive to things and people around her, especially Jordan.

"Sounds good to me, Ash. I'll let you know when I'm free." Jordan brushed strands of hair over her shoulders.

The featherlight contact tingled through her. "Uh, right," she said breathlessly. "But I'll probably know before you do."

Jordan arched a thick brow. "Is that a fact? Do you have connections here I should know about?"

"Well, not really." He still hadn't figured out that she was his superior. Although she hated to break the moment between them, she had no choice. "It's just that Petersen has to give me a weekly report and—"

"You?" His eyes narrowed. "What position did you say you held here?"

So that's why things had gone so smoothly until this moment. He hadn't been paying attention to her words the first time. Judging by his indignant tone, he seemed to have taken offense now that he finally realized that she was his boss. "I'm assistant to the hotel's general manager," she answered, almost apologetically.

Jordan laughed without a shred of amusement. "How old are you?" he sneered. "Twenty-three? Kind of young to have such a prestigious job, eh, Ashley?"

"What are you implying?" Ashley snapped, stepping away from him to glare at him better. He was over six feet, but at five feet eight inches, she was tall herself and not easily intimidated.

"Not what you think!" he snarled. "You're twenty-three years old, Ashley, and you're my boss."

"If you have a problem with that, you know what your options are," she retorted. "I'm twenty-three, but that doesn't mean I'm a brainless fool. A smart twelve-year-old could do my job!"

Not comprehending why he felt so threatened by Ashley's position, Jordan glared at her. He'd never thought of himself as a chauvinist. He doubted the fact that Ashley was a woman was what bothered him, but she was just a kid. That rankled the hell out of him. He certainly wouldn't mind a seasoned, older—*much* older—woman as his superior.

But Ashley? She was immature and his best friend's *baby* sister—and dressed in a red suit, the skirt reaching only the middle of her thigh, showing her long legs to perfection. The formfitting jacket outlined round breasts and a slim waist. The shiny red pumps added a certain sexiness to her toned calves, while the gold earrings and bracelet completed the power look.

He'd insisted to Zach that she wasn't a baby, and the job she held in the hotel business wasn't for an infant. But she was his boss, and he had to answer to a . . . a *fledgling*.

That galled the hell out of him. Even more galling was the fact that at that very moment he wanted to haul Ashley into his arms and kiss those pouty lips on that beautiful face with the annoyed expression.

His emotions roiled in confusion. On the one hand, he felt Ashley Douglas *wasn't* a baby, considering what he was thinking about doing to her—even with the threat of losing Zach's friendship. On the other hand, he felt she was too damned young to be his boss.

Ever since he'd touched her silky hair, he'd held on to his control, while sensations sparkled through him. Whatever madness claimed him he didn't know. He only knew that as he gazed into her hazel eyes, the fragrant scent of her hair curling between them, a fierce need to learn about the person she'd become seized him.

Yet he'd acted like a complete ass and he needed to make amends. Instead of railing at her, he should have been complimenting her accomplishment. He drew in a contrite sigh.

"Ashley, look, I've known you forever, and it's hard for me to imagine you as anything other than the little kid bouncing behind Zach and me. I'm proud of you. You've made big strides. Congratulations. I apologize for my narrow-minded outburst."

He patted her on her shoulder, where her hair flowed down her back. Caressing the irresistible pull of the wavy strands, he drew her closer to him. He could no longer deny the urge to kiss her. "Ash," he murmured.

Twin pools of liquid jewels gazed at him. Without further hesitation, he locked his mouth to hers, meeting no resistance. The kiss started out sweet and exploratory, but the sensations spiraling through him urged him to more fervor. It was as if he'd waited a lifetime to experience this with Ashley, to feel so alive and vital. It was as if someone had waved a wizard's wand and cast a spell over him. She was a feather in his arms, and every curve of her slim body molded to him. He felt the rapid beating of her heart, heard her soft moan, smelled her spicy perfume. He wanted more of her, all of her. He wanted—

A throat cleared, loud, *very* loud, snapping him to his senses. Instantly they broke apart. The dazed expression in Ashley's eyes mirrored his feelings. Noticing the amused looks Curtis and Arthur directed their way, the color in her flushed cheeks deepened.

"Yo, Jordan, my man. This ain't the place for that stuff," Arthur said, not unkindly.

"You're right," he managed, embarrassed to the tips of his toes. "I'm sorry, Arthur. I was just apologizing to my boss."

Was he nuts? What the hell had come over him? He had a lust attack in the middle of the restaurant, not only jeopardizing his new position, but also leaving Ashley open for ridicule and gossip.

Not lust, he corrected, but desire, plain and simple. For Ashley. His best friend's little sister.

She was certainly lovely enough. Still, that was no excuse. She deserved better than his rabid public attention. He glanced around. The restaurant was closed until two P.M. and thankfully only the four of them were present in the area. Busboys and waiters were a bit away from them, hauling tablecloths, napkins, and silverware to the tables. He hoped they'd been too involved in their own activities to take notice.

"Listen, man," Arthur continued, "I don't know what you did to Ashley, but we ain't never felt the need to apologize to her in that manner." When both Ashley and Jordan remained silent, he smiled. "Ashley, I'm sorry, too. Not for what I did today, 'cause I ain't done nuthin' wrong, but I might do somethin' wrong tomorrow." He stepped closer to her. "So let's get on with the apologizin'."

Jordan stepped between Arthur and Ashley. "Go chop an onion or something and take Curtis with you."

Curtis looked up from his place at the table in surprise. "Me?" he asked with indignation. "I ain't said nuttin'."

"Give me a break, guys, will you?" Jordan implored. "This is embarrassing enough as it is."

"It should be, man. You were all over the woman. But I feel for you. C'mon, Curt, let's split, man."

"Well, can't we at least get a hug, Ashley?"

"Not even a handshake, Curtis," Jordan emphasized. "Get lost, both of you. Meet me in the kitchen in ten minutes."

"Man, I tell ya. Come on, Art."

Hands in the pockets of their white pants, they strolled away. Ashley laughed at the silliness of Curtis and Arthur. They'd already been working at the hotel when she started there almost three years before. The three of them had become good friends; the two men were easy to like.

"Ashley, what can I say?" Jordan began quietly. "What I did was inexcusable. It'll never happen again. I promise you."

Her body tingled from her neck to her toes. To think that Jordan would never kiss her again was unimaginable. "I don't know whether to be insulted or flattered."

"Don't be either. I'm not a flatterer and I'd never intentionally insult you. I just got this overwhelming urge to kiss you and I couldn't control myself. I hope I didn't offend you."

Offend me? Oh, silly man. How could he offend her when his kiss so contradicted his words? In her heart she felt she had a fighting chance to win his love. "You didn't offend me, Jordan," she said, her voice huskier than usual. "I enjoyed it. I really want you to see the bowl, so should I expect to see you on your next day off?"

With a chuckle, Jordan fisted her chin, her ivory skin smooth and soft. "Count on it," he said softly. "I'll see you then, boss. I thought I'd see you tonight as well, since Zach invited me to the weekly dinner you all have together at the mansion, but I'm going to decline. Wouldn't want my nose broken for giving you a torrid look."

Gazing at him a second, Ashley swallowed hard. But even the fact that she'd have a lot of explaining to do to her family about her telephone call to Zach this morning didn't matter. "I'll see you at my place, then," she said, and glided away from him.

Her bowl. Her lovely bowl had something to do with Jordan's actions. But in what way? Of course, she wasn't questioning her good fortune, but Jordan had barely glimpsed the bowl, and only one time. Perhaps whatever contact she had with it transferred to others.

Her thoughts crashed to a halt. It was her hair! Jordan had touched her hair, and the bottle of shampoo had been in the bowl. Her hair had somehow acquired magical powers, too.

Oh, she'd have to find a way to keep Jordan's hands buried in her hair. Or maybe find something else that could work as well. If a mere touch of her hair affected him, how would he react toward her if he *drank* something from the bowl? Would wine become a love potion? Or would it have the opposite effect? She doubted that. She believed the bowl would yield only positive effects and couldn't wait to see if her theory was correct.

Delighted with her discovery, she couldn't have been happier if she'd found Aladdin's lamp. Her bowl was proving to be just as magical.

Overcome with doubts, her heart tumbled in her chest. This could very well be wishful thinking. But Jordan had never acted in such a manner toward her. The bowl had to be magical, and somehow its magic had touched him.

Four

"Darling, I adore what you've done to your hair," Glynis Douglas said, fingering Ashley's curls.

"Thanks, Mom." Smiling primly, Ashley grabbed another grape from the tray that sat in front of her on the coffee table. She'd arrived at her parents' home early, ready to explain why she called Zach about the hundred dollars. But now any explanations that might mar her weekly visit seemed unnecessary, since her mother didn't mention the phone call, and her father hadn't made it home yet. Once again Zach had protected her from the wrath of their parents.

Sighing in relief, she kicked off her pumps and folded her legs beneath her. She sat on the soft leather sofa in the family room of the mansion, the airy, bright space a cheery reminder of the happy times spent there. The pool table where Zach and Jordan taught her to play still sat in the far corner, polished and with new felt; the video games she used to best them at, *Donkey Kong* and *Pac Man*, stood abandoned on an empty bookshelf.

The photograph of her and Jordan dancing at her sixteenth birthday party hung above the built-in wet bar. It was that very night that she'd promised to love Jordan, and only Jordan, for the rest of her life. How humiliated she'd been when he'd gently but firmly told her they had no future together. For years that picture had brought back bittersweet memories; now it represented a beacon of optimism.

Jordan had been in her life forever, and she marveled that she had loved him so long. After their earlier encounter, she felt confident that there *was* a future between them.

She hadn't seen him again after she parted company with him in the restaurant, but that didn't worry her. Today they had made a tentative step toward . . . *something*.

Seduction was far out of the realm of her experience, but she was willing to purchase a few guides for a crash course. Then, on the night Jordan visited her apartment, she'd be ready for him . . .

"How are you going to manage that, Ashley?"

Ashley jumped at the sound of her mother's voice. In the past, she swore Glynis could read minds, but this wasn't one of those times. Her mother would've been hysterical had she known that Ashley was thinking about seducing Jordan and buying manuals to aid her.

Casually taking another grape and popping it into her mouth, Ashley leaned back on the sofa. "How am I going to manage what, Mom?"

"To keep your hair up in this humidity? Or have you found a new hairdresser?"

Forcing thoughts of Jordan at bay, she said smugly, "No, Mom. I merely changed shampoo. Great job, huh?" She tossed her hair back, and it covered her shoulders like fine silk thread. She'd never mention her theory about the bowl to Glynis. She'd never believe her.

Besides, Ashley didn't want her parents to know she'd spent a hundred dollars to purchase the bowl. Counting on

Zach not to announce her spree, *she* wouldn't muddy the waters either. No matter how angry he was with her and how often he threatened to expose her, he never would.

Mentioning the bowl would also mean seriously considering the possibility that Jordan might have responded to her because of forces outside of himself, instead of his own basic, human desire.

"You mean you achieved that look from a mere shampoo?" Glynis asked incredulously.

"Yep." Ashley sipped from her glass of iced tea. She brushed a few errant strands of her mother's champagne-blond hair away from Glynis's smooth forehead. "Cost me all of five dollars. It'll probably work wonders on your hair as well."

Glynis laughed. "Well, it did work wonders on your hair, Ash. It's even lighter. I'm so proud of you. Five dollars, and you look like a million! You're learning at last."

Her mother rewarded her with a tight hug, which Ashley eagerly returned. It had been years since she'd received any praise from Glynis, and Ashley more than welcomed it. She reveled in it.

"Well, there's my beautiful, extravagant daughter!" a booming voice sounded throughout the room, as the tall, fit figure of Murray Douglas appeared. Deeply tanned from years spent in the sun, Murray smiled at his daughter and threw his overloaded golf bag in the corner. He wore business attire, which meant he'd probably had a morning game. At fifty-five, he still had a young, virile appearance and was quite handsome with his graying hair and moss-colored eyes. "How are you?"

"Hello, Daddy." Ashley stood and pecked her father on his cheek. "I'm fine."

"I think our daughter is finally learning the value of money," Glynis inserted proudly. "Extravagance didn't cause that drastic change in her looks. It was a five-dollar bottle of shampoo."

"A five-dollar bottle of shampoo did *that*?" Jordan asked, walking into the room behind Zach.

Sans his chef's uniform and dressed in denims and a red T-shirt, he was still the most handsome man she'd ever seen. Memories of their kiss heated her insides, and she smiled intimately at him. He'd said he wasn't coming tonight, but his appearance added a special touch to an already lighthearted evening.

"Wow!" Zach let loose a whistle. "Look at you, Ash."

"Please!" Ashley said with a laugh. "You all make it sound like the 'before' in this picture was a regular bow-wow." She concentrated on Jordan once again, her heart doing a break-dance at his close proximity. "Hi, Jordan. I didn't expect to see you here."

Jordan embraced her warmly and glided his fingers through her hair, allowing them to linger. Electric currents sizzled through her at his touch.

"Zach wouldn't take no for an answer, Ash," he said in a husky whisper. "Since my duties don't really start at the hotel until tomorrow, I couldn't refuse." His blue-gray gaze sharpened with interest as he took in her full appearance. "I'm glad I didn't."

"Why?" Murray asked with irritation, his eyes narrowed at Ashley's and Jordan's familiarity.

Confused embarrassment registering in his features, Jordan lifted his hand from Ashley's head and stared at his host, ignoring Zach's scowl. "Why? Well, it's obvious, Uncle Murray. It's the lure of Nellie's cooking."

"It didn't look like Nellie's cooking was on your mind just now," Murray snapped.

"Daddy, please!" Ashley protested, stepping between the two men. Her father's vehemence shocked her. She thought he'd welcome a relationship between her and Jordan.

"You're embarrassing me *and* Jordan. Have you forgotten I'm not a little girl anymore? I don't need your protection. I can take care of myself."

"Oh, hogwash, Ashley!" Murray pointed an angry finger at her. "It's Jordan who needs protection from you. He got all excited over what you did with a five-dollar bottle of shampoo, as did your mother and brother. What I want to know is, how much money did you spend for the red suit to go with your new look? Now, there's the true test, young lady."

So that's where his burst of anger came from. He fully expected her to have spent a fortune on a wardrobe to complement her shiny curls. She congratulated her frugality, forced though it might have been. This fabulous suit was eight months old!

Ashley wrapped her sleeveless arms around her blustering father's neck and kissed him again. He fingered her hair. "Daddy dearest, I should be insulted by your lack of confidence in me. But I'm not. It's just the kind of reaction that keeps me on my toes. In answer to your question, I haven't bought a dress in over eight months." Her voice rang with triumph.

"Eight months?" Murray asked in happy surprise. "Well, this just won't do! With that new look, you're just begging for a new wardrobe. Where's my checkbook?"

Positive her father was joking with her, Ashley stood with her mouth open as Murray patted his chest, reached inside his coat pocket, and extracted the blue leather case that held his checks.

"Let's see. Let's see," he said thoughtfully. "You'll need shoes, purses, stockings, and whatever other accessories young ladies use."

"Sure, Dad," Ashley said sardonically, going along with his game for the hell of it. She wanted to tell him to throw in a couple of thousand for her bills, but couldn't. Her parents believed she had her finances under control.

"Five thousand ought to cover your shopping spree." Rapidly he began scribbling on the check, while everyone stood astounded at his actions.

Her mouth agape, Ashley stared at her father's bent head. Was this the same man who just last week threatened to disinherit Zach if he gave Ashley any monetary assistance?

"I don't believe this!" Zach sputtered, furious. "Dad, you're Ashley's biggest critic where money is concerned. Now you're writing her a check for five thousand dollars?"

"You keep your comments to yourself, mister! This is my little girl, and she needs a helping hand," Murray said. He beamed in her direction. "Look how beautiful she is. Do you want her to go around in rags with a face like that? Even Jordan noticed how lovely she is."

Zach glanced at Jordan and frowned. Jordan's remorseless shrug only added to her brother's annoyance. For the time being, she wouldn't stress herself out over why her family seemed so dead set against any relationship between her and Jordan. It was still too early for that. But when she finally won Jordan over, she'd warn everyone not to interfere. They'd have enough hurdles to overcome, without the extra problems that her father and brother's disapproval would create.

"This is insane," Zach muttered. Stomping to the sofa, he sat and lifted his long legs on the table, then closed his eyes. "I hope you're not becoming senile at such a young age, Dad."

Everyone ignored Zach's comment as Murray handed the check to Ashley. Fingers trembling, Ashley accepted the piece of paper. This was a dream come true! After years of making her eke out a living to make up for her shopping sprees, her father had handed her the means to pay her bills without worry for several months to come. She stared down at the check. "Daddy," she whispered, truly astonished, "I don't know what to say."

Without a doubt, she knew the contact with her hair was responsible for her father's changed attitude. Jordan and her mother had touched her hair as well. Sourpuss Zach was the only person who *hadn't* glided his fingers through her tresses.

Something wonderful was happening to her, something she couldn't explain. Nor would she want to, because no one would believe her. Her father, her staunchest critic, had parted with five thousand dollars for the sole purpose of a long-overdue shopping spree for his little girl.

"You deserve it, darling," Glynis told her. "You're proving to us how hard you're trying."

Zach straightened in his seat, and he and Jordan exchanged wry glances. For the first time in memory, Ashley feared Zach would expose her spending. Beyond his ironic smile, Jordan remained passive. They must have been thinking of the money she'd spent on the bowl. *Well-spent money, boys.*

"Thank you, Daddy. You, too, Mom, for not objecting."

"Object, darling? Never," Glynis assured her. "A girl needs to release a little frustration sometimes. What better way to do that than by shopping? We expect you to take this gift at face value."

Her mother was right, as she'd proven to Ashley time and again over the years. Ashley might've cried buckets on Zach's shoulder after Jordan's rejection when she was sixteen, but her parents sent her shopping for the African safari she and Glynis were going on. Trips to Disney World, Six Flags, and Astro World had dominated her childhood. By the time she was fifteen, she'd gone to Europe twice and had seen and bought things other kids only dreamed of.

Why shouldn't she take this money and go shopping?

For eight months, she'd worn the exact same outfits day in and day out. It wasn't the way she'd been brought up, and to her it was downright obscene.

Surely she wouldn't spend the *entire* five thousand dollars. A portion would be left to pay a bill or two. Her parents expected her to spend the money on herself, not waste it on bills. If by some accident, she spent *all* the money, then she'd come back to her parents, let them bury their hands in her hair again, and ask for more money.

Really, that bowl was the wisest investment she'd made in years. She couldn't wait to return home and show her allegiance to it. By then, Jordan should be well under *her* spell as well.

Just as Ashley opened her mouth to ask Jordan to take a walk with her, Nellie bustled in.

"Dinner be ready, Mrs. Douglas," the little woman announced. Her keen black eyes were set in a tawny-colored face. When she saw Jordan, she smiled. "Jordie! You've finally made it home."

Jordan wrapped his arms around Nellie in a bear hug. "Good to see you, darlin'. I sure missed your cooking."

"Well, I'm glad you're back." That knowing gaze focused on Ashley. "Maybe now you'll discover what's really good for you."

Rising from his seat, Zach went and placed a kiss on Nellie's cheek. "Oh, no, Nellie! Please don't give this rascal any ideas. Besides, I think Jordan already knows what's good for him. Right, pal?"

"Sure, Zach." He gazed at Ashley. "Care to escort me into the dining room, sweetheart? I am the invited guest here."

"Like hell." Zach snorted. "And even if you *were* considered a guest, you'd be *my* guest, so I'd do the escorting."

Hands on hips, Ashley scowled at her brother. "Since when have you become so mannerly, Zachery? As I recall, you're the guy who left Fawn to her own devices in this mansion over the weekend, because you received a last-minute golfing invitation."

"Kids, please!" Glynis clapped her hands for order. "I see no problem with Ashley escorting Jordan into the dining room. You know, women's lib and all? Besides, they're old friends. Why are you being so retentive over this, Zach?"

"Forget it, Mom." Zach started off. "I wouldn't want to ruin our meal."

"Yeah, let's just ruin our evening afterward and discuss this," Jordan responded.

"Boys, that's enough!" Murray ordered sternly. "This power play you two have always had over Ashley is a thing of the past. She's a grown woman, quite capable of handling both of you."

"That's right," Ashley put in, grabbing her suit jacket from the back of the sofa and putting it on, then stepping into her pumps. "I love you both dearly and—"

She halted as the impact of her words hit her. To admit she loved Jordan was harmless; to admit to the *way* she loved him wasn't. Until yesterday, he hadn't known she existed. Such an avowal this early in the game might scare him away completely.

At the moment, everyone was staring at her with expectancy. But only Jordan's reaction mattered. Beyond an arching of his perfect brows, he showed no emotion at all.

"And?" Zach asked.

She resented Zach's persistence as much as she resented his overprotectiveness. "And, uh, I'm hungry." She held out her arm to Jordan. When he took it, they preceded everyone into the small, intimate dining room, used only for family dinners.

The next two hours passed swiftly. The earlier tension fell away, replaced by easy camaraderie, good food, and fine wine. Ashley couldn't remember when she'd had a more pleasant evening in her parents' company.

Devoid of questions and accusations about her finances, the conversation about the hotel was spirited, and Jordan was breathtaking. No matter how she tried to avoid it, her gaze kept straying in his direction. Every time she did so, she found his smoky scrutiny focused on her as well.

Their interaction wasn't lost to her family. While Glynis and Murray smiled with satisfaction, Zach glowered his disapproval, which didn't daunt Ashley at all. Jordan became less bold with his glances, however.

When the evening finally ended, Ashley stood by the front door, watching as Zach followed his usual custom and prepared to take her home. He quietly spoke to Murray about what needed to be done at the office first thing in the morning. Now that Zach's attention was diverted, she and Jordan stared openly at each other.

Jordan pointed to himself then the door, and Ashley nodded quickly, not daring to pass up the chance of having Jordan all to herself.

"Excuse me, Zach, Uncle Murray, but I'm leaving. By the way, buddy, I'll take Ashley home. Save you the trouble."

Zach scowled at him. "It's no bother, Jordan," he snapped. "I've been doing this for two years."

"Then you need a night off," Ashley said pleasantly, hurrying into the fray. She kissed her brother's firm jaw. "You've already gone above and beyond the call of duty, Zach, and I love you. I'm tired, and you and Daddy are going on and on." She glanced at Jordan. "I'd better get my purse if I want to get into my apartment. My keys are in there. Be back in a jif." In a flash, she disappeared down the hall to the den.

Angrily, Zach turned to Jordan. "What's with you, man?"

"Listen, Jordan," Murray inserted before Jordan could

respond. "Be careful. My little girl has become very persuasive these days. Before you know it, she'll have you in a position you might regret. Excuse me, boys." With that, the older man strolled away.

"Dammit, Jordan, what's with you?" Zach asked again, as if his father hadn't spoken.

"What are you talking about, Zachery?"

"The looks you gave Ashley all through dinner and the rest of the evening. And now this. You don't even own a car. How do you expect to get her home? You seem to have completely forgotten the conversation we had the other day."

Jordan threaded his hand through his hair in annoyance. "I haven't forgotten anything, Zach," he replied. "Besides, I'm sure you're here to refresh my memory if I did. To answer your question about getting her home, the buses run 'til midnight."

"Buses?" Zach shouted. "Still equating *cheap* with frugality, eh, Jordan? Don't you think my sister at least deserves a cab?"

"Here I am, guys." Breathless, Ashley rushed back to where they stood. "Ready?" She looked from Zach to Jordan and blinked at the anger she saw on their faces.

"Do you mind a bus ride, Ash?" Jordan asked, without taking his angry regard from Zach.

"Of course not, Jordan," she quickly answered, unsure of what was going on. Jordan and Zach had been at odds before, but tonight they were downright hostile toward each other. She knew she was the reason for their present animosity, but Zach's attitude would change soon enough. First and foremost, he and Jordan were friends. As long as Zach wasn't pulling rank and playing the bullying, older brother with his best friend, they would resolve whatever differences they felt offended by. "I'm looking forward to it."

She hugged Zach affectionately. Automatically his arms went around her shoulders, her abundant hair spilling loosely over them. "I'll talk to you later, Zachery the Daiquiri."

He chuckled at the nickname she'd given him years ago, the scowl disappearing from his handsomely rugged features. "Right, Rash Ash," he said, reaching his hand out to Jordan. "Maybe it's the moon, but I've just made a complete ass of myself, Jordie. I apologize."

Jordan took the proffered hand. "Accepted," he said. "I'll catch you later. Come on, Rash Ash, we're outta here. Say good night to Aunt Glynis and Uncle Murray for me." Opening the double entrance doors, he waited until Ashley walked outside before following her and closing the doors behind him. In silence, they walked down the curving pathway, bordered on each side by lush, green lawn that glistened with dew in the darkness.

Stars dotted the sky like glittering diamonds, while the slivered moon hardly penetrated the indigo night. The scent of night jasmine and sweet olive was prevalent, and Ashley mourned the loss of a perfect evening.

But her jitteriness prevented her from truly enjoying Jordan's nearness. What indeed was happening? Daddy had turned generous, Mom was agreeable with everything, and Jordan and Zach had nearly come to blows.

Was it really the bowl that was creating this madness, or was it the shampoo itself? At some point or another, they'd all touched her hair.

Perhaps she was merely dreaming. She had accepted all the strange occurrences without explanation, adopting a cavalier attitude that needed serious reevaluation.

A *bowl* with special powers? Preposterous! But if the upside-down attitudes of her loved ones hadn't been an indication, then her hair and the sudden appearance of the hundred dollars certainly were.

A chill passing through her, Ashley's heart skipped a beat, and she held on to Jordan's arm. She wondered if the bowl really did possess magic powers. Or was it merely haunted?

Five

Jordan sat quietly beside Ashley, who occupied the window seat and gazed out the window of the nearly empty streetcar onto which they'd transferred from the bus.

Tension filled him, heightened by his deep awareness of Ashley. He'd always liked Ashley, disregarding a few parts of her personality that he couldn't tolerate, but since he'd returned he was thinking about her more and more in an intimate sense. The matter seemed to have been taken completely out of his hands, as if magnetic fields were drawing them insistently together.

Uncontrollable images of enjoying Ashley's wit and energy had run rampant in his mind ever since he'd kissed her earlier in the day, when every delicious curve of her tall frame had been molded to him. Then he'd walked into the mansion tonight, and the times they'd spent together there as friends rushed back to him, along with the dazzling desire he'd experienced for her at the restaurant.

Though he'd long ago set himself above her as her brother's friend and the experienced man who was off-limits to her, they'd always been friends. He enjoyed being around Ashley, and part of his attitude was because of the fact that Ashley had been a mere child when she'd declared her love for him. The other reason was because of his friendship with Zach. Jordan had correctly perceived Zach's disapproval of a relationship between him and Ashley. Yesterday Zach hinted at it. Tonight he'd left little doubt in Jordan's mind.

Tonight, though, Jordan didn't care about Zach's reaction. Nor did he care that he and Ashley weren't compatible enough to involve themselves in an affair. He resented her complete disregard for money, reinforced by her parents' coddling of her. Even now, he felt irritated that Uncle Murray had blithely handed Ashley five thousand dollars, which she happily accepted. For a day at the mall she'd ignored her option of refusing the money.

He could never accept Ashley's views about money, which left a long-term future together in serious doubt. Yet the unheralded attraction that began yesterday, at the noisy intersection of Carrollton and Bienville, lured him just then. *Him*, a man who'd mastered his meager finances and amassed a small fortune.

Jordan squinted his gaze at the glittering restaurant the streetcar rattled past, and knew Ashley's exit was two stops away. Her head was still averted, and he wondered what went through her mind—not that he'd delve.

He was afraid that she'd invite him inside her apartment so they could talk, and that things would get out of hand. Someone needed to put a halt to their attraction. He'd played the bad guy once; he could do so again.

"I think the stop coming up is yours, Ashley."

"Right." Quietly Ashley pulled the buzzer cord, then stood and looked at him expectantly.

Guiltily he stood as well, and together they went to the rear of the vehicle. He hated to admit that he actually considered letting her depart without him. When the streetcar

halted fully, they exited and hurried across the street. They
had two full blocks to walk before they reached her apartment.

"Thanks for the company, Jordan."

Her long legs easily kept pace with his fast strides, and
Jordan smiled. She'd always been athletic. And competi-
tive. And outgoing. Before her disastrous declaration of
love, he'd enjoyed spending time with her. Setting himself
up as another brother had been safe for him. It had also
been misleading to her. By the time she was fifteen, he'd
known that she was wild for him. But he thought if he
ignored her fascination with him, it would eventually go
away.

It was a fool's paradise. Until she told him she'd never
love anyone other than him, he'd never discouraged her
attention. Then he broke her heart by denying what she felt
was real. No wonder Zach wanted him to stay away from
her.

If he had any sense, he would do exactly that. Apparently
he didn't have an *ounce* of sense. Because at the moment
there was nothing he wanted more than to repeat the kiss
they'd shared earlier. "It's my pleasure to keep you company, although I'm sure you would've gotten home safely.
Zach is always there to protect his baby sister."

The glaring streetlamps briefly illuminated Ashley's soft
skin. Even as tired as she looked, she was quite pretty. But
at his sarcasm, she frowned and shrugged her shoulders, no
longer the little girl who pouted.

"Maybe," she conceded, "but I *am* a grown woman now.
Plenty capable of protecting myself. Isn't it obvious yet?
I've lived alone for two years and haven't felt the need to
run back home in fear of the bogeyman."

The five-thousand-dollar check flashed in his mind again,
and his irritation with her increased. He laughed derisively.
"Why should you run back home? Zach is always there to

protect you from any bogeyman. And your father. Ha! Ol'
Uncle Murray. In spite of what he says, you can be sure
he'll be there to dole out the big bucks. Tell me, Ash, how's
five thousand dollars going to teach you anything about
managing your finances?"

"Whoa! What's your problem, Jordan? I didn't ask
Daddy for that money—"

"No, but you certainly didn't have to take it!"

"The hell I didn't!" Ashley fairly snarled. "It's been two
years since my father's given me a penny. Whatever
sparked his generosity tonight, I wasn't about to look a gift
horse in the mouth."

"Not that you'd try, even if you could." Her angry flush
released his own pent-up emotions in a firestorm. Because
of Ashley, he'd nearly come to blows with his best friend
and ignored their incompatibility. "I thought you'd at least
give it the old college try, Ashley. But I was wrong. You'll
never change."

"How dare you, Jordan?" Ashley snapped. Outrage
sparked a golden glow in her hazel eyes, the full, sweeping
lashes fluttering furiously. "That's not fair. That money is
a *gift* from my father, and I didn't solicit it. I was as astonished as everyone else when he gave it to me. Tell me, if
you had been given five thousand dollars, would you have
returned it?"

"No! Why should I?" Jordan asked, realizing how futile
his arguments were, proving just how right his belief was
that Ashley would never change. "But the difference between you and me is that *I* would put it to good use. I
wouldn't blow it on some silly clothes!"

"Oh, you're impossible! You probably have fungus
growing in your wallet from lack of use. For your information, Jordan Bennett, I'm not as openhanded with money
as I used to be. But I do spend money enough to enjoy life.
Something you need to try occasionally. Good night!" In

long, angry strides, she covered the few remaining yards to
her building.

"Ashley, wait a minute!"

"Bite me!" she yelled. Slamming the iron gate closed,
she stomped out of Jordan's view.

He started to follow her but foresaw one of two things
happening. Because of their simmering desire for one another, either the argument would spiral so far out of control
that irreparable damage would be done to their friendship,
or he'd give in to the urge to make love to Ashley.

Rubbing the back of his neck in frustration, he blew out
a sigh. Indeed, just what madness had possessed him?

Ashley ran up the few steps to the porch and unlocked the
entrance door. Without a backward glance, she went inside
and kicked the door closed.

Things had been going along so well between her and
Jordan. What had happened for the night to regress so?
Unless she did something drastic, Jordan would always see
her as the spoiled little rich girl she'd once been.

Weary suddenly, she flipped on the overhead light,
walked on leaden legs to her sofa and sat down. With a
sigh, she opened her purse and retrieved the check. What
indeed should she do with her gift? Although she thought
she'd settled that issue with herself at her parents' house,
the thought had plagued her the entire ride home. Until
Jordan's self-righteousness asserted itself, she'd thought to
discuss it with him.

How wrong she'd been about the bowl's effect on Jordan. Perhaps she was also wrong in thinking some magic
power caused her father's change. Maybe he'd given her
the money as a simple act of parental pride over her prog-
ress these past two years, though less significant than her
parents believed.

And she wasn't brainless. She knew what she *should* do

with the five thousand dollars. Her wardrobe was suffi-
ciently appropriate for her job, and it wasn't as if her dance
card was filled with hot dates. Still, "dress for success" was
a borrowed motto, a creed she'd been weaned on. Besides,
Daddy specifically said to buy a new wardrobe, and she
certainly wouldn't have it said that she disobeyed him
again.

Not giving it another thought, she decided to put her bills
on hold for another month and visit Canal Place after work
tomorrow. The mall was a shopper's dream, boasting such
stores as Saks Fifth Avenue, Kenneth Cole, Ann Taylor,
Joan Vass, Caché, Inc. and a variety of other specialty
shops. It was also close to her job, which meant she
wouldn't have to trek across town to another mall.

Dropping the check in the bowl, she stood and went to
her bedroom, anticipating the pulse-pounding excitement
that would steal into her when she set foot in Canal Place
after months of deprivation.

Six

Like a life force, the shampoo tingled through Ashley's hair the next morning as she worked it into a fluffy lather for the second time. The powerful fragrance surrounded her, and she breathed in deeply, energized by the warm water flowing through her hair and the floral essence permeating the confines of the shower.

She'd overslept and, if she didn't want to be late for work, she needed to get a move on. Regretfully she turned off the flow of water, opened the shower door and stepped onto the soft mat, then grabbed a fluffy towel from the rack. Quickly wrapping it around her body, she got her hair dryer from the shelf, turned it on, and hurriedly dried her beautiful tresses.

Once she was completely dressed, she double-checked her appearance in the mirror. Satisfied with the results of her grooming, she went into the living room. Noticing the time, she smiled happily, having dressed in record time. With ten minutes to kill before getting to her bus stop, she deserved a pat on the back.

She'd awakened in a jubilant mood, hardly able to contain her excitement for her after-work excursion. She was even considering starting her shopping spree on her lunch hour. First she needed to deposit the check into her bank account. Such a hefty amount might take several days to clear, but the same went for any checks she wrote later that day at the mall.

Her heels clicking on the hardwood floor, her fragrant hair bouncing sexily around her shoulders and breasts, she took her purse from the sofa where she'd left it last night. Quickly taking out a deposit slip, she scribbled down the necessary information, then got her check and looked gratefully down at it.

Her horrified scream stuck in her throat. Instead, a faint squeak squeezed past her throat muscles. Bringing the check closer to her eyes, her nose nearly touched the paper. She found the same thing she had a moment ago. Absolutely nothing! The check that promised such a lovely day was blank!

"Wha . . . ?" Faint hysteria threading through her, she stared in wide-eyed amazement at the bowl. "Oh, my God! Oh, no, this isn't happening! This *couldn't* happen." Frantically she looked into the dish. Perhaps her father accidentally handed her two checks. Knowing how implausible that theory was, she threw aside the bills laying in the bowl all the same.

Dropping down to her knees, she reached her hand beneath the small space of the sofa table, finding nothing but the dusty, cold floor. A sob escaped her; she crawled around the floor searching for the check she'd brought home last night. "Oh, God! Daddy must have used invisible ink to create this elaborate joke and finish teaching me a lesson about money. No, he wouldn't do that. He was too sincere." She passed a trembling hand over her tear-filled eyes. "This is serious. Not only am I talking out loud to myself, I'm answering myself as well."

Flushed with exertion and anxiety, she got to her feet and dusted herself off. "Dammit!" she cried when she saw the small run in her stockings. "I'm nearly late for my bus." Brushing away angry tears, she scowled at the bowl and threw the check back into it. "I warn you, you thieving hunk of metal, I expect to find the amount of that check fully restored when I return, or I'll take a sledgehammer to you!" She leaned into the bowl's cavity, not caring in the least that her family would believe she was a candidate for the asylum if they saw her just then. "Do I make myself clear?"

She could have sworn that for a moment a ray of heat emanated from the piece, and she reeled back, frightened.

This was all a bad dream! The moment she stepped outside into the sunny morning and made the mad dash to reach the bus on time, she'd awaken.

Sadly that didn't happen. Instead, just as she reached the bus stop, the doors of the big white bus, with the purple, green, and gold stripes, snapped shut as the vehicle started off.

"Hey! Hey, mister, *stop*!" Running alongside the vehicle and beckoning the driver with frenzied hand gestures, Ashley screamed at the top of her lungs. "Hey, you big oa—"

The bus halted, and the doors opened. A stoic driver greeted her. Breathing rapidly, Ashley climbed the three steps, thankful for her tennis shoes. Before she reached the money machine, the mustachioed man put the bus in motion. She grabbed the steel pole to steady herself.

Glaring at the driver and the other passengers who appeared annoyed with *her* and hating buses just a little more than usual, Ashley went to a seat in the back, grumbling. Miserably holding on to the bag that contained her wallet, pumps, and other necessary items, she leaned her head back.

She wasn't looking forward to seeing Jordan at the hotel.

She knew this wasn't her day. Besides, the possibility that she'd lost her mind was very real.

What sane person would scold and threaten a *bowl*?

"Ashley, are you all right?"

Gritting her teeth at Carson Wood's question, Ashley nodded. For the hundredth time that morning he'd asked the same thing, and each time she wanted to snarl at him to mind his own damned business. But that would be unprofessional, not to mention unexplainable. So with amazing control, she'd managed to follow the thread of conversation in the meeting that had eaten away most of the morning.

"I'm fine, Wood." Tapping her pen against a legal pad in agitation, she rubbed her eyes. "Just a little tired, as I've already said."

"Well, we're about done here anyway."

Instead of being a project manager of the Blackwell Corporation, he could've easily been a male model. Possessed of a weight trainer's physique and a chocolate complexion, he was quite handsome. He also had quite a head for business and was hell to bargain with. Somehow Ashley managed to do so, securing his agreement that Blackwell would hire the necessary people to complete the hotel's refurbishment within the fifteen-month time frame she'd recommended. He'd also agreed to lower the price.

This would have been quite a coup had her day started off differently.

"Fine, Wood. I'll call Zach and tell him to expect a call from your people to set a time to sign the contracts. As soon as he knows something, I'll make sure Mr. Russell's schedule is clear. In the meantime, I'll do my report on ideas for the renovation and send it to you on Monday. I'll also make sure to have copies for my father and Mr. Russell."

Wood nodded. "Sounds good, Ashley." Standing, he extended a muscled arm. "You're one tough cookie, lady."

Accepting the proffered hand, Ashley laughed distractedly. "You're rather obstinate yourself, Wood."

"So my wife tells me constantly. Of course, I don't agree."

"Of course." She followed him to the glass doors of the meeting room and out into the carpeted hallway as they headed toward the elevator bank. "It was good seeing you."

"You, too, Ashley. By the way, you look great. I love what you've done to your hair."

"Thanks." Mentioning her hair brought to mind that sorry little bowl—and her belief that it was possessed. Until this morning, she'd thought it an enchanted creation, out to do lighthearted magic. But it was an evil, mean-spirited piece of metal, cursed with wickedness.

It was all right when it was giving, but she wouldn't tolerate *taking. Stealing* was more appropriate for what it did. The one-legged bandit.

For eight months, she'd dealt with the disappointment of not being able to shop and had come to terms with it—or so she'd thought. The bitter defeat she felt at the moment told her it had only been a temporary acceptance of a situation that she'd had no control over.

Yet she did have control. She had credit cards. Why shouldn't she splurge a little? Everyone expected her to do so anyway. She'd worry about the bill some other time.

A *ding* announced the elevator's arrival. "I'll have my secretary call by Friday, Ashley," Wood said, stepping into the dim interior.

"That'll be fine," Ashley responded. "Talk to you later."

Once the elevator doors closed on Carson Wood, Ashley headed back to her office, where she immediately dialed Zach's office number. If she paused for one moment, she'd fall into deep reflection and she couldn't afford that, not when she was so confused. She'd stretched the meeting out with Wood as long as possible because she didn't want to face her other duties, mainly seeing Jordan, since *she'd* suggested an overhaul of the restaurant as well and *she'd* suggested hiring a new chef.

Just as she was about to hang up, Zach answered.

"I was about ready to give up on you," Ashley announced, her ever-present cheeriness missing.

"Hi, Ashley. What can I do for you?"

Ashley sighed at Zach's less than friendly tone. "Carson Wood just left my office, and I wanted to apprise you of what happened."

"Make it quick. I have to pick up Fawn for lunch."

"I can call you later, then."

"No, you called now, so you obviously wanted to talk. Talk."

With studied calm, she explained Wood's decision to Zach, hating his short responses and the underlying disapproval in his voice, which she knew had nothing to do with her accomplishments on the Blackwell bid.

This conversation only added to her self-pity. Zach was becoming far too bossy. If she'd wanted to be scrutinized and disciplined like a schoolgirl for every little thing, she would still be living at home. Only now she wasn't sure if Zach was angry with her because of the money their father gave to her or because she'd left with Jordan.

At the end of her explanation, Zach asked, "That all?"

"Yeah."

"All right, then, I'll talk to you later."

The buzzing of the dial tone greeted her. Setting the receiver on its cradle, Ashley buried her face in her hands. She and Jordan were on opposite ends on the totem pole; therefore, she really shouldn't allow him to threaten her close relationship with her brother.

"Ashley?"

"What?" she screeched in irritation, lost in thought, her eyes widening when she caught sight of Jim Russell backing out of the door he'd silently opened.

"I-I'm sorry, Ashley. I can come back if you're busy."

Her cheeks burning with embarrassment, Ashley stood and rushed to where Mr. Russell stood. "Oh, Mr. Russell, I didn't mean to yell. I was deep in unpleasant thoughts. Please, come in."

"Whoa-ho," Mr. Russell said with a chuckle. He pulled his handkerchief from his front coat pocket and mopped his brow. "I thought *I* had done something to offend you. That's a relief. Well, Ashley, what can I do for you?"

Returning to her desk and reseating herself, Ashley smiled. Mr. Russell was one of the wonders of the ages. He'd made a fortune in the hotel business with his shrewd management, yet he was the most absentminded person she knew. "I didn't summon *you*, Mr. Russell," she said patiently. "You came seeking me, remember?"

"I did? Whatever for?"

"Beats me."

"Oh, now, I remember!" Mr. Russell exclaimed happily. "I just saw James Brown in the lobby—"

"James Brown? The singer?" Ashley popped from her chair again, patting her hair and heading to the coat rack where her suit jacket hung. "Why doesn't someone tell me about these things?"

"He sings, too? What a talented young man."

Her heart sinking, Ashley stopped in her tracks. "Who sings, too?"

"Why, the new chef. Isn't that what you just said?"

"No. I . . . oh, never mind." Thoroughly aggravated with her boss, Ashley marched back to her desk. Instead of sitting in the chair behind it, she propped herself against the desk, crossing her ankles. "What about the new chef?"

"Nothing important. How's he working out?"

Her thoughts drifted to last night. On a personal level, he wasn't working out at all. On a professional level, she wasn't sure. "This week will be his first full week, Mr. Russell. We can judge better later. But I was going to seek you out because Carson Wood was here this morning." She quickly briefed Mr. Russell on the meeting.

"Good, good, I knew you could do it. Carry on, Ashley," Jim Russell said and departed the room, just as her phone rang.

Hoping it was Zach, she hurried to it. "Hello?"

"Ash?"

Her insides tumbled at the sound of the masculine voice. "Jordan?"

"Yeah." A rich chuckle accompanied the answer. "Listen, have you eaten yet?"

"No, I haven't." *Be still my heart.*

"Well, how's about I cook you lunch? My treat and my way of apologizing."

Twirling her hair around her finger, Ashley giggled. "How many ways do you know how to apologize? Personally, I liked the way you apologized the first time."

Laughter soared through the phone, and tingles raced through her being. He hadn't taken offense to her forwardness. In fact, he seemed to appreciate it. That heartened her for the moment and she forgot her earlier distress.

Jordan cleared his throat. "You don't mince words, do you? After hearing the invitation you threw at me last night, I was tempted to join you and take you up on your offer."

So he had heard her. Only he'd ignored the anger that accompanied the words "bite me," and turned it into something wild and provocative. Hearing the wicked note in Jordan's tone and having absolutely no experience with men left her feeling embarrassed and unsure. The manuals she'd considered buying were becoming more and more practical, if she meant to have Jordan see her as a full-grown woman now.

She laughed, uncomfortable. "My stars, did I really say that?"

The pause in Jordan's voice seemed endless. She wondered what crossed his mind.

"Yes, Ash, you did," he said finally, the warmth in his voice not disguising the underlying seriousness. "But if I were inclined, kissing you seems less violent."

"I'm all for doing away with violence," Ashley responded breathlessly. Flirting with Jordan was like dancing with fire. Even if they didn't have inherent money differences coloring their attraction, a relationship between them jeopardized Zach and Jordan's friendship. She knew Zach forgave *her* anything. Yet it almost felt as if words were being put into her mouth. It also felt so right that she ignored her better judgment. "Especially in such a pleasurable way."

"I'll keep that in mind. See you in a little bit."

When she hung up the receiver, she leaned back in her chair. She was throwing herself at Jordan and she didn't have to do that. She wasn't sixteen anymore. If Jordan wanted her, he'd have to make the first move.

The millennium was near to hand and women's priorities *had* evolved, but she still had her pride. She refused to go after him and risk rejection again.

During lunch, she wouldn't get personal. Business and food would be the topic of conversation, not kissing and certainly not *biting*. Maybe she'd even talk about her bowl.

Nah, that would be a mistake. In a way, that was too personal because it had to do with her finances—the source of their argument last night.

He'd said she wouldn't change. She'd bet that she would. At least she was trying. But was Jordan? Would he always be . . . frugal? Really, he was too tightfisted for his own good. Or anyone else's for that matter.

Suddenly she dreaded seeing him again. Her heart didn't always listen to her head where Jordan was concerned. Trying to discipline her spending urges, she'd had setbacks occasionally. She couldn't allow a setback to occur with Jordan. Her emotions would come unraveled all over again.

In her opinion, she really had too much to contend with. Until Jordan began working at the hotel, her job had been ideal. Now she could look forward to unbelievable stress.

Stress at work with seeing Jordan everyday and getting the hotel refurbishment completed at cost and within fifteen months. Stress within her family because of her brother's overprotectiveness and her father's sudden generosity. Stress at home with a bowl that had her at its mercy.

Perhaps not. She just wouldn't put anything inside it anymore.

Going to the door, she opened it and stepped into the hallway. When she reached the lobby and headed toward the restaurant, another thought occurred to Ashley.

She could also get rid of her bowl. But that would be like throwing away a hundred dollars. And *that,* according to her family, would be frivolous.

Seven

With precision born of experience, Jordan deftly chopped fresh garlic, oregano, basil, parsley, and chives, then mixed the seasonings together.

Placing the mixture next to the crushed white pepper and mopping his brow with a nearby hand towel, he got his bottles of oil and vinegar and poured a measure of each into a salad dressing carafe. Once he'd shaken the combination vigorously, he added his seasonings and pepper, replaced the stopper, shook the carafe again, then opened his creation and sniffed.

Marvelous! A perfect addition to the Gulf shrimp, plump and pinked from boiling, vine-ripened tomatoes, and crisp green Romaine lettuce he had for the salad. Jordan couldn't wait for Ashley to taste his latest addition to the menu. He hoped he'd have time to sit and enjoy the salad with her, instead of having the waiter bring it to her as was the case with the soup du jour.

This wasn't what he had planned when he'd invited her to lunch to apologize, but it seemed as soon as she seated herself, customers began filing into the restaurant, and orders started pouring in for Jordan.

When Zach tipped him off to the opening here, he had told Jordan that restaurant sales had declined in the last two years, just as they had in the hotel. Jordan's love for his profession showed in his tasty creations, and Zach felt he'd be a welcome addition to the hotel staff.

Yet seeing the crowds today, Jordan wondered what the restaurant had been like before sales declined. New Orleanians loved food, and word spread quickly about a good chef, but this was amazing! His first full day here and the restaurant was abuzz.

Poor Ash! She came down expecting to eat immediately and almost passed out from starvation instead. Jordan smiled, remembering the faces of hunger she'd displayed after a full thirty minutes had gone by and he hadn't taken a break yet. Licking her lips, sniffing, sighing, and pretending to pass out from hunger, were just a few theatrics she'd exhibited. Taking pity upon her, he'd asked Curtis to bring her a bowl of the artichoke and chicken soup that would be the Wednesday lunch special from now on.

"Salad ready yet?"

"Just a second," Jordan answered the waiter, who seemed impatient to receive his order. Rechecking the ticket that had come back ten minutes earlier, he began arranging the salad on the china. "Crowd thinning out?"

"Two tables are left."

Jordan paused. "Ashley's gone?"

"Miss Ashley? No, she's still at the corner table, waiting for her next course."

"Ask her to give me a few more minutes." Proud of the salads he'd created in record time, he smiled at the waiter as the man took the filled plates from him.

"Sure thing, Mr. Jordan."

Now that the mad rush was coming to an end, Jordan

surveyed his domain. Dirty pots and pans filled the huge, stainless steel double sink; tea and water glasses, sweaty with melting ice, lined the butcher block table next to it, along with bowls and plates that needed scraping before being washed.

The lingering smells of strawberry glacé and fresh seasonings combined with brewing coffee and baking bread; the powerful central air conditioner warded off the heat of the big oven.

He really didn't have to help clean up. That's what he had assistants for, but he enjoyed the cooking process from beginning to end and everything between. Ashley awaited him, however, so he'd help clean up once she returned to her office.

Last night sleep had eluded him, while her parting words wreaked havoc with his aplomb. He realized he'd still been smarting from the argument he'd had with Zach, and just as he resented the label of cheapskate that Zach pinned on him, Jordan understood how Ashley resented being called a spendthrift. Her anger had been justified, but putting five thousand dollars in the hands of a shopaholic like Ashley was tantamount to putting liquor into the hands of an alcoholic.

Last night he also decided he wouldn't see her anymore than he had to—only on a professional level. If he could, he'd avoid *that*. He really didn't have to see her at all. Communication between them could be relayed through the restaurant manager, Petersen. Something had to be done. Every time he was in her company, his feelings for Ashley escalated to a dangerous level.

The gangly, lively sixteen-year-old he'd left behind had been all legs and arms. But she'd turned into a beauty who provoked images of those long, now-shapely legs wrapped securely around his back in passion. It was those thoughts that could get him into serious trouble. Even weighing her positive points against her negative points didn't help. To him, she was beautiful, smart, funny. In a word: delightful. He had trouble remembering that she could also be wayward and stubborn, in addition to being a shopaholic and a horrible cook.

Yet she *had* made an effort to change. She couldn't have remained on her own for two entire years and still be the same Ashley he'd left behind. For that reason, he'd decided to break his self-imposed rules one last time and invite her to lunch.

A hand flashed in front of Jordan's face. "Hey, man, you in a trance or somethin'?"

"Arthur!" Jordan snarled. He was in no mood for the man's antics today. Even if he had given the impression of staring into space like an oddball. Thoroughly confused, he was entitled to his wandering thoughts.

"Hey, easy, Fido," Arthur teased. He snatched his hat off his head, revealing the small plaits that would grow into dreadlocks. "Somebody been feedin' you raw meat?"

"Arthur!" Ashley's voice floated to them. "Leave Jordan alone."

"Hi, Ash," Jordan said smoothly.

She wore a pale blue suit that looked fabulous on her tall, willowy frame. When she came closer to him, her long, thick hair brushed against his arm. His loins tightened, and he sighed.

"What have you made?" she asked, her appreciative hazel gaze piercing his shallow defenses.

"Seafood salad." Busying himself with getting two plates from under the counter and arranging the salads, he started talking again. "Sorry it didn't work out the way I planned, but this is the first break I've had since morning."

"What you gonna do, Jordan? Apologize to her again?" Arthur asked with a wicked chuckle. He propped himself on the tall wooden stool and winked at Ashley.

Ashley burst out laughing. "Don't you have any control over your help, Jordan?" she teased.

Hands on hips, Arthur glared at Ashley with feigned indignation. "Who you callin' *help*, Ashley? I am a *chef's assistant.*"

Ashley stepped aside to let Jordan get to the table with the two plates filled with the salad. "A sous-chef," she corrected.

"Don't call me that either," Arthur said. "Don't sound ritzy enough. And I'm a real ritzy brother lately."

Jordan shook his head. "Assistant Chef, would you be so kind as to put some napkins and crackers and eating utensils on the table for me and Ashley?"

"*Read my lips, Jordan.* I said I'm the assistant *chef,* not assistant *waiter.*"

Exasperated with his teasing new friend, Jordan shoved the items in Arthur's hands. "Get your ass off that stool and get these things on the table. Or you'll be assisting yourself in the employment line."

"Okay. That's how you want to be, huh, bro?" Arthur slowly slid off the stool, replacing his hat. "Throw your weight around on the po' lil' guy—"

"Arthur, shut up!" Ashley ordered, laughing hysterically. "Why don't you look over the ingredients for the dinner menu and stay out of trouble?"

"Right, but my man here owes me an apology. And I don't mean the way he apologized to you, Ashley." Grumbling under his breath, Arthur lumbered away toward the entrance to the dining room.

Alone now, Jordan found himself the recipient of one of Ashley's brightest smiles. Leaning over, he rested his elbows on the table, entranced by the breathtaking vision before him, the mesmerizing smell of her hair, the delicate curve of her chin.

"Don't be cross with Arthur," she admonished softly.

"He's a great guy, and it's just his make-up to cut up."

"I know," Jordan admitted, believing he would have handed her the moon had she asked for it at that moment. "It's just that sometimes I'm not in the mood."

"Well, you're obviously not having a good day. Can I do anything to make it better?"

What a perfect opening to tell her exactly how she could make him feel better. He gave her a torrid look. "Yes, you can," he said huskily. "The question is, will you?"

"Damn table's ready." Arthur burst into the room and, like two guilty kids caught red-handed in the candy bag, Jordan straightened abruptly as Ashley jumped from her seat. "Why don't I just serve ya'll?"

"Th-thank you, Arthur," Ashley said unsteadily. "I'll just wait for you in the restaurant, Jordan."

Jesus, what had he been thinking? Frustrated, he rubbed his hand over the back of his neck. That had been the perfect opening, all right. The perfect opening for Zach to castrate him!

Once they were seated in the now empty restaurant, they ate silently for a time. Ashley methodically stabbed one shrimp at a time, while Jordan jabbed forkfuls of food into his mouth, unsure of how to continue after his provocative question. Giving inane conversation the old college try, he drank deeply from his water glass, then smiled.

"How's the salad? I put my heart and soul into that creation."

"The salad's excellent. You seem to be a big hit. This morning's radio advertisement worked, and you backed it up with two new delicious additions to the menu. You're in solid, Jordan. I'm very happy."

"You have that much faith in me that you spent money on radio spots before I had one full day on the job?"

Ashley sipped from her water glass. Gold-flecked hazel eyes gazed at him, filled with deep longing. It would be so easy to accept the silent invitation she sent him.

"Yes. You're worth that and more. You're excellent at whatever you do."

Indeed? Was she merely referring to cooking or was she speaking of his kisses as well? The intensity in her soft, clear voice suggested just that. He wanted to do something else with her that he'd been told he was very good at. Something that would entwine her beautiful body with his, as he buried himself inside her wet heat over and over again.

Noticing her confused stare at his continued silence and agitated at his swirling emotions and erotic thoughts, Jordan drew in a breath. He was flattered by her confidence in him and impressed by her business acumen. He mustn't muddy the waters with any romantic entanglements. "Thank you."

"No, thank you. I'm flattered by the lunch. Your apology was delicious and accepted."

"My pleasure, Ms. Douglas," Jordan said with a grin. It faded as Ashley stood.

"I'm sorry to have to cut this short, but I need to get back to work, Jordan."

Disappointment reverberated through him. "Right."

"So long."

"Yeah. Take care, Ash."

Watching her glide away, he realized then that she was going to fight her attraction for him just as he was fighting his for her, tooth and nail. It was just as well.

So why did he feel so rotten?

Eight

By the time Ashley left the hotel that evening, dusk was turning the sky a rosy red. A warm breeze blew from the Mississippi River; Canal Street teemed with people making the mad rush to their respective homes after a long work-day. Music from the calliope on the Natchez Steamboat filled the air, while the streets vibrated beneath the wheels of the buses and big rigs heading for various destinations.

Deciding to walk the short distance to Canal Place, Ashley hummed with excitement. She hadn't been shopping in eight months! Despite the setback that that nasty little bowl handed to her, she'd found a way to outsmart it.

The reason why it stole her money was unimportant at this point. The fact that her father had actually encouraged her to go shopping was all that mattered. While he wouldn't believe what had actually become of his money, at least she had enough left over on several different credit cards to pretend it was his money she'd spent.

She was almost there, almost inside the amazing shopping center that would end her self-imposed drought. Anticipation dried her mouth and accelerated her heart rate.

The urge to buy, to *spend,* pulsed through her veins, an uncontrollable need far out of her control.

She ran up the steps, reaching the glass doors that opened to her salvation, in record time. Pulling a door open, she walked in. And stopped.

A young mother pushed a carriage with a toddler crying inside. Mall security strolled by. The sound of the falling water from the center fountain pounded in her ears. Globe lights surrounding the glass-enclosed elevator flared as it halted on the first floor; the doors opened, and a slew of passengers milled out.

Shop! Shop! Shop! The words chanted through her brain.

She wouldn't feel any guilt. It seemed as if she'd always have bills due. The bowl had helped her and given her a hundred dollars to pay her Entergy bill. Her rent wasn't due until her next pay period, and she'd already asked for an extension on her phone bill. No, there really wasn't any need to feel guilty. She deserved this shopping spree.

Pushing forward, she smiled grimly. If by some accident she became frivolous, there was always the bowl.

Unfortunately it was the same dish that had prompted such desperate measures.

Smoke from burning cigarettes polluted the air in the small, poorly lit French Quarter bar where Jordan met Zach later that evening. For the past two weeks since he'd moved back to the city, the two of them had met somewhere almost nightly. With Jordan becoming reacquainted with Ashley two days ago, Zach would never rest easy again.

Jordan suspected Zach was keeping tabs on his whereabouts to make sure he didn't go anywhere near Ashley. While he considered Zach the brother he never had and enjoyed his company, the reasons for this inordinate amount of attention wore on Jordan's nerves. Especially since his involvement with Ashley seemed to have uncontrollably deepened. If Zach had thought Jordan and Ashley would become romantically involved, he might never have tipped Jordan off to the position at the hotel.

Straddling a stool, Jordan gestured to the waiter that he was ready to order. After the guy placed his beer in front of him and walked away, Zach spoke.

"I'm starving. Why don't we get something to eat?" Zach tasted the drink the bartender placed before him. "We can call Fawn and Marie—"

"No," Jordan interrupted, not wanting to lead the lushly curved Marie Hastings on. She was a nice girl, but he really couldn't garner the enthusiasm he needed to involve himself with her. She had the prettiest blue eyes this side of a summer sky. Their evening at the movies a couple of nights ago went well, and she seemed fun loving and not overly expensive to take out. They'd talked on the phone after he returned from dinner at the Douglases last night, but something kept him from asking her out again. "You and Fawn go ahead, Zach. I'm fine. Besides, I can't see spending money needlessly. I can eat when I get home. In this case, however, I ate before I left the hotel."

"Sure you did, buddy," Zach said with biting sarcasm. Disapproval shadowed his face. "A penny mooched is a penny saved. The only reason you agreed to go out with Marie the other night was because *I* sprang for it."

Jordan glowered at him. That wasn't the only reason he'd accepted Zach's offer. He'd just been plain damned tired of Zach pulling him in every direction in an effort to keep him away from Ashley. But after two weeks of Zach's manipulations under the guise of getting Jordan settled in quickly, fate intervened. He'd run across Ashley by accident on a busy street corner. "I don't know why I even bother going out with you, Zachery. You can be a first-class jerk at times. *I* spend my money for what I consider important. You'd do me a favor if you minded your own goddamn business."

"Right," Zach said, smiling tightly. "When we leave here, there's a place I'd like you to see. I'm sure you'll consider it real important. In the meantime, I apologize for stepping on your toes." He extended his hand. "Pals?"

Not quite trusting Zach's droll tone, Jordan accepted the proffered hand. "One of these days, Douglas, I'm going to punch your face in." He chugged his beer, then stood. "Let's get to this important place."

"Hey, I haven't finished my drink," Zach protested. Pointing his finger for emphasis, he frowned.

Jordan shrugged, undeterred by Zach's annoyance. "You can afford to leave it."

"This from Mr. Waste Not, Want Not?"

"That only applies to *me*." Jordan stressed, stepping closer to Zach. "You and your family have always been a little free with your money."

"We used to be, Jordie," Zach said seriously, the hard edges that had accompanied his words softening. "But after Dad's business crashed, we tightened up a great deal. Well, most of us," he added as an afterthought. "As you know, we're still working on Ashley."

At the mention of Ashley, Jordan merely smiled. If only she'd learn to tighten her pocketbook the way her family had. Considering the habits that had plagued her for years— habits exacerbated by her family—he was much too attracted to her.

A couple of days ago, he'd witnessed her lapse. Last night, he'd been a spectator to the huge amount of money she required to keep her happy. He wouldn't put it past her to go off the deep end and buy out the malls.

But what could he expect? Her family *encouraged* her behavior.

Hating how emotionally dangerous it was for both of

them, Jordan scowled. Zach's disapproval didn't help matters. Ashley had always been rather wayward and headstrong. If she felt her brother stood in the way of a relationship with him, she'd never forgive Zach. Jordan wasn't certain he wanted the guilt of knowing he was responsible for destroying the love Ashley had for her brother.

"Damn!"

"I beg your pardon?"

"Nothing," he growled. Slamming a bill down to cover his tab, he walked out into the dusky twilight, aware that Zach followed him.

People crowded the street. A scraggly mule pulled a small, empty carriage, urged on by the driver atop the perch. The crowd parted briefly to allow the conveyance to pass, then just as abruptly closed ranks once again.

Zach grinned at two girls sashaying past, their heavy makeup, huge wigs, and stiletto heels not quite disguising the fact that they were female impersonators. "The place is starting to percolate."

"Yeah," Jordan agreed. "Let's get to where we're going, Zach. I don't have tourist money for these joints."

"You wouldn't," he retorted, then smiled. "Only kidding."

"Bite me," Jordan mumbled, echoing Ashley's words from last night.

Heading toward Decatur Street where Zach's Land Cruiser was parked, they passed the Lucky Dog stand. Smelling the roasting wieners, Jordan's stomach rumbled, but he refused to spend almost two dollars on one hot dog when that could buy a whole pack at the grocery store.

Zach sidled a glance at him, looking pointedly at Jordan's stomach. Jordan ignored the look and continued on.

When they came to the little boys tap dancing on the sidewalk in an effort to make money, Jordan hurried past.

He glared as Zach made a huge production of setting a dollar bill in the hat near the boys.

Soon they came to Jackson Square, which sat between the historic Pontalba Apartments. Andrew Jackson astride his rearing stallion fronted the majestic and architecturally beautiful St. Louis Cathedral, Presbytere, and Cabildo. Muted light from streetlamps threw the three buildings into bold relief, against the clear, darkening skies.

The Quarter was a beautiful, old place, wrought with interesting facts and amazing stories. But for Jordan it was an expensive trap he didn't care to frequent.

Even if the nearly empty Café DuMonde, with its outside seating and tasty beignets and café au lait, would be a perfect spot for him and Ashley to pass time together. Afterward, a carriage ride through the streets of the Quarter, then a hurricane at Pat O'Brien's to spice up the evening . . .

Had he completely lost his mind? He was just complaining that her family advocated her spending habits, but he was thinking about wasting a good seventy dollars.

They finally reached the parking lot where the SUV was parked. After Zach paid the exorbitant fee, they rolled off the lot into the slow traffic of the Quarter, heading toward Esplanade Avenue.

As Zach sped past huge, old oak trees lining the street and away from the Vieux Carrè, Jordan wondered what Ashley was doing at that moment. The need to see her possessed him. He couldn't get rid of Zach soon enough to do just that.

Leaning back in his seat, his muscles tensed. He should've been man enough to broach the subject of a possible relationship between him and Ashley with Zach. Honesty was the best policy, and this case was a prime example.

Last night Uncle Murray suggested that there was a power play going on for Ashley. Perhaps he was right. Zach felt threatened that she would no longer rely on him as she did, if Jordan was there; and admittedly Jordan had always liked it when Ashley deferred to *him* for anything.

It was a sorry situation, but it needed to be out in the open. Maybe then Zach wouldn't feel so put out.

Then again, they were adults, and Zach should mind his own damned business. From the time of his father's death, Jordan had been the man of the family, answerable only to his mother until he came of age. Why should he suddenly capitulate to Zachery's tyranny?

That question plaguing him the entire ride, Jordan frowned when Zach pulled into parking lot of the Saturn car dealership on Causeway Boulevard.

Narrowing his eyes, Jordan tensed. "What's this?" he asked suspiciously. He gazed around the leather interior of the year-old Land Cruiser. "Are you going to buy another car?"

"Come on," Zach said, opening his door and ignoring Jordan's question. "I want you to tell me what you think."

Jordan followed Zach to the showroom, where a salesman rushed out and shook Zach's hand. The man was solidly built and ruggedly handsome, with iron-gray hair and piercing blue eyes. He was also obviously acquainted with Zach, judging by the familiar exchange they engaged in.

Surely Zach didn't need another car. He loved that Land Cruiser. Jordan refused to believe that Zach was attempting to force him into purchasing a car. Just the thought of spending so much money made a cold sweat break out on his forehead.

"Hey, Jordan," Zach said, smiling broadly. He gestured to the man next to him. "This is Tony Reynolds. He's going to give us a demonstration in a great little vehicle. But I want you to drive it first and tell me what you think."

Why would Zach want him to test drive a car *he* intended to buy? Zachery's tactics smelled of pure trickery. But he was badly mistaken if he thought he'd cajole Jordan into purchasing a car.

Jordan laughed nastily. "Sure, Zach, why not?" He started toward the dark green car that was already parked and waiting. His blood boiling with fury at Zach's low-handedness, Jordan paused when the two men didn't follow. "You guys are riding with me, aren't you?"

"No," Zach answered smugly. "Can't have us sitting there influencing your decision to influence mine."

Big mistake, pal! Outwardly calm, Jordan nodded. "Whatever."

Tony hurried to the car as Jordan pulled it open. "Let me point out some features to you, Mr. Bennett. Makes it easier for you and the car to get acquainted."

"Anything you say," Jordan said easily, sliding into the driver's seat. He barely refrained from barrelling into Zach and waylaying him. If he wanted to waste thousands of dollars on a car and its care, that was his business. But he had a hell of a lot of nerve attempting to force Jordan to do the same.

After preliminary explanations of the car's functions, Jordan was soon on his way. Struggling to remain composed and to keep focused on the road, Jordan seethed with anger over Zach's deception. His *friend* needed to be taught a lesson.

Jordan's hunger remained a dull ache in his belly, so he drove to his home on Prytania Street, miles from the car dealership. Let them stew for a while. Zach never should have played this game.

He'd been considering the ramifications of being honest with Zach about his burgeoning feelings for Ashley. Then Zach had the nerve to do something so underhanded and sneaky to him? He didn't think so.

Pulling the car into his driveway, he allowed the engine to idle as he considered what a nice ride it had been. It was also quite a pretty car, with its dark green color and tan interior. The radio sounded clear, the AC kept the temperatures comfortable, and there was nothing like that new-car smell to tempt you to make a purchase.

If he wanted to be honest with himself, he *needed* a car. Besides his own personal transportation, there was Ashley to consider. If he ever took her out on a real date, how would it look if she was wearing a fabulous little dress and the high heels she favored—on a bus?

With a sigh he turned the ignition off and got out. Once inside his house, he fixed himself a salami sandwich, then turned on the television to watch a segment of *Dateline*. Since the showroom closed at nine-thirty, he was careful to keep track of the time.

After forty-five minutes, Jordan decided to return to the Saturn dealership. Knowing he couldn't part with the money to purchase the car, Jordan got into it, regretting his frugality for the first time in a long time.

In less than twenty minutes, he arrived back on Causeway Boulevard to face a furious Zach and a worried Tony. Jordan's own anger returned. Slamming the door shut, he walked toward Zach and threw him the keys.

"Your turn," he said, grinning without humor.

"You bastard!" Zach yelled, shoving the keys at Tony. "Where the hell have you been?"

Feigning calmness, Jordan stood nose to nose with Zach. "Zachery, calm down." His voice rang with challenge. "You still have to take me to that place you consider real important."

"I ought to let your ass walk home," Zach growled, his fists balling at his sides. "Or better yet, you'll *have* to buy the car to get home, you cheap jerk. When will you see that in most cases a car isn't a luxury but a necessity?"

Jordan's jaw tensed. Why was Zach so anxious to see him spend his hard-earned money? More than anyone else,

Zach should have understood his need to save. By the time Uncle Murray almost lost the Douglas fortune, Zach had already been a grown man. For Jordan, the loss was complete. He'd lost his father *and* monetary security at a young age.

Well, he wouldn't buy the car. Especially not just to get home—not when the buses were running. If Ashley truly cared about him, she'd have to understand that.

Spending thousands of dollars to get from point A to point B, when for a small fee public conveyances performed the same service, was ridiculous. He was sure he would be a good candidate for financing the vehicle, but he didn't want another monthly bill. He already had a mortgage to contend with. Which meant the only other option he had was paying for the car outright.

After taxes, title, license, and insurance, he would have to shell out nearly sixteen thousand dollars. Bile rose in his stomach at that thought, and a tremor passed through him.

No, he just couldn't do it.

Before things turned ugly, he stepped away from Zach. "Nice try, Douglas," he spat, enraged that Zach had presented temptation to him. Angry, too, that he was refusing to buy it. He nodded to the salesman. "You, too, Tony, but the fish aren't biting today."

"Damn you, Jordan!" Zach began.

Jordan ignored him. "Are you going to make an ass of yourself over *my* finances, or do I get a lift back home?"

Glaring at him, Zach shook his head. "Come on, tightwad," he said, resigned. "You know I'll drop you off."

"Thanks."

After they bid farewell to Tony Reynolds, Zach and Jordan got into the big, comfortable Land Cruiser and headed for Prytania Street. For a time Zach concentrated on the road, while Jordan watched the cars around them on the Interstate.

It was a clear night, enabling him to see the bright New Orleans skyline in the distance. He loved Chicago, but he'd missed home terribly. Now that he was back, he didn't want to ruin his friendship with Zach. Still, Zach needed to remember his place. They weren't kids anymore.

"Do me a favor, Zach," Jordan began tiredly. "Stop trying to get me to spend money on what *you* think I need."

His hand tightening on the steering wheel, Zach snorted. "If I didn't think Ashley had her eye on you, Jordan, I wouldn't give a damn what you spent or didn't spend. But with her free regard for money, you're at the opposite end of the spectrum. I believe Ashley will learn to save before you learn to spend."

Ashley *saving* money? That would be the day. He chuckled in self-derision. The day *he* learned to spend. Both acts would require the same magic that pulsed between him and Ashley. Yet he understood what Zach was saying. It was the same argument he would use to stay away from Ashley. Zach's words and actions only reinforced their incompatibility.

"You don't have to worry, Zachery. I told you before, Ashley and I are just friends," he lied. *Like hell we are! One of us had better worry!*

The rest of the drive passed in silence. It came to Jordan that he and Zach had been at odds frequently these past two days. He didn't like that. It also saddened him to think that if his feelings for Ashley kept escalating, he and Zach might no longer remain friends.

When Zach pulled the SUV in front of Jordan's house, Jordan got out quietly. "See you, Zach."

"Yeah, Jordan. Later, man."

As soon as Jordan closed the door, Zach zoomed away. Jordan glanced at his watch. It was near ten o'clock. The vibrant image of Ashley crystallized in his mind.

Despite the odds, he couldn't help his feelings for Ashley

any more than he could help his fear of trying to survive without money. And that frightened him.

The urge to take a walk hit him suddenly, and, instead of going into his house as he'd intended, he headed down Prytania Street for an unknown destination.

Nine

"Arrrggh!" Ashley slammed the door in her darkened apartment and leaned against it, the heat from the stuffy interior surrounding her. Dropping her purse and packages on the floor, she flipped on the overhead light, then clicked on the AC. She leaned against the wall. "I hate buses!"

She wasn't too happy with herself at the moment, either. What had she done by going on that misguided shopping spree? The letdown she always experienced after spending an inordinate amount of money seemed more acute this time. All pleasure had long since deserted her, leaving her with inexplicable emptiness—and huge debt. Repudiation accompanied those feelings.

Although her family expected her to lull her evening away shopping, she'd let herself down. Why had she done it? After eight months of proudly curbing her spending habits, she'd blown a hundred dollars at the antique shop and hundreds more tonight at Canal Place.

"Oh, God."

The usual nausea and dull ache began. Her irresponsibility sickened her. Despite her boast that she was changing, it seemed she never would. Like a drug addict who searched for the next high, she found any excuse to spend money. And now, coming off that high left her ashamed and out of sorts.

If only she'd left well enough alone after the ink on her father's check disappeared. If only she hadn't bought that thieving, silver bowl in the first place.

Glaring at it, she started toward the sofa table where it so innocently sat. The loud ringing of her telephone stopped her advancement. Praying it was Zach, she dashed to where she'd left it in her bedroom to pick up the receiver. "Hullo?"

"Ashley?"

The youthful voice sounded familiar. Her turmoil prevented her from immediately remembering the caller. Besides, none of her former classmates knew where she now resided. "Yes?"

"How are you?"

"Fine," Ashley answered automatically, still uncertain about the caller's identity, recognition at the edges of her mind.

"Don't you recognize my voice?"

"It can't be!" Ashley squealed in response, the image of a petite, redhead forming in her mind. "Sydnee? Sydnee Golden?"

"Yes!"

Delighted to hear her friendly voice, Ashley leaned back on her bed, not caring that the closed draperies made the room nearly pitch dark. "When in the world did you get in town?"

"An hour ago," Sydnee squeaked, her girlish voice making her sound as if she were ten years old instead of twenty-three. "I'm only passing through."

"When can we see each other?"

"Ash, I'm on my way to Paris and I've been trying to

get in touch with you half the day. I wanted to surprise you, so instead of leaving from New York, I decided to fly here first to see you, then leave out of Atlanta. Unfortunately you put a dent in my plans, young lady. Now we're back at the airport, waiting to board. But I'll see you on my way back to New York."

"Oh, Syd, I feel cheated," Ashley lamented. Sydnee's breathy cheeriness amazed her. Wondering how Sydnee got her home number, but not her work number, she asked, "How did you know where to reach me?"

"Your mom told me. Said she didn't want me to bother you at work, since we never took responsibility seriously. She thought you'd take the rest of the day off."

It seemed as if the magic that had softened her parents' attitude the night before had all but deserted them today. Only Jordan remained affected—because he had touched her hair. What would happen if he actually *drank* something from the bowl's cavity? Bad idea. The thing was a little monster that would probably send Jordan running away from her in the opposite direction. "Guess what? Remember Jordan Bennett?"

"Sure do . . ." Sydnee's voice trailed off. "Yeah, honey, I'll be there. Listen, Ash, I gotta go. I'm pregnant and I'm getting married. Bye—"

"Don't you dare leave me hanging with news like that, Sydnee Golden!"

Sydnee giggled. "Forgive me, Ashley, but I'll write to you about it, I promise. Bye now."

"Damn you, Sydnee!" Ashley shouted to the dial tone. Shaking her head in frustration, Ashley slammed the receiver down, lonely all of a sudden. Just when she was about to expunge her confusion over Jordan, Sydnee dropped a bombshell, then hung up.

She and Sydnee had met in grade school. Three years ago Sydnee had left home for a tour of the friendly skies.

Since both her parents were deceased and Sydnee had no other ties, her job as a flight attendant took her all over the world.

When Sydnee left, she and Ashley cried on each other's shoulders and promised to keep in touch. In three long years, Ashley hadn't heard from her. Until today, and with such tidings.

Dejected, Ashley stood and switched on her lamp. Should she feel happy for her friend? Sydnee certainly *sounded* thrilled, and she loved Sydnee like a sister. At the moment, Ashley wanted to be Sydnee—rushing off to marry Jordan and pregnant with his child.

Damn, if only she could give up on that impossible dream. During lunch today, she'd sworn to put her emotions in check. In all fairness to Jordan, he really didn't have any control over what he was feeling toward her. By some impossibility, a possessed bowl was wreaking havoc in Ashley's life. She couldn't fool herself and believe Jordan had generated true sentiments. She had no doubt that he liked her, but not in *that* way.

Yet each time she was in his presence, her shallow defenses dissolved like ice in hot water, and she believed the impossible. Now Sydnee's call made her profoundly sad. But she wouldn't allow her momentary envy to rule her.

"Good luck, Syd," Ashley said in a small voice and trodded back to the living room. She looked at her packages again, scattered on the floor by the door. With a deep sigh, she brought the packages to her bedroom and put them in the closet without taking them out of their bags and boxes.

Then she returned to the living room. Weary, she sat on the sofa, her back to that hellish bowl. It was almost nine-thirty, and she realized she hadn't eaten a thing since her wonderful lunch with Jordan. She wished she could see him at that moment. This afternoon had been like a dream come true, but what would their next encounter bring?

Forlornness descended upon Ashley; oddly, she felt like crying. The only bright spot to her day had been her time spent with Jordan and then Sydnee's call.

Resting her elbow on the back of the sofa, she leaned her head in her hand and picked a piece of lint from the couch. She smiled sadly. She hadn't known how much she missed her friend until she'd heard Sydnee's voice. Thinking a hot bath might soothe her agitation, Ashley rubbed her temples.

Tomorrow when she returned from work, she'd have to face the objects of her shame and begin the task of saving her purchases. Damn her overspending anyway.

A flashing light, much like a bright neon sign, flared around her, startling her. Turning, her gaze fell on the bowl. It shone with white brilliance, then dimmed. Ashley jumped up, gasping in surprised fear. The flash repeated itself several times, then became a soft, silvery glow.

Sheer terror raised the hairs on her nape and arms. She clenched her fists, her fingernails digging into the tender flesh of her palms. Her back against the door, Ashley's eyes widened as a beam from the bowl settled on her.

Thinking the bowl was about to vaporize her, she raised her arms defensively, and a scream tore from her throat. The glow widened, penetrating her shield.

A deep sense of peace entered her being. Lowering her arms and wiping away tears she hadn't realized were falling, she drew in a breath.

Slowly she walked across the room, unsure where her courage and tranquility came from. When she reached the table where the bowl sat, she squinted her eyes. Without touching it, she examined the antique piece, transfixed. The birds, flowers, and bows appeared fluid, almost lifelike. The delicate wings on the doves fluttered ever so slightly, and a heavenly sweetness permeated the air around her.

A euphoric laugh escaped Ashley. This was pure insanity. She felt drunk with contentment. All the shadows that had plagued her earlier seemed to have brightened, and she *believed* in the one person with whom she warred the most—herself.

The feeling, however, was fleeting. Gazing into the cavity of the bowl, the pulse-pounding giddiness abruptly left her. The check that her father gave her last night was still there. Although there was no dollar amount or signature, Ashley's name was again written on it. Directly under her name were the words: *Blank memo page, please. Thank you very much.*

She drew her brows together in confusion. "A blank memo?" She was afraid to question why she automatically rushed to the kitchen and opened the cabinet drawer to get a blank notepad. "Will a notepad do?"

Where the previous words had been on the check, the word *yes* appeared.

Ashley clutched her arms to her chest. *Oh, my, the bowl really is magic!* "Why are you here?"

Are you a total dolt? You brought me here.

"Hey, I don't have to take that from you! At least I'm not a thief. When are you planning to give me my money back?"

I'm not. You don't deserve it.

"What!" She felt absolutely no fear from the glowing bowl, only a seething indignation at its autocracy. Of course, she should have run shrieking from her apartment when this little episode first began.

Ashley Douglas, you'll get what you deserve. Believe me. But nothing more and nothing less.

"Why, you . . . you . . . You're nothing but a con artist!"

Bright light flashed several times before the bowl's glow dimmed, then receded inward, leaving it just a shiny, beautiful piece of silver with a blank check and a blank notepad inside it.

"Hmm." An interminable amount of time passed while Ashley stood and gazed at it, waiting. When no other phenomenon occurred, she returned to the sofa and reclined back.

She didn't exactly know how to feel. Like a healing laser, the bowl's beam had taken away her initial fright, convincing her that it wasn't an evil entity, but true magic. Yet only small children believed in such nonsense. Why did she so readily accept what had taken place?

She doubted she was as immature as others accused her of being. Well, maybe where her finances were concerned, but that was a different matter entirely. She definitely wasn't so jaded that she needed to suspend reality for escapism.

So now what? Where exactly did she go from here? It was unbelievable, but she owned a magic bowl with an attitude. She was sure the bowl had become ticked off at her for calling it a con artist.

Well, fine. She certainly wouldn't apologize to it. After all, it had no right to take her money, then tell her she didn't deserve it. How did it know what she deserved?

No, this couldn't be happening! She needed to think in a sane environment; she needed a cappucino from the coffee shop. Jumping up, she snatched her purse from the floor, then glared at the bowl. "You have some gall, Miss FannieMae," she huffed, rushing to the sofa table and plucking the bowl's rim. "Ow!" She kissed her smarting finger. "I rescue you from that antique shop and shine up your tarnished hide, and this is the thanks I get. You are the most ungrateful wretch I've ever seen!"

The bowl glowed a bright red, and Ashley stepped back, watching in fascination as words once again began to appear on the pad.

First of all, missy, never call me FannieMae. It's em-

barrassing. I am not a FannieMae. *My peers would laugh me out of the realm if they heard you!*

"You have peers?"

Quiet! I'm magic. I can have anything I want! I am also of the male gender.

The words flashed across the pad like Teletype. Beginning to enjoy this oddity, Ashley ventured closer. Captivated by the bowl, she forgot her anger. "What's your name?"

Elvis.

"No way!"

You may call me Elvis. Although my master called me Ambrose.

"Come on," Ashley said with a laugh. "Elvis is not your real name. Neither is Ambrose."

Ha, ha, ha. I see you have a sense of humor. I like that. I have taken many names over the centuries. This century I have taken the name Elvis. You will address me as such.

"All right," Ashley said with a dramatic sigh. "*Elvis* you are."

Now, then. I believe you were insinuating to me in a most impolite manner that I should be grateful for your rescue. Am I right?

"Um, yes."

Yes, well, I do owe you a debt of gratitude, my dear. In time we'll settle that debt.

"Thank you," Ashley said primly. Kneeling on the floor and resting her chin on the cool wooden surface of the table, she stared at the bowl. "May I know who or *what* you are?" she whispered. "And what your origins might be?"

You may not, Ashley. I believe you were on your way to the coffee shop for a cappucino. Don't let me delay your intentions.

Frowning at Elvis, Ashley raised her head, incredulous.

"H-h-how did you know that? Are you . . . are you a mind-reader as well?"

Bingo, my girl. So be careful what you think.

"Well, I won't stand for you reading my mind," Ashley protested with great indignation. "It's an invasion of privacy."

Oh, puh-leaze, Ashley. I don't bother myself with trivialities.

"Oh! My thoughts aren't trivial."

Calm down. Do not have a hissy fit. I respect your privacy. I was peeved at your attitude, so I decided to read your mind to see what your plans for me were. Not that it matters. I chose you. Which makes me yours until I decide differently. I promise I'll no longer read your mind. Now run along.

The writing disappeared, and the bowl dimmed. If the words had been spoken, they would've done so with an unmistakable finality, taking the matter out of Ashley's hands. For the time being, the bowl was through with her.

Still bursting with questions, she took her purse and slipped out of her apartment, heading in the direction of the coffee shop, three blocks away.

Ten

Other than a couple who'd seated themselves just as Ashley walked up to the coffee shop, the outside tables were empty. The dark, cloudless sky boasted bright stars and a half moon; the fluorescent streetlamps afforded a well-lit, safe atmosphere in the uptown neighborhood. A warm breeze blew around her, carrying the scent of brewing coffee and freshly baked pastries in the night air. Going into the small shop, where baker's racks with containers of a variety of coffee beans stood against the walls, Ashley placed her order, then returned outside and seated herself.

Carefully tasting her piping-hot cappuccino, a zillion things floated through Ashley's mind. The anger and disappointment she experienced at finding the blank check this morning, and later the fear and amazement she felt when the bowl pulsed with energy. Her success at negotiating the Blackwell deal. Sharing lunch with Jordan. Sydnee's telephone call.

A picture in her head of her and Sydnee on Sydnee's last night in town, before she moved to New York, formed in Ashley's head. Since Sydnee had chosen overseas flights based out of the Big Apple, the move was necessary.

At first Ashley had missed the bubbly redhead dreadfully. She'd had no one to confide in. She'd made other friends since Sydnee's departure, but they weren't Sydnee. As time went on, Ashley felt less and less lonely, filling her days with mundane things—until her twenty-first birthday, when her parents cut off her allowance and virtually disowned her financially.

If they knew what she'd done tonight, Glynis and Murray would have considered their decision wise. Sure, they wanted her to enjoy the money her father gave to her. But they didn't expect her to break her budget for the sake of shopping. That was the bone of contention that had led to their tough-love approach in the first place.

Sydnee would understand. Sydnee shared Ashley's propensity for shopping. She'd also always loved her job, but now that her circumstances had changed, Ashley wondered if her friend was taking a leave of absence or giving up her career altogether. She did say she was pregnant and getting married. In that order.

She couldn't wait to hear Sydnee's story. They had always been able to tell each other anything. Once Sydnee explained things to Ashley, she would tell her friend about Jordan and . . . and Elvis. Sydnee would sympathize with her over Jordan, and they'd both share a good laugh about Elvis, then try to get it . . . him . . . the bowl, to make them rich.

Ashley paused in her thinking. Elvis said he was of the male gender. Clearing her throat, she giggled, wondering how he knew. If she told her present acquaintances about Elvis, she'd find herself scrambling to get away from the little men in the white coats with the big nets!

Taking a generous swallow from her cup, Ashley glanced guiltily about. The couple who sat two tables from her shared a passionate kiss, enraptured with one another.

When they broke apart, they stared at each other lovingly.

Ashley sighed. Could she convince Elvis to assist her in her efforts to win Jordan's heart? She reminded herself that she wasn't supposed to be entertaining such an unlikely possibility. She was supposed to be distancing herself from Jordan, because they shared vastly different views about money. And because her overprotective brother stood between them.

Shoot, maybe Elvis could help her to stop thinking of Jordan in romantic ways, if for no other reason than the detriment it would cause to her and Jordan's relationship with Zachery.

She just wished she could see Jordan right then, for good or bad.

"Ashley?"

She gasped at the sound of the unmistakably husky voice, her mouth flying open in astonishment. It seemed as if Jordan had materialized out of nowhere!

The absurdity of this entire situation struck Ashley. Only by sheer willpower did she swallow her laughter and compose herself. "Hi, Jordan." Visions of being in his embrace danced through her mind. His dark hair was mussed, as if he'd run his fingers through it countless times. She refrained from standing and smoothing her hand over the silky strands. Her heart knocked against her chest like a sledgehammer, making her placidity all the more surprising. "What are you doing here?"

Releasing a deep breath, he rubbed the back of his neck. He opened his mouth to speak, then closed it again, hesitating. After a brief struggle, he said, "I finished up at the hotel and decided to stretch my legs."

Keenly aware of his lustful expression that mirrored her own feelings, Ashley tasted her cappuccino again, nervous. She might not be that schoolgirl anymore, but Jordan was still the man of her dreams. If she made one wrong move, she'd ruin everything. Her ludicrous spree tonight swirled through her mind.

She must never, ever let him know of that. He'd swear she was the same person she had been back then.

Placing one hand on the back of her wrought-iron chair and the other on the matching table, Jordan leaned toward her. A faint scent of cologne reached Ashley, and she took another swallow from her cup. Some of the frothy milk remained on her lips.

"Hmm," Jordan murmured, low and husky. "That looks delicious. Cappuccino?"

Warmth surging through her at his double meaning, Ashley licked the froth from her lips. "It *is* delicious," she said softly, her gaze colliding with his smoldering blue-gray one.

The fragrance from her hair danced between them, entrancing them in a dream world. She tilted her face toward his, her whole being filled with anticipation. His nearness made her pulse pound, and she ached for his touch. But she was afraid to make the first move. Afraid that she'd make a complete fool of herself.

"May I join you?"

His sensuality mesmerizing, Ashley caressed his stubbled cheek in a feathery touch. Swallowing her excitement, she nodded. "Please do," she said softly.

He straightened to his full height, so stunningly virile that her breath caught.

"Good," he murmured. His smile was devastating. "I'll be right with you, Ash. Let me order one of those and get a refill for you."

Don't suck in another huge gasp, girl. You'll pass out from lack of oxygen! Jordan is actually springing for a cup of coffee. That's truly something to shout about.

"Thank you," Ashley smoothed imagined wrinkles from

her skirt, appreciating the firmness of his derriere as he strolled away, ignoring her wicked thoughts. He had a well-proportioned body with slim hips and long, muscular legs, discernible even through the white pants he wore.

He'd always been a sportsman, enjoying the outdoors with a zest that was unsurpassed. She, too, had a love for sports and nature. They had a lot in common, a fact she'd recognized when Jordan noticed her as nothing but the pesky kid who trailed behind him and Zach.

But there was one sticking point that always brought about arguments, and that was money. Unfortunately she couldn't overlook that. Doing so asked for heartache. Money and finances—and differing views—sometimes ended marriages.

Jordan placed a fresh cup of cappuccino, filled to the rim, in front of her. Seating himself next to her, he sipped from his cup. "It *is* good," he agreed. He tasted the cappuccino again, then smiled at her, his even, white teeth contrasting perfectly with his tanned skin. "So tell me, Ash, what are you doing here?"

"Drinking coffee," Ashley said with a laugh. She'd cherish whatever time she had with him.

Chuckling, Jordan nodded. "Touché."

"Actually I didn't feel like sitting in tonight," Ashley confessed, enthralled by his high spirits.

"Funny, neither did I. It's weird. What are the chances of us meeting like this?"

From head to heel, her body tingled from Jordan's nearness. "What, indeed? You've really walked a distance. Maybe it's fate." *Or Elvis.*

"Well, I suppose it is a distance from the hotel to Uptown, but I live only eight blocks from this coffee shop. A brisk leg stretch is always welcome."

Another warm breeze blew, lifting Ashley's hair across her face and spreading the exhilarating fragrance that she recognized as her shampoo around them. She raised an un-steady hand to push her hair back and felt Jordan's hand in her hair. It appeared they both had the same idea, but his touch electrified her and upset her balance.

She smiled at him, suddenly shy. "Where did that breeze come from?"

Annoyance flickering across his features, Jordan smoothed back her hair, then removed his hand. "It's just a strange kind of night. I don't usually walk this far, but something urged me on." He gave her a half smile, then rubbed his neck. "I'm glad, Ash. You're very persistent in my mind. Shall we try to renew our friendship?"

Friendship? Although she'd half expected this announce-ment, disappointment careened through her. How could she be just a friend to this man? For as long as she remembered, her feelings for him went far beyond friendship.

But she wouldn't complain. One of the few things she'd learned these past two years was that there was always a starting point, no matter how small. For now she'd content herself with his friendship. Until she changed his mind.

"Yes, Jordan," she responded. "Let's be friends. Oh!" she blurted, forcing herself to change the subject, her emotions too overwrought to continue the conversation. "I heard from Sydnee tonight."

"Sydnee Golden?"

"*Oui*," Ashley said in an exaggerated French accent. "She's pregnant and off to Paris to get married."

"Get out! Not Sydnee. You two lived for the mall."

"She sounded thrilled," Ashley said wistfully, not daring to comment on Jordan's potentially inflammatory statement about her spending habits. Something might inadvertently slip about Canal Place. "Isn't it wonderful?"

"Fantastic," Jordan responded, his attention diverted away from money. "Did she say when she'll get back?"

"She said she'll write me all the details and will stop by on her way back from Paris."

"You must have been pleasantly surprised to hear from her."

"Stunned is the word."

Ashley wondered how long the small talk would continue between them. Although learning about Sydnee was notable, it was mundane and nothing compared to her tumbling emotions. Unfortunately she'd started this conversation *because* of her tumbling emotions. Hurt and confused at his announcement, she hadn't known what else to do.

Besides, if they pursued any serious discussion, it would eventually lead to Jordan's disapproval of the way she handled her finances and her own displeasure over his views on money. That wasn't the way to start a romance.

Given that, maybe small talk was best.

"It's getting late." Ashley swallowed the last drop of her second cup of cappuccino. "I think I'd better leave." *No point in prolonging the agony.*

When she stood, Jordan quickly downed the remainder of his coffee and stood as well. "I'll walk you home, Ashley."

She resented his brotherly tone. That's what Zach was for. She wanted so much more from Jordan. "That's not necessary, Jordan. You'll be that much farther from your house."

"Nonsense. What are friends for? Besides, I won't take no for an answer. Come on, let's go."

As they walked toward her apartment, they found the streets all but deserted. Every now and then, a car passed them. At one intersection, a man cycled by at breakneck speed. Farther down the block, a big dog ran to the fence of a house they were passing. Ashley jumped at his loud barking, which continued until they cleared the property.

To calm her, Jordan told a silly joke about a racecourse,

a man, and his deceased wife. His ploy worked. Forgetting entirely about the rottweiler, Ashley laughed so hard she was breathless. And quite delighted. She had forgotten what a keen sense of humor Jordan possessed.

"Jordan, where have you been hiding that funny bone lately? You've always been hilarious when you wanted to be." She halted as they reached her gate. "Here we are."

"Yeah." The disappointment in his voice mirrored her own.

Not wanting the evening to end, Ashley smoothed back a lock of her hair. Zach had always called her "Rash Ash," and at the moment she was feeling very rash. This was the chance she'd been waiting for.

Jordan mightn't ever come to her apartment again. But the present was all that mattered. Her magic bowl sat just beyond the perimeter of her walls, along with a bottle of red wine hidden in her kitchen cabinet. What harm would it do to persuade Jordan to have a drink with her and see if Elvis could help her out?

He owed her a great debt anyway. He'd stolen her money, which resulted in her once again overspending.

"Jordan, would you like a glass of wine?"

Hesitancy flickered across his handsome face. Just when she thought he was going to say no, he nodded. "Sure, Ashley. Why not?"

It wasn't long before Ashley was carrying Elvis into the kitchen, wiping out his cavity and opening the wine, then pouring it into her bowl.

The dark liquid bubbled suddenly, like boiling water, and the usually heady scent seemed just a little more potent. When the ripples calmed, Ashley carefully brought Elvis back into the living room and placed the bowl on the table. Ignoring Jordan's surprise, she hurried into the kitchen, got her only two wineglasses, then returned to where Jordan sat and dropped down beside him.

"A new approach to drinking wine, Ashley?"

"No," she responded lightly, ignoring the hint of sarcasm in Jordan's voice. "Well, maybe. I thought it would be cool to showcase my bowl with some fine wine."

Jordan's blue-gray gaze widened. "That's your bowl? The same ugly thing you had on Carrollton Avenue?"

Ashley laughed nervously, afraid Elvis might take umbrage and turn their wine into hemlock. "One and the same. He . . . uh, it's beautiful, huh?"

"Sure is. But why pour our wine into it?"

Ashley shrugged, her pulse racing. She couldn't tell Jordan the truth, but neither did she want to lie to him outright. And Elvis mightn't cooperate. This mad idea might be a waste of time, though in the kitchen, the wine had gurgled and roiled like a witch's brew. It would do something to them.

Laughing nervously, she stretched her neck from side to side. "Who knows? Drinking from it might turn the wine into some type of magic—"

"Elixir?" Jordan supplied.

Instead of laughing at her, he seemed intrigued by the idea. "You read my mind, Jordan. I hope you don't hold such whimsy against me?"

"Never, Ash. It's one of the things that endears you to everyone. You do have a wonderfully fanciful side that allows you to believe in things others would never think twice about and see the beauty in everything around you. Now, let's drink our wine."

Pleased at Jordan's candor, she stared at the nearly full bowl. "I think the best way to do this is to dip our wine-glasses."

"I'm all for it. The night does seem bewitched. Why not yield to such romanticism?"

After dipping both their glasses and filling them with wine, Ashley sank back in her seat, holding firmly to her glass. She was almost afraid to try it—not because she honestly believed Elvis would poison them. He was a gentle sort, if slightly impressed with his own abilities.

She wondered if she would do something she'd eventually come to regret. Would drinking wine from the bowl make her forget her inhibitions? Not only sexually, but all the obstacles of conflicting differences between her and Jordan. Once the wine was out of their system and the euphoric feeling deserted them, she might not like the end result. Just where would they be?

Right where they were now, she reasoned, so why hesitate?

Jordan sniffed his wine, seeming to have the same reservations. "It sure smells good. I've never smelled wine with such a potent scent." An eyebrow arched. "Aren't you going to taste it?"

She laughed, eyeing him nervously. "I'll try it, if you will."

"Why don't we do it together, Ashley?"

Ashley cleared her throat. It was only fair that she sample the wine she offered him, knowing the powers of the bowl. "Sure."

Taking a tentative sip, Ashley saw Jordan swallow generously from the glass. Resting the glass on his knee and twirling it about, he quietly sat for a moment, before tasting the wine again.

Encouraged, Ashley drank deeply, appreciating the full-bodied flavor as the semisweet liquid rolled down her throat. Searing sensuousness erupted in her soul. Her bones felt liquid, her body light, her being languid.

As if in a trance, she set her glass down on the coffee table, then stared at Jordan. Sexual magnetism exuded from him.

"How's Zachery?"

Jordan's voice was low and erotic. Desire quivered

through her limbs. Her nipples hardened, and her belly tightened. Wet heat flared in her secret place. She scooted closer to him, all doubts and fears deserting her. Vaguely she remembered his question. "I'm not sure. He's angry with me about last night."

"Then I know he'd want to kill me if he saw me tonight," Jordan said, drawing her into his arms. "Ashley, we should do this more often," he muttered before lowering his mouth to hers.

Kissing her with fervor, he delved into her sweetness like a man possessed. Hungrily his tongue explored her recesses while he roamed his hands over her figure. His madness invoked the same response in Ashley. She wrapped her arms around his neck and kissed him wildly. Jordan buried his hands in her hair as he gently pushed her back onto the sofa, then settled his body against her.

The skirt she wore afforded scant protection against Jordan's movements. Ashley wrapped her legs around his, his hardness contained within the confines of his pants, nestled securely between her thighs. His hands found the buttons of her blouse.

Rocking against his maleness, Ashley kissed Jordan feverishly—

A blinding light flashed around them. Halting his movements, Jordan raised his head. "What the hell was that?"

"I-I have no idea." But she did and she glared at Elvis. He'd promised not to read her mind. At the moment he seemed to be doing more than that. He was intruding upon her dreams. "Please, Jordan."

She buried her fingers in his thick hair and attempted to draw him back into the kiss, but the mood was already lost as reality set in.

"Damn!" The word exploded from Jordan. With the speed of a lightning bolt, he sat up. "Are you all right?"

"I'm fine," she whispered. She really wasn't. Her body

ached for succor. Her liquid gaze met and melded with Jordan's.

"I'm sorry, Ashley. My intentions are truly for us to be friends."

"Of course," Ashley said numbly.

"I think I'd better leave."

"Sure." She smiled at the modern-day Adonis standing so dejectedly before her. Still, Elvis's powers continued to astound her. Maybe if Jordan drank the wine alone, it would help him to sort out his feelings. "Would you like to bring the wine home with you?"

"Why not?" Jordan answered without argument.

After she found a funnel and returned the wine to its original container, Ashley stood at the door and bid Jordan good night. Alone again, she stared at Elvis. As angry as she should have been and as much as she wanted to know all of Jordan, she realized Elvis had saved her from making a disastrous mistake, even though *he* had precipitated the matter.

It was her manipulations that had brought her and Jordan to the brink of making love, however. *He* wanted to be friends. She'd do well to remember that.

"Thanks, Elvis," she whispered.

In response, the bowl glowed softly, and she smiled sadly.

The brisk walk away from Ashley's small apartment only added to Jordan's discomfort.

How would he ever keep his hands off her? He was a practical man and honestly believed he and Ashley would never succeed as lovers. Inherent differences stood between them, not to mention an overprotective ass named Zachery Douglas. Ashley was impulsive. Jordan was cautious. He was a saver. She was a spender. Besides, Jordan would never be able to resist Ashley's demand for spending, and she'd bankrupt him within a year. She had that effect on him.

Where would that leave him? Regardless of what her parents said, she'd always have a roof over *her* head. He doubted, however, the Douglas men would welcome him back into the fold if he ever crossed the line with Ashley.

Yet, despite his better judgment, Jordan kept being steered in an altogether different direction. A direction he swore he wasn't ready to take with anyone.

He should have refused the wine, but he hadn't wanted the evening to end. The invisible bond that reeled him insistently to disaster with her made her invitation impossible to resist. What the hell was happening?

He'd kissed Ashley in the restaurant yesterday, but he'd dismissed that as a little kiss between friends. A little kiss between friends? It was more like a kiss between him and a woman who was stealing his heart without even trying. A woman who probably had captivated his heart years ago.

His dilemma now was finding the will to resist her. He seriously doubted that he could. His thoughts were unsettling at the least, challenging at the most.

Jordan reached his house. It was a two-storied Victorian mansion with a wraparound veranda and huge French windows. With pride, he went up the wide steps and walked across his porch to the entrance. Unlocking the door, he stepped into the cool interior of his nineteenth-century home located in the Garden District.

Walking from the entrance hall, which was lit by two wall sconces, to the living room, he stopped and took in the well-appointed room. The entire house boasted high ceilings, pickled floors, and wooden moldings. It never ceased to amaze Jordan how far he'd come from that homeless boy of so long ago.

This was *his* home, bought from the wealth he'd painstakingly acquired over the years. Nothing and no one would take it away. Not ever again.

Guarding his money took a lot out of him. Perhaps he didn't want to be as carefree with his finances as Ashley was, but he knew he could be a little less frugal as well. Yet a sick dread welled within him every time he thought of spending a huge amount of money. Anything could happen, at any time. It always helped to have money stored away for an emergency.

After tonight's fiasco at the car dealership, he realized he needed to slowly adjust to delving into his pockets. It wouldn't mean he had to break his bank account. It simply meant enjoying his money every now and then.

He doubted he would have bought the two-dollar cup of coffee for Ashley had they run into one another at the coffee shop last week. To some, he might live a miser's existence, but it was the only way he *knew* how to live. To help his mother, he'd held small jobs—cutting grass, delivering newspapers, washing cars, and anything else he could do—from the age of ten. He'd taken his duty as the man of the family seriously.

For years, grief along with her career and parenting duties hadn't allowed Karen to become involved with anyone. But now his mother was finally happily remarried. His sister, too, had married well. Tracie and Karen both lived in Chicago. Yet he was *still* the head of the family, and if for any reason either of them ever needed a place to live, his home would be theirs to share. He'd made sure that Karen and Tracie would never again have to depend on the kindness of strangers.

Once his sister and mother were happily secured in relationships, he had decided to return to New Orleans. After hosting Tracie's wedding several months ago and walking her down the aisle, he'd contacted Zach and informed him of his decision, then asked him to refer a good real-estate agent his way. Jordan believed that owning a house was a necessity, but instead of buying it outright, he'd paid for three-fourths of it, then financed the rest. He knew the practicality of having a good credit history, but if he paid for everything outright he'd never acquire one.

One day he wanted to open his own restaurant. The time never seemed right. He never seemed to have the right amount of money accumulated for him to feel comfortable making such an investment. There was always the possibility that the business would fold; he'd lose a huge amount of money for following a dream, when he could content himself making money and working for someone else.

When Zach called and said a chef's position had come up at a hotel where the Douglases had a small interest, Jordan jumped at the chance. With sterling references backing him, Jordan was quickly hired and came to New Orleans two weeks early to get settled in.

In all that time, he hadn't run into Ashley, mostly by design. Now, in two days' time, she was threatening his lauded control as if a spell had been cast over him.

Realizing he gripped the wine that Ashley had given to him, he set it on the cherrywood liquor table, then placed a CD in the player. Once the soothing piano music began to play, he sat on the plush sofa and leaned his head against the overstuffed pillow. He massaged his temples.

He had to make a firm decision and stick to it. Something stopped him from asking Marie out again. Or maybe a *someone* stopped him.

A vision of Ashley rose in his mind. How could he have been so careless to allow himself to become attracted to her? He thought of Ashley telling him Zach was angry with her about last night. Surely Jordan's attitude hadn't helped the situation. He'd made such a fool of himself in front of her family.

Zach was angry for all the wrong reasons. Or maybe they

were the logical reasons. Zach thought he was too cautious with money and not cautious enough with his emotions, regarding Ashley.

It seemed at every turn, Ashley was there. In his vision or in his arms. Once Zach had dropped him off, Jordan had walked without thought.

Then he saw her, as if something had led him straight to her. Her beautiful face animated with deep thought, she'd actually smiled before taking a sip from her cup.

The scent from her hair electrified him, a silent siren's song that left him powerless. Jordan couldn't remember when he'd enjoyed a simple outing more. At her apartment, he'd been a hairbreadth away from making love to her. She'd responded so sweetly to him, but the odd light had brought him to his senses.

Still, he couldn't imagine having spent the evening with anyone else, anywhere else, tonight. The significance of that daunted him.

The bonging of the grandfather clock announced the arrival of midnight, the witching hour, a time when sorceresses met to practice their dark arts. As if such nonsense existed. Even the feeling that Ashley had bewitched him was a foolish excuse to assuage his guilty lust.

Unless he encountered Ashley by accident, he wouldn't seek her out again. He'd avoid her as much as possible. What he needed was a diversion, something or someone to get his mind off of Rash Ash. The *someone* immediately came to mind.

Remembering that she'd called him close to one o'clock last night and hoping she was still awake, he reached for the cordless phone that sat on the end table next to him and dialed Marie Hastings's telephone number.

Eleven

Ashley lounged lazily on Zach's white leather couch in his living room. Last year, when he decided to move into the luxury condominium located on Poeyfare, he'd had two of the units turned into one spacious apartment. Perfect for entertaining, it had a sumptuous view overlooking the courtyard and Olympic-sized swimming pool, but Zach was hardly ever there to enjoy any of it.

A true workaholic, he loved the family business; he also loved to travel. Business excursions took him away from home often, while, besides golf, his free time was filled with pleasure trips to one exotic location after another.

Ashley had been to Zach's apartment a total of four times in the entire year he'd lived there. Now, for some odd reason, he'd decided to phase out his old furniture and redo his decor completely. As if he'd truly gotten the chance to enjoy the old style.

Today she'd gone with her brother to his place to inspect the coffee table he was giving to her as a peace offering. She'd seen it before and considered it a beautiful piece of furniture, but she pretended she'd forgotten how it looked and wanted to see it again before she accepted it.

Actually she wanted to ask Zach about Jordan. Just over four weeks had gone by since he'd stumbled across her at the coffee shop. Since that time she'd talked to him twice over the phone in her office and had seen him in the restaurant six times, all related to work. It was as if that night never happened. Jordan made no mention of it, and she wondered why, because she couldn't forget how he'd felt against her. As his friend, she should've been able to discuss her feelings with him, but he seemed unapproachable, even hostile.

Her bowl, too, had fallen silent. It had ceased to write messages to her, and the last time it glowed was the night she and Jordan almost made love.

The money her father gave to her seemed lost to her forever. With her shopping spree a distant dream, she diligently and dutifully paid small amounts toward her overdue bills at each pay period. Although still slightly peeved at Elvis's thievery, it felt good not to have to live with the shame of overindulging at high-priced shops when her bills were due.

She'd seen her parents four additional Tuesdays at their weekly dinner since her father's generous gift, but she'd been careful not to allow them to touch her hair. She believed any other checks would have been safe as long as she didn't place them in the bowl's cavity, but she couldn't be sure. After all, it was Elvis's flash that had ceased her and Jordan's out-of-control kissing.

Neither had she mentioned her shopping expedition. It shamed her that she'd used money she didn't have. Pretending she used the money her father gave to her would have been an outright lie.

Deep down, she'd always understood the reasons her parents cut her off. If she hadn't before, she certainly had a better understanding now. If she didn't learn to control herself, she could bankrupt the richest Rockefeller. The trick was finding a happy medium.

Her thoughts plaguing her, she smiled as Zach joined her on the sofa, handing a cola to her.

"Thanks," she said. "I see you've already replaced most of your traditional furniture with high-tech modern pieces."

"Yeah," Zach answered. He waved his hand to indicate the stylistic art pieces. "I felt futuristic. I want to hit the millennium in a big way. High-tech and modern. So are you interested in acquiring the table?"

"You bet," Ashley responded with a laugh at her brother's explanation. "Thanks, Zach. It'll certainly add style to my living room. What did you do with the old couch and end table?"

"My girlfriend's aunt lost almost all her belongings in a fire a few weeks ago, Ash, and Fawn asked me to help in any way that I could. I'm sorry. I hope you don't mind that I gave her the sofa and end table."

Ashley brought her hands to her chest. "Oh, my stars, Zach. Of course not! The poor thing. Why didn't you give her the coffee table, too?"

Zach's eyes widened in surprise. "I wanted you to have it. After all, you need one, too."

"What's the look for, Zachery?"

"It just surprises me that you didn't chastise me for not running out and buying her everything that she needed."

"It didn't even cross my mind," Ashley said honestly. "Maybe I'm learning, huh?"

"That depends, Ashley," Zach answered, giving her a level look. "What did you do with the money Dad gave to you?"

Ashley drank from her cola. "Absolutely nothing," she said wryly. "As a matter of fact, I haven't even deposited it into my bank account yet."

"Seriously, Ashley?"

"Seriously, Zach." Ignoring the reasons *why* she hadn't deposited the check, she couldn't deny the guilt and misery she felt at Zach's proud tone. He thought she hadn't deposited the check because she was finally becoming responsible with money. If only he knew the full story.

"Listen, honey, I'm damned proud of you for that. And I have to apologize for being such a butthead these past weeks." He sighed. "But it has less to do with your spending habits, which I'm used to unfortunately and—"

"More to do with Jordan," she interrupted softly, her stomach clenching with despair. Zach really had no reason to be proud of her. Somehow, this time, she couldn't bring herself to confess.

"Yes. I have absolutely no right to dictate to you whom you should and shouldn't date. I'm not your father, only your brother, and you're a grown woman. But I still don't believe Jordan is right for you. If you two became romantically involved, it would only ruin the friendship you have with him."

"And what about the one you two share?"

Zach bowed his head and studied his hand before answering her. "I tried to convince myself that it would have no effect on our friendship, but, deep down, I know it would."

"I see." Ashley's tension increased. Zach's statement wasn't a great revelation. She knew he didn't want her and Jordan to get involved. She just didn't understand his motivations. "Why?"

"For the reasons I stated, Ashley," he said, shrugging his broad shoulders. "I don't believe a relationship between you two has the chance of a snowball in the desert. I think he should discourage such a likelihood. I don't want you to become a brokenhearted divorcée." Loosening his tie and pulling it off, he opened the top two buttons of his shirt.

"I've been informed, however, that I have nothing to worry about. Jordan says you two have talked it over and have decided to be friends."

"Right." She feigned a bright smile and quickly changed the subject. "So when am I going to meet your new femme fatal?" she teased.

"Fatale," Zach corrected. "If you stick around a while, maybe today. We're double-dating with Jordan and Marie, and they're all coming here first."

Ashley lifted her cola to her mouth, a slight trembling of her hand the only visible reaction to her brother's unconcerned announcement. But her heart slammed against her chest at Zach's words, and she felt ill.

She'd thought, no *hoped*, that she and Jordan had had something going. Could it have only been her imagination? The answer lay in Jordan's actions. Four weeks had passed without a single word or act of encouragement on his part. Now he was taking out another woman.

Wanting to leave before they got there, and before she embarrassed herself, she grabbed her purse from the coffee table. But she couldn't bring herself to move off the sofa. Her knees would buckle.

The thought of another woman stealing Jordan's heart made her eyes water, but Ashley blinked furiously, determined to keep her tears at bay.

"Fawn's a great girl, Ash," Zach went on, oblivious to the turmoil he'd caused her.

How could he know? From what Jordan told him, Zach believed they were only friends. He also believed that fact sat quite well with Ashley.

"I'm sure you'll like her. Oh, by the way, Jordan also told me you two had some java together several of weeks ago. He met you at a shop by accident or something. I'm glad he did. Be careful venturing out alone, baby sister."

Ashley shrugged her shoulders. It was a deflating feeling

to think that Jordan believed their encounter so casual that he could nonchalantly discuss it with Zach. He'd almost taken her virginity, after all. But it appeared to have been just another girl for him to kiss and dismiss.

She'd never realized that Jordan Bennett was so callous.

A spark of anger swept aside her intense hurt. How could she even think to let this happen again? She'd pined for Jordan as a teenager. She refused to fall into that treacherous trap again.

Intending to leave before the lovebirds arrived, she pushed herself off the sofa. The doorbell chimed melodiously, rooting her to the spot where she stood. As Zach went to the door and opened it, she cursed under her breath.

A dark-haired young woman flung herself into her brother's arms the minute he opened the door.

"Gads, Fawn. Give the man a break. Have you no shame?"

Rich with amusement, Jordan's voice floated to Ashley, and she sucked in a breath, torn between anger and anguish.

"Of course she has," said the woman who could only be Marie in a throaty alto. "She just has no resistance to Zach. As I have none to you, love." She slipped her arms around Jordan's neck and kissed him fully on the lips.

In spite of her brave intentions, Ashley could feel her heart almost break in two. She was already ensnared in the trap, a place where she realized she'd never fully freed herself from, since her teen years.

No, she wasn't just now falling in love with Jordan. In the seven years that had gone by without seeing him, she'd never fallen *out* of love with him. Spending time with him again had only reinforced that love.

Well, she didn't need to be around these people with their raging libidos. She had to get out of there so she could go home and cry.

She drew in a breath of courage. "Um, excuse me." Her

insides were trembling, but her strong voice surprised her. "Before you four put plan *B* into place, you should make sure there are no onlookers viewing the action."

"Ashley!"

The utter astonishment in his voice vindicated her anguish; the horrified shock in his expression was priceless. The teary feeling left her, and she smiled. "Hi, Jordan. Good to see you again."

Unable to respond vocally, he nodded, then stared at her.

"Ladies," Zach said with pride, either unaware or ignoring the dramatic tableau going on, "this is Ashley. My baby sister."

"Hello, Ashley," Fawn said with a pretty smile framing her olive features. "So nice to meet you. I've heard so many wonderful things about you. We're cruising the Natchez tonight. Would you care to join us?"

"Yeah," Marie said smoothly, openly assessing Ashley. She narrowed her eyes at Jordan's obvious discomfort. "I can always get an extra complimentary ticket. By the way, I'm Marie."

"Thank you both, but I'm afraid I have to decline. Too many irons in the fire."

"Spending time with your boyfriend, then?" Marie asked innocently.

"No, actually, I'm quite available at the moment," Ashley said sweetly. "There are just minor things I have to see to."

Zach frowned at her. "Will you be okay, Ash?"

"Yeah, sure," Ashley responded, her emotions in knots. "You guys enjoy yourselves. I suppose there's no point in telling you don't do anything I wouldn't do, since you probably will anyway." Her comments were directed solely at Jordan. She gave him a pointed look and had the satisfaction of seeing him blush.

Fawn laughed, and Marie joined in.

"We should be so lucky," the blue-eyed, lushly curved Marie commented.

"Speak for yourself," Fawn said with a chuckle.

"That's enough," Zach said good-naturedly. "G'bye, Ash. Take care, and I'll probably see you at Mom and Dad's on Tuesday. Maybe after dinner we can come and get this table and take it to your place."

Nodding, Ashley walked to the opened doorway, where she paused. "Pleasure meeting you both," she said to the women. "Have fun. I'll talk to you later, Zach." Unable to resist, she glanced at Jordan. The pain of guilt showed clearly in his blue-gray gaze, and embarrassment shadowed his features. "So long, Jordan."

She dashed out while she was ahead—while she still held on to her dignity.

Twelve

The next morning, Ashley sat on her sofa waiting for her coffee to brew. Pulling her favorite robe tighter around her waist, she rested her head in her hand. Early-morning sun filtered through the half-opened blinds, giving the living room an aura of warmth and light, antagonizing her gloomy mood.

Her door buzzer rang, warding off approaching sour thoughts. Wondering who could be calling on her at that hour, she stomped to the door and swung it open.

There stood Harry, a silk bathrobe hung open, revealing a bare chest and black silk pajama bottoms. His long, black hair lay around his shoulders, and his dark eyes gleamed with amusement.

Ashley scowled at him, in no mood for Harry's flirtations. "What?"

"Ashley, geez, girl. You look terrible in the morning. Maybe I'm lucky that you refused to go out with me after all."

Shoving an annoyed hand through her limp, unwashed hair, she narrowed her eyes at Harry. "*What* do you want?"

she asked testily, unable to deal with her dippy landlord this morning.

Harry tried to peek around her shoulder. But since she was an inch taller than he in her bare feet, it was virtually impossible. "A favor, Ash."

One hand on her hip, the other on the door in preparation to slam it shut, Ashley asked through clenched teeth, "What favor?"

Wickedness gleamed in his eyes. "Not what you're thinking, sugar. I just need you to keep my garden ornaments in your apartment until I have my patio spruced up."

In no mood to argue, Ashley agreed and stepped aside. Stooping beside him, Harry picked up a big, pink flamingo and brushed past her, heading straight for her bedroom. Drawing in a long-suffering sigh, she watched as he followed with a large frog and a fountain with two frogs on lily pads.

His task completed, Harry walked to where she waited by the open door with her arms folded. He kissed her jaw. "Thanks, Ash. Not only will my babies be safe, but I now have the perfect excuse to visit you. You know I—"

"Good-bye, Harry," she said, pushing him out the door. "I'll talk to you later."

"Fine. Ashley," he began.

She closed the door before he finished, and returned to the sofa. Maybe she'd been rude and unfair to Harry, but she wasn't up to entertaining him or anyone else.

Last night had been a horror show for her. After seeing Jordan and Marie together, she took in a late movie alone at Uptown Square, but didn't remember what she'd seen. She felt empty, totally alone, and completely betrayed. She understood now why Jordan had avoided her so efficiently these past weeks. Despite how it galled her, his actions devastated her as well.

The "we should be so lucky" comment made by Marie

hinted that she and Jordan hadn't been intimate. But it didn't abate Ashley's distress. He had given her hope, then abandoned her. Even the friendship he insisted he wanted seemed unimportant to him.

Intellectually, she now knew she had little chance of winning Jordan. She just had to be firm and get that message through to her wayward emotions. If only she could get her heart in sync with her head. For the life of her, however, she couldn't.

She knew Jordan felt something for her. She had merely to break through his stubborn resistance and somehow keep Zach's mouth shut. His discouraging attitude didn't help matters.

With a sigh, she stretched tiredly out on the sofa and looked at her bowl. It was easy to believe that she'd imagined that the bowl had special, magical powers. For more than four weeks it had been nothing but a beautiful, decorative object. She might even say she'd become unraveled, except that the check her father had given her was inside it with Ashley's name and Murray's signature, but still no dollar amount.

And the heat of Jordan's body pressed against her, after he drank wine from the bowl, invaded her dreams at night. None of that was imagination. It had been a real occurrence, caused by Elvis.

Hearing the *ding* from the state-of-the-art coffeemaker her mom had gifted her with, announcing the brew's readiness, she wrinkled her nose at the pleasant aroma drifting through the living room. She raised her hands above her head and stretched delicately.

Saturday was usually her day to relax, catch up on laundry, read, or just do whatever caught her fancy. This weekend she was supposed to start initial sketches for the hotel's refurbishment so she could pass it along to Wood, Mr. Russell, and Zach and Murray for the Douglas firm's shareholders. Whatever she did on Saturdays, however, she always started with a cup of coffee. Only today she felt as if she'd lost her best friend.

Sitting up, she rested her chin on the back of her entwined hands.

"Oh, enough of this, Ashley!" she said suddenly. "Snap out of it. There's always another bus coming." *Yeah,* a little voice whispered, *but it might be crowded.*

Ashley giggled at the thought of comparing a womanizing man to a crowded bus. Both were hazardous to one's health. Still chuckling, she went into the kitchen and poured herself a mug of coffee. Glancing toward the living room, a brilliant white light illuminated the doorway.

"Elvis!" Cup in hand, she dashed back into the living room and headed straight to the dazzling bowl. "Elvis, you came back."

Immediately the fine-scripted Teletype started across the notepad.

I never left.

"Well, you stopped communicating," Ashley pouted. "I thought you had deserted me, too."

Too?

"Yes. It's a long story, Elvis. One I don't care to divulge at the moment. And don't you dare read my mind," she added as an afterthought.

Ho, ho, ho. Don't flatter yourself, kiddo.

Ashley scowled and set down her cup. "Does your mother know how rude and insulting you are?"

How could I have a mother? I'm a bowl.

"Well, you had a *something*," Ashley argued, feeling rather foolish at being so summarily chastised. "A creator, then. Is that better? But someone made you and shaped you into the beautiful bowl that you are."

Thank you.

"You're welcome. How come you don't talk?"

Young lady, do you see a mouth on me?

"No, smarty-pants, but neither do I see ears, and yet you can hear me."

Well done, Ashley. You're very observant. I've borrowed my hearing from the creatures designed on my sides, if you must know.

Picking up the bowl, Ashley turned it this way and that. The metal was warm beneath her fingers, vibrating with energy. Tingles shimmied through her and filled her with peace. She set the bowl down.

"The only creatures I see on your sides are butterflies. The other designs are bows, bells, and flowers. I didn't know butterflies had ears."

Look at me a little closer, Ashley. On the base of my stand.

When Ashley picked up the bowl again, she remembered the figures of two birds that had appeared to come alive during her first encounter with Elvis. She smiled. "Why, there are birds! Where did they come from?"

It's an image of two doves. My source of hearing. However, unlike the beautiful birds, I am immortal.

"Oh, but this is truly amazing, and so wonderful!"

I'm glad you approve. I sense a sadness about you. What is the source of your unhappiness?

The abrupt change of topics told Ashley Elvis had ended his generous revelations to her. But she wanted to learn all she could about the bowl's mysteries and magic. For the moment, however, she'd revel in what it had told her. What *he* had told her, she corrected. Shoot! It was hard to constantly put a gender to a *bowl*. And even harder to imagine that she was beginning to acquire an affinity for Elvis.

But she was. Especially since he was so concerned about her well-being. He'd *sensed* her despondency. That was more than she could say for almost everyone she knew.

"You're really sweet to be concerned," she said softly.

Thank you. And you're really soft.

"I beg your pardon?"

Your hands, my dear. When you were inspecting me, you touched me all over. From my rim to my stand.

Heat rushed to Ashley's cheeks, and embarrassed laughter escaped her. *His stand?* She'd touched his *stand?* She couldn't believe she had a lecherous bowl on her hands.

"Are you flirting with me?" she snapped, her surprise evaporating.

Ha ha ha ha ha ha ha ha. You really are naive. I was only paying you a compliment, Ashley. I'm not allowed to flirt, even with someone as lovely as you.

"You can see, too?"

Of course. The birds have eyes, don't they?

"They also have a mouth. How come you don't use one?"

I tried to, about six hundred years ago, but the only sound I could make was peep, peep, peep and coo coo, coo coo.

"Why did you choose me?"

Because of your sincerity to become responsible with money, Ashley, and because you've such a kind nature. I used my powers to deter others who appeared interested in me, until someone with your characteristics came my way. Then I beckoned you to buy me.

Yes, the bowl most certainly had. Trembles racked her just remembering the tingles she'd experienced when she'd first laid eyes on the dish.

Trust me, Ashley. I cannot reveal to you all the things I can do. Not until you've earned the right to know. And I determine that, by telling you a little at a time. Now cease your questions! I have already revealed too much to you. And you have yet to answer my question. What is troubling you?

"An affair of the heart." Ashley sighed. "Oh, I have a

wonderful idea. Do you recall four weeks ago when you sent Jordan Bennett to join me in a cup of coffee?"

I did?

"You know you did, Elvis. Now you can help me win him over."

How?

"Using magic," Ashley answered in exasperation. "Like you did before."

Ashley, I don't know what you're talking about. I don't even know a Jordan Bennett. But cheer up, I promise I'll be rooting for you to win over your young man.

Not believing Elvis's denial for one minute, Ashley pressed her lips to the bowl's rim. "Thank you, Elvis," she whispered, close to tears. Her heart was beating fast and furious, and she hoped the rash actions she was taking to gain Jordan were worthwhile. "I knew I could count on you. You're the best."

The silvery light turned a crimson red, glowing like a brilliant fire. Slowly Elvis reverted back to the beautiful ornamental piece she'd bought, and the pad went blank.

"There's a lot to be said about a bowl that can blush," Ashley said with a laugh. "It's nothing short of sheer magic." Her coffee cold and now forgotten, she went into her bedroom to dress and plan a strategy to break through Jordan's reservations and conquer his heart.

Later that afternoon, she found a pleasant surprise when she returned from the Laundromat that Harry kept for his tenants. Zach sat on her sofa, watching television, his feet resting on the coffee table he'd given her.

Dropping her basket of folded clothes by the living room closet, she went and kissed Zach's jaw. "You brought it!" she exclaimed, more than happy to finally have a table in her living room. She refused to ask about Jordan. She didn't want to hear what a fabulous time the four of them had the night before together.

"Yeah," Zach said, grinning at her delight. He watched her closely. "I hope you don't mind that I used my spare key?"

"Of course not, Zach." Uncomfortable beneath his scrutiny and wondering if he guessed at her heartache, she hurried to the kitchen. She quickly returned with a can of spray-on wood polish and paper towels. After polishing it, she patted it lovingly. "Do you know how long it's been since I've had a *real* table in here?"

"Never?" Zach asked glibly, flicking the television off.

Ashley poked her tongue at him and stood. Her pulse pounded with the need to know about Jordan, but she refused to give in to the urge. She'd rather confess her shopping spree first. And *that* would happen after a rainstorm drenched the fires in hell. "Let's celebrate. I'll fix us something to eat, and we can eat at the table."

"Oh, God, she's trying to kill me!"

"No, silly," Ashley said, not taking offense. Her track record in the kitchen was worse than Napoleon's defeat at Waterloo. "I'm going to fry eggs. How hard can that be?"

"Ashley, you can't *boil* an egg," Zach reminded her, resting an arm on the back of the sofa. "How the hell do you expect to fry one?"

"Just trust me. Okay?"

Ashley went into the kitchen and took out a small frying pan. She had all kinds of pots and pans and cooking and serving dishes, as well as recipe books. One day she meant to learn how to cook, and today was a good day to have another go at it. So what if the last time she'd dealt with eggs she burned them? So what if Harry threatened to evict her because the fire department had to come out?

Those were minor setbacks.

Taking two eggs and a stick of butter from the refrigerator, she nodded firmly. "I can do this," she muttered, sure of herself.

Peeking into the kitchen and grinning at her frown of concentration, Zach shook his head. "Need any help, Ash?"

"No. I can do this," she reiterated firmly.

"Okeydokey." Zach left her alone, and Ashley turned her attention back to her task.

Turning the burner on beneath the frying pan, she put the entire stick of butter in the pan. Then she got a bowl, cracked the eggs, allowing them to drop inside, and proceeded to scramble them with a fork.

Humming softly, she waited until the butter was smoking and turning brown before pouring the eggs into the pan. They sizzled and fried, swimming in the burning butter. Fastidiously she stirred them, adding salt and pepper to the mixture. Satisfied that the eggs had soaked up all the butter, she frowned at their dark brown color. *That* wasn't supposed to happen.

Unsure of what she'd done wrong, she emptied them onto a plate and stared at them. Should she eat them? Most importantly, should she serve them to Zach? She didn't want to end up killing him with one of her creations. At least these eggs didn't have the same foul odor as the burnt boiled eggs nor were they as black.

With a shrug, she got two plates and divided the eggs, then brought them out and put the food on her new coffee table.

For a moment, Zach stared at the plates, then he burst out laughing. "Poor Ashley! Cooking isn't one of your strong points, I see."

"Oh, shut up," she said crossly.

Zach grabbed one of the plates. "As a gesture to your gallant effort, I'll try them." He took a forkful and chewed carefully, before swallowing hard. "They're not half bad," he declared.

Tasting them herself, Ashley frowned. She couldn't taste the eggs for the burned butter. "They're too greasy for *my* tastebuds," she said primly, pushing the eggs aside.

Setting his own nearly full plate down, Zach laughed. "Call Warehouse District Pizza. How's about a large barbeque chicken pizza?"

Ashley jumped to her feet, relieved. Hurrying to the telephone, she thanked her lucky stars for having Zach for a big brother.

Thirteen

Bright and early Monday, Ashley stood gazing out of the window in Jim Russell's office, which overlooked Canal Street on one side and a side street leading to the French Quarter on the other side. A light drizzle fell over the city, but far in the distance, Ashley noticed a glimmer of sunshine, a beckoning ray of hope.

Talking to Elvis this past weekend was like adrenaline pumped directly to her heart. At no time after their discussion had thoughts of Jordan consumed her. She had every confidence that she'd win him over. Because Elvis had already begun to work his magic, she felt self-assured in her quest.

Sorrow went out the window, and she'd never enjoyed her house or her very own company more. She was even able to find extra money for a couple of long overdue bills and write out the checks, then tidy up a bit.

Even the couple of hours Zack was there had passed productively as they went over the plans she'd come up with for the hotel. Now she supposed Mr. Russell wanted to hear what she'd decided upon, to give his final approval.

When she got in a few minutes earlier, she'd found a message on her desk, stating Mr. Russell's immediate desire to see her. But she'd been there for five minutes, and there was no sign of her boss. Agitated with waiting, she paced to his sharkskin-covered desk decorated with ivory drawer pulls. Frowning at the huge monstrosity, she got a notepad and scribbled a message, indicating that she'd been there.

Just as she was leaving, the office door swung open.

"Ashley, good morning." Mr. Russell rushed inside, carrying a buttery croissant. Taking a bite of the flaky roll, he stared at her. "Don't tell me. Don't tell me," he chanted. Narrowing his eyes in concentration and finishing off the croissant, he shook his head. "Yes, tell me. Or at least give me a hint." He wiped his mouth with the napkin that had been wrapped around the bread. "Why are you here?"

Silently Ashley held out the memo to him.

"Oh, that!" Mr. Russell stepped closer and read the note. "Did I send that?"

Drawing in a deep breath, she nodded.

"Hmm, I wonder why. It had nothing to do with little Hades or the housekeeper's shoes that he chewed up. She decided to work in her bare feet this morning, while my wife goes to buy her another pair of shoes. If I didn't need you to go to my house . . . hmm." He stroked his chin, deep in thought, then snapped his fingers. "Petersen," he announced triumphantly. "He took emergency sick leave yesterday. Something about falling out of a tree trying to put up his son's swing."

"Omigod! Mr. Russell, is he all right?"

Mr. Russell shrugged. "Well, I suppose. But we'll know more when he regains consciousness. They're trying to play down the broken leg thing, however."

If she hadn't known what a flaky sort Mr. Russell was, she might have taken offense at what seemed like an insensitive comment. "My stars!"

"Yes, isn't it a shame. Poor man. But he's getting the best of care. Remember, Ashley, if for any reason I forget, the company is going to pick up the twenty-percent that his insurance doesn't pay for."

Ashley smiled. This was just the type of generosity that set her boss apart from some of the boors in life. "Good. I'll send flowers to him and a fruit basket to his family as well."

"Excellent idea, Ashley. But while he's recuperating, you'll have to take over his duties. You'll have to get to-gether with Jarvis Berton about the food supply. That young man is going far someday. He's a great cook. His croissants are light and fluffy with butter coming out the yang-yang on them. Now, are you up for the job?"

Biting down on her lip to keep from laughing at Mr. Russell's description of Jordan's baking skills, Ashley pat-ted her hair and nodded. "You bet, Mr. Russell."

Am I up for the job? You bet your sweet patooty, I am, sir. Thank you, Elvis. I only hope you didn't seriously injure Mr. Petersen on my account.

The thought bothered her. The only reason she'd asked for Elvis's help was because he seemed like a gentle . . . soul. But she refused to have bodily harm committed to attain her goals.

"Handle your extra duties however you see fit, Ash. Tell Mr. Berton hi for me."

"Will do, sir, and thanks. I won't let you down." "Jarvis Berton" mightn't appreciate her though. Ashley wondered with amusement what was so hard about remembering Jor-dan's name. "Will there be anything else, Mr. Russell? I have the initial idea for the plans that Carson Wood re-quested last week."

"Good. I'll get them from you later. By the way, I'd like to set up a meeting between Wood, Murray, Zach, you, and me—"

"You want me there?"

"Of course, Ashley. Why wouldn't I? This is your baby. You just need me for signatures. With our renovations and expansions, however, I need to target consumers. I'm developing an idea that will help to bring the hotel to national prominence. With your brilliance and that young hotshot in our kitchen, we can go all the way."

Ashley blushed at the compliment. "Thank you for your confidence in me."

"Someone has to have faith in you, wouldn't you say, Ashley?" Mr. Russell asked in a rare moment of insight. "I'm not saying that your father and brother aren't proud of you. I've just noticed they expect you to be the baby of the family who's always in need of them one way or another. It's more convenient for *them* to think that."

Mr. Russell's words remained with her as she returned to her office. She appreciated whatever had precipitated his wisdom, because it gave her something to think about.

Her family *did* think of her as a baby. Even if she failed in the renovation project, it was time she demanded the respect she was due from them. The way to start that transition was to stop relying so heavily on them, especially Zach.

She also had to take care not to start relying too heavily on that bowl.

She felt Elvis was somehow responsible for the way everything was turning out. His powers seemed far reaching, certainly beyond her living room.

Once she'd ordered the flowers and fruit for the Petersens, she started to dial the extension for the kitchen. When Jordan suddenly appeared in the open doorway, she paused.

"Ash?" His voice was tentative. "May I come in?"

Ashley placed the receiver back on the cradle, her jerky movements betraying her tenseness. "Hello, Jordan," she said, crisp and cool. Which was just the effect she wanted to impact upon him. She wouldn't have him thinking she was pining over him, even if he was looking sexy in his chef's whites. And impossibly handsome. And remarkably contrite.

She was well enough acquainted with him to know that he was squirming over last Friday's incident. Her fondest wish was that he thought enough of her to *want* to explain why he'd so abruptly halted what was happening between them.

Her demeanor calm, her heartbeat wild with excitement, she indicated the chair in front of her desk. "Come in. As a matter of fact, you're the person I was about to call. Close the door, will you, please?"

When he had closed the door, Jordan walked to the chair and dropped wearily into it. She refused to pity his hangdog expression and instead raised her chin in a haughty pose. "I take it you've heard about Petersen?"

"Yes. A pity," Jordan replied, a frown darkening his handsome features. "I understand he's still unconscious."

"Yes, unfortunately. He also has a broken leg."

"I know," he said tersely. "That was a pretty stupid thing for him to do."

"Well, for star's sake, Jordan!" Ashley gritted, throwing her hands in the air. "He was only trying to make his little boy happy. You can't condemn him for that."

"All right, Ashley, all right. Let's not debate the merits of Petersen's judgment. I'm here to talk about the food supply."

"Fine, but tell me, Jordan. Are you irritated at Mr. Petersen because of his accident, or is your wrath directed at me for some reason?"

Unfathomable blue-gray eyes studied her, and tense fingers gripped the cushiony handles on the chair. Jordan breathed in sharply, closed his eyes, then opened them again. Hot desire turned his gaze to molten silver.

Passion pulsed between them, a lightning rod sizzling with currents. That wild, vibrant scent from her hair swirled in the space around them, conjuring images of raw passion. Shivers of awareness racked Ashley's body, and her breathing came in ragged bursts.

Jordan jumped from his seat, walked around the desk, and pulled her out of her chair. He hauled her against his chest and lowered his mouth to hers, kissing her savagely, possessively, thoroughly.

His tongue inside her mouth sent sweet need through Ashley. Her senses sang; her toes tingled. When he ended the kiss, she buried her face in the warmth of his neck, drugged by his male scent, electrified by his closeness.

"Goddammit, Ashley," he growled in her ear. Briefly he tightened his arms around her, before releasing her and walking away. He thrust his hands through his hair. "How can you be so unassuming over this whole matter?"

Her jaw tightening, she took a step away from him. How could *he* be so unassuming as to think his kiss wouldn't affect her? But she was determined to remain in control and ignore her shaky legs and pounding heart. Returning to her desk, she straightened a stack of papers and sat down. Purposely she misinterpreted his meaning. "I have not ignored Mr. Petersen's misfortune, Jordan. I am very sympathetic to his plight and plan to pay him a visit later today."

Jamming his hands in his trouser pockets, Jordan pinned her with an angry stare. "You know what I mean, Ashley, and it has nothing to do with Petersen's accident."

"Oh?" Ashley leaned back in her chair and folded her arms. "Then by all means enlighten me, Jordan. I haven't the slightest idea what you're talking about."

"Give me a break and stop being coy," Jordan ordered. He sat back in the chair, his aggravation obvious by the rapid movement of his leg. "It's not your style. You and I can't have a relationship. We have nothing in common. Can I be any clearer than that?"

"Well, I don't know—"

"Besides," Jordan continued defensively, as if she hadn't spoken, "I have not slept with Marie, regardless of what you may think. Marie and I are just friends. Is *that* clear?"

"Of course, Jordan. But what has all that to do with me?" She knew she was still being coy, yet she couldn't let him know how she rejoiced at his words.

"I don't know," Jordan answered, calmer now. "I just don't want you to get the wrong impression, that's all."

Ashley tapped her fingers on the desk. "The wrong impression of what? You and Marie? Or the kiss you just gave me?"

"Neither," he said facilely. "It was just a regular date with Marie. Nothing more."

"I see," Ashley responded in the same tone. "And the kiss?"

"Just another . . ." Jordan's voice trailed off as he gazed into Ashley's hazel eyes. The kiss had shaken him to the core. He hadn't realized how much he'd missed Ashley, yet he hadn't forgotten how lovely she was. Her flawless features remained in his mind constantly and not even the fun-loving, cheery Marie could budge it.

Knowing he'd eventually have to face Ashley after Friday night, he'd dreaded this moment. He thought she'd be devastated, or at the least angry. The last thing he'd expected was indifference.

He should have been happy, but, perversely, her attitude surprised and annoyed him. Maybe all the stress and worry he'd been under that he and Ashley could fall for one another had been unnecessary. Certainly her response to his kisses were as passionate and spontaneous as his had been. He hadn't imagined that. She'd kissed him back. But the stubborn little brat would never admit she felt something, too. Besides, she'd never, ever said again that she was in love with him or that she wanted a long-term relationship with him.

Everyone had merely *assumed* that she wanted that because of her avowal when she was sixteen.

He smiled at her. Her lips were kiss-swollen and red; she had been utterly delicious. "The kiss, Ashley, was wonderful," he finally said, not wanting to sound like a first-class jerk, but feeling like one anyway—or at least an immature one. He told her he wanted to be just friends with her. Now that she seemed to be adhering to that, he resented it.

"Yes, it was," Ashley confessed, returning his smile with an enchanting one of her own. "Incidentally, I have a recipe I intend to try next Saturday. Drop by if you're free, and maybe you can give me some pointers."

Jordan's grin widened at her adroit change of subject. She was good at getting her way. "Thank you, Ashley. I'll make it my purpose to be free. But it's your show. I'm sure whatever you prepare will be fine. Without any pointers from me."

Ashley laughed. "Oh, so you like living dangerously, huh?"

"Don't be so hard on yourself, Ash." His casual demeanor was fully in tact once more. One day they would have to get past the small talk and try to have a heart-to-heart without arguing. "You never know what you can do unless you first give it a try."

"Right," Ashley agreed. "So, shall we get on with today's food business?"

"By all means," he said huskily and settled back in his seat. "Let's do."

Her beautiful face was animated, and her hair was glorious, the wavy golden-blond strands inviting his touch. There were a number of other things he would've preferred to be doing with her at this moment. But *he* had laid the ground rules. She was merely following them.

Fourteen

When Ashley arrived home that evening, she dashed inside and threw her things down. Flipping on a light, she went straight to her bowl. Thoughts of Jordan consuming her and anxious to talk to Elvis, the dreaded bus ride was a blur.

"Elvis," she whispered, looking into the dark cavity. "Can you hear me? I want to thank you for giving Jordan a little nudge my way. But did you have to hurt Mr. Petersen in the process?"

The bowl flashed its brilliant white light, and the Teletyping began.

I take it you're excited about something, Ashley?

"Yes, I am." She pressed her lips to Elvis's rim. "I'm excited about how wonderful you are."

The bowl turned a deep red again. *You* must *stop doing that, Ashley.*

"But why? You can only see and hear. You have no other senses. Besides, you deserved a kiss."

Thank you, Ashley. But for your information, I am also sensitive to touch. And yours is very soft and sensual.

"Elvis! You're a bowl, for heaven's sake."

My point exactly, Ashley. Being an inanimate object, I cannot give back what I receive or what I feel.

The words seemed bittersweet; they touched her. She'd thought the bowl was charmed. Maybe it was cursed. "I'm sorry for touching you, Elvis. I was only expressing my gratitude."

I know. But think of another way. Perhaps you can polish me up a bit.

"I can certainly do that," Ashley quickly said. "But, then, I would be touching you again. Aren't you sensitive to a polishing cloth, too?"

Not really. Although it will probably be just as pleasurable an experience as when you first cleaned and polished me.

"Only me," Ashley said sardonically, gazing heavenward before refocusing on Elvis again.

Only you?

"Yes, only I would acquire a magic bowl that showed the signs of a pervert."

Me? A pervert? Don't be dramatic. I'm the most normal, enchanted bowl in existence. Never mind that I'm the only one. Ha, ha, ha.

"You're turning out to be quite a character, Elvis," Ashley said with a laugh. "But I pray you're not mean-spirited. Poor Mr. Petersen may have a serious head injury, since he's still unconscious."

Do not fear, Ashley. Mr. Petersen is merely asleep. You must have time to put a bloom on your romance with Jordan Bennett. A few more days of rest won't harm Mr. Petersen. Because when he awakens, he will be able to resume his regular duties. Although he'll do it on crutches.

"How much time do I have?" she asked, trusting implicitly that Elvis would see to Mr. Petersen's well-being.

A week.

"Fair enough. I invited Jordan over for dinner on Saturday for an evening of dining, wining, and relaxation."

And you intend to pull out all the stops?

"I'll do my best." She frowned. "Although I'm not exactly sure what that means."

You'll be fine. Just be sure to have me well polished for your guest.

"I will. But I'm not too certain about how to proceed with polishing your, uh, stand. You know, you're rather sensitive to the touch. And well . . . you know what I mean, Elvis," Ashley mumbled, feeling the heat creep up her neck.

Oh, ho, ho, ho. Indeed I do. But I am a cold, inanimate object, remember? What do you care?

"I swear you're impossible, Elvis. I'll polish you, but the second you start to glow crimson, that's it. I'm stopping."

Fair enough, Ashley. You have my word. I'll be a perfect gentleman.

Ashley giggled. "You'd better be. Excuse me," she said in response to the ringing of the telephone. "Let me catch that." She rushed to the cordless phone she'd left on her newly acquired coffee table. "Hullo?"

"Ashley? This is your father, baby," Murray boomed, as though Ashley wouldn't recognize his voice. "I've sent a cab over to pick you up. It should be there momentarily, so be ready when you hear the horn."

"Daddy, I just got in. I'm not coming over there tonight."

"Yes, you are," Murray ordered sternly. "We have a big surprise for you, so get your behind over here ASAP."

"Daddy!"

A dial tone rose in her ears, and Ashley imagined the fierce frown her father wore because of her refusal. Apparently today wasn't the day she started standing up to her family. She slammed the phone down in frustration as a car horn blew outside.

"Damn." Sighing, she grabbed her purse and patted Elvis's rim. "See you later, pal."

A soft glow followed her as she dashed to the door.

Fifteen

The taxi ride from her apartment was quick and uneventful, and she arrived at her parents' mansion too soon for her sake. Having no idea what her father wanted, she hoped the evening wouldn't be too long and drawn out.

She'd really intended to have a relaxing evening at home, which included washing some of her delicate lingerie. Maybe she'd finally unwrap all the things she'd bought a month ago and hid in her bedroom closet.

She hoped her father didn't ask about the money he'd given her. Hating to lie to her parents, but knowing they'd probably have her exorcised, placed in therapy, or locked up if she told them about Elvis, she really had no choice. She could just see her mother blaming her father for cutting off Ashley's allowance in the first place.

Ashley chuckled. Perhaps that would be a way to get back into her family's good graces again. The only disadvantage to that would be the loss of Elvis. Her bowl was company. He was fun. He was *magic*! And he would use that magic to bring her and Jordan together.

Grouching to herself, Ashley opened the door to her parents' home with her key. Quietly closing the door behind her, she stopped in the darkened entrance hall and drew in a deep, steadying breath.

Not seeing or hearing anyone, she surmised everyone was lounging in the den. Shoring up her courage, she scooted down the hallway toward the family room.

"Well, it's about time you showed up, young lady," Murray said sternly as she passed the kitchen. "Your mother's waiting for you in the den. What kept you?"

Ashley stopped inside the doorway of the country kitchen. The humor glinting in his moss-colored eyes surprised her, considering his tone. A tray with two glasses of sherry, a glass filled with ice, and a bottle of Coke sat on the butcher-block table. Her heart sank. Company *did* mean a long, drawn out, boring evening. She looked at her father in question. "Looks like you have guests, Dad. I'll just come back another time."

His brow creased, and he pursed his mouth into a thin line. "The hell you will! I'll bring in an extra Coke for you. Now, go and join your mother in the den!"

Narrowing her eyes at her father, she exhaled a long, noisy sigh. When was she going to develop a backbone and stop letting her family push her around?

Setting her purse on the hall table, she went to the den and sat down next to her mother on the couch. Expecting to find guests, it surprised her to find Glynis alone, stifling a bright smile.

Tired, hungry, and irritated at her father's bullying, Ashley realized her parents were trying to surprise her with someone. But at the moment, she wasn't in the mood to see one of their old friends from their college days, who insisted on seeing Ashley right then. She'd been subjected to such evenings before.

Folding her arms, she looked sideways at Glynis. "Mother, there are a number of things I could be doing at home, so why have you allowed Dad to play tyrant and force me to come here?"

Glynis patted Ashley's arm. "Don't be so hard on your father, darling," she said with a laugh. "You know there's always a reason for what he does."

Ashley sighed contritely. "I know, Mom. So what's his reason this time?" She looked around the room pointedly. "Where are the guests?"

"Since we practically grew up together in this house, I don't exactly consider myself a guest," a youthful female voice said, following Murray into the den.

Ashley's squeal reverberated throughout the house. "Sydnee!" She bounded off the sofa, missing her father by mere inches as she rushed to Sydnee's outstretched arms. "I don't believe this!"

Hugging each other fiercely, they bounced up and down.

Murray set the tray on the coffee table, smiling sheepishly. "And you were bad-mouthing me."

"Which you really didn't deserve this time, Daddy."

"You can blame me, Ash," Sydnee said. "Your parents wanted to drive me to your apartment to surprise you, but I didn't want to intrude on you. Besides, I thought surprising you this way would be more fun."

"Maybe, but certainly not less surprising!" She hugged her friend again. "What's going on with you, Sydnee?"

"Everything wonderful," Sydnee responded with a gleeful laugh. "We'll talk later." She winked at Ashley. "Right now, I'm enjoying my visit with my second parents."

On pins and needles, Ashley willed the evening to end quickly. Sydnee looked wonderfully radiant, fairly glowing with happiness. Ringlets of rich red hair softened her pale features, lightly dusted with freckles. Tranquility glistened in her eyes, which were the color of warm honey. And with her slim figure, she surely didn't look pregnant.

A twinge of envy spiraled through Ashley. To her, nothing could be more fulfilling or cause such joy than to love a man who returned your love with the same intensity with which it was given. Sydnee appeared to have found such a man—and then some. She was carrying his child.

Hating her negative feelings and determinedly pushing them aside, Ashley enjoyed the inane talk, which went on for hours. Sydnee skillfully dodged questions she didn't want to answer, keeping the banter away from a personal level and focusing on the past and the changes that had taken place since she'd left the city three years ago.

They even talked about Ashley's addiction to spending money, but Ashley's parents said she'd learned a great deal about economizing in the two years since she'd moved out. Sydnee assured them all she hadn't lost *her* fondness for spending and in fact, never stopped; also contributing to that fact was upon her parents' passing, Sydnee had been left a large sum of money.

When the evening finally ended, Ashley's parents insisted the girls spend the night there. Ashley was just as insistent, however, that she and Sydnee go to her apartment. In the end she won out, and Murray drove them to her place.

"Oh, Ash, how charming. It's so *quaint*," Sydnee exclaimed, after she'd given Ashley's small apartment the once-over.

Ashley laughed good-naturedly. "Quaint isn't what I was striving for. Charming? Yes. Do you think it looks a bit *old*?"

Sydnee waved her hand, her wedding band sparkling in the lamplight. "Oh, perish the thought. It's lovely. I really mean it. The things you have in your bedroom are rather whimsical."

"What things?" Ashley asked, beckoning Sydnee to the sofa to sit next to her.

"The pink flamingo, the statue of the two frogs in a pond, the—"

"Those things belong on the patio." She laughed at Sydnee's exaggerated cheeriness as she spoke about Harry's belongings. "My *landlord*'s patio. I'm waiting for him to remove them from the premises."

"Then they're not yours?"

"No way!"

"Thank God!" Sydnee finally plopped down beside Ashley. "They're too tacky for words."

"*Sydnee!* You said they were whimsical and charming and quaint."

"Yes, but that's when I thought they were yours. Besides the apartment *is* charming and quaint. I know it's been a while since we've seen each other, but I just couldn't believe your tastes had changed so drastically. Especially given how stunning *you* look. You are absolutely gorgeous, Ash."

Ashley patted her hair and smiled at the compliment. "Thanks, Syd. So are you. And I'll tell you all about me, *after* I hear about you. We had enough small talk at my parents. What gives? How did you meet Mr. Right? Is he French?"

"Slow down, Ash." Sitting on her folded leg that rested on the sofa while her other one hung to the floor, she turned to Ashley. "Before I begin, let me apologize for not keeping in touch. It was rough at first. I don't mean financially. Dad left me and Cal fixed for life. I mean emotionally."

"Oh, Syd." Ashley grabbed Sydnee's hand. "I had no idea."

"I know you remember the year after I left Dad and Cal moved to Chicago. Then, last year Daddy died. I felt as though my anchor had broken and left me adrift."

"But you were always so strong. When your mom passed

away, six months before you left, you were the one who
kept everything together."

"That was the hardest thing I'd ever had to do, Ashley.
Cal lost himself in women and work, while my dad was
devastated. I *had* to be strong for him. I don't think he ever
got over my mother's death and simply grieved himself to
an early grave."

"I'm so sorry, Sydnee. I wish I had known, but I just
took it for granted that you had accepted your mom's passing. The cancer had ravaged her so terribly."

"I know, and her death was inevitable, but it still hurt.
But now I've never been happier. Cal and I are even starting to mend the fences that were destroyed when he was
being such a jerk. I only regret my folks aren't here to meet
Matt."

"Tell me about him," Ashley urged, sensing Sydnee's
need to move on to a happier topic.

"Okay, okay!" Sydnee said excitedly. "While on an out-
bound flight from New York to Paris, I met Matthew Albert
Fields, the most devastatingly handsome man I've ever
seen. He's Consul General at the American Consulate in
Paris. I was positive that I'd hidden from the passengers
my heartbreak and turmoil behind my smiling facade." She
made a parody of a big grin. "Matt saw right to the core
of me and saw what no one else had. He saw the raw grief
I carried with me day in and day out. When the plane finally
landed, he persuaded me to have coffee with him, and I
reluctantly accepted. From that point, he coaxed me into
another date and another and another. Finally it led to the
next level in my life, a level where I confronted my grief
and finally let go."

"My stars!" Ashley said, enthralled by Sydnee's story.
She placed her hand on her chest. "What a romance!"

"I know. When I finally opened my eyes and got a good

look at Matthew, I discovered that besides being a compassionate human being, he was a hunk!"

Ashley laughed. "How old is he?"

"He's fifteen years older than I am, Ash, which makes him thirty-eight. He has super dark blue eyes and golden hair."

"He sounds wonderful!"

"He *is* wonderful. I kept refusing his proposals until I got pregnant. Oh, Ash, he was so cute. He threatened me with bodily harm if I didn't marry him and give his son *his* name legally—"

"You're having a son?"

"I'm having a baby, Ashley. It's too early to tell its gender. But you know how men are about having sons. It's always 'that's my boy.' "

"Yeah, tell me about it," Ashley said. "Except, of course, when those boys turn out to be little princesses like you and I, then they can't stop bragging."

"All right! Enough about me," Sydnee ordered, straightening in her seat. "Tell me what's been going on with you. Is there a man in your life?"

Ashley smoothed a strand of hair behind her ear and bit down on her lip. Where would she begin? There certainly was a man she wanted in her life, but nothing short of magic would put him there.

She wanted—no, *needed*—to confide in someone, and she and Sydnee had been as close as sisters. Ashley would tell her about Jordan and how she'd yearned for him almost all her adult life; and how hard she'd tried to change about spending money carelessly.

Yes, she wanted Sydnee to know about her own inner struggles, but that conversation would sound normal in comparison to what she craved to talk about—Elvis. And that's where normalcy would remove itself from the conversation.

She imagined Sydnee subtly inching away from her on the sofa, and asking when was the last time she'd seen a doctor, preferably a shrink. Of course, if Elvis cooperated with her, therein would be proof. He'd probably eavesdropped on their conversation and hadn't heard any mention of him from Sydnee. She'd talked about the frogs and the flamingo, but not one word about Ashley's beautiful bowl.

"Ash?"

"Forgive me, Syd. My mind wanders sometimes." She chuckled uncomfortably and shifted her weight. "I don't know how to say this, but it's still Jordan."

Sydnee's copper brows drew together in a fierce frown. "Jordan Bennett?"

"Uh-huh."

"After all these years, Ash?" Sympathy laced her voice. "Has he even given you the time of day?"

Their encounter on the sofa came to mind. "That and more. We're kind of seeing each other." When Sydnee looked at her sideways, Ashley wrinkled her nose and shrugged. "Well, sort of," she amended.

"Do you think something will come out of it?" Sydnee asked mildly, removing lint from her summer sweater.

"Hopefully."

"Has he gone blind? Can't he see what a vision you are? You look like a model with your tall, slim frame and wavy, light blond hair. Besides, I've always liked Jordan. He's kind, macho, and—"

"Devastatingly handsome," they chorused together, then giggled like schoolgirls.

"But he is, Ash. Although he keeps his pursestrings a little too tight for my taste."

"He's loosening up, Sydnee, although rather slowly. A few nights ago, he bought me a cup of cappuccino. Before that, he paid my bus fare from my parents house to here."

"So he's not blind after all. Keep it up, girl. You may still get him to buy you that wedding ring." Sydnee turned toward the sofa, her gaze falling finally on the bowl. "Where did you get this bowl, Ashley? It's beautiful." In awe, she traced her fingers across the rim, then slid her hand down its stand.

"Oh, no," Ashley murmured weakly as Elvis glowed crimson.

Letting out a yell and pushing the bowl away, Sydnee jumped from her seat.

Ashley leaned her head against her palm and closed her eyes briefly, then stood and picked up the bowl. "This is Elvis," she said with a sigh. "Don't touch his stand. He's s-sensitive there." Blushing at how utterly insane she sounded, Ashley smiled blandly. She set the bowl back on the table. "He's also a magic bowl and very perverted."

Sydnee's head bobbed back and forth as she looked wildly from Elvis to Ashley and back again. Sydnee started inching toward the French doors. "Ash! What is that? Did you make it glow?"

"Didn't you hear me?" Ashley asked crossly, annoyed that Elvis was scaring the wits out of her friend.

"Yes!" Sydnee snapped. "I heard you and I think you've lost it. There's no such thing as magic. What's going on, Ashley Douglas? You should be ashamed of yourself, playing such a nasty trick on a pregnant woman."

"If you come back and sit down, I'll tell you the whole story."

Her gaze never leaving Elvis, Sydnee tiptoed back to the sofa and sat close to the end. "I'm listening."

The silliness of this entire situation striking her, Ashley grinned mischievously, then related the tale of how she came to possess Elvis, including the strange pull it had on her in the antique shop.

"My God!" Sydnee said in awe. She glanced wide-eyed

at the silver bowl. "C-couldn't you have settled for a puppy? Or a goldfish? Don't you feel eerie with that thing in here?"

Ashley lifted her jaw obstinately. "As I explained, Sydnee, Elvis can see, feel, and hear. So try to refrain from calling him a *thing* and other such derogatory names."

"Oh, silly me." Her high-pitched laugh sounded frantic. "How could I have been so insensitive? I thought a bowl *was* a thing. But who knows? These days, everything isn't what it appears to be anymore."

Wanting Sydnee to have a chance to digest this new discovery, Ashley briefly changed the subject. "Where's your husband, Syd?"

"He's . . . he's in New York," she answered, still not taking her gaze from Elvis. "I want him to meet you and your family. He's coming down in a couple of days, and we'll fly back to the Big Apple for Paris connections."

"Good." Ashley rose from her seat. "That'll give you enough time to get acquainted with Elvis. I'm going to pop some popcorn. You can join me in the kitchen if you'd like."

Hurriedly standing, Sydney walked behind Ashley and glanced warily at the beautiful bowl. "You better believe I'd like."

Sixteen

After popping the corn, Ashley persuaded Sydnee to return to the sofa. Breathing in deeply of the fresh, buttery smell hanging in the air, Ashley placed two glasses of lemonade on cork coasters on the coffee table.

Setting the bowl of popcorn between them on the couch, Ashley folded her legs and quietly munched on the tasty treat. In spite of all she'd told Sydnee about Elvis, her friend still looked apprehensive. Ashley hoped Elvis would put Sydnee's fears at ease, as he did her own. Although she trusted Sydnee not to tell anyone about the magic bowl, she was beginning to regret that she'd been honest about it all. She didn't want Sydnee to be frightened of him.

"So." Sydnee popped a kernel into her mouth, her distinct discomfort obvious by her chalky complexion. "You said the thi—I mean, Elvis sort of beckoned to you to buy it?"

"Righto." Hoping her calmness soothed Sydnee, Ashley leaned toward the coffee table and reached for her lemonade. She took a sip. "Yum! This is my best creation to date."

"Dammit, Ashley," Sydnee protested, bounding to her feet. "I just don't know what to think. I know there's something strange about Elvis. But magic? Come *on*! And if it's true that he is magic, why doesn't he use his powers to become human? In all honesty, that bowl gives me the creeps." To emphasize her point, she shivered.

"Syd—" Ashley stopped when Elvis flashed his brilliant silvery light, training a beam on Sydnee.

For a brief moment, the aura encased Sydnee, wrapping around her like a cocoon. Soothing warmth radiated from the brightness, immobilizing Sydnee. Her mouth open in astonishment, she gazed at her glowing skin. As the glare diminished to a soft glow, Sydnee drew in a tranquil breath.

"Ash, I've never felt such serenity before. It's amazing. It's . . . it's really magic."

"Yes, Syd, it is," Ashley said quietly, the mysterious powers of the bowl taking her breath away. With Elvis's help, she herself had transcended into a similarly peaceful acceptance. Watching someone else experience the same thing was wondrous! "I was afraid of him, too, but that same silver beam found me and calmed all my fears."

A Teletyping sound suddenly rang out.

"He's writing a message," Ashley explained at Sydnee's questioning look.

"A message?"

"Yeah. Let's see what he's writing."

Together they went to the sofa table and gazed down at the bowl.

"What is it writing?"

Ashley pointed to the words appearing on the notepad. "Look."

I do apologize for frightening you, Sydnee.

She blinked, then looked in awe at Ashley.

"I told you." Smiling brightly, Ashley nudged her forward. "Say something to him."

Her fingers tentative, Sydnee touched the rim of the bowl. "Thank you for removing my fear, Elvis. And I apologize for calling you a thing."

Thing, Sydnee, sounded so barbaric to me. You may, however, refer to me as an enchanted object on occasion. All other times you may call mè Elvis.

"My pleasure," Sydnee responded. Leaning closer to the bowl, she drew her brows together in a frown. "Who named you Elvis?"

I named myself. My creator, Merlin, gave me my first name.

"Whoa!" Ashley took position on the other side of the bowl and knelt down. "Merlin the Magician? King Arthur's helper?"

One and the same. He fashioned me out of pure gold for His Majesty and Guinevere, his queen. Of course, that was before the Lancelot Scandal.

Ashley and Sydnee exchanged confused looks.

"But you're silver," Ashley reminded him.

I had no powers before that Lancelot thing, Ashley. I was just a beautiful, golden bowl, kept on the queen's chest in the royal bedchamber. After Lancelot, I was a constant reminder to Arthur of happier times and the reason I was given to them. So the king returned me to Merlin.

"He's going so fast, Ashley, I can hardly keep up. The words are erased and replaced by others in a blur. Can't you get a bigger notepad?"

I'll go a little slower.

"Thank you, El—"

Please, no more interruptions. Where was I? Oh, yes. As I was saying, Merlin named me Ambrose and covered me with a thick layer of silver. He was loath to destroy me, but would never again show my golden facade to the world, in deference to His Majesty.

"How did you end up in that antique shop?" Sydnee asked.

I've been many places through the centuries, Sydnee. I've been well cared for and, at times, horribly neglected. The day I saw Ashley, I knew she was a patron of beautiful objects. So I commanded her attention. Even as tarnished as I was, she still bought me.

Ashley smiled fondly at her bowl, not feeling half as insane now that Sydnee seemed as taken with Elvis. "Be honest, Elvis. You put a spell on me to buy you."

Ho, ho, ho. Do you regret your purchase?

"You know I don't," Ashley quickly responded. "One other thing, Elvis, since you're in such a revealing mood. How did you acquire your magic powers?"

Merlin empowered me. Arthur and his heralded knights were living legends, and he wanted a legacy left behind, as proof that once upon a time there was a place called Camelot. He diminished two of the most beautiful doves in the kingdom and cast them in gold and silver and attached them to the base of my, er, stand. Through Merlin's magic, they accord me the senses of sight, touch, and hearing. The powers Merlin gave me are limited, but they are infinite and eternal. I cannot become human, however. Nor would I want to be. I would never be able to endure the stress.

"But—"

Enough! Elvis interrupted Sydnee. *Go to your door, Ashley. Jordan is on the other side, about to knock.*

His light fading, his last words on the pad disappeared. In an instant, the knock sounded. Going to the door, Ashley giggled at Sydnee's astonishment.

"Hi, Ashley," Jordan said when she opened the door. "I know it's rather late, but I'm just leaving work and I had a few questions about the food supply." He held out a bottle of chardonnay and grinned. "Oh, this is for you."

Ashley swallowed hard, feeling as if her heart lodged in

her throat. Smiling brightly, she accepted Jordan's generous gift. She must remember to have a talk with Elvis about his unexpected surprises. Considering who the surprise was, however, she didn't truly object. "Thank you, Jordan." She stepped aside. "Please, come in."

When Jordan walked into the living room, Ashley closed the door.

"Hi Jordan," Sydnee greeted from where she stood near the sofa.

Jordan did a double take. "Sydnee?"

Smiling brightly, she gave him a small wave. "In the flesh." She rushed to him and hugged him.

"My gosh." Jordan squeezed her tightly. "It's good to see you again, honey. You look great." Releasing her, he turned to Ashley. "I'm sorry. I should have called before I barged in on you like this. We can talk business some other time. You two must have a lot to talk about. I'll just make myself scarce."

"Not on my account," Sydnee piped up. "Ashley and I need more than one evening to catch up on three years. I'm tired and I hope you don't think me rude if I leave you two alone."

Ashley looked at her and winked. "Not at all. Maybe Jordan and I can come up with some exotic recipe for the restaurant."

"Yeah, a signature dish." Sydnee reached for the wine. "Let me chill that for you." Going to the bowl, she absently took out the blank check and notepad, then set the bottle of wine inside. "I'll get some ice," she said, padding toward the tiny kitchen.

Smiling, Jordan perused the room, his gaze falling on Elvis. "I still can't believe *that's* the same bowl you bought that day, Ashley," he said incredulously and went to have a closer look.

"It certainly is," Ashley responded, following him. She

started to ask about Marie Hastings, but decided against ruining the sublime moment.

Taking the bottle of wine out and placing it on the table, Jordan lifted the bowl and examined it from the rim to the stand. Ashley hid a smile, wondering what Jordan would do if he knew how sensitive Elvis's stand was.

"Wow, it's heavier than I realized. It's incredible what you did to it, Ashley. I meant to tell you that. This bowl is quite beautiful."

Carrying a tray of ice cubes and two wineglasses, Sydnee returned.

Jordan quickly returned the bowl to the table and replaced the bottle of wine where Sydnee had placed it. "Oh, I'm sorry."

"I think it's beautiful, too." Sydnee arranged the ice around the bottle, then set the glasses on the table next to the bowl. "And a great discovery. I'm out of here, guys." Making her way to Ashley's bedroom, she noisily closed the door.

After Sydnee's departure, an awkward silence ensued. Sitting with her hands in her lap, Ashley wasn't sure what to say, uncertainties plaguing her. The last time Jordan had been there, the situation had flared out of control, then he'd all but deserted her.

"Popcorn?" she asked, shoving the bowl in his direction.

Jordan laughed. "What are we doing, sweetheart? We're better friends than this."

Ashley put the popcorn down and gazed levelly at him. "I hope so, Jordan," she said softly. She folded her arms to keep from throwing them around him. "Why did you really come over?"

Drawing in a long breath, Jordan didn't remove his glance from her. "I really came to see you," he admitted, sitting on the sofa. "And I wasn't exactly truthful when I said I just got off from work."

"I know. It's after one in the morning, and I know your hours, remember?"

"Actually, I didn't remember," Jordan said with a weary chuckle. "I was already at home, Ash, when I got this irresistible urge to see you. I can't explain the . . . the *pull* I felt. I just knew I needed to see you, so I called a cab to get me here as fast as possible."

"Oh, Jordan," Ashley murmured, scooting closer to him, her heart singing. *He spent money to get to me!*

"Another strange thing happened," Jordan went on. "Before I hung up the phone, the taxicab driver was tooting his horn at the curb in front of my door."

"Well," Ashley said with a guilty laugh, "he probably was already in the neighborhood." *Or whisked there by magic.*

"I guess so," Jordan conceded. "Taxicabs are abundant in the city, after all." Reaching over, he twirled a strand of her hair through his fingers. "What are you doing to me, Ashley?" he asked thickly. "I can't get you out of my mind."

Ashley rubbed her cheek against the fingers holding her hair close to her face. If she had been a kitten, she would have purred. "Is that a bad thing?" she whispered.

"I wish I could say no, Ashley," he murmured, "because my attraction for you grows stronger each day." Leaning toward her, he kissed her on the forehead. "Your hair is like silk falling through my fingers. You're simply exquisite." He kissed the tip of her nose. "Your skin is flawless, and your lips . . . your lips. . . ." A slight dip of his head and he locked his mouth to hers. Kissing her tenderly, he held her face between his big hands.

Ashley's entire being quivered. The contact of his tongue in her mouth sent surges of electricity throughout her body. She ran her fingers through his hair, then slipped her arms around his neck as his kisses became more demanding.

Her body throbbed with need, and just as she started to lean back and bring him with her, he ended the kiss, once again leaving her unsated and frustrated.

Pushing her out of his embrace, Jordan stared at her. "Have I become so bedazzled by your beauty that I am forgetting my principles?"

At the abrupt end of their passionate contact, Ashley blinked, her body humming with desire. She forced a smile. "Heaven forbid your principles become clouded by, uh, *bedazzlement,*" she said, resenting his tedious argument.

Jordan sighed. "Don't be angry, Ashley. I'm just not the right man for you, sweetheart. It made me sick to my stomach to spend six bucks on a cab tonight, when I could have just as easily seen you tomorrow. Inevitably, those differences will catch up to us."

Incipient anger threatening to burst forth, Ashley stood. "Don't patronize me, Jordan. I'm not sixteen anymore."

"Ashley—"

One strange glow from her bowl reminded her that Elvis had sent Jordan over for a brief interlude, not a long argument. Distracted by Jordan, she didn't turn toward her bowl. She remembered the effect the red wine had had on Jordan and hoped the potency wouldn't be as high since this wine remained in its bottle. "Where are my manners? Would you like some wine?" She gazed into Jordan's eyes a second, willing him to say yes, imagining she saw the love there that he refused to admit he carried for her.

"No," Jordan said. "I think I'd better leave, Ashley. I won't apologize for kissing you again because I'll most likely do it again. And again. And again. Until you either slap me silly or tell me to get it right." He stood. "It's late. May I use your phone to call a cab?"

Spending more money? And he'll probably kiss me again? Thanks, Elvis. She finally glanced over at the bowl. It was electric blue. "Elvis!" she screeched.

"Who?" Jordan frowned at her in confusion as he picked up the cordless phone. "Elvis? Must be a new cab company," he said absently. "Thanks, I prefer the tried and true."

"I-I said *Avis,*" Ashley mumbled, trying to cover up her mistake as Jordan gave the address to the dispatcher.

After listening a few moments and giving an affirmative response, he clicked off the telephone and set it down. "Avis is a rental car company, honey. Not a taxi service."

"My mistake," Ashley said lamely, worriedly glancing at the bowl. A horn blew outside. "Wow! If that's the cab, that *is* fast service." She went to the door and opened it. "It *is* your taxicab, Jordan."

"What are these people doing, hanging around waiting for my call?" he asked, annoyed. The horn blew again. "Hold your beeswax!" he yelled. "I'm coming! Ashley, when I'm able to understand my weird behavior, I'll explain it to you. I hope that happens the next time I see you." He pecked her on the cheek. "Good night, gorgeous."

"Good night, Jordan." Closing the door, she dashed to the sofa table and stared in horror at the blue bowl. It was frigid to the touch. "Sydnee! Hurry! I think we killed Elvis!"

Seventeen

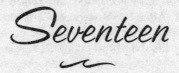

Ashley picked up the bowl with the bottle of wine and melting ice cubes still inside and dashed to the kitchen.

"What are you talking about, Ashley?" Sydnee asked, hot on her heels.

Putting the wine in the refrigerator and pouring the ice into the sink, Ashley grabbed a dish towel. She dried the inside of the bowl, then rushed back to the living room.

"What's happened to him?" Sydnee asked, still following her. "He's very blue."

Her hands shaking, Ashley placed the bowl back on the table. "I don't know, Syd. I think it was the ice that turned him blue. He feels very cold."

"Maybe he'll tell us what happened."

Ashley and Sydnee looked down into the bowl.

"He hasn't started writing yet, Sydnee." Pressing her lips together, she gave Sydnee a wounded look. "What am I going to do? He's so cold and blue."

"It's my fault, Ashley. I'm so sorry."

"Don't blame yourself, Syd. . . . Hey! I just had a brainstorm. If he's really blue because of the ice, maybe hot water will bring his silvery color back."

"You're brilliant!" Sydnee exclaimed.

Elvis in Ashley's hand, they raced back to the kitchen. Ashley sat the bowl in the sink and turned the hot water on full blast. After a few seconds, Elvis slowly began to regain his shiny silver sheen. When the change was complete, Ashley lifted the bowl out of the sink and again dried it thoroughly. As she dried the stand, she even detected a pink hue.

Unable to swallow an exasperated chuckle at the sight, she brought the bowl back to the sofa table and replaced the check and notepad. Immediately, the Teletyping began with an uneven clicking noise.

Y-y-you two witless d-dolts. D-do I l-look like an ice b-bucket to y-you? I-I nearly fr-froze my stand o-off.

"Please forgive us, Elvis," Ashley implored. "We didn't know. How can we make it up to you?"

A few minutes passed before Elvis responded, and when he did, his words were once again even. His silvery hue returned as well.

Since Sydnee put the ice inside my cavity, I'll settle for a hug from her.

"A hug?" Sydnee asked with a perplexed frown. "How do you hug a bowl?"

Frowning sternly, Ashley shook her head. "What a lech."

"A lech?" Sydnee echoed. "Even if I knew how to hug a bowl, I'd never attempt to hug a lecherous one."

"You should be ashamed of yourself, Elvis," Ashley scolded. "Taking advantage of our ignorance. We didn't know how cold would affect you."

Click, click, click. *Surely you're not scolding me? After all,* I'm *the injured one here.*

Detecting surliness behind the words, Ashley giggled. "*How* did you get to be the way you are, Ambrose?"

Bite your tongue, Ashley Douglas. It has been fifteen centuries since anyone uttered that saintly name to me.

"I'll make a deal with you. Accept Sydnee's and my profound apology and our sympathy for the discomfort you suffered, and I'll cease and desist from calling you Ambrose."

Is there another choice?

"No," Sydnee answered firmly. "Take it or leave it."

All this because I wanted a hug. You girls drive a hard bargain. I'll accept, however. Answer your phone, Ashley. It's Jordan. And a good night to both of you.

His glow dimmed, and the words cleared from the pad.

"What phone?" Sydnee asked, just as the phone began to ring.

"That phone." Ashley sighed. She felt strange knowing who was on the other end of the line before she answered. But she pretended to be surprised to hear Jordan's voice as he immediately explained how fast he'd gotten home.

"Granted, traffic was light, but to get home in less than a minute from your apartment is worse than warped speed."

"Jordan, you've been gone longer than a minute. Are you sure your watch is still running?"

A moment of silence followed that, then a soft, "Damn, you're right. It's actually been fifteen minutes. That's more rational. The ride *felt* normal. It really did not seem like a speed demon was behind the wheel."

Ashley didn't miss the euphoria in Jordan's voice. It was a rarity hearing Jordan's composure slipping, and it worried her. "Are you all right, Jordan?"

"I don't know. I just feel . . ." His voice trailed off. "Listen, Ashley, I'm going to let you go. Say good night to Sydnee, and I hope to see you at work tomorrow."

With that he hung up. Ashley stood motionless for a moment before she replaced the receiver on the cradle. Elvis wouldn't respond to her again tonight, but she needed to impress upon him not to confuse Jordan. He could end up thinking she had something to do with his bafflement. Although with Elvis's help, she did, of course. If he ever found out, Jordan would never forgive her. As independent as he was, he wouldn't appreciate having the matter taken so thoroughly out of his hands.

He might have been able to fight off a lot of things he didn't want to deal with, but magic was rather impossible to hold back.

Maybe she should take more responsibility herself in trying to win Jordan's heart. If anything ever happened to Elvis, then so, too, would her romance end with Jordan. She wanted to have him in her life forever, yet Elvis had hinted on more than one occasion that he'd chosen her. Which meant he could also un-choose her at any time.

The thought frightened her, and she realized she was already depending too much on Elvis's magic.

"I'm bushed." Sydnee gazed expectantly at her.

Although Ashley wasn't in the mood to talk about Jordan right now, not even to Sydnee, she had a request of her friend. "Um, Syd. Saturday . . . uh, can we go to the bookstore? I need to buy a couple of books."

"Sure," Sydnee said automatically. "But what's so important about books?"

Sydnee never had been much of a reader. Fortunately the books Ashley wanted to invest in would have a lot of photographs and illustrations. "B-because they're going to help me seduce Jordan."

"Huh?" Sydnee narrowed her eyes. "Ashley Douglas, exactly what kind of books are you talking about?"

"Guides. Manuals. Anything you'd like to call them."

"Are you serious, Ash?"

"Yes!" Ashley answered quickly. "Don't make it seem so sociopathic."

Sydnee laughed. "I'm sorry. I think you've misunderstood my reaction. I'm just wondering if you know what you're doing."

"Dammit, Sydnee, what do you think I need the books for?"

"No, Ashley, you've misunderstood again," Sydnee said, laughing harder. Her features becoming serious again, she studied Ashley carefully. "Are you sure you want to go all the way with Jordan? I mean, suppose once you two make love, he walks?"

That distinct possibility plagued her. If they made love, it would either cement their relationship or rip it apart forever.

Deciding her brain couldn't process anymore, she gave an exaggerated stretch. "I'm tired, too. There are jammies in the dresser drawer in the bedroom, Syd, and we can share the bed comfortably. It's a king."

"So I've noticed." Sydnee smiled in the direction of the bowl. "Good night, Elvis."

After Sydnee departed for the bedroom, Ashley went to the sofa table where Elvis sat unlit by his glow. Hearing Sydnee voice her own deep-seated fears frightened her. Maybe there wasn't any harm in attaining Elvis's help. "Sorry again for what happened, Elvis. And about Jordan? I think he's confused about his feelings for me. I want him to kiss me without reservation—to hold me and never let me go. If you can get him to do that without confusing him, I'll love you forever. Of course, that wouldn't be hard to do. You're quite loveable." Kissing the tip of her index finger, she placed it on Elvis's rim. "Good night, Mr. Enchantment."

She headed toward her bedroom. Just before she closed the door, a glow brightened the living room, and she knew Elvis had heard her.

Eighteen

The following Saturday, Ashley stayed in the terminal at New Orleans International Airport until Sydnee's plane took off.

Staring dejectedly through the plate-glass window, watching the taxiing vehicle slowly lift off into the sunny skies, Ashley sighed. She really wasn't happy with the way her day had begun. She and Sydnee had had a wonderful day planned, but right after breakfast Matthew had called. He apologized to both of them, but said he couldn't come down to meet them. Something urgent had come up, although he didn't say what.

He'd already booked a flight from New Orleans to New York for Sydnee, and, once there, they'd take connecting flights to Paris. Though terribly disappointed because she wanted Sydnee to stay longer, Ashley nevertheless understood the urgency of the mysterious matter. Once Sydnee said good-bye to Matthew, Ashley immediately telephoned Zach and asked him to take them to the airport, but he told her he had an extended meeting set with Carson Wood and would be unavailable to drive her there himself. Instead, he allowed Jordan to borrow his Land Cruiser, drop him off at the Blackwell offices, then take Ashley and Sydnee to the airport.

Jordan touched her back and wordlessly escorted her back to the airport parking lot. "I'm sorry things turned out the way they did, Ashley," he commented once they were on the road again toward Orleans Parish.

"So am I, Jordan. Unfortunately, some things can't be avoided."

Deciding to forsake the Interstate in favor of the longer, more scenic route, he glanced at her briefly as he took the appropriate exit. Nodding his head, he smiled.

He could've told Zach that he, too, was busy and couldn't oblige Ashley and Sydnee, but he needed to see Ashley. Knowing she wouldn't be at the hotel this evening when he reported to the restaurant, he jumped at the opportunity. Because of Sydnee's sudden departure and Jordan having to work this evening, the dinner Ashley was going to prepare for him had been postponed a week.

Halting the big SUV at a stoplight, he looked at her again. A hair band pushed her glorious locks off her face, all the better to see her exquisite features. Glorious blond waves flowed onto her shoulders and down her back, inviting his touch. High cheekbones accentuated creamy skin, beckoning his caress.

She was an amazing and beautiful creature, unafraid of challenges and resistance.

Before the day Ashley changed her appearance so drastically, he'd barely noticed her—at least not the way he was noticing her now. She'd always been pretty, but never in the alluring way she was now. The change in her looks was almost magical.

But what of her attitude? She'd said she hadn't touched the money her father so rashly gave to her. If that bowl was the last impulsive thing she'd bought, then her attitude was indeed changing as well. And maybe her purchase of the bowl hadn't been so terrible or hard to figure out. It was a unique and beautiful piece of artwork, and she'd always had a discerning eye.

Last night, the bowl's surface appeared to change from the shiny silver to a strange, metallic blue. Of course, he could've been mistaken. The lamplight released only a soft glow and might have played tricks on his eyes. He had also been frustrated himself with his desire for Ashley that he was willing to believe just about anything to have her.

The honking of a horn alerted him to the go-ahead signal. He zoomed off. "Have you considered getting your bowl appraised?"

Her sleek, dark sunglasses gave her the appearance of a movie star, making her features impossible to read, as she reclined in the leather seat. Smooth and tanned, her long legs looked fabulous in the khaki shorts she wore. They would feel great wrapped around his back.

"Why would I want to do that?"

Jordan eased up on the accelerator as a small car maneuvered in front of him. "You might have purchased something of infinite value."

"So I take it you like my bowl?"

He liked more than her bowl. He wouldn't elaborate on what a perfect fit her breasts would be in his hands. Or how her slim, well-toned body seemed a perfect complement to his. "Yes, very much. I-it was a wise investment, I would think."

Sliding her glasses to the rim of her nose, she gazed at him. Amusement lit her hazel eyes, even as her look appeared to probe the depths of him. "Really? I never thought I'd hear you say such a thing."

"You have the wrong idea, Ashley," Jordan explained, wondering if this was the time to discuss his feelings for her with Zach. But what would he say? "Hey, Zachery, man, I've got the hots for your baby sister." Nah. That wouldn't do. Not only would that be the quickest way to lose a friend that he loved and admired like a brother, but also it would be the quickest way to get punched in the mouth. He could never use so crude a phrase as "having the hots" to describe his feelings for Ashley. Whatever they were, they'd begun to transcend mere lust. Last night he realized he didn't actually want to put the skids on their budding romance. He liked liking Ashley. "Have you ever thought about why I feel the way I do about money?"

Ashley rested her hands on her flat belly and shrugged. "Not really," she admitted. "I just always thought you were, well, stingy."

"Thanks, Ash, for that vote of confidence," he said wryly. "People aren't born, uh, frugal."

"You're right, but I can also say that others aren't pre-destined to be spendthrifts. Circumstances and environment make us what we are."

How perceptive she was. And how right. Her spending habits weren't *entirely* her fault. Everyone around her had contributed in one way or another. Just as he expected her to change her ways, it was high time he did the same.

As long as she understood that he didn't see the need to have the unnecessary expense of owning a car. He'd never own a credit card, nor was he interested in extravagant va-cations and lavish outings.

"We both thank you, for that matter."

The realization that Ashley had still been talking to him struck him, and acute embarrassment reddened his cheeks. "Thank me?" he managed, unsure of when the change in conversation had taken place.

"Yeah," Ashley answered, unaware of his inattention. "If you hadn't been sweet enough to bring us to the airport, we would've probably had to get a taxicab. That would've cost a fortune, and Lord knows I couldn't afford that. That really would've busted my budget."

Pleased at her attempt to curb her spending, Jordan
grinned at her. Would wonders never cease? He never
thought he'd see the day that Ashley Douglas was on a
budget. "It would have cost a pretty penny, sweetheart," he
agreed. His decision to allow his feelings for Ashley to run
their own course delighting him, he pulled into a gas sta-
tion. "It's quite a distance back to your apartment, Ashley.
I'd better replace the fuel in Zach's cruiser. You're not in
a hurry, are you? I'll only be a few minutes."

Watching out of the sideview mirror as Jordan pumped
the gas, Ashley admired his air of self-confidence and inherent strength. Whatever demons he battled regarding
money, he seemed to be winning. At the coffee shop, he'd
started to loosen his pursestrings, and she felt like throwing
herself into his arms. He was spending money on his own
accord to replace the fuel in Zach's tank, but it was because
of her. Silently she thanked Elvis.

"Would you like something to drink, Ashley?"

"Yes, um, water would be good, thank you."

She glanced at her watch. At two o'clock it was still too
early for Dom Pérignon. But perhaps that would've been
pushing it. No point in urging Jordan to spend his money
too fast. There was time enough to teach him to enjoy the
finer things life had to offer.

Right now she wasn't sure he'd consider spending a hundred dollars or more, depending on the vintage, for a bottle
of champagne. Still too frivolous, when a ten-dollar bottle
would suffice. Hmm. Was Jordan familiar with the old ad-
age, you get what you pay for?

She wouldn't do this. Becoming judgmental would do
nothing but hinder their fledgling romance. He was a thirty-
one-year-old man who had no doubt already noticed the
quality in the more expensive items on the market. Anyway, *she* bought inexpensive wines and found them to be
very good.

She took last night's gesture to pay for taxicabs and today's announcement as a sign that he was becoming free-
handed. He'd always been free*hearted*—with time, advice,
recipes. Anything, except money. But that was changing.

Jordan slid in the driver's seat and handed her a cold
bottle of water. "Evian all right?"

"Perfect," Ashley said, reaching for the water.

He strapped on his seat belt and started the ignition, then
drove off. "It's turning out to be a beautiful day, Ashley. I
don't have to be at the hotel until six this evening. Why
don't I pick up something in town, and we can have a
picnic by the lake. Are you game?"

Butterflies fluttered in Ashley's belly, and her heart
started beating a rapid tattoo. Her day was going from bad
to beautiful to absolutely perfect. Was she game?

Was Elvis magic?

Unequivocally yes to both questions. Stretching her neck
from side to side, Ashley adjusted her sunglasses. "That
sounds simply wonderful, Jordan." She hoped her tone was
demure and not too eager, which was how Jordan made her
feel.

Although she wanted Jordan to be the one who made up
his mind to have a relationship with her, she considered
asking Elvis to delve into her future to see if Jordan was
in it. Merlin had been Elvis's creator. The bowl could probably foresee hundreds of years down the road. Besides,
knowing whether or not Jordan was in her future with Elvis's help would be more enlightenment than magic.

Another rash thought on her part. Oftentimes, her im-
petuosity only worsened matters. Look at what happened
when she'd decided to ask Jordan to have a glass of wine
that she'd poured into Elvis's cavity.

What would knowing of her and Jordan's future together,
or lack thereof, gain her? If she discovered he *wasn't* in

her future, it would break her heart. If he was, then that meant whatever she did wouldn't matter because they were destined to be together. That would only take the fire out of the courtship.

No, she didn't want to know. Nature would take its course, without any fortune-telling.

On Veterans Highway near the Orleans-Parish line, Jordan pulled into the parking lot of Martin's Wine Cellar. Together they went into the store and selected a small variety of gourmet goodies, including goose liver pâté, smoked oysters, Edam cheese with caraway seeds and Gouda, thin water crackers, fat green grapes, fresh strawberries, and a cold bottle of sauvignon blanc.

With untold satisfaction and too astounded to speak, Ashley watched as Jordan placed treat after treat into their basket, then shelled out nearly eighty dollars for their spur-of-the-moment picnic. His actions spoke volumes. For him to spend that much money on her, she had to be something special to him. He even bought a checkered yellow and white tablecloth!

Only a short distance from the lake, they arrived at their destination within fifteen minutes of getting out of the checkout line. As Jordan guided her to a cozy spot near the seawall, beneath an oak tree, anticipation hastened her steps, and she couldn't thank Elvis enough for the rendez-vous.

Nineteen

~~

Sultry, warm breezes blew gently across the placid Lake Pontchartrain, then around Ashley and Jordan as they picnicked and gazed up at the cloudless blue sky.

Pleasure boats dropped anchor not far from shore, while the masts of numerous sailboats dotted the horizon. A brown pelican skimmed the water and swooped up a small fish. Not far from where Ashley and Jordan lounged on the tablecloth, a family played volleyball. They'd invited Ashley and Jordan to join in on the fun, and left the invitation open when the two agreed they weren't up for it right then, having just raced each other to the levee and back.

Jordan lay back, looking at Ashley out of compelling eyes, filled with expectation. Noticing that he nursed the same glass of wine he'd first poured, Ashley casually sipped from her second glass.

"What new creations do you have in store for the restaurant?"

"Several that I'm sure you'll like."

His lazy smile made her pulse race. Unable to stop herself, she smoothed back an errant lock of dark brown hair from his forehead. She allowed her fingers to linger in his smooth silkiness.

"I've always liked whatever you did, Jordan," Ashley whispered, his passionate surrender thrilling her. If they had been alone, she was sure he would have brought their mutual desire to fruition. "I hope you'll feel the same about my cooking."

Positioning his arm behind his head, he caressed her cheek. "I'm sure you've graduated from burning boiled eggs to fine cooking."

Ashley leaned into his hand and sipped her wine again. "If you say so," she mumbled around the liquid in her mouth.

So far she had graduated past the boiling stage in her cooking experience, and those times hadn't been pretty. Two months ago, she'd attempted to do pasta for her and Zach, but she hadn't set a timer. Becoming preoccupied with a business call, the pasta had boiled overlong and turned into one big lump. Of course when she'd confidently invited Jordan to a home-cooked meal, she planned on Elvis's aid.

"I could never match what you do in the kitchen."

"You're too hard on yourself, Ashley," Jordan reprimanded. His fingertips glided over her arm, briefly touched her belly and hip, before settling on her thigh, where he circled her leg with expert finesse. "I believe you'll do just fine."

Enjoying the feel of Jordan's hand on her, Ashley closed her eyes, aware of her pounding heart, her taut nipples, her hot need. But people were milling about, making it impossible for them to act on their feelings. Sitting up, she drained her glass and set it aside, then drew her knees close to her body.

"Thank you for the vote of confidence, but I really don't deserve—"

A fingertip over her lips interrupted her. "Of course you do. You wouldn't have invited me over if you couldn't cook, so don't even worry about it." He sat up as well. "Want to race again?"

It was an offer she couldn't refuse, and when she won again, she laughed in abandon and playfully smacked Jordan on the arm. "You faker, you let me win again."

"Did I?" he asked innocently. "I would think those long, gorgeous legs of yours had something to do with it."

"That might be true," Ashley conceded, aching to be crushed in his embrace. "I can outrun most girls and even some guys. But your legs are longer than mine, and you're so much stronger than I am." She kissed his firm jaw, afraid to do much more. "I appreciate your chivalry, however."

"Do you? Well, I wonder if you'll think this is so chivalrous." A sensuous flame danced in his eyes, turning them a molten silver. His aim perfect, he covered her lips with his own. He delved deeply into her recesses for a moment, then broke the contact. "I could devour you, but we're in plain view of everyone, so let's keep it chaste."

"Of course," she said. His words were as powerful as any drug. This intimacy between them was a dream come true, and she doubted anything could have made her happier. But they still had so much to settle between them that this Utopia couldn't last forever.

Look in the dictionary under the word "perfect" and you'd find a picture of this day. That was Ashley's thought as she stood in the doorway two hours later, saying good-bye to Jordan.

They had spent the entire day together and most of the afternoon. Now, a half hour after he was due to go in to the restaurant, he was bringing her home.

The rest of the picnic had been heavenly. She thoroughly enjoyed the food, and the wine made her giddy. She'd laughed at almost everything Jordan said. He'd been genuinely funny, with a wonderful and carefree side that she had never truly been privy to.

"Would you come in for a minute?"

"I'm sorry, I can't." He smiled to lessen the politeness of his tone. "But I can't remember having a better time, Ashley."

"Neither can I," she responded calmly, her senses rioting. "We must do this again sometime."

Placing his hand on her shoulders, Jordan kissed her on the forehead. "It's a promise. G'night, Ash. I'll see you Tuesday."

"Right."

Ashley watched as he got into Zach's Land Cruiser. When Jordan blew the horn and beckoned her to go inside, she quickly did so, closing and latching the door.

An unknown, soul-reaching contentment filling her, Ashley went to the sofa table. Leaning down, she placed a kiss on the rim of her magic bowl. "Thank you, Elvis," she murmured softly.

She waited a few seconds for a response, but frowned when no light brightened the room and no Teletyping began. Making her way to her bedroom, worry punctuated her happiness.

Elvis hadn't ever ignored a kind word from her. Had he somehow lost his powers?

Twenty

The next day, partial sunshine gleamed through the thin curtains in Jordan's kitchen and bounced off the metal sink. The thermostat was adjusted to a comfortable degree and afforded a welcoming coolness throughout the mansion.

His mind on Ashley, Jordan watched as a stick of butter melted in the skillet. Once everything was almost ready, he'd telephone her and invite her over for breakfast. The conversation they needed to have was overdue, and given the fact that he'd been frivolously spending money these past days, he couldn't put it off any longer.

He added the lump crabmeat, then a dash each of salt and pepper. Turning the fire under the seafood up, he looked at his watch. He needed to sauté this portion of the recipe for several minutes. Before he poached the eggs in water and vinegar, he'd make the telephone call. Wondering if the discussion would dampen their burgeoning feelings, Jordan sighed. They both were set in their ways about money. From the beginning he'd had mixed emotions about getting involved with Ashley. Thinking he'd settled that once and for all yesterday, it surprised him when he'd awakened this morning to the same old uncertainties. It was almost as if a brief spell had indeed been cast upon him, urging him to act on his attraction for Ashley.

He was still quite attracted to her, but the madness that made him believe there could be a future between them no longer claimed him. A place deep within him really didn't want to fight his feelings any longer, but now that he was thinking clearly, he knew he must.

The singsong of the doorbell abruptly cut into his thoughts. Weighted down by his problems, he went to his front door and peeped through the peephole. Zach stood on the other side, a thunderous expression on his face.

Cursing roundly, Jordan opened the door.

Zach brushed past him. Jordan closed the door and turned to find Zach staring at him, fists clenched at his sides.

"What the hell's gotten into you, man?"

Jordan narrowed his eyes at his best friend, anger vibrating through his body at Zach's demeanor. He warned himself to remain calm—at least until he discovered why Zach was so angry. "What's gotten into *me*? I'm not the one who just barged into my—"

"Go to hell," Zach interrupted ruthlessly. He thrust a tense hand through his blond hair. "I thought you and I settled the fact that you were to stay away from Ashley."

"You and I might have discussed it, but Ashley and I feel differently about the matter." Jordan's voice was cold and precise. Disappointment hit him hard. He'd sincerely believed that Zach would adjust to a relationship between him and Ashley, despite his previous objections. This was only an added reminder of why he and Ashley would never work. "You have a hell of a lot of nerve, Zachery. Ashley's a grown woman, and she can damn well choose whomever she wants to have an affair with."

"An *affair*!" Zach boomed, the veins in his neck nearly

popping out. "That's what you have Marie for, remember? I swear to you, Jordan, if you've touched Ashley, I'll beat you to a bloody pulp, *then* make you marry her."

"As if you could make me do anything," Jordan snarled, ignoring Zach's references to Marie. It had been a mistake to go out with Marie in the first place. She wasn't . . . Ashley. "Forced weddings are relics of the past, in case you've forgotten. As are overprotective brothers. Or so I thought. Stop making a fool of yourself over your sister, Douglas. She wouldn't like your interference anymore than I do."

"Damn you, Jordan!" Zach paced in front of Jordan, his body tense, his jaw clenched. "You're no good for Ashley. She needs a man whose closer to her own age and who isn't such a stingy bastard! Someone with less hang-ups."

"This from the man who relegated his sister to the work-force, instead of speaking up for her?" Jordan sneered. He refused to tell Zach how much money he'd spent these past days on Ashley. "How sympathetic you've suddenly become to her outrageous spending habits. Let me remind you again—Ashley is old enough to do her *own* choosing. Not someone *you* pick for her to date. As for my age, eight years isn't as big a difference as it once was. She's no longer sixteen, but a twenty-three-year-old woman, in case you haven't noticed."

"I should swipe that smirk off your ugly face, Bennett!"

"Go right the hell ahead."

Accepting Jordan's furious invitation, Zach swung and braised Jordan's jaw. Not to be outdone, Jordan returned the punch and caught Zach fully on the cheek.

Of practically the same height and each strong and well built, neither gave an inch. Weeks of pent-up hostility burst forth. A planter filled with a flourishing English ivy crashed to the ground; dirt and glass and plants exploded every-where.

Zach landed against the wall as Jordan swung again. A

fine painting crashed to the floor. With a ferocious howl, Zach came at Jordan and landed a blow on Jordan's eye. . . .

A high-pitched whirring sound screamed throughout the house. Immediately water rained down upon them. A stream of smoke filtered from the direction of the kitchen, the acrid smell filling the air.

The shock of smoke detector and sprinklers going off momentarily immobilized the two men. They stared at each other as if they'd only just been introduced.

"What the hell!" Holding his hands out as if in supplication, Zach gazed about, the water from the sprinklers still beating down upon him.

"Goddammit!" Jordan exploded.

Squinting his eyes to ward off the steady stream of water falling, he looked around at the mess. Gooey mud from the overturned planter coated the floor. Furniture was overturned; paintings hung crookedly on the wall or lay haphazardly on the floor. And the damage from the water would be obscene.

In a daze, he watched as Zach stood and went to the kitchen. Returning after a few moments, he stood quietly in the door.

"Don't just stand there, damn it. You're going to help me clean up this mess!" Jordan snapped.

Once they turned the sprinklers off, they began the phenomenal task of cleaning. Neither spoke to the other. Jordan wondered if the spell that seemed to have been cast over him had suddenly turned into a curse.

Tied back in a bow, Ashley's straight, dark blond hair hung nearly to her waist in a ponytail as she sat at her desk bright and early Tuesday morning.

Yesterday she'd used the last of her magic shampoo, and the golden waves she'd become accustomed to had deserted her this morning. She needed to replace her shampoo, but wondered if Elvis would use his powers to change its properties again.

She had a real fear, however, that the magic in her bowl no longer worked. Elvis hadn't responded to her at all yesterday, nor did he write anything this morning. She hadn't realized how dependent she'd become on his bright light and wisecracking replies to her queries. Now she somehow felt disconnected.

Just what had happened?

Knowing she wouldn't find her answers right now, she sifted through the papers before her to get an idea of where to begin her day's work. Unable to concentrate, her thoughts hopscotched across her mind.

At the airport, Sydnee had promised to call within a few days. Actually Ashley wished she'd call today. As the only person with whom Ashley could freely discuss her wonderful bowl, Sydnee would understand Ashley's concern for Elvis.

"Knock, knock."

Ashley looked up at the sound of Mr. Russell's voice as he walked through the already open door.

"Good morning, Ashley," he said cheerily.

"Good morning, Mr. Russell," Ashley said with a smile. "How can I help you?"

"Did you ever set a time for the Blackwell Corporation to begin initial work on the hotel?"

"It'll start in four weeks." She made a neat stack of the papers on her desk, hoping there weren't any new problems. She really couldn't handle going back to the drawing board in search of a new contractor. "Is there a problem?"

Mr. Russell rubbed his chin. "I hope not."

"What gives, sir?" Ashley asked impatiently.

"Got a call this morning. Blackwell wants to change some design in the refurbishing of the hotel. And that isn't what we're about. You know that, Ashley. You didn't misrepresent our intentions to Mason Good, did you?"

"Carson Wood," Ashley corrected with a sigh. She'd always taken pride in how much trust Mr. Russell put into her abilities. Now he seemed doubtful of her. Her hurt surprised her. "No, Mr. Russell. I didn't misinterpret or misrepresent. Have you talked to Zachery and Daddy about this?"

Surprise widened his gaze. "Did you want me to?"

This was her baby, and if her family thought she was somehow allowing the Blackwell Corporation to screw them out of money, they'd demand Jim Russell remove her from the project. "No."

"I didn't think so. I thought you'd want to handle it yourself."

"I do," Ashley said quietly. This was insane! She and Wood had settled everything. Or so she'd thought. "I'll talk to Mr. Wood immediately and find out what's going on."

"Good, good," Mr. Russell said, approval lacing his tone.

She picked up a pen and began tapping it on her desk. Now that Elvis wasn't working, someone else came to mind, and dread sickened her. "How's Petersen doing?"

"Who?"

The tapping paused briefly as she frowned at Mr. Russell. "Petersen. Mr. Randy Petersen, the restaurant manager."

"Oh, him!"

Ashley nodded.

"He's the one who injured himself when he fell out of that tree, isn't he?"

Again Ashley nodded.

Striking the pose of a great thinker, Mr. Russell laid a finger upon his jaw. "I really don't know, Ashley. I saw him yesterday at the hospital. Would have asked him, but I didn't want to wake him up. He slept so peaceful."

She'd have to find a way to restore Elvis's powers. "Mr. Russell, I believe he's still in a coma. Not asleep."

Mr. Russell's arms fell to his sides, and his mouth dropped open. "A coma? Well, damn. He must have fallen on his head. Here I thought the clumsy fellow only broke his leg. Call a florist, Ashley, and have a plant or flowers delivered to his room."

"Of course, Mr. Russell," Ashley agreed easily. She didn't remind him that had already been done. Because he was so absentminded, it would only start a new round of explanations. Maybe this was the onset of senility. But he was only fifty-two. "Anything else, sir?"

"No, Ashley," Mr. Russell said. "By the way, your hair looks nice that way. Although I prefer the wig you'd been wearing these past weeks. You know, Ashley, even with *that* hair, you're still very beautiful. Should I keep a close watch on the male staff?"

"What for?"

"Well, you know, one of them might get fresh."

Ashley laughed. "A little compliment now and then would be welcome. I'm sure that's all it would be."

"Good for you, Ashley. How's Jim Bond working out?"

"Huh?" Recognition dawned as she associated the initials *JB* with a handsome man who wore a chef's uniform like no other. "Oh! He's doing great, Mr. Russell. He's developed a menu around the hotel's new signature dish, and the customers love it."

"Wonderful. Is there anything else you need to tell me while I'm here?"

"Not at the moment, sir," Ashley assured him. "But I'll call you the minute I get off the telephone with Carson Wood."

"Very well, Ashley, carry on."

Without further ado, Mr. Russell turned and walked out of the office.

Wondering how *James* Bond got skipped over for *Jim*

Bond, Ashley chuckled. More than likely that's who he meant, but couldn't remember the name.

Placing thoughts of her boss' poor memory to the side, Ashley picked up the telephone and dialed Carson Wood's office. She was immediately put through by his secretary.

"Hello, Ashley," Wood greeted. "I was expecting your call."

"Good," Ashley said, leaning back in her chair. "It saves me the trouble of explaining why I'm calling. Exactly what's going on, Wood? This is an historic building, and we don't want it changed by any means. I thought our meeting covered the basics and the plans I submitted would be taken into consideration—"

"Blackwell Corporation, supported by my personal observation, shares your sentiments of not changing the hotel," Wood interrupted. The excitement in his voice encouraged Ashley to listen. "Our intention isn't to *change* the hotel, Ashley, but to *restore* some of its original facings. The plans you submitted are fantastic. The footnotes on the building's history underscored the need for preservation. You mentioned the third-floor atrium's original wall paintings date back to the late eighteen hundreds. But they have been covered up with paint, wallpaper, and God knows what else. I think the hotel can be brought back to its original beauty, but we won't touch a thing without the go-ahead from your people."

Ashley reflected a moment. She'd always loved the historic architecture of the building that had been so long neglected. Antique walls. Intricate frieze work. Wood carved banisters.

Nothing fascinated her more than antiques, which is the reason she'd been inspired to add the footnotes to her report. Having the hotel restored to its original form, would be quite an achievement for her. Yet the cost would go well above the already quoted price.

Mr. Russell could be convinced, even if he had some reservations, but her father and brother were also on the board of directors, and she'd need *their* permission to go ahead with the project.

"Ashley?"

"Sorry, Wood," Ashley said of her prolonged silence. "I'm going to have to get back to you on this. I need to discuss it with the directors, so I'll call you in a couple of days."

"That's fine, Ashley. I understand perfectly. I'll be waiting."

"Talk to you soon."

As she placed the receiver back on its cradle, Ashley thought of how she would approach the board with such news. It wouldn't be an easy task. Her family would believe this was her roundabout way of being a spendthrift. Yet the challenge would be convincing them how seriously she took her business dealings and make them realize that she'd never jeopardize their holdings or her reputation.

For the moment, however, she had to put that problem aside. Today was Tuesday, her day to meet with Jordan to discuss the food supply for the week.

Strolling to the kitchen, she realized that Jordan hadn't dominated her thoughts, even though she hadn't spoken to him since he'd left her at the door on Saturday. Actually Elvis had, and she wondered what to make of that.

" 'Lo, Ash," Curtis called as she made her way through the restaurant.

Ashley paused as she saw her friend. He sat at a table counting out silverware. "Hi, Curtis."

"Casanova's in the kitchen. But I tell you, his ass is some sorry-looking."

"What do you mean?"

"Go see for yourself."

Puzzled by Curtis's mysterious tone, Ashley hurried to

the kitchen where she found Jordan huddled with Arthur at the counter, his back to her.

"Hi, guys," she said, her curiosity nearly overtaking her. The smell of filé gumbo filled the air and she didn't miss the tensing of Jordan's body. "Looks like I'm interrupting something important."

"You are," Jordan grumbled.

"Whoa!" Arthur said with a whistle. "I don't know what you've done to him, but he was pleasant until you arrived, Ash. Did you have somethin' to do with his black eye?"

"What!" Ashley rushed to Jordan. An indignant gasp escaped her at the sight he presented. His left eye was horribly swollen and blackened; his lips were discolored as well. Abrasions marked his chin and cheek. "What happened to you?"

"I don't want to talk about it."

"Were you mugged?"

"Dammit, Ashley, drop it!"

"How can you ask me to drop it when it looks like someone tried to beat you to a bloody pulp?" she snapped.

"You should see the other guy," Arthur chortled. "He ain't none too pretty either."

"Arthur, shut up!" Jordan ordered, walking to the industrial-sized coffeemaker. "Would you like a cup, Ashley?"

Ashley put her hands on her hips and looked at Jordan. "Considering your grudging tone, are you sure you want me to *have* a cup, Jordan?"

"You're my boss. I can't tell you what to do, can I?"

"No, thank you, Jordan. Keep your coffee." She glared at Arthur. "Tell me who did this to Jordan."

"If you say one word, Arthur, I'll sew your mouth shut," Jordan warned.

"Ouch, man! Do you know how much that'll hurt?"

"Do you take anything seriously?" Ashley asked crossly. "Now tell me who did this to him."

Arthur looked from one to the other, then he shrugged. "Ash, I think you're a fine woman and a good friend, but in this case I can't betray Jordan. It's just best thatcha don't know. Ya know?"

"Arthur—"

"How can we help you, Ashley?" Jordan asked, setting a cup of coffee before her, in spite of her earlier refusal.

He grunted as he placed his own coffee cup against his sore lips to drink. Ashley's heart went out to him, but he didn't want her sympathy. Sitting on the stool to keep from taking him into her arms, she tapped her fingers on the table. "I thought maybe you'd need me to go over the food supply with you."

"That's what I was helping him with, Ash," Arthur commented, grabbing her untouched cup of coffee and tasting it. "Why don't you just go on back to your office. We got it covered."

"We were doing the menus, Ashley," Jordan corrected, "not food supplies." He shook his head at Arthur. "I thought I taught you the difference."

Arthur laughed. "All right, then. *I'll* make up today's menu. Put in a touch of soul food for the more discriminating palate . . . Greens, pig tails, cornbread, fried okra, pork chops, and ribs."

Ashley and Jordan looked at each other and nodded with approval. This was their first "connection" today.

She smiled brightly, cringing at how frightfully swollen Jordan's eye was. "Soul Food Day," she exclaimed, refusing to comment on the state of his face anymore.

"Yeah," Jordan said excitedly. "One day a week we'll add soul food to our menu."

"Serious?" Arthur asked, surprised.

"Uh-huh," Ashley said happily. "I think it would be a

wonderful addition and will enable us to reach an exciting new clientele."

"Right," Arthur agreed, his brown eyes lighting up in pleasure. "You can be known as the hotel of international flavors. Added to your regular menus, you could serve an ethnic dish."

"Great idea, Arthur," Jordan said, sitting on the other stool and tasting his coffee again. "*Great* idea. We could do Indian, Chinese, Irish—"

"And don't forget soul food," Arthur reminded him.

"That's at the top of the list," Jordan told him. "Great input, Art."

Ashley smiled at the wide grin splitting Arthur's face. "I wish my dilemma was so easily solved."

"What dilemma?" Jordan asked as Arthur excused himself and went into the dining room.

Ashley explained about the painted walls on the third-floor atrium, and her concerns about the cost of the restoration, if they went ahead with plans to refurbish the original architecture. "Of course, I feel in the long run it would be less expensive than the simple cosmetics we had in mind for the refurbishing. The publicity alone would draw patrons just to see the genuine works of some unknown nineteenth-century painter. And who knows, once the paintings have been uncovered and revealed, the author's signature may be scrawled in a corner someplace."

"I admire your sagacity, Ashley. I'm sure your father and Jim Russell will trust your judgment. Cosmetics can be attractive, but it could end up covering a treasure trove. If I were asked my opinion, I would say go with the refurbishing rather than the remodeling."

"That's how I feel, Jordan." His aloofness didn't escape her. And although he was more civil to her now than when she'd first walked in, he still wasn't the same man with whom she had picnicked on Saturday. "I don't think I'll get an argument out of Mr. Russell. But my family is a different story altogether." She flipped her ponytail over her shoulder. "I'm going to buy a case of my shampoo on my way home tonight."

"And you expect your family to agree to the Blackwell deal, talking like that? They know how wasteful you are, and that statement just proves it."

"Wasteful?" Ashley said, stunned at the resentment in his voice. "Excuse me, but my personal spending habits have nothing to do with my business decisions."

"They do when your father and brother are on the board of directors," Jordan returned. "Tell me, Ashley, how long will it be before you go wild at a department store again as you encouraged me to go wild on our picnic?"

"What?" Ashley spat, standing from her seat. "I didn't force you to spend that money."

"But you didn't stop me, either."

"I thought maybe the chains lassoed around your wallet would do that job. How dare you sit in judgment of me, when you're just as bad about money as I am, only at the opposite end of the spectrum."

A sneer curled his bruised lip. "I'd prefer to be on my end than on yours. A case of shampoo when a bottle will do? Is there no end to your frivolity?"

"My frivolity ends where your frugality begins," Ashley responded tiredly. "I have had enough of this—"

"So have I, Ashley. Whatever went on between us is over as of now!"

"Fine!" Ashley yelled, angry and hurt at Jordan's abrupt change. The magic that had existed between them had been extinguished. Her heart sank. "Good day, Jordan."

Devastated, she made her way back to her office. Elvis had somehow lost his powers, and everything was going mad. The deal that she'd worked so hard on was in arrears;

Mr. Petersen remained in a coma; Jordan had been terribly beaten; and worst of all, his burgeoning feelings had reverted to the old disdain.

What would she ever do without Elvis's help?

Twenty-one

~

Fluffing the pillows on her sofa, Ashley leaned back tiredly.

She'd been home for a full hour and had taken care of all of her needs, then rolled her television into the living room to spend the evening watching her programs, if not fully relaxing.

Although there was nothing special about it anymore, she wanted to be near her bowl. She glanced sadly at it. Now most ordinary, it was still a beautiful piece.

She didn't find it unusual that she'd so readily attached herself to Elvis. Her capacity to believe in the extraordinary had always been extreme. It helped her to suspend the realities of everyday life, which she was in desperate need of now that Jordan had turned so viciously against her. For the time being, though, she'd give him the benefit of the doubt. Maybe he was upset because of how badly he had been beaten. And Arthur said the other guy was in the same shape.

Hmm. It was almost as if Jordan *knew* his attacker. Of course! That was the only explanation. How else would

Arthur have seen the man responsible for Jordan's cuts and bruises?

Elvis would have been a big help just now. She was sure he'd have been more than able to give her some insight about Jordan's attacker. But she didn't want to become a candidate for the loony bin now that Elvis had returned to his ancient solitude. Somehow she'd make do with the resources she had and try to readjust to life without her bowl.

Surfing through channels with her remote control, she realized she had too many other things to occupy her time, and her mind wandered to the events of the day. After returning from the disastrous meeting with Jordan, she'd sought out Mr. Russell and told him about her conversation with Carson Wood and why Blackwell had decided they wanted to extend the refurbishing.

Jim Russell was delighted, seeming to be a different person at the news. He was all business and in total control. He assured her *he'd* talk to the other board members and that she should not worry about her father and brother. He'd then instructed her to call Carson Wood to give him the go-ahead to begin work.

It occurred to her that trivial matters bored her boss. His surge came from being in the driver's seat. Complete authority was also what gave her dad his charge. She hoped Daddy was as enthused over the project as she and Mr. Russell were. Otherwise, egos would clash and take serious beatings—and so would the hotel. But she knew her father. Even if Mr. Russell did approach the idea first, Murray would never let pride stand in the way of a solid idea. Or, most importantly, making money.

If only Jordan approved of something she'd done, and admired her for it. But, no, he'd accused her of being wasteful. Ugly words had been fired from both sides, and she regretted that. Her hopes for a lasting relationship weren't completely extinguished, but with matters the way they presently were, they'd be lucky to have a friendship once the smoke cleared.

If only she'd stop loving Jordan.

If only he'd start loving her.

Shifting her body, Ashley turned in her seat. Maybe Elvis had been only a figment of her imagination—a different kind of dream. Whether a dream or imagination, she *missed* her figment. Elvis was a constant source of amusement and company for her. Tears welled in her eyes at the profound loss she felt.

How could she have dreamt or imagined what Sydnee had witnessed and confirmed along with her? For that matter, whatever would she tell Sydnee?

"Oh, Elvis," she said in a shaky voice. "What happened to you?"

Still, there was no response. Swiping at an escaping tear, she turned away and raised the sound on her television.

A dim glow cast its light about the room. Ashley straightened in her seat, turning once again to Elvis. The dim glow erupted into a brilliant, white light.

"Elvis!" Ashley shouted, jumping off the sofa and rushing to the bowl. "You came back!"

The beloved clicking sound began.

I didn't go anywhere.

The word "anywhere" was written in bold, red letters and underlined.

"For star's sake, what happened? It's been two days since you've responded to anything I said. I thought you'd lost your powers."

Please! Me *lose my powers? Don't be gauche. My powers are infinite. Eternal.*

"I swear you're trying to be sarcastic, Elvis," Ashley snapped. "And smug. Are you going to tell me what happened or not?"

Nothing happened, Ashley. You and your friend have the

worst manners of any humans I've come across.

"What are you talking about?"

You rushed out of here Saturday without a by-your-leave, or a "Thank-you, Elvis." All this after I was kind enough to arrange your day with Jordan.

"W-what? Y-you're responsible for Sydnee leaving?"

Guilty.

"But what did you do? How . . . ?"

It's done, Ashley. I arranged a minor emergency for Matthew that would keep him in Paris for a month.

"But why?"

Silence yourself, Ashley!

The big, bold letters were the equivalent of shouting. She silenced herself.

Matthew had planned to surprise Sydnee and stay here two weeks, which would not have been good for your budding romance with Jordan—

"Elvis! Did you go to New York and read Matthew's mind?" Ashley asked, thoroughly indignant.

One more outburst and I won't respond to you for a year! Now be quiet. How could I go to New York when you have me sitting here? I read his mind through the phone conversation he had with Sydnee.

"Oh, I see," Ashley responded. Her hackles were raised at Elvis's audacity. "You promised you wouldn't read minds, Elvis. How could you go back on your word?"

I promised I wouldn't read your *mind, Ashley. And please don't argue with me. You can't have a romance with your friends looking on, so be grateful for small favors.*

"I am grateful, Elvis. I just worry that Jordan's feelings are your creation and not about me. Because of your magic."

Don't you know that true love is *magic?*

Ashley laughed softly. "So it is," she conceded. "But

since you admitted giving me such a big boost, why did
you stop glowing for two days?"

*The boost was only supposed to last a couple hours into
the day, but you didn't get back home until after dusk.
What's more, you and Sydnee didn't even say good-bye.
You just left me alone for hours!*

"So you were pouting?"

Yes.

"I'm sorry, Elvis," Ashley said contritely. "Forgive me.
I was remiss. There may be other times I'll be away for
extra-long hours, however. That doesn't mean I don't think
about you or care about you. I promise from now on I will
tell you whenever I know I'll be longer than usual in coming home. Okay? Saturday couldn't be helped. You worked
your magic to perfection. It was Jordan who suggested the
picnic."

There was a moment of silence before Elvis responded.
When he answered, Ashley knew it was grudgingly.

Okay.

"Thank you, Elvis," Ashley said primly. "Tell me. Did
your magic really keep me with Jordan all those hours on
Saturday?"

*No, Ashley. Give the man some credit. That was his very
own idea. I only had him programmed to bring you and
Sydnee to the airport.*

"What's happened to him if that's the case? He—"

*Fear not, Ashley. Internal and external differences be-
tween you two are gnawing at his confidence. He'll come
around.*

"Oh, Elvis, may I kiss you?"

Yes, but be gentle.

Ashley touched her lips to the bowl's rim. Elvis's glow
muted and turned a pale pink.

"Will you ever stop blushing?" Ashley said with a laugh. "How can I repay your kindness?"

Let me listen to a CD by my namesake.

"Your namesake?"

Yes, Ash. Elvis Presley. The King. If I had a voice . . . Man, I love all his songs and would sing them every day.

Ashley patted his rim. "Your wish is my command, master." She went through her CD selection and took out one by Elvis Presley, then slipped it on the player. *"Love Me Tender"* filtered through the room in the singer's soothing baritone.

The clicking of the Teletype sounded, and Ashley went to see what Elvis was writing.

Thank you, Ashley. I've always liked Elvis's music. That's why I took his name. Although Ray Charles is still my all-time favorite. Perhaps tomorrow you can play his CD for me.

"Of course."

Forgive my thoughtlessness. You were watching television, weren't you? I really don't want to keep you from your program.

"Perish the thought," Ashley said. "I like Elvis, too." Flicking off the muted television, she settled herself back on the sofa. "May I join you, sir, while Elvis entertains us with his wonderful music?"

In response, the bowl's light flashed a brilliant white, then dimmed itself to a pale, shimmering pink glow.

Drawing in a satisfied breath, Ashley smiled. Radiance flushed the room. All that was missing from this romantic atmosphere was Jordan. But for the moment, she'd gladly accept Elvis—and his music.

After the trials of the day, she found it to be a profoundly pleasant way to end it, reminding her that there was always hope for tomorrow.

Twenty-two

_∼_

The next afternoon, Ashley sat tensely at the long, ebony table in the boardroom, awaiting the appearance of her father and brother. She smiled grimly at Jim Russell who, along with Jordan, had accompanied her to Douglas Enterprises. Mr. Russell insisted Jordan attend to underscore his plans for the restaurant.

Ashley knew she'd have to be sharp and focused to get Murray and Zach's approval. For the entire morning, she'd called the other shareholders at Mr. Russell's request and gotten their votes to upgrade the project according to her notes and Carson Wood's request. The only holdouts had been her family. A mere phone call wouldn't appease their mistrust. She had to meet with them face-to-face and convince them that she was serious about this project and that she wasn't out to just waste money.

That wasn't the only source of her anxiety. Beyond polite words, Jordan remained stoic, and she needed to break the ice. This coming Saturday was the day of their dinner, so after this conference ended, she'd pull Jordan aside and remind him of her invitation.

She was putting her feelings on the line, but she couldn't sit back and do nothing. She needed to take a step in a positive direction. She wouldn't achieve anything by waiting for Jordan to make the first move.

She leaned back in the leather chair, impatient for the meeting to get under way. Wondering what delayed Murray and Zach, she surveyed the boardroom where her father had almost lost everything the family owned several years before.

Huge picture windows encircled the seventeenth-floor office. Outside, a gentle rain fell, but the light blue sky peeping from the horizon promised sunshine. A live ficus stood in a huge planter in each of the four corners of the room. A telephone sat directly in the center of the table. Floor-to-ceiling shelves dominated one wall, where a television and VCR sat behind glass doors.

Not much had changed since the near takeover, and Ashley wasn't certain if that was by design or by accident.

The door swung open, Zach followed Murray into the room. The first thing Ashley noticed was her brother's face, as bruised and cut as Jordan's. Narrowing her eyes, she looked from one to the other.

"What are you doing here, Bennett?" Zach growled, touching his blackened right eye. "This is a closed-door meeting. Since you aren't a family member or a shareholder, you have to wait outside."

"There you go again, Zachery," Jordan shot back. "Opening your mouth before you know the facts. As a matter of fact, Mr. Russell asked me to attend this meeting."

Zach slowly made his way to one end of the table and sat. He glared at Jordan and flexed his right hand, which was encased in sterile white bandages. "This meeting is going to be even more insufferable with you here."

Standing, Ashley cleared her throat. "Guys, is there something I should know about?" she snapped. "It seems strange that both of you appear to have had your faces battered."

"There isn't anything you should know about, Ashley," Jordan ground out. "Just mind your business for once."

"You mind your damned manners, Bennett!" Zach yelled, pounding the table with his undamaged hand. "That's *my* sister."

"So you remind me at every turn."

"Boys, enough!" Murray shouted, passing a warning look to both of them. "This isn't the time or the place to discuss personal problems. Whatever they may be. After this meeting, I want to see both of you in my office pronto!"

"I'll be there as well," Ashley grumbled, reseating herself. "I can't believe you two. You've been best friends forever. What in the world could be so important to come to blows over?"

"Enough, Ashley," Murray said sharply.

"Who says *we've* come to blows, Ashley?" Jordan asked, his eyebrows lifted, ignoring Murray's words.

"Are you saying it's mere coincidence that you both are beaten and bruised?" Ashley sputtered incredulously.

"Yes, that's exactly what I'm saying, Ashley.

She wasn't sure why Jordan's story sounded so lame, but it did. Yet what reason did he have to lie to her? Unless Zach and Jordan had fought because of *her*.

"Finish this discussion later!" Murray said, exasperation clear in his tone. He gave Ashley an annoyed look. "Now, then, what is the reason for this urgent meeting?"

Ashley looked at Mr. Russell, who gave her an encouraging nod. Taking a deep, fortifying breath and placing her personal problems aside, she opened her leather folder. She found the necessary figures and passed out a copy to each man present.

"Uh, Dad." She swallowed hard, hesitating about how to address her father properly in this setting. The thought that her father and brother—and even Jordan—expected her to be financially inept pounded through her. For a moment she wished Mr. Russell hadn't put so much responsibility for this project on her shoulders. It placed her in an odd dilemma. Whose expectations would she live up to? Her family's and Jordan's? Or Mr. Russell's? Today she couldn't satisfy both sides, so maybe she should satisfy herself. She shifted in her seat "I mean, um . . . Carson Wood has asked to change the renovation plans."

"In what way?" Zach asked, focusing his full attention on her. "I thought everything was settled and he was about to begin."

Ashley squirmed in her seat. This was the touchy part. "It was. B-but he asked for my input. He wanted me to pass along my ideas for the refurbishment, right down to a suggested color scheme—"

"Well, damn, he doesn't know you very well, does he?" Zach scoffed.

"He does," Mr. Russell put in indignantly. "And that's why he asked for Ashley's pointers." He gave her an encouraging nod. "Continue."

"Jim, why is my sister speaking? You're the general manager of the hotel who, along with this family, own part of the stock—"

"She's speaking, Zachery, because I've promoted her to Senior Vice President of Operations. She does a crackerjack job over there and has become indispensable to me. I suggest you listen to her."

Her eyes wide, Ashley listened to Mr. Russell's blithe announcement, speechless and astonished. Had he forgotten to mention her elevated status, or was this his way of showing his full support in front of her family? Either way, everyone was staring at her—her father with trepidation; Zach with annoyance; and Mr. Russell with expectation.

Only Jordan's features remained unfathomable and impassive. She stiffened her shoulders.

"Thank you, Mr. Russell, for your confidence in me. Zach—"

"Ignore, Zach," Murray interrupted. "He's had a burr in his behind for two days now. Talk to me. I'm listening. Tell me what scheme you and Carson Wood have devised."

"Um, Daddy, when I turned in my report to him, I added historical footnotes about certain sections of the hotel. Murals beneath mounds of paint in the third-floor atrium, frieze-worked ceilings that once dominated the hotel, intricately carved banisters that had been stored away in the attic because of their state of disrepair. He liked what he read and wants to return the hotel to its former glory."

Murray rubbed his chin and gazed down at the sheet with the figures on them. "Which means he'll need more money?"

"Yes," Ashley said in a small voice, "but not more time."

"Why should we agree to this, Ashley? As shareholders, we must look at cost versus profit. You're talking a 115 percent increase in restoration fees. How long will it take us to recoup that?"

"Not long, Daddy. Not with the plan we have." At ease discussing the hotel, she smiled and when she spoke, it was with passionate purpose. "You know the phrase 'everything old is new again'? Every year, New Orleans is attracting more and more visitors. We can tap into that market. We'll have a hotel restored to its former glory and a restaurant that boasts a hotshot young chef, who's already drawing in crowds. Pre-opening day publicity centered around the restoration will garner interest months ahead. We already advertise nationally. It won't take any additional money to rouse public awareness to what we're doing."

"Ashley—"

"Daddy, listen to me," Ashley continued, worried that he

was about to turn her down and accuse her of wasting company money as she was so apt to do with her own.

"Uncle Murray," Jordan said, leaning forward in his seat, undeterred by Zach's ferocious glare, "We have to admire Ashley's sagacity. Cosmetics can be attractive, but it can end up covering a treasure trove. I think you should go with the complete remodeling."

"Thank you for that input, Jordan," Murray said. "But it was unnecessary. Since my mind is already made up, there's nothing you or anyone else can say for or against this thing to sway me."

"Murray—" Jim Russell began, only to have her father raise his hand for silence.

Ashley's heart sank, and she shrank back in her chair.

"Honey, I have to say I'm shocked," Murray went on in an unyielding voice. "I never knew you had this . . . this, shall we say, business side to you." A huge grin lit his face. "I'm damned proud of you, baby. Tell Carson Wood if he wants to tear down and rebuild the whole damned building, I'm all for it as long as you approve of what's being done."

The tension in her body released itself as her father's words sank in. Although he hadn't come right out and said so, he trusted her, and that delighted her. She had to bow her head to hide the rush of tears in her eyes. When she recovered she raised her hand and smiled. "Thank you, Daddy."

"No, Ashley, thank you. You've shown me another side of you." He stood. "I know Jordan was supposed to outline the plans for the restaurant, but we'll have to do that another time. I have a golf game to get to. But first, Jordan, Zach, I want to see you in my office. *Now*."

"I'm coming, too," Ashley said, standing as well.

"No, you're not," Murray announced. "Some things are best left unsaid in your presence. No offense, Ashley."

"I'll wait for you downstairs, Ashley," Mr. Russell said happily, beaming a proud smile her way.

"Thank you." Once her boss was gone, she looked at the three men in her life and decided not to press the issue of what brought Jordan and Zach to blows. Although with her brother acting like a complete jerk, she was ready to uppercut him herself. "Jordan will be along shortly. I need to talk to him alone."

"No—"

"Fine," Murray interrupted Zach, indicating with a nod that they leave.

When Ashley found herself alone with Jordan, she wasn't quite sure what to say. She had just accomplished her most stunning career achievement and now she felt like a young girl. Well, she'd taken control of the boardroom. Now she must take control of the bedroom.

"Jordan, this isn't the time or place to discuss the argument yesterday."

"No, it isn't, Ashley."

"Then I'd like you to come to dinner Saturday night. No strings attached."

"I don't know."

Ashley shrugged, pretending indifference, praying he'd accept. His aloofness irritated her. He'd praised her to her father, but he was still shutting her out. "It's up to you. If it's Zach—"

"Leave Zach out of this." Jordan started for the door, where he paused without facing her. "I'll be there, Ashley. You'd mentioned this long before the events of this weekend. See you later."

With that enigmatic statement, he opened the door and sauntered out.

Twenty-three

~

Ten minutes later, Zach quietly listened to his father berate him and Jordan for their childish behavior. Murray knew the full story of what had happened Sunday, but somehow Ashley hadn't gotten wind of the fight. He was damned glad. She'd never forgive him for trying to waylay Jordan.

As much as he disapproved of Ashley's spendthrift ways, he absolutely despised Jordan's stinginess. Not that he'd given it much consideration before Jordan had taken an interest in Ashley. Part of the reason he'd introduced Jordan to Marie was because he hadn't wanted *Ashley* to get any ideas about Jordan. Zach never dreamed he had to worry about a reverse situation.

A relationship between his sister and his friend was a disaster in the making. Zach feared that the friendship he and Jordan had enjoyed for most of their lives would be irrevocably damaged if the man hurt his little sister.

At the moment, the continuation of their friendship didn't look too likely. But as Ashley's brother and Jordan's friend, he felt it his duty to be the reasonable one in this situation, even if his methods were *un*reasonable.

Zach realized silence had descended. Both Jordan and Murray were staring at him. He glanced beyond where his father sat in a burgundy leather executive chair to the window behind Murray. The light rain had stopped completely, and a hint of sunshine peeped from behind the lingering clouds.

"What do you have to say for yourself, son?"

"Nothing, Dad," Zach answered. "I told you that I don't think Jordan and Ashley are right for one another."

"Dammit, Zach!" Jordan shouted. "That's not for you to decide. It's up to me and Ashley."

"You and Ashley?" Zach snapped. "When she's fancied herself in love with you since forever? And because you're just thinking with your—"

"Enough!" Murray commanded in a tone that forbade more arguments. "This is ridiculous. You boys have been friends for over twenty years. Zach, Jordan is right. As much as we might approve or disapprove, this is between him and Ashley. She's a grown woman. Start treating her like one. As for you, Jordan, you should understand Zach's worries and need to protect Ashley. He is, after all, her brother and wants the best for her.

"And neither of you think I'm best for her?"

Jordan stared at Murray, his look as hard as his tone. It hurt that the people he considered family thought so little of him, and it disappointed him that he'd misjudged Zach so greatly. Although he'd never considered how Uncle Murray would feel about a relationship between him and Ashley, he sincerely believed Zach's disapproval was all bluster. How wrong he'd been. And yet even though the madness that had driven him to Ashley time and again these past weeks had lessened, he still thought of her in a romantic way.

Seeing her today, the consummate businesswoman, only added to his fascination. Her hair had returned to its normally straight, dark blond condition. Still she was pretty with her hazel eyes alive with laughter and a touch of makeup coloring her cheeks and luscious lips.

She also seemed more mature than she'd ever been, and Jordan knew that was because of the aura of power she'd presented. Jim Russell had put the utmost confidence in her to have given her such a promotion—and such praise. If only Ashley practiced the same in her private life, then Jordan wouldn't have such reservations.

Even the nastiness he'd shown to her yesterday hadn't sent her into a fit of anger. Remembering her sweet dinner invitation, he was embarrassed all the more. As usual he owed her an apology for being a first-class jerk. He needed to adhere to his self-imposed rules and be a friend to Ashley. With Zach in such a snit, irreversible harm could be done to Ashley and Zach's relationship as well.

Jordan didn't want that. Ashley loved Zach dearly, and eventually she might blame Jordan for any split between them. He sighed. "The picnic that Zach nearly destroyed my house over was an innocent afternoon spent between friends."

"Is that good enough for you, Zach?" Murray asked quietly.

Zach shrugged. "It has to be, doesn't it?"

"Just so you don't think I'm hiding anything from you," Jordan continued, "Ashley invited me over to her house for dinner on Saturday, and I accepted."

"Dinner?" Murray and Zach boomed together.

"Listen, it's not—"

"You don't understand, son," Murray said, on the verge of laughter. "Ashley can't cook an egg."

"Yeah, and that's a literal assessment. Her landlord, Harry, threatened to evict her for excessive pollution a couple of months ago." Zach laughed and straightened in his seat. "She attempted to boil eggs for us and burned them to a crisp. They were the color of tar and about as hard. And the stink! I swore never to touch another egg in my life, although Ashley has since *fried* an egg for me. But I tell you, man, anyone who's never smelled boiled eggs shriveled and burned to a crisp should consider themselves lucky."

"Blessed, really," Murray added with a chuckle. "Have fun."

"Thanks, Uncle Murray," Jordan said dryly. "Anyway, Ashley assures me she has everything under control."

"Okay," Zach said. "By the way, send the bill for the damages to your house to me."

"Thanks, but it isn't necessary."

"It is," Zach responded in a neutral voice.

It wasn't the friendly tone Jordan was used to, but neither was it icy anger.

"If it'll make you feel better." Smiling to take the sting out of the words, Jordan stood. "I think it's time for me to go. I have to get back to the restaurant. I left my two assistants, Curtis and Art, in charge, and I need to go help out in my kitchen." He made his way to the door.

"Jordie!" Murray called, halting Jordan just as he opened the door. "You're wrong to believe that I don't think you're the best for my little girl. You're a good man and would be a fine addition to any family. But if your feelings aren't as deep for Ashley as hers are for you, she could end up deeply hurt. I'm not asking you to stay away from my little girl. I'm just asking you to take care."

"Thanks, Uncle Murray." Feeling a modicum of satisfaction, Jordan nodded to Zach and then walked out.

The rest of the week passed in a blur. Saturday arrived much too quickly for Ashley. Today she'd entertain Jordan with a meal cooked with her very own hands. The thought enthralled her greatly—and worried her terribly. After all of her failed attempts at the stove, could she really prepare a three-course meal?

She sipped her coffee and considered her question.

Yes, she most certainly could! She wasn't a Douglas for nothing. Douglases were stubborn and proud go-getters. They also planned ahead. She'd bought several cans of pork and beans and four packages of hot dogs as backup if her dinner didn't work out. Her microwave was in good shape, and she'd become an expert at heating wieners and beans.

If all else failed, she had Elvis.

"Knock, knock, knock."

Harry's voice floated into the kitchen, where Ashley stood gazing at her bags of groceries. She jumped at the sound.

"I do hope you're decent, Ash."

Her landlord's voice was closer.

"Because I'm coming in."

"Thank goodness I am," Ashley said, annoyed, as Harry traipsed into the room. "Otherwise, you'd certainly get an eyeful. How many times do I have to stress to you to wait on the *other* side of the door until I let you in, Harry?"

"Don't be so grouchy," Harry admonished, peeking inside the bag nearest him. He took out her bag of grapes and opened it, pulling a few of the fruit into his hand. "I knew you were dressed. I saw you come in carrying these bags of groceries. They looked like more than your usual canned goods to me. My curiosity got the best of me. I want to know if you're planning to cook real food so I can have the fire department standing by. After all, you'll have to use real heat."

Leaving the items she wouldn't use for her dinner, she placed those that she would need on the counter, Ashley chuckled. "Are you trying to be funny, Mr. Roberts? Or is that a form of sarcasm?"

Harry went to the cabinet, took a mug out, and then

poured himself some coffee. He tasted the dark brew as
Ashley turned on the faucet and began washing the crisp
Romaine lettuce she'd purchased. "Sarcasm? From me?
Now, Ash, you know me better than that. I was merely
joking. Besides, I'm curious. I noticed your coffee table is
set for two. You're washing real salad greens like a real
person. Are you expecting a guest for dinner, and is it me?"

Ashley tore off another piece of lettuce. "You wish."

Harry stared at the counter. Several containers lined the
limited space, including a package of fresh shrimp and another with beef fillet tips. There was a jar of cocktail sauce,
a package of noodles, and a bag of dinner rolls. Next to
that sat a bottle of chardonnay, which Harry promptly put
in the refrigerator.

"Ambitious, aren't we?" he asked with keen humor.

"I'll be fine," Ashley responded with smug indignation.
She turned the faucet off and laid the last of her lettuce in
the strainer. "After all, one has to start someplace."

"Yes, indeedy," Harry agreed. He frowned at the beef.
"I noticed you'll be serving white wine with beef—"

"I *like* white wine," Ashley interrupted. "Anyway I have
two bottles of Beaujolais right over there." She pointed to
the far end of the counter. The bottles stood next to her
newly bought shampoo that she'd use tonight—once Elvis
worked his magic on the stuff. Since Jordan had accepted
her invitation without any help from Elvis or his charms,
Ashley didn't feel the least bit guilty. "Besides, I will also
be serving shrimp."

"Well, maybe you should use a rosé."

"And maybe you should mind your own beeswax," Ashley snapped, becoming thoroughly vexed with her annoying
friend. This was hard enough for her. His expertise only
compounded her inexperience.

"And leave you to your own dangerous devices in an
unprotected kitchen? Never! Should I have an ambulance

on standby along with the fire department, just in case?"

"In case of what?" Ashley asked, stifling a laugh. And at her own expense, too. Harry's sense of humor made it hard to stay angry at him. She opened the cocktail sauce, then got a spatula and a bowl.

"In case some dumb fool actually eats your food."

Giggling, Ashley led the way into the living room, still holding on to the spatula. She pointed to the exit. "Close the door behind you and thanks for your input, but I really don't need it. Or your company. So get out!"

"Go figure," Harry said, heading for the door and carrying his mug of coffee. "I was only trying to be helpful. Remember to keep your fire extinguisher within reach."

Ashley threw the plastic spatula at him, but he ducked in the nick of time, and she missed him by mere inches.

"I'll return your mug later. *Much* later. Maybe just in time to aid your distressed dinner guest." He hurriedly closed the door behind him.

Back in her kitchen, Ashley stared at the uncooked food. She hated the doubt that Harry had placed in her, but maybe he was right. Perhaps her choice of menu was really a little too ambitious. She'd remembered a recipe she'd seen in a magazine and decided to try it. It sounded simple. Beef fillet tips in a noodle casserole. Any fool should be able to prepare it.

Well, maybe she wasn't just *any* fool, but a special kind. She'd lost the recipe long ago and now had absolutely no idea where to begin. How long should she boil the noodles? Cook the meat? Boil the shrimp for the shrimp cocktail?

Oh, brother! What had she done?

After she placed the food in the refrigerator and tidied up the counter, she went to her bowl. "Elvis, can you hear me?"

Of course I can hear you. Haven't I told you so?

"Well, sometimes you can't," Ashley reminded him, folding her arms.

Young lady, I can always *hear you. When I don't respond, that just means I'm ignoring you.*

Ashley leaned over him. "How can you be so ill-mannered? To ignore me when I need to communicate with you?"

You do have a flair for dramatics, Ashley. Sometimes you can be bothersome. So, like you humans would say, I simply tune you out.

"Well, please don't tune me out tonight, Elvis," Ashley implored. "Tonight I need you."

Do you have any inkling of how provocative that sounds?

"Elvis! Do you always have to be so . . . so wolfish? Turning everything I say into something . . . um . . . wanton. Are you sure you weren't a lecherous human male at one time, and got turned into a bowl for your licentious ways?"

Ha, ha, ha. Me? Licentious? Never! I am a romantic, Ashley. Rooting for lovers the world over. I was never human. My master named me after St. Ambrose.

Ashley sniggered. "A saint? Why St. Ambrose and not St. Valentine? Since you claim to be so romantic."

I was fashioned for romance, Ashley. For King Arthur and his queen. But let's not get into that Lancelot thing again. It grieves me to recall such betrayal. Especially since my purpose for being became useless to the king.

"Gosh, that must have been awful."

Ahh, it was. It was. For a fortnight Merlin sang Ambrosian chants, which were introduced by St. Ambrose in Milan around 384 A.D. Anyway, Merlin called me Ambrose because he liked the chants, not for the powers he gave me. He was heartbroken for the king. He asked me only to use my powers for the good of humankind. Particularly human lovers.

"So you promised Merlin to be kind always?"

I did not! Be kind to humans who are not always kind to each other? Never!"

"But—"

Make no mistake, Ashley. My wrath equals my benelovence. And my benelovence only goes to those deserving of it.

"Oh," Ashley said in a small voice, wondering if she was still considered deserving of magical kindness.

Don't despair, Ashley. I chose you, remember? Because of your innocence and unpretentiousness. I grant your wishes at my discretion. I sense now that you have a request of me.

"Elvis, you're so perceptive. I invited Jordan over for dinner tonight and I don't know how to cook."

Ha, ha, ha, ha, ha, ha, ha, ha.

The Teletyping clicked across the pad in rapid fire, erasing and rewriting the page over and over again with the laughing words.

Ashley scowled. "Gee, I had no idea I was such a comedienne," she said with annoyance. "Maybe I should try my hand at show business."

The clicking accelerated, and *ha-ha's* covered the check, which Ashley feared would remain blank forever, and the notepad on both sides.

"I have a damn bowl—a *bowl* for heaven's sake—laughing at me," Ashley snapped. She thumped Elvis's rim. "You medieval reject, stop it this minute! Or I promise you I will fill your cavity with ice and put you in the freezer for good measure."

The clicking slowed down.

Ashley, you're priceless. This is the first time ever that my birds have tears in their eyes. Forgive me, my dear. I did not mean to disparage you. But anyone who can't cook shouldn't invite people over for dinner. Oh, ha, ha, ha—

"Stop it, Elvis!"

Yes, my dear. It's my pleasure to help you, Ashley. Tell me what you have in mind.

Ashley gave him the name of the recipe and admitted she'd forgotten what to do.

Take each package of everything you're going to have and set it inside my cavity for one minute each. Then place it back into the refrigerator. When you're ready to cook, it'll turn out perfect.

"How will I know when it's ready?"

I will turn off the heat under your pots. Jordan has to see you cooking, in order to appreciate your efforts.

"Thank you so much, Elvis," Ashley said, relieved. "I simply adore you."

You adore me? This medieval reject?

"Well, you're not a reject. You have a fabulous history behind you."

That I do. But don't stand there gabbing. Get the food and do as I told you. Who knows? Jordan may decide to surprise you and come early.

"Oh, right."

Filled with confidence and feeling luckier than anyone she knew, Ashley scurried to the kitchen.

Twenty-four

~

"Hello, Jordan, do come in," Ashley greeted four hours later, holding the door open for him.

As Elvis had predicted, Jordan indeed arrived early. The sun was just beginning to set, and the heat of the afternoon still remained outside.

Jordan stepped into the cool apartment. "Thanks, Ash."

She gave him the once-over, and her heart began to pound. Dressed for relaxation, the light tan polo shirt he wore clearly defined his broad shoulders and wide chest. His arms bulged with corded muscles, and brown shorts exposed his strong, perfectly sculptured, long legs. The bruises that had been so outstanding when she'd last seen him on Tuesday had all but healed.

She fingered her freshly washed hair, and the powerful floral scent she'd missed surrounded them. Jordan's appreciative gaze roamed over the newly restored honey-blond curls that hung free to her waist. His gaze took in the V-neck, red summer sweater and black miniskirt, continuing down to her bare legs and the spaghetti-strap sandals that encased her pedicured feet.

She smiled at him. "Dinner isn't nearly ready, Jordan. But I have some appetizers right there on the sofa table. In the meantime, would you care for a glass of wine? I have chardonnay."

"Sounds like a winner to me," Jordan said, following her to the sofa and sitting down.

Hot sensation rushed through Ashley at the smoky promise in his eyes. First they needed to talk. "I'll be a minute or two. I must check to see if the water's ready for the noodles."

Where did that come from? She hadn't even turned the fire on under the pot yet. Nevertheless, when she entered the kitchen, the pot of water was already heating on the stove. *Elvis!*

Confidence engulfed her. She absently reached for her plastic tray and frowned at the weight and cold metal texture. Glancing at it, she discovered the plastic tray was now an ornate solid silver server. Her wineglasses, too, had become tinkling crystal.

Laughing happily, she extricated the wine from the refrigerator, placed it on her new silver tray, and carried it to the living room. Her hair fanning around her, she leaned over and set the tray on the sofa.

Taking in his fill of her display, Jordan rose from his seat and picked up the bottle opener. "Allow me," he said softly. "What a beautiful tray, Ash." He forced the metal spiral into the wine cork and twisted the handle. "Another antique shop purchase?"

Wondering if he was hinting at whether or not he thought she'd spent more money recklessly, Ashley's guard went up. "I beg your pardon?"

"The tray, Ash. It's a perfect match to the bowl," Jordan said innocently. He pulled the cork out with a triumphant *pop,* then poured out two glasses into her antique crystal.

Holding his glass up, he inspected it from all angles, then took a sip. "So are the glasses."

"Huh?" Stupefied, Ashley studied the glasses and tray closer. "Omigod!" What she'd failed to notice in the kitchen, Jordan immediately picked up on and pointed out to her. The long-stemmed crystal glasses had doves on their bases, gold around the rim, and bells, bows, flowers, and butterflies just under. Exquisite! And the exact replica of Elvis. So was the silver tray, minus the stand.

"Did you find the complete set of glasses, Ashley, or just these two?"

Elvis, what are you doing to me? Unsure of how to answer that, she wished she could run to her bowl for advice. She only had two, very inexpensive wineglasses that Elvis had turned into beautiful pieces of artwork. In her cabinet were ordinary drinking glasses, plastic cups, and three mugs. Would they still be there when she opened the door, or would she find a cabinet filled with glorious antique crystal?

Was Elvis trying to create problems between her and Jordan?

With a sigh, she handed the glass to Jordan. "Hold this. I have to check on the crystal. Um, I mean the *dinner*." Without another word, she hurried to the kitchen.

When she walked in, she covered her mouth to stifle a yelp. The pan from the stove was emptying the noddles into the colander sitting in the sink. She gasped and rushed over to grasp the pot handles, just as Jordan joined her.

"Oh, hi, Jordan," she said with a nervous giggle.

"Problem?" he asked.

"No, of course not."

Her hands shook, and she set the pot down on the counter, the loud *bang* startling her further. Biting down on her lip because her heart felt as if it was about to beat right out of her chest, she turned on the cold water and allowed it to run over the steaming pasta. Aware that Jordan watched her every move, she went to the stove and checked the pan that was on the fire.

"Are those beef tips you're sauteing?" Jordan asked just as Ashley gasped at her new discovery. He leaned over and took a whiff of the meat cooking on the stove.

Blinking in disbelief, she pasted a wide grin on her face when she saw Jordan staring at her as if she was a candidate for Bedlam. "Yes, they are beef tips." Her voice was reed thin. Elvis was turning her house into a magical wonderland, and she wasn't sure she was comfortable with it. At least, she wanted to *know* what was happening before it happened. When she'd left the kitchen just minutes earlier, the beef tips had been in their package in the refrigerator.

"Smells wonderful," Jordan said. "I can't wait to taste it."

"Neither can I. If you're really starving, you can snack on the paté, cheese, and crackers. Dinner won't be much longer."

"I'm fine. What can I do to help?"

"I already have the glasses and silverware out, but you can get the plates from the cabinet over there." She pointed to the place. "I hope you don't mind eating at the coffee table—"

"Wow!" Jordan exclaimed.

Dreading what she'd find and realizing her mistake too late, Ashley turned toward the sound. Ivory-colored china, rimmed with gold and sporting the same patterns as Elvis and his other creations, sat inside. The dishes gleamed and sparkled.

Seeing the question in Jordan's eyes, Ashley swallowed hard. *Elvis, you double-crosser! I wish you'd read my mind now!* "Well, um. . . ."

In awe, Jordan shook his head, then opened the cabinet next to the one with the china. A complete matching set of crystal lined the shelves. "I've never seen anything so beautiful. How could you possibly afford them, Ash?" he asked without rancor.

You simply bought them on the time-pay plan.

The thought flooded Ashley's mind, obliterating everything else there.

Detecting Elvis's handiwork again, Ashley sighed. "I can't afford them," she said honestly. "I simply bought them on the time-pay plan. I didn't know Elvis . . . um . . . I mean the bowl had matching pieces when I bought it."

She really didn't know about the other pieces, all of which she was certain hadn't existed until now. She was seriously thinking about caving Elvis in with a sledgehammer for conjuring them up in the first place. And for making her fib about how she actually got them.

"Ashley, not only are these beautiful, but they are also a wonderful investment. I think you made a very wise purchase. I'm quite proud of you." He leaned over and kissed her gently on the mouth. "I believe you're finally growing up." Taking out two beautiful salad plates and matching dinner plates, he handed them to her. "There you are. Now, are you ready for more wine?"

"Yes, please," Ashley managed. She should have known that whatever Elvis did was for her good and to further advance her quest to win Jordan's heart. *Elvis, you darling! You're so smart.*

When she opened the refrigerator for the salad, she found that not only was it prepared, but so were the shrimp. The seafood was mounted around the perimeter of two small, widemouthed, ornate crystal glasses. A few shrimp nestled in the cocktail sauce, while sprigs of parsley and lemon slices dangled between each. She wouldn't gasp again. She'd already promised herself to stop that.

The completion of the dinner took care of itself out of Jordan's view, and Ashley asked him for a hand in serving it. For the time being, she hoped Elvis had no more surprises in store for her.

Twenty-five

~

Dinner over and done, Jordan relaxed on the sofa, drinking the red wine Ashley had emptied into her beautiful bowl before pouring into the glasses.

She had promised to cook him a gourmet meal and she delivered—way past what he truly expected from her. If he hadn't seen with his own eyes that she had cooked the savory meal they ate, he never would have believed she had prepared it. She was just full of surprises.

Everything had been done to perfection. He'd never before eaten such a tasty meal that he himself hadn't cooked. Even Ashley's shrimp had a sauce foreign to his taste buds, but she refused to give up her recipe.

Instead, she turned her beautiful smile on him and boasted that it was a secret. It didn't matter. He'd get it from her eventually. In all the years of their association, she had yet to refuse him whatever he asked of her.

She stretched her slender arms above her head. Her high, round breasts pushed provocatively against the tight little sweater she wore. Since he first walked through the door, he had watched her, but had pretended nonchalance. Now

he applauded his self-restraint for not hauling her into her
bedroom, stripping off that skimpy little skirt she wore, and
showing her what life was all about.

That black skirt, revealing legs that seemed to stretch to
her beautiful neck, was a siren's sheath. It tempted and
titillated. Her hair shimmered like golden strands of corn-
silk, while her face was perfect from any angle.

He took another sip of his wine, applauding her positive
change. Although he was sure Ashley had used some of
her father's money to purchase the matching pieces to the
bowl, it was money well spent. It was the most elegant set
of dishes he'd ever seen. It would also be a perfect compliment to the dining room in his home. . . .

Well, hell.

The only way that would happen was if Ashley came
with them. In all honesty, he'd like nothing better. No other
woman compared to the beautiful and whimsical Ashley.
Marie, who was a sweet girl, couldn't compare. The magic
he felt near Ashley was lacking with Marie and every other
woman he'd met since his return to New Orleans.

That sparkle outweighed his doubts and Zach's disapproval. Whatever drew him to Ashley wouldn't, couldn't,
be denied.

Although she did seem more mature and less of a spendthrift, he wanted additional proof of those changes before
he confessed his love for her.

He knew he loved her. Thoughts of Ashley occupied his
every waking moment. But the love he carried for her was
flawed. Otherwise, he'd accept her faults; he'd accept
everything about her *unconditionally*. For that reason, he'd
temper the urge to make love to her. Once they crossed that
barrier, their relationship would be forever altered, and he
still feared that their huge differences would make a long-
term relationship between them impossible.

There didn't seem to be anything he could do about his

fear of living without money. And he'd be damned if he'd put himself in a position to worry over how to keep Ashley happy and at the same time hold on to his fortune.

He tasted the wine again and smiled lazily in her direction. The wine was mellowing him. Ashley's lips looked succulent and inviting. With a sigh, he straightened himself in his seat and sipped from the glass again. How would he ever keep his resolve when his loins throbbed so?

"Jordan?"

Ashley's voice added to his incipient and erotic thoughts about her. He hoped the wine didn't alter his better judgment not to make love to her. The urge to pull her into his arms and kiss her senseless almost overpowered him.

He cleared his throat. "Yes, Ash?"

"Do you like Elvis's music?"

"The King?" He smiled and tasted the wine again. "Some of his music is great. But some I could do without."

Bedroom eyes, the color of emerald and topaz, wreaked havoc with him. She slid her tongue across her lips to catch a drop of wine.

"I have a wonderful collection of his recordings. Would you like to hear a ballad or two? Or would you prefer something with a beat?"

Glad for the diversion, he stood and set his glass down. "Allow me. Let me surprise you." Going to the CD player, he shuffled through the discs until he found what he was looking for. He slid the disc into the player, then turned to Ashley and held out his hand. "May I have this dance, my lady?"

Ashley glided into his arms as the soft baritone voice drifted from the stereo.

"Love me tender, love me true . . ."

Resting her arms on his shoulder as he glided her around the small room in a slow rhythm, she wondered if he detected the erratic beat in her racing heart. Maybe the song he'd chosen was meant to tell her something. Did he want her to love him?

Did he love her?

"That's one of my favorites," she whispered into his ear.

"Mine, too," Jordan murmured, gazing down at her. "I'm very impressed with you, Ash. You've just shown me what a perfect evening is like."

"I'm glad you enjoyed it," Ashley whispered, refraining from mentioning their last argument as he brought his head down and pressed his lips against her own. Tightening her arms around his neck, she gave in to his scalding kisses.

He slid his hands down her back to her derriere and held her in place against his swollen arousal. Lightning scorched through Ashley's body, and a soft moan escaped her.

"Ash," he intoned hoarsely, grinding against her.

In rapid succession, he kissed her eyes, her cheeks, and her neck, before he found her mouth again with hungry intensity. He groaned, ravaging her recesses, their tongues meeting, mating.

Jordan slipped his hand beneath her skirt, invading her panties with deftness. His fingers glided through her tight feminine curls, reaching the core of her mad desire with agonizing slowness. His whisper-soft caress teased and tormented, adding to her exquisite need for release.

She moved with restless energy against his hand, encouraging him to give her surcease. His fingers moved faster against her erected bud, stoking her liquid fire to the sweet climax she craved. Her knees buckled, and she moaned senselessly.

Jordan refused to relinquish his passionate control. She glided to and fro as he cupped her completely, the rapturous feeling he invoked within her becoming more and more intense.

"Jordan!" Ashley cried, her heart pounding, her emotions spiraling.

In response, he slipped his finger inside her warmth. Her body trembling, she drew in a breath and closed her eyes in surrender.

In. Out. In. Out. He massaged her with an accelerated burst of speed.

"Please," she murmured senselessly between ecstatic murmurs. She collapsed against his chest, his male scent adding to her arousal. "Make me yours."

A brilliant white flash brightened the room for an instant.

Jordan held her close, the pounding of his heart almost as fast as her own. "What was that?"

"What was what?" Her voice was low and retiring.

"I thought I saw a light flash," Jordan said huskily. "It must have come from outside."

Acute embarrassment engulfed her hot desire. How could she have forgotten about Elvis? Her face heating, she pushed out of the arms that held her with such firm gentleness. Jordan reached for her again, but she turned away.

"No," she said, her voice almost inaudible.

"Don't be ashamed of what just happened, sweetheart," Jordan said tenderly.

Ashley remained silent. How could Jordan know that her embarrassment stemmed from Elvis witnessing their passionate moment? A moment she relished and of which she could never be ashamed. How could she explain to Jordan that it wasn't what happened between them that caused her such humiliation?

Being in his arms was sheer enchantment, something she wanted to experience time and again. If he thought such an occurrence had caused her such distress, however, he might temper his own desire for her. Instinct told Ashley that what Jordan felt for her went beyond carnal urges. She didn't want his budding feelings for her to wither before they had a chance to fully bloom.

"Ash, forgive me," Jordan continued. "The fact that you

threaten my sanity should have nothing to do with me wanting to make love to you on a daily basis." He grinned and
caressed her cheek.

Knowing he was trying to put her at ease, Ashley smiled.
"I-I'm not really embarrassed, Jordan. It's just that I've
never done this before. It . . . it took my breath away. It
was wonderful." She wanted to tell him that she wanted
more of the same that very minute. Passion still burned in
his blue-gray eyes, darkening them to the color of storm
clouds. She had no doubt that he would comply with her
wishes.

Before she spoke, Jordan gathered her into his arms again
and held her snug against his arousal. The long, ragged
breath he drew in sounded poignant. It also signaled his
retreat. Ashley hugged him tightly, hating the withdrawal
that would only bring the same chasm between them that
it always brought.

Jordan closed his eyes. Thoughts of his phallus resting
deep within Ashley swirled through his mind. After all, she
was willing. Why not accept her invitation? He'd already
decided he loved her; now it was only a matter of accepting
her totally. In the meantime, their physical relationship
could get off to a wonderful start.

Knowing the myriad of other problems this would create,
he groaned aloud.

That same flash happened again. His eyes flew open. He
released Ashley abruptly, wondering if he'd imagined the
bright lights, wondering if perhaps they were a beacon to
his inner turmoil.

He wouldn't let desire cause a riff between himself and
the Douglases. If Ashley became pregnant before he had a
chance to marry her, that's exactly what would happen. He
was part of that family, as angry as Zach was with him
right now, and he loved them.

He had to either conquer his demons or accept Ashley

as she was, *before* making a commitment to her. And he couldn't bring himself to do that. Not while the ghost of his childhood haunted him. Reluctantly he released her with a kiss on her forehead.

Ignoring his desire-filled organ bulging his shorts, he gazed into her eyes with heated intensity. "Maybe we should call it an evening," he said quietly, his heart pounding, his head throbbing.

"If you'd like to." Her gaze falling to the swell in his pants, Ashley giggled nervously. He didn't miss the disappointment settling in her features. "Um . . . would you care for another glass of wine before you leave?"

"Maybe not quite a full glass. While I'm waiting for a taxi. Would you join me?"

"Being the hostess, I could never let you drink alone." She poured the wine while Jordan dialed the phone and called for a cab.

"I had a great time, Ash," Jordan said, accepting the wine, then taking a sip. "Even the wine tastes special."

"Would you like me to put the remainder back in the bottle so you can take it home again?"

Jordan laughed. "No, thanks, witch. I'll content myself to drink it here. Tell you what. Save it. Randy Petersen should return to work Monday. I'd like you to fix a meal for him like you fixed for me. I'll buy whatever you want to prepare. If he's as impressed as I am, you may find yourself in a two-hat job."

"A two-hat job?"

"Yes. Assistant manager and chef," he teased.

Ashley chuckled. "That's very flattering, Jordan, but I think I'll stick with my new job as Senior Vice President of Operations."

"I wouldn't expect you to do any less. You are so good there." A horn blew outside, and Jordan downed his wine with one gulp. Ashley walked him to the door, where he kissed her thoroughly. He could do that now. He was leaving. His desire wouldn't overcome his resolve. "Good night, Ashley," he said hoarsely. "Sleep well." *He* wouldn't, not until Ashley was at his side.

Blowing a final kiss in her direction, he went down the walkway to the waiting cab parked at the curb.

Twenty-six

Ashley closed the door behind Jordan and leaned against it, her body afire. The remembered feel of his swollen manhood increased her own need. His maleness was huge, and she wondered how it would have felt to have Jordan filling her.

They had gone further than they ever had, and that fact only heartened her. If it hadn't been for Elvis's interruptions, she and Jordan surely would have made love.

Thoughts refocused on Elvis, Ashley cringed. She'd have to face his censure for her behavior. With dread, she slowly directed her steps to the sofa table that held her bowl.

Wine filled it. Sighing, she poured the wine from the bowl back into the bottle with schooled efficiency. She hurried into the kitchen and washed the cavity, carefully dried it, then put it back in its place on the table. The bowl glowed softly, and Ashley returned the check and pad to the bowl, dreading the words he'd write.

She stroked the rim. "Elvis," she said softly. "I'm so sorry you saw what you did. I apologize for not remembering you were here."

A moment of silence ensued. Thinking Elvis too disgusted to respond, Ashley bowed her head. The clicking began, and Ashley leaned over to see the disparaging remarks.

You already called me a pervert, Ashley. Am I to understand you are about to add voyeur to that?

"I didn't say that, Elvis. But you couldn't help but notice what went on between Jordan and me."

Couldn't I?

"What do you mean?"

I would never intrude on your private moments, my dear. And I didn't. I suspended my senses of sight and sound for your benefit.

"But how?"

Don't interrupt me, Ashley. I have magical powers and can do anything.

"Why did you flash your beam, if you weren't . . . um . . . intruding? That was the second time after all."

This time was an accident. I wondered if your guest had departed, so I reactivated my hearing. It was at that moment that I heard groans and moans of an extremely passionate nature. In my surprise, my light went on accidentally. I do apologize for that, Ashley. But the first time, well, I wasn't sure you were ready for such an occurrence. I'm sorry.

"Apology accepted," Ashley responded. "You are indeed a true gentleman. And by the way, thank you for tonight. The china, crystal, and silver . . . I mean *gold*ware were perfect. And the food was like nothing I've ever eaten before. Simply superb. But you could have given me a clue to what you had planned for me. Everything happened without warning."

Ha ha ha. Softly, Elvis wrote, getting the point across that he was chuckling softly. *Don't you find surprises titillating, Ashley? It wouldn't have been as much fun if you had known what was coming next.*

Ashley laughed. "You're right, of course. Anticipating your every action would have had me on pins and needles. But your way, you clever bowl, only had me on the edge of insanity. Especially when I saw the noodles emptying themselves into the colander."

My compliments, Ashley. Sort of . . . What is it you New Orleanians say? Lagniappe? Well, that's what it was. A little something extra. A gratis service.

"Elvis, I think you're wonderful. I'm glad you chose me."

So am I. Good night, Ashley.

Ashley slid her fingers around the bowl's rim, and its light glowed, soft and muted, filling her with a peaceful contentment. At that moment, she had absolutely no doubt of her feelings for Jordan. She loved him.

Yet even after the passion between them, she wondered about his feelings for her. He didn't use her to sate himself, he sated *her*.

Convinced that Jordan was fighting his growing love for her, Ashley shook her head. That wasn't a good sign. He might win his argument with himself and decide she wasn't worth the gamble.

Twenty-seven

~

"Hello, Mr. Petersen." On learning that Randy Petersen had
indeed returned to work on Monday, Ashley went down to
his office to welcome him back. The office was a small,
claustrophobic affair with one lone window. She didn't
know how Petersen could stay in there, sometimes for
hours on end, doing paperwork. "You were missed. Nice
to have you back."

She spoke sincerely. The poor man could have been injured worse than he was. Fortunately, because Elvis insti-
gated the accident, Petersen had only suffered a broken leg.
His return meant less frequent encounters with Jordan on a
day-to-day basis, however, since Mr. Petersen would resume his duties.

Jordan had reverted back to kind. After their erotic encounter Saturday night, she hadn't heard from him.

"Call me Randy," Mr. Petersen said. A warm smile lit
his mocha complexion. He sat at his desk, resting his cast-
covered broken leg on another chair, his crutches leaning
against the wall. "Thanks much for taking over for me."

"Think nothing of it, Mr. Pete . . . um . . . Randy. It was

a real pleasure. I suppose you know Jordan has created a signature dish for the hotel, and an ethnic food day called Savor the Ethnic Flavor Night. Different ethnic foods served one night a week—"

"I know," Randy interrupted. "We'll see how that works out. Of course, we'll still serve our standard menu for patrons who aren't ethnically oriented."

Ashley smiled. "That's a good idea. I'm sure Jordan intended to do that anyway."

"By the way, Miss Douglas—"

"Call me Ashley."

They both laughed.

"Ashley," Randy said, humor glinting from his dark eyes. "Jordan told me what a delicious meal you fixed him."

So he had been thinking of her. Ashley smiled. "He did say he was going to tell you about it. I'm thrilled he liked it so much."

"Well, he liked it better than that. He's invited me over to your place one day soon to savor your culinary skills. My question is, was the invitation your idea?"

"Who else's?" Ashley responded, twirling her hair through her fingers. *Who cares? As long as it keeps Jordan's attention focused on me.* "We'll pick a day and let you know. In the meantime, try to stay off your leg. I'm going to the kitchen to say hi to Jordan before I go back to my office. I'll see you later. So long."

"So long, Ashley. Thanks for stopping by."

Ashley reached the kitchen just in time to overhear one of the perpetual arguments between Jordan and Arthur. Curtis, who was pulling out pots and pans, listened intently but remained quiet for the moment. Ashley stopped by the huge refrigerator, out of sight for the time being.

"I said *no*, goddammit," Jordan growled. He paused in his furious chopping of shallots to glare at Arthur, then return to the vicious movements. "The odor would foul up the atmosphere."

Arthur threw garlic on the table by Jordan. Sitting on the stool, he began separating the cloves. "Yo, Jordan, my man. I can cook it at my house and *bring* it here. All you'd have to do is reheat it."

Grabbing another onion, Jordan shook his head. "Are you familiar with health laws, Arthur?"

"So?" Curtis asked, arranging two frying pans next to Jordan.

Jordan cleaved the onion in two additional sections. "So food served at the hotel must be cooked in *our* kitchen."

"So in other words what you sayin' is my kitchen ain't healthy?" Arthur asked indignantly.

"That must be 'xactly what he's sayin', Art," Curtis put in. "Since you ain't died from eatin' anything you cooked out of it, I don't see the problum."

"Hi, guys," Ashley said with a laugh, seeing the annoyed amusement on Jordan's face. He glanced at her and nodded. His sexy, half smile and raking gaze sent a dizzying charge through her body. "At it again, huh?"

"Ash, hey, baby," Arthur said, smiling at her. "Would you mind tellin' your friend here what a delicacy chitlins are? I mean, granted, they may stink up the place while you're cookin' 'em. But it's the eatin' we're aimin' at."

Ashley wrinkled her nose, very aware of Jordan watching her. She'd never tasted the stuff, but had heard of their rank odor. They were supposedly delicious once they were cooked. "Sorry, Art. You can't go by me. I've never eaten chitterlings."

Looking her up and down, Curtis frowned. "Chitterlings? Who said anything about chitterlings? It's *chitlins.* You people is too proper for me. You eat brains and kidneys and other organs, and think chitlins is below yo' taste buds."

"No, Curtis," Jordan growled, laying aside his knife and narrowing his eyes at his two assistants. "I just think they *stink*! And anything that doesn't *smell* like food can't possibly be edible. No chitterlings! Excuse me, *chitlins*! Now, if you don't mind, I'd like to have a word with my girl . . . I mean my *guest*. See how you guys confuse me?"

Arthur laughed wickedly and stood, abandoning his garlic. "That ain't confusion, man. That's lettin' us know where your mind is and what you wish. Ashley ain't interested in you, Jordan. You're too mean—"

"Arthur, shut up," Ashley commanded, her voice shaky with laughter. "Go cook something."

"Yeah, anything but *chitlins*," Jordan put in.

"Awright, Jordan," Arthur said, hands on hips, "make jokes. But that dish is a delicacy in my community. Tell you what, Jordie. I want you and Ash to come to my house for a dinner like you've never had before."

"I can believe that," Jordan mumbled.

"What's the matter, man, you chicken?" Arthur challenged.

Ashley giggled. Considering how much fun Arthur was on the job, on his own time he was probably a riot. Besides, she couldn't allow Jordan to lose face. Even if that meant eating pig intestines. "Just name the time, day, and place, Arthur, and we'll be there."

"Ashley!" Jordan yelled in disbelief, horror in his handsome face.

"My girl!" Arthur said, patting her back heartily, before waving a dismissing hand to Jordan. "Just forget him, Ash. I'll set it up for next Wednesday afternoon—"

Jordan's long-suffering sigh interrupted Arthur's plans. "If you're game to try it, Ash, I won't let you go it alone. Count me in, Arthur."

Arthur grinned broadly. "You won't regret it, man."

"I sure the hell hope not," Jordan returned, watching as

Curtis and Arthur told Ashley good-bye, then headed for the dining room.

Now that they were alone, awkward silence replaced the friendly sparring that had taken place. He remembered Ashley's embarrassment Saturday night. Part of the reason he'd neglected to telephone her yesterday was because he wasn't sure what to say to put her at ease. She had seemed happy Saturday night and she'd assured him she wasn't embarrassed, so maybe he should take her word for it.

It was so like her to be full of bubbly energy, despite whatever circumstances she faced. He'd intended to seek her out today to talk about Saturday night, but her visit made that unnecessary. Fearing she'd run off, he'd ease into the subject.

He massaged the back of his neck. "Petersen's back."

Ashley sat at the stool Arthur vacated. "I know," she responded, twirling her fingers on the butcher-block table.

He wished his body was beneath that whisper-soft touch instead of the inert object she offhandedly caressed.

"I just left his office," she continued, unaware of his thoughts. "He told me you invited him over to my place for a meal."

Jordan chuckled and sat across from her. That brilliant scent from her hair floated between them. "I hope you don't mind, Ash," he whispered. "I'm so proud of your accomplishments. I just want to shout them from the highest roof in the city."

Ashley glanced at him from the corner of her eye, the shy, flirty look enthralling. "That won't be necessary," she said with a laugh. "Why don't you and Randy plan to come over Saturday night?"

"Sounds good," Jordan said, his mouth dry with anticipation. He brought her hand to his mouth and placed a soft kiss on her palm. "Right after work. Providing, of course, Arthur's meal doesn't kill us on Wednesday."

"I heard **that**!" Arthur yelled, loping back into the kitchen.

"Me, too," Curtis replied, hot on his heels. "Arthur's gonna make you eat those words."

"Yeah? Well, that may be better than eating what he plans to serve," Jordan responded sardonically.

"Oh, God, not again," Ashley said, chuckling. Standing from her seat, she looked at Jordan. Fire heated his veins at the need in her eyes. "I believe this is where I came in. I just stopped by to say hello. And to tell you it's all right for Randy to have dinner with us."

Jordan kissed her cheek. "I'm glad you stopped by, Ash," he said huskily. "I've been thinking about you. About *us*."

"So have I," Ashley admitted shyly, refraining from looking at their captive audience. "I-I had a good time the other night."

"Yes, Ash. It was special." He brushed a silky lock of her hair behind her ear. "If I don't talk to you before Wednesday . . ." He turned to Arthur. "Exactly what time Wednesday are you expecting us?"

"About three-ish. The address is 3000 St. Charles Avenue."

"You live on St. Charles Avenue?" Jordan and Ashley chorused in surprise.

"You two got a problem with that?" Arthur asked.

Ashley arched her brows and bit down on her lip before responding. The apartments and houses on St. Charles Avenue were high-priced. "Why, er, no. No, not at all, Arthur," she managed. "We'll see you there on Wednesday. Thanks for inviting us, Art."

Appearing to enjoy the shock on Ashley's and Jordan's features, Arthur grinned. "My pleasure."

"I'm very impressed, Arthur," Jordan said, recovering from his surprise. "The Avenue is a very prestigious address. Grand old mansions. Expensive apartment buildings—"

"So?" Curtis interjected.

Jordan scowled. "What an instigator. But not this time, Curt. I'm not biting. I probably won't get to see you until Wednesday. I'm going to be very busy here in the restaurant. I also had a, er, small accident at my house, and to defray costs I've been helping the contractor redo the wallpaper. I'll do my best to call you tonight. That, I promise."

Ashley hugged Jordan. "That's fine," she said, tempering her happiness in the presence of Curtis and Arthur. "So long, guys. Try not to torment Jordan too much."

Back in her office, Ashley stared unseeing out of her window, arms folded. A sixth sense told her Elvis was somehow responsible for the invitation she and Jordan got from Arthur. But to a meal of *chitlins*?

Obviously Elvis seemed to be helping her obtain her goal. He appeared to get some sort of perverse satisfaction in making her squirm for that aid, however.

If he had to plant a dinner menu in Arthur's head, why couldn't it have been lobster? Or steak? Or pheasant and truffles? Why pig parts?

Oh, well. Anything worth having is worth fighting for. Even if the menu caused her to lose one battle, she still had confidence enough to believe she'd win the war.

Settling herself at her desk for her day's work, she couldn't wait to get home to confront her magic bowl with the devilish sense of humor.

Twenty-eight

~

You're late.

Ashley had been in only long enough to turn on a light, drop her things on the sofa, and peer into the bowl's cavity. She'd gone to her parents' house for dinner tonight, where Zach had been conspicuously absent. He probably thought Jordan would be there.

Your phone's been ringing most of the evening. It's Jordan. Must be urgent. He's been quite persistent.

"Hi, Elvis. I can't imagine what urgency it could be. I think he's only keeping his promise to call me."

I see. I've missed you, Ashley. I find I've grown accustomed to your incessant chatter.

Ashley patted Elvis's rim, the only other way, besides talking to him, she could communicate her feelings. "Thanks, Ambrose. I'm quite fond of you, too."

Ambrose? How would you like to be turned into a grass inhabitant?

Ashley laughed. "I'm sorry, Elvis. I just couldn't resist. I want to thank you for getting Arthur to invite me and Jordan to dinner, but did you have to make it chitlins?"

The rapid clicks produced *ha-ha's* on the pad. *Ashley, my dear, I fix it so you and Jordan can be thrown together as much as possible. But what you do or eat when you're together, I leave up to you.*

"Well, I can't refuse to eat Arthur's food, Elvis," Ashley lamented. "He'll probably put a lot of time into it."

Of course he will. He'll do his best. You and Jordan are his friends. Just show him that he is yours. By the way, young lady, where were you this evening?

"Well, sir, if it's all right with you, I went to my parents house for something to eat, even though this is Monday and Tuesday is my usual day to eat there. Is that okay with you?"

A-okay, Ash. Would you be kind enough to put an Elvis CD in the player, please?

Ashley smiled. "For you? With the greatest pleasure."

Elvis glowed a muted white just as the phone started ringing.

"Hullo?" she said, going to the CD player. Once she inserted the disc, she turned the sound low.

"Hi, Ashley."

"Jordan?"

"Yeah. Am I disturbing you?"

Ashley sat on the sofa, giddy. "Oh, no, not at all. Elvis told me . . . er . . . um . . . I mean *you* told me you would call, remember? So I was expecting your call."

"Who's Elvis?" The confusion was clear in his voice.

"Who?" Ashley asked, feigning surprise, damning her slip. "Elvis? Did I say Elvis?"

"Yes, Ashley, you did."

She searched her mind for a plausible excuse. Either Jordan would believe there was another man in her life or he'd think her a complete do-do brain. "Ah, yes, I know. I have a one-track mind, Jordan. I just put on an Elvis CD, and his name became indelible in my brain." *God, I'd better start thinking before I speak.*

"You're quite an Elvis fan, aren't you?"

"Quite." One word should suffice to keep her out of trouble.

"Ashley, I had an idea—and it wasn't about Elvis—that I wanted your input on."

Wanting to discern the reason for the seriousness of his tone, she wished she could see his face at that moment. Still, it surprised her that he wanted her input on anything. Jordan thought enough of her to ask her advice about something. "Me?" she asked, all ears to whatever it was.

"Yes, you," he said with a chuckle. "What would your reaction be if I told you that I am seriously thinking of opening my own restaurant?"

For a split second, Ashley sat speechless. Jordan was talking about spending a lot of money, which is what it took to open a restaurant, even with investors. Could he possibly have *that* kind of money?

"Ash?"

"Um, yes, Jordan. I think that's a sterling idea. But you're talking about a lot of money. If you would like, I can look into the particulars for you, to see how much money you'll need up front. Then, if it's more than you can afford, you might consider a partner. You're looking at a lot of hard work, but it sounds quite exciting."

Jordan's rich baritone laughter floated through the receiver. "I didn't expect such enthusiasm from you, Ash. I must confess, my admiration for you grew by another leap when you said considering a partner could save me money."

Ashley wished she could dissolve through the phone and fall into his arms. He admired her for trying to save him money. Never mind that he was thinking of loosening his pursestrings to spend money, she was trying to show him how to be frugal. That wasn't lost to him. Could life get any more ironically sweet?

"Suppose we discuss this further on Wednesday after dinner, sweetheart? I'd really like your input."

"All right, Jordan. I'll see you then."

"Good night, darling. Pleasant dreams."

The phone went silent, and Ashley clicked it off, then placed it back on the coffee table. "Good night, my love," she whispered.

Twenty-nine

~

Ashley saw the same look of astonishment on Jordan's face that she knew was written on her own when they arrived at Arthur's place Wednesday afternoon.

A housekeeper dressed in a black and white uniform opened the door to them and led them to a strikingly beautiful living room.

"Mr. Franklin is gonna be right wid you," the woman said. "He say look aroun'."

"Okay," Ashley said, dumbfounded.

"I'll tell Mr. Franklin ya'll here. Please make yourselfs comfo'table. By the way, I'm Emma."

"Thank you, Emma," Jordan said quietly, indicating the rendition of Picasso's *The Old Guitarist* above the sofa.

Ashley's mouth dropped open, and she barely noticed Emma's departure through the adjoining door.

Ashley and Jordan took a quick tour of the spacious apartment. It was a showplace, appointed with beautiful, traditional furniture and one-of-a-kind knickknacks. Expensive artwork—Degas, Renoir, Monet, and Cassatt—lined the walls. A plush Persian rug laid beneath the mahogany dining room table.

By the time they returned to the living room and sat on the sofa, the door opened and Arthur appeared with a young woman holding on to his arm.

"Ashley. Jordan. So glad you could make it," Arthur said warmly, advancing to where they sat. "I'd like you to meet my lady. This is Okimba. She's from Ethiopia."

Thick, black braids fell past Okimba's shoulders. Full lips, a small nose, and high cheekbones in a tan, heart-shaped face gave the sloe-eyed beauty an exotic look.

Ashley smiled and extended her hand to the girl. "Hello, Okimba. I'm pleased to meet you."

Okimba took the proffered hand and pumped vigorously. Her broad smile revealed perfect white teeth. "Hello, Ashley." She nodded to Jordan. "Hello, Jordan. Welcome to our home. Arta has told me much about you."

A smile lit Jordan's eyes. "Can't say the same about him," he muttered. "But thank you for the warm welcome, Okimba."

"Ain't she something, man?" Arthur asked proudly. "Don't get me wrong now. Although there's nothing wrong with American women, they couldn't touch my Kimby. She hangs on my every word."

"We'll have to fix that, won't we?" Jordan asked with a straight face.

Ashley pinched him, then turned to Arthur. "She's very beautiful, Art."

"Thanks, Ash." Arthur walked to the bar. "Yo, Jordie, my man, name your poison. I got it right here." He gestured with a sweep of his hands to the many bottles that lined the shelves on the wall behind the counter. "You, too, Ash."

"Do you have any chilled white wine?" Ashley asked, near to bursting from curiosity. Arthur was obviously wealthy. Or was it Okimba's money he lived off?

"Yes," Okimba piped up. "Arta said he chill white wine especially for you. Allow me to get for you."

"Yo, yo, yo, Kimby, baby," Arthur chastised. "That's what I pay that woman in the kitchen for. Just chill and let *her* ass serve."

"Of course, Arta," Okimba responded in her delightful accent.

"Yo, Emma!" Arthur yelled. "Front and center, baby."

The door swung opened immediately, and Emma emerged. A dish towel flung over her shoulder, she placed her hands on her hips. Fire in her eyes, she moved her head in a manner that suggested she was ready for war. "Listen, you stunted lil' fur ball. I ain't yo' baby. And don't *ever* yell at me like I'm some kinda soldier. Front and center, my ass! Winnin' that lott'ry last month might have given yo' ass money, but you still ain't got a ounce of class, you lil' toad." She threw the dish towel on the floor and kicked it toward him. "On second thought, you lil' sumbitch, I quit!"

"Wait, wait, is that a way to treat me? I'll pay you double. Keep your ass from workin' in that hot sun diggin' them ditches anyway."

Emma took a step toward him, and Arthur backed away.

"Yo, Emma, just kiddin'. You can hate me all you want to, 'cause you ain't rich and beautiful like me, but don't hate my poor little Okimba. You can't leave all this mess for her to clean."

"What!" Ashley jumped to her feet. "Arthur Franklin!"

"Stay out of it, Ashley," Jordan ordered, pulling her down. "I'm enjoying this."

"The hell I'll stay out of it, Jordan Bennett!" Ashley snarled. "I won't even stay and eat if Okimba has to clean up after us."

"Maybe that's one way for us to get out of eating pig shi—"

"Jordan!" Ashley interrupted.

Glaring at Emma and ignoring everyone else, Arthur grunted. "Now see what you went and did, Miss Emma? My guests are leavin'."

"*Miz* Emma, huh, rat face? Is you ready to respeck me now, Arthur?"

"Yes, ma'am," Arthur gritted through clenched teeth. "I'm ready to respect your ass. I'm sorry, big sister."

"Sister?" Ashley sputtered. "You're his sister, Emma?"

"Surely is," Emma said. "At the moment, though, I feel like disinheritin' his sorry ass."

"Arthur!" Ashley shouted.

"*Tsk, tsk,*" Jordan put in, shaking his head. "That's low, Arthur."

"Now ya'll jus' calm down," Emma said. "Art's a good boy. He give me and Mama everything we want, includin' a house. But he likes ya'll and wanted to impress ya'll. So he done ask me to help out. Only thing is, he forgot his place."

Bowing his head, Arthur sighed. "I apologize to everybody. I guess I made a good ass out of myself."

"Surely did," Emma told him. "And fo' that, you'll be the waiter, the cook, and the clean-up crew. Now get in that kitchen and fetch that wine. Make sure you remember to put 'nuff glasses on the tray to serve me, too."

Order was eventually restored—after a fashion. But Emma threw barbs to a chastened Arthur on a whim, leaving Ashley and Jordan to be the amused spectators, while Okimba looked on without a hint to her thoughts. They enjoyed a round of drinks, then Arthur made his way to the kitchen. When he finally announced it was time for dinner, he was wearing a flower-designed apron, which threw Jordan into a fit of laughter.

"Man, shut your damned mouth," Arthur said with traces of laughter in his voice. "You ain't funny."

"You sure the hell are," Jordan said. "If only Curtis could see you now."

"Ah, hell no. I'd have to tape that boy's mouth up to keep it shut. Be right back." Arthur returned in moments, carrying a glass tray loaded with plates of salad.

This course consisted of avocado, lettuce, grapefruit, and orange slices, bacon crunch, and oil and vinegar dressing. Ashley thought the salad was filling all by itself, but Arthur insisted they try his oyster soup before eating the main course.

Ashley didn't protest. If he continued to serve courses before the entree, she'd probably be too full to eat the chitlins.

Jordan laid down his spoon after devouring the soup. "Arthur, you're an excellent cook. The soup was delicious."

"Ain't it, though?" Arthur slurped a spoonful. "Outdid myself this time."

"So you won the lottery, Arthur, and kept it a secret, huh?" Ashley asked, filling her spoon with the soup again. "I'm hurt."

"I didn't keep it a secret, Ash," Arthur said, pushing his bowl away from him. "I just forgot to tell you. Listen, I'll just give you an extra helpin' of chitlins to make it up to you."

"Oh, no!" Ashley blurted. "Don't do that, Art. I'm not *that* hurt!"

"Okimba?" Jordan asked, frowning as Emma picked up her bowl and downed her soup. Arthur threw his napkin at her. "Uh, do you like chitlins?"

"I don't think so," Okimba answered softly.

Laying her fork aside, Ashley widened her gaze. "You don't? Have you ever tasted them?"

"No."

"You know how some people are, Ashley," Arthur said. "They don't eat pork. But once she tries this, she'll love it." Standing up, he brushed the wrinkles from his apron. "The moment of truth has arrived." He went into the kitchen and soon brought out two plates for Ashley and Jordan, then two more for Emma and Okimba, and finally one for himself. "Ain't you gonna eat them, Ashley?"

With a nervous laugh, Ashley looked down at her plate. The aroma tantalized her nostrils. Seasonings, parsley, scallions, and green pepper colored a red tomato sauce, ladened with curly pieces of meat and spread over white rice. She glanced at Jordan, who rubbed the back of his neck.

"Smells delicious," she said, tentatively testing the food with her fork before tasting it.

"Brave girl," Jordan murmured.

"I heard that, Jordan!" Arthur shouted.

"Shut up, fool!" Emma said around the food in her mouth. "You can't help but hear the man, since you sittin' at this table."

Ashley speared another piece of meat and put it in her mouth, chewing thoughtfully. "It's good." She nodded to Jordan. "It really *is* good, Jordie."

Scowling ferociously, Jordan tasted his food. "Hmm," he said, surprised. He tasted more. "Umm, you're right, Ashley. It's quite tasty."

"Told you," Arthur said triumphantly. He frowned at his girlfriend. "Kimby, you haven't tried yours, baby."

Okimba smiled serenely. "Thank you, Arta, but I pass. If I am going to try pork, I would rather start with bacon."

"Good for you, Okimba," Ashley said. Although eating chitlins wasn't as disgusting as she'd first imagined, it was definitely an acquired taste. The small amount she'd sampled, though very good, was enough for her. Just knowing what it was proved a turnoff. She pushed her plate back. "I have a tiny empty space left," she said when Arthur raised his eyebrows in question, "and that's for dessert."

Emma pushed her empty plate aside and stood. The woman really didn't waste time eating. "I'll get the dessert. You start clearin' the table, Artie."

"Yes, ma'am, Miss Emma," Arthur said, saluting his sister.

The dessert, warm apple pie topped with vanilla ice cream, cloves, cinnamon, and rum, was the piece de resistance to Ashley, a delicious end to a somewhat ambiguous meal. Afterward, Arthur led them back to the living room for after-dinner liqueurs.

"Ashley, Jordan," Emma said, coming in carrying her purse. "Been a pleasure meetin' ya'll. I gots to go, but I hopes to see ya'll again. Bye."

"Bye, Emma. The pleasure was all mine," Ashley said, smiling.

"Yeah, we'll see you again, I'm sure," Jordan put in.

"So long, big sister." Arthur hugged her tightly. "Thanks."

"Good-bye, Miz Franklin," Okimba said shyly.

"Call her ass Emma, Kimby," Arthur said.

Okimba looked from the intimidating pose Emma presented as she narrowed her eyes at her brother, to the mischievous Arthur, who smiled at his sister innocently.

"Baby, that's okay. By the time I get around to poppin' the question, you'll be used to it."

"By the time you gets around to poppin' the question, that lil' girl will need to call me Miz Franklin, 'cause I'll have one foot in the grave."

"Bye, Emma," Arthur said, ignoring her latest barb.

Emma departed, and Ashley listened to the mundane, sometimes boring conversation with little interest. By six o'clock, she was long ready to excuse herself with Jordan and end the evening, but Arthur's antics turned serious and commanded her attention.

He mentioned to Jordan that he'd given most of his million-dollar lottery winnings away to help friends and family—and, of course, to pay the taxes on the money. He had a couple of hundred thousand left and wanted to invest in something. "Do you have any ideas, man?"

Jordan glanced at Ashley. Seeing her nod, he cleared his throat. "Have you ever thought about opening your own restaurant?' "

"My own restaurant?" Arthur echoed. "Man, I wouldn't know the first thing about runnin' a restaurant."

"Do you know how to run a restaurant, Jordan?" Okimba asked.

"What I don't know I could always learn," Jordan answered with a shrug.

"Really?" Arthur sat up straighter in his seat, his dark brown eyes lighting up. "Jor-*dan*, my main man," he said, rhyming the last syllable of Jordan with man.

"Cut the crap, Art," Jordan said.

Ashley held her breath for what was coming next. This was the backer Jordan needed in his quest to open his own restaurant.

"Yo, Jordie, what I don't know I could learn, too. Maybe we could learn together."

"Exactly what are you saying, Arthur?" Jordan asked.

"Well, er, we could kinda, like, go in together, Jordie."

"As partners?" Ashley questioned, exasperated at how long it was taking them to get this out in the open.

Okimba clapped her hands together. "How wonderful. Do you agree, Ashley?"

She nodded vigorously. "Wholeheartedly. But it's up to them."

Arthur stared at Jordan, all fun and games gone from his features. "What d'ya say, Jordan? Even our ladies want to see us give it a try."

Our ladies? Ashley glanced in Jordan's direction to see

his reaction to that. He merely smiled seductively at her and turned his attention back to Arthur. Ashley's breath caught. Was he truly beginning to think of her as *his* lady? Did they in fact have a future together?"

"There seems to be something strange at work lately," Jordan said. "Ashley and I discussed my opening a restaurant a few days ago, and now the very same idea hits you. Well, I suggested it, but you're all for it."

"Sure am," Arthur said. "We could train my main man, Curtis, to become head chef—"

"I'd love to go in with you, Arthur," Jordan interrupted, "but I'll have to give it some thought and there are differences we have to iron out. If we can't agree on a specific thing, we either compromise or throw it out. There'll be no bosses. We'll be *equal* partners."

"Listen, Jordie, man. I know you've had experience in running restaurants for other folks, so you know what you're doing. I've seen your work. You're a great cook. I have a lot of learning to do, so I'd appreciate it if you were at the helm. That means being the boss. For a while, at least," Arthur said with a chuckle.

Jordan grinned. "Couldn't keep it straight, huh, Art? All right. I'm grateful for your confidence. It's a big step, and I prefer caution over rashness. If I decide to accept your offer, I promise I'll steer us in the right direction. Give me a year. In that year, I'll expect you to learn everything there is to know about the restaurant business. After that we'll sink or swim. As equal partners."

Arthur swiped at his eyes with his hand. "Jordie, my man," he sniffled. "You're a good dude."

"So are you, dude. Now knock off the crocodile tears."

Thanks, Elvis, Ashley found herself thinking. *What a roundabout way you have of doing things.* She had absolutely no idea of Jordan's finances, but Arthur's offer would certainly ease the burden of going it alone. She hated to admit that she was actually worried about Jordan's finances, when *he* didn't seem to be. Now all she needed was for him to admit his true feelings to her.

"Would you like another drink, Ashley?" Okimba asked, gently interrupting Ashley's satisfying thoughts.

"Yes, Okimba," Ashley responded. "Only this time make it a Coke." She didn't want alcohol giving her a false impression of the evening. Thoroughly enjoying herself again, she wasn't even in a rush to leave anymore.

The conversation, the company, was great. Okimba was gracious and exquisitely beautiful. And Arthur . . . well, was still Arthur. No matter how serious he became, his playful personality always exhibited itself. Thinking further, she had no problem believing that he'd given away most of his lottery winnings. Arthur Franklin was one of the kindest men she knew.

Glancing around the room, her gaze fell on Jordan where he sat at the bar with Arthur. Jordan winked at her, and she smiled back.

Shoot! If her heart wasn't embedded safely in her chest, it would have burst right through! Elvis had better damn well hurry and work his magic before she succumbed to love sickness or made a fool of herself over Jordan in some unladylike way.

Okimba handed her a glass of Coke with ice. "Here you are, Ashley."

"Thanks, Okimba," Ashley responded, as Arthur handed Jordan a CD.

"My Kimby likes reggae music, Jordie," Arthur said proudly. Frowning at the apron he still wore, he cursed softly, then took it off and threw it on the bar. "Ya'll mind listening' to that? Or do you and Ashley have a preference for any music?"

"Doesn't everyone?" Jordan countered good-naturedly. Winking at Ashley as she and Okimba joined them at the bar, he handed the CD back to Arthur and laughed. "We like reggae, Art. Put something on and show us how to dance to it."

Arthur hooted with laughter. "I can't wait to see that!"

"Ignore him," Okimba said, waving her hand in dismissal, in a perfect imitation of Emma. "You don't necessarily have to dance to the riddums. You can take your movements where the music brings you." She swayed to and fro, left to right, her body fluid and sensual in its motion, her long braids swinging.

"We can do that," Ashley said happily. She hoped her movements were as erotic and had the same effect on Jordan that Okimba's seemed to have on Arthur.

He pulled Okimba into his arms and kissed her shamelessly, then whispered something into her ear. She giggled and playfully swatted his shoulder.

Sitting on the bar stool, Jordan drew Ashley down onto his lap. She wrapped her arms around his neck and nuzzled his ear. "Are you game?" she whispered.

His soft groan was low and primitive. " "For you, I would try anything. I'll even risk Arthur's ridicule, if you'd join me in making a fool of myself."

Laughing, Ashley rewarded him with a brief kiss on his lips. "How can I refuse when you put it that way?"

"All right, Art," Jordan boomed with confidence, his raging arousal pressing against Ashley's buttocks. "Bring on your music."

"Ha-ha! Jordie, my man!" Going to the entertainment center on the other side of the room, Arthur soon had the room vibrating with the Caribbean music.

Jordan held Ashley around her waist with both hands; she slid her arms around his neck. Gazing into each other's eyes, they swayed rhythmically, before Jordan stopped and kissed her feverishly. Delicious sensation coursed through

Ashley, and she nibbled his tongue, returning his kiss with all the pent-up frustrations within her.

When he lifted his head, she buried her face in his neck, the faintly spicy cologne mingling with his male scent. Their bodies molded, melded, their movements sensual, sensuous, transporting her with utter pleasure.

Ashley glanced over at Okimba and Arthur. They, too, were lost in their own world, their motions in tune to the music, a visual aphrodisiac, fluid, erotic, and beautiful. As the music died down, Jordan gave her one last, quick kiss.

"Jordan, you are matchless," Ashley said, breathless.

"Matchless?" Arthur echoed with a laugh, still holding onto Okimba. "Ash, don't fill him with false confidence. He might make a mistake and dance in public like that. People might think he's a comedian instead of a great chef."

Jordan laughed. "Thanks, Arthur. But I think Ashley and I did as well as you and Okimba. Now try to remember you're the host here and get me another drink." He finished his wine. "I'm trying to drink enough to make me forget that main course you served tonight."

"That's uncalled for, Jordan." Arthur feigned indignation. "That has nothin' to do with the fact that you can't dance."

Okimba leaned her head against Arthur's chest. "But he can. He and Ashley danced to the music's rhythm, Arta."

"I know, Kimby. I know. I was just teasin'," Arthur said, running his fingers through her braids. "Would you and Ash care for somethin' to drink?"

"We're drinking Coke," Ashley announced, pointing to her glass.

"*Coke!*" Arthur sputtered.

"Yes, Coke," Ashley repeated. "I don't want to drink anything stronger."

"You ladies just leave that to me," Arthur said gleefully,

heading for his wet bar. "I'll fix you a drink that's tasty and mellow. Strictly a ladies' drink. I call it Willin' Lady Punch."

Ashley glanced from Arthur to Jordan. Noticing Jordan's encouraging nod, she laughed. "Willing Lady Punch? I don't know if I like the sound of that."

"I certainly do," Jordan put in. "What's in it, Art?"

"All kinds of fruit juices—fruit punch, orange juice, grapefruit juice, pineapple juice—and a few other things. Also, there's a little alcohol. Rum and tequila."

"Sounds delicious," Okimba said enthusiastically.

"Yeah," Ashley agreed. "I'd like to try it."

Arthur grinned slyly and nudged Jordan. "Two Willin' Ladies coming up!"

After the first drink, Ashley felt her inhibitions loosening. Responding to Jordan's kisses and hugs, she was mellow and definitely willing. By the third drink, she was living a dream; she also had boundless energy and amazing rhythm. But after a few hours of reggae music, Caribbean beats, and two more drinks, her strength ebbed.

In a fog she heard Jordan comment on the late hour. Then she hugged Okimba and Arthur good night, before she and Jordan got into a waiting taxicab, the magical evening dancing in her head.

Thirty

Ashley stirred in her bed as the insistent buzzing of the alarm clock seeped into her brain. "Go away," she murmured sleepily. But the noise was relentless. "Umm . . . wha . . . ?" Abruptly she sat up and held her head in her hands to cease the pounding. "Ohhhh," she moaned.

Squeezing her eyes shut, then opening them again, she looked at the clock. Nine-thirty! That couldn't be right. The alarm was supposed to go off at seven o'clock. What happened? She should have been at work a half hour already.

She swung her legs over the side of the bed, vowing her next project was to slay Arthur in a vicious, inhumane manner. That damned drink he'd concocted! Strictly a ladies' drink, he'd said. Well, her head was pounding in a most *un*ladylike manner.

Granted, she'd enjoyed the evening immensely. She had been with Jordan, after all. Ensconced in Arthur's beautiful apartment, they'd been a true couple. For Ashley, it was a lifelong dream come true. Okimba and Arthur had been in their own little world as well, and barely noticed Ashley and Jordan's loveplay because of their own.

When they had finally left, at nearly four in the morning, Ashley fell asleep in the cab, and Jordan deposited her inside her apartment. Everything after that was fuzzy.

She stood up, but one of the layers of clothes she wore bunched around her middle. Frowning, she looked down at herself. What the hell was she wearing?

A silk nightie covered a pair of long-sleeved, cotton pajamas. A summer robe hung from her body, fastened to her by the belt that was tied around her waist. On her feet, she wore thick booties.

"Oh, God," she lamented. "I couldn't have been that drunk!" She had started for the bathroom when she noticed the bright beam under the crack of her closed door. "Elvis!"

Already late for work, a few minutes with Elvis wouldn't make that much of a difference. When she went to the bowl, the clicking sound began immediately.

Good morning, Ashley. You seem vexed about something.

"Good morning, Elvis. Yes, I am vexed," Ashley gritted, squeezing her throbbing temples. "I'm late for work. Even *I* consider getting drunk and not being able to get to work on time irresponsible. I can just imagine what Jordan is thinking."

What an actress you would make. You are quite dramatic, Ashley. Don't go on so.

"Well, if you were about to lose the man you love and your job all in one fell swoop, you would go on, too!" Ashley complained.

Be at ease, Ashley. You're not expected at work today until noon. Therefore, Jordan won't think you're irresponsible.

"But . . . but how? What did you do?"

Poor Ashley. You must have been more intoxicated than I realized. I instructed you to place a call to your boss this morning when you went to the, uh, ladies room. Don't you remember?

"No."

Tsk. Tsk. You told Mr. Russell not to expect you before noon and that you'd explain when you saw him.

"What? What am I supposed to tell him, if I don't even remember calling him in the first place?"

Come on, Ashley. You don't expect me to do everything, do you? I was kind enough to dress you for bed last night. Well, more like this morning.

"*You* dressed me?"

Yes.

"Did you have to put more than one outfit on me?" Ashley grouched, then frowned. "How exactly did you do it? Birds don't have hands, after all."

I merely commanded your favorite night garments to clothe you.

Ashley giggled at the thought. No wonder she had three different outfits on. "I'm sorry, Elvis. You're too good to me. Did you know Jordan and Arthur may go into business together?"

Indeed I do.

"Was that the purpose of the dinner?"

The purpose was twofold. One, so you could learn of Arthur Franklin's generosity. Two, and most importantly, to get you and Jordan together for an evening.

"Did you have anything to do with the food?"

No. Arthur really is a good soul food cook.

Ashley smiled. "Thank you, Elvis. Now, I must get ready for work."

Elvis's light receded, and Ashley went into the kitchen to put on some coffee.

Thirty-one

~

"Harry, if you don't get your junk out of my bedroom post-haste, I'll put it out on the trash heap where it belongs." Ashley issued that ultimatum to her landlord two days later as she spruced up her apartment for her dinner with Petersen and Jordan that night.

"All right, all right," Harry relented. "I know when to quit. What's this guy got that I haven't got anyway?"

"Me!" Ashley answered smugly. She watched Harry carry his pink flamingo to the front door and make three more trips for the other garden items.

"Thanks for keeping 'em, Ashley," Harry said when he'd taken the last piece out. "Are you sure you won't come over for a drink and some hanky-panky? You never know until you try it if you'll like it."

"Trust me, Harry," Ashley said, opening the door, "I already know. In any case, I'll pass. Good-bye, Harry."

Harry placed his hand on his heart. "Not good-bye, my dearest. So long until we meet again."

Ashley slammed the door on his last annoying word, then

went back to her chores. She expected Jordan to drop by later with the food he wanted her to cook.

Since Wednesday she had been constantly at Jordan's side while he and Arthur discussed their business deal with great excitement. She'd been so enthralled she hadn't even conversed with Elvis. She and Okimba were becoming fast friends, making outings all the more pleasurable.

Supreme contentment surging through her, Ashley collapsed on the sofa, surveying her sparkling premises. She'd done such a superb job of cleaning up, even she had to compliment herself. Noting how far she'd come in the months on her own, she smiled to herself. At her parents' home there was always someone to clean up behind her. She never dreamed she'd ever have to clean up after herself, or that she'd even know how to do so.

When she rested her legs on the coffee table, it dawned on her that it wouldn't be able to accommodate three for dinner. Well, she had a set of cherrywood snack tables. She would set them up with placemats.

Ashley reached over and patted Elvis's rim. The bowl glowed softly, just as a knock on the door sounded.

"Not now, my friend. I still have things to do. I have to set up the snack tables and prepare the food Jordan brings. Besides, I don't want him to know about you just yet."

The knock sounded again, and Ashley stood. Elvis's light receded slowly.

Opening the door, she found Jordan on the other side, his arms filled with grocery bags. He followed her to the kitchen and dropped the bags on the counter, then stood back while she took the groceries out.

He'd brought rock cornish hens, wild rice, peas and carrots, and the special recipes that he wanted her to replicate. Stuck in the bottom of one bag was also his recipe for crepes with strawberries and cottage cheese.

"Want some help?" Jordan asked, watching her intently.

"Not on your life," Ashley answered smugly, happily confident of Elvis's magical assistance. She shoved the recipes back at Jordan. "And I don't need these. I have everything covered."

Jordan stuffed the pieces of paper into his top pocket. "Then I won't disturb you. I'll just see what's on TV, if you don't mind."

"Go ahead. Just remember, this kitchen is off limits."

"Fine," Jordan said with a laugh, brushing her lips with a kiss before leaving her alone.

As though she knew what she was doing, she went about preparing things for cooking. Putting the peas and baby carrots in a sauce pan, she decided as an afterthought to add water before turning on the heat.

Next, without removing the three Cornish hens from their wrappers because she remembered a dish her mother liked that called for the fowl to be cooked in a wrapping, she greased a baking dish for good measure, then placed the birds inside. That done, she put the wild rice into a large pot and filled it with water.

Anticipating the tasty dishes Elvis would create, she moved on to the crepes. Washing the strawberries, then opening the package of cottage cheese, she poured the fruit over it, then folded the entire box of crepe dough into that mixture. Over that, she dumped a quart of milk. All of this she put into the refrigerator to chill until Elvis was ready.

To make her cooking seem legitimate, Ashley put the hens in the oven and turned it on. She wasn't sure how high to make the heat, so she turned the dial until it caught and couldn't go anymore.

She nodded, satisfied with her work. Seeing the vegetable and rice boiling furiously, she lowered the heat under each burner as a precaution. As she joined Jordan in the living room, she felt confident that Elvis would signal her when the food was ready.

Thirty-two

~

Five minutes after she went into the living room to join Jordan, Randy Petersen arrived. While she was disappointed that she didn't have more time alone with Jordan, she was genuinely happy that Randy was so enthused about tasting her cooking. She went into the kitchen to get refreshments for the three of them, and checked her food for good measure.

Noticing that Elvis hadn't yet worked his magic, she frowned. Immediately shrugging away her concern, she returned to the men, carrying a tray with glasses and a bottle of chardonnay, as well as a Seven-Up for herself.

For the next half hour, the talk centered on the new venture Jordan was considering. Randy approved but was loath to see Jordan leave the restaurant, especially since he'd be taking both Arthur and Curtis with him.

"I'm going to do my best to persuade Ashley to join me as well," Jordan replied.

Joy flared through Ashley. Such a statement clued everyone in to his true feelings. When would he ever confess them to her?

"Is that so?" Randy asked good-naturedly. "I don't think Mr. Russell will let her go that easily."

"Yeah, Jordie," Ashley inserted, catching a whiff of burning cellophane. Frowning, she sniffed the air. It wasn't a pleasant odor. "Uh—"

Arcing a brow, Jordan stared at her. "Ash, did you forget about something?" he asked casually.

"No! No," she said, jumping from her seat. "I'll check the pots. Excuse me." She fairly flew to the kitchen—and was sorry she did when she got there.

The water had boiled out of the rice and vegetables. The peas and carrots were stuck to the pot, where smoke was just beginning to fan the air. But the hens caused her the most horror.

Extricating them from the oven, burned and melted cellophane covered their surface. What had she done wrong? The last time she'd prepared the dinner, Elvis did all the work. Now he'd allowed her to ruin everything?

Panicked, she glanced at the bowl. "Elvis! I need you." She waited a moment, hoping Elvis would change the food to a delicious creation, but nothing happened. *"Elvis!"*

"Ashley, can you use some help in there?" Jordan's concerned voice floated to her from the living room.

"No!" she snapped, trembling with mortification. Realizing her tone would have Jordan rushing in, she swallowed hard, striving for calm. "I mean, thank you, but I can handle it."

If only she were being truthful; but Jordan was counting on her to impress Randy. She just couldn't fail him. He'd never forgive her. Elvis *had* to help her.

Rushing to the refrigerator, she checked the crepes. Strawberries floated on the top of the bowl, mingling with lumps of flour. She gasped in horror.

What was Elvis doing to her? After all the help he'd

given her to win Jordan over, he couldn't desert her now. How could he let her down so cruelly?

Close to tears, she slammed the refrigerator door closed. Well, she wouldn't be defeated. The dinner didn't look all that appetizing, but maybe Elvis was using his magic in a different way tonight. Perhaps this food was as tasty as the first meal she'd served.

Immediately Ashley set to work scraping the wrapping and burned skin off the Cornish hens. She carefully removed the crisp meat, placing them on individual plates, followed by the scorched vegetables and mushy rice.

Forgetting entirely the salad Jordan wanted her to prepare, as well as the water and wine, she brought the plates into the living room and placed them before her guests.

Jordan and Randy exchanged puzzled glances, and Ashley closed her eyes in dread, her heart sinking.

"Taste it," she murmured, praying for salvation.

Narrowing his eyes at the mess on the plate, Jordan pointed to it. "What's this, Ashley?" he asked testily.

Ashley smiled timidly. "It's . . . it's the main course. Dig in, guys."

Staring at her in confusion, Jordan picked up the plate and took a forkful of rice. He tasted the rice, swallowing it after a couple of chews. Throwing her a menacing look, he tried the vegetables. Same reaction.

Randy tested the Cornish hen—and gagged. With high drama, he took his napkin, covered his mouth, and released the food into it.

Twisting her hands nervously, Ashley shifted her weight. She didn't know what to say.

"Are you sure this is the same woman whose food you've been raving about, Jordan?" Randy growled, glaring at Ashley. "Why, the little poultry bag is still inside my hen."

"Mine, too," Jordan snarled, setting his plate on the coffee table and jumping to his feet. "What the hell kind of joke is this, Ashley?"

Ashley raised her hands in supplication. "I-I can explain," she said in a beseeching voice.

"Explain what? How you just made a fool of me?"

"No, Jordan, it isn't what it looks like."

"Oh?" Jordan said nastily, rubbing the back of his neck. He flung his hands in the air. "You mean what's on those plates isn't the garbage it looks and tastes like?" He took a step toward her.

Refusing to be intimidated, she held her ground.

"What happened, Ashley? I know you know how to cook. I *saw* you make dinner. Yet you deliberately humiliated me tonight."

Randy rose unsteadily from the sofa and limped to his crutches where he'd left them in the corner. "Listen, Jordan, I'll just wait in my car for you, if you don't mind."

"No, Randy, please don't leave—" Ashley began.

"Thanks for inviting me, Ashley," he said tightly. "These things happen. Please don't feel bad. Good night." Steadying himself on the crutches, he opened the door and let himself out.

As still as stone, Ashley watched the door close after him. Crushed and embarrassed, she was now compelled to make Jordan understand what happened. Considering the anger flushing his features, it might not be possible tonight.

"Please listen to me, Jordan," she implored, rushing to him and grabbing a handful of his shirt. He tensed beneath her touch. "I didn't cook the meal the other day—"

"The hell you didn't!" Jordan gritted, moving away from her. "I *saw* you."

"You saw me go through the motions," Ashley said desperately. "But it was the bowl—"

"Bowl? What bowl? What are you talking about, Ashley?"

Ashley hurried to the bowl and held it up. "This bowl."

Jordan laughed contemptuously. "Have you lost your mind?"

"Please believe me. I know it sounds crazy, but this bowl has magic powers."

"You obviously take me for a complete fool."

"No, I don't, Jordan. The least you can do, however, is have an open mind. The bowl really did cook that food. It also created the glassware and china and silverware—"

"Stop, Ashley, before you go too far. I thought you'd grown past committing any more irresponsible acts. This wild story has just proven me wrong. For the sake of argument, why didn't you follow the recipes I brought over?"

Ashley lowered her head. "I didn't think I had to. I thought Elvis would do it for me."

"Elvis? Who the hell's Elvis?"

"Um, th-that's the bowl's name."

His anger abating, Jordan looked at her in concern. "Maybe I should contact your family. You seem to be losing your grip on reality. You've named a *bowl*!"

Her remorse slipped away as anger took hold. If Jordan chose not to believe her, that was his prerogative, but she'd be damned if she'd let him mock her. Regardless of how wild her story sounded.

"*I* didn't name it, Jordan," she snapped. "He named . . . himself. And I do apologize for the way things turned out, but there's nothing more you can say if you don't believe my explanation."

Jordan gave her a challenging look. "Prove it, Ashley. Command your bowl to perform some kind of magic."

Ashley had never put Elvis to that kind of test. Yet she had to prove her story to Jordan. She only hoped Elvis cooperated with her. She knew how touchy he could be sometimes.

Going to the sofa table, she looked down at Elvis. "Elvis, can you hear me?"

She waited for the flash and the clicking to begin. A few minutes passed, but nothing happened, so she went back to the sofa and sat.

"I'll be damned," Jordan nearly spat the words. "It doesn't appear to be working."

"Maybe he just doesn't like *you*," Ashley retorted.

"Whatever," Jordan responded furiously. "I don't know what you did to the food, Ashley, but the small taste I took has already given me heartburn."

"I'm sorry."

"Me, too," Jordan said in that same tone. "I should sue for food poisoning."

Ashley jumped up. "Just try it, you wuss!" she flared. "When my bowl does respond again, I'll have you turned into a wart on a frog. Everything you ate here that night was enhanced by magic. Including the wine. Too bad you're so hard to convince. I think you'd better leave now, Jordan. Randy's waiting for you. Don't slam the door on your way out."

Turning her back to Jordan, she summarily dismissed him. She hoped he'd change his mind and announce his understanding, but instead he simply took long quick strides across the floor. The opening and closing of the door followed. It was only then that she turned around again.

The silence overwhelmed her. She'd lost Jordan. Not only that, she'd humiliated him, and he'd never forgive her. The vale of tears she wanted to dissolve into refused to come. All she felt was numbness.

Staring into the empty space, she glimpsed the void without Jordan. She knew she must resign herself to her loss—and her fate.

Whatever it was.

Thirty-three

~

An endless amount of time passed while Ashley sat staring into nothing. The weeks spent with Jordan passed before her mind's eye. In that short amount of time, she'd done more growing up than she had in the entire two years she'd been on her own.

She might have wanted to make her family proud that she'd curbed her spending habits, but she'd known Jordan might discover any lapses in judgment. She had known that his disappointment in her would be worse than anyone else's—except her own.

Really, it had been easier than she'd thought. Once she stopped obsessing over what she couldn't have and concentrated on the Blackwell contract and Jordan, she hadn't really thought of shopping very often. Even her misguided need to buy sex manuals had been deterred by Sydnee's abrupt departure.

Spending money wasn't a cure-all.

In the past, if she suffered some emotional upheaval, the very first thing she would have done was hit the department stores. Now the only thing she could think of was how could she have been so stupid?

Instead of impressing Jordan, she'd humiliated him. It seemed as if she'd once again relied on someone—or in this case some*thing*—to make everything right for her. Once her family had turned her loose, how could she have come to rely so heavily on Elvis?

Perhaps that's why she wasn't taken seriously. Was she truly so inept that she couldn't survive as a self-sufficient woman?

The question left unanswered, twilight became darkness, and the candles she'd lit for her dinner suffused the dimness with brightness from their many meager flames.

She had to get up and clean her cooking mess, but she just couldn't bring herself to face her defeat. She had begun to believe the relationship between her and Jordan was growing beyond friendship. But he was too stubborn to listen to reason. Perhaps it was just as well that she discovered his mulishness before they committed to each other.

Yet even that logic didn't lessen the heartbreak she felt.

And Elvis. How could he have allowed this to happen? She'd put such confidence in him. With his help, she knew she'd win Jordan's love, something she'd never been able to do on her own.

Instead, Elvis helped to insure Jordan's everlasting scorn of her. Swiping at a tear that finally broke through her deadened emotions, sobs tore from her, piercing the silence.

The room suddenly radiated with light, and she sucked in a breath. Looking over her shoulders, she saw that Elvis had returned, the brilliant beam around him illuminating the silver. When the clicking sound started, she went and stood by the table to discover what Elvis was writing.

Ashley, what has caused you such profound sadness?

"As if you don't know!" Ashley cried furiously, swiping at her tears with the back of her hand.

I don't. I made a vow not to read your mind, my dear. Remember?

"Elvis," she sniffled, ignoring his words, "I've lost Jordan, and it's all your fault."

Please explain.

Ashley explained how she'd expected him to create another gourmet delight for her to impress Jordan and Randy, but he'd let her down. Because of that, Jordan was mortified with embarrassment, and they'd had another bitter argument.

"It wasn't about money this time, but somehow he still found a way to tag what I did as irresponsible. Jordan was so angry when he left, but because of the past, the label he pinned on me again tonight will become an indelible stamp on his brain. He'll never see me as anything else."

Ashley, I'm sorry you quarreled with Jordan. But what you did was irresponsible.

"In what way?"

You led Jordan to believe you could cook. Not only was that irresponsible, but it's also dishonest.

Lifting her head, Ashley looked around the room before responding. "For my folly I'm left with a broken heart," she said, glancing at Elvis again. "Why didn't you come to my rescue this one time, Elvis? I thought you cared about me."

I do care about you, Ashley. I knew nothing of your plans for a second dinner for Jordan, however.

"You didn't?" Ashley responded, surprised. "I thought I mentioned it to you. Or at least I thought you might have overheard me."

You didn't mention your plans to me, nor did I hear you mention them to anyone else. Which wouldn't have mattered anyway. I would not have helped you this time.

Ashley bristled. "Why not? I thought you were committed to helping me win Jordan's love. How can you be so hypocritical?"

Me? Hypocritical?

"Yes!"

EXPLAIN YOURSELF, ASHLEY!

The big, bold letters suggested displeasure.

"You led me to believe you were dedicated to my cause. Just when you have the chance to prove yourself, you allow me to make a fool of myself!"

I allowed you? Believe me, my dear, the choice was all yours. Have you given the slightest thought to your actions tonight, Ashley? You sought to deceive Jordan, the man whom you profess to love. Would you appreciate such deception from him?

Ashley sighed. Elvis's written words seemed to convey a certain annoyance, and his ire was justified. She *had* tried to deceive Jordan. If she'd secured Elvis's help, she would have made him an accessory.

"No, I wouldn't appreciate it," she answered, her actions filling her with regret. "I don't think Jordan would ever attempt to mislead me, though. Please accept my apology, Elvis. I was wrong."

Apology accepted, Ashley. But I can understand your confusion. Jordan was no less deceived the first time I assisted you with a meal. I had confidence, however, that you would make an effort to learn to cook by using recipes. To perfect any craft, practice is the key word. You must also remember you can't build a relationship on deception.

"I know," Ashley admitted softly. "Thanks for the advice, Elvis. Although it's a bit late. I've already lost Jordan."

Perhaps he isn't lost, after all, Ashley.

She touched the rim of the bowl. "I have to tidy up the kitchen," she said, walking away from the table.

When she reached the kitchen, a pleasant surprise greeted her. It was spotless, with everything back in its place. No odors. No leftover food. Nothing to remind her of her deceitful disaster.

Her heart melted at Elvis's generosity. After changing into her bedclothes, she poured herself a glass of wine, then took it back into the living room with her. Glancing at the bowl, she whispered thanks, went to the sofa, and sat down. Taking a sip of wine, she then placed it on the coffee table, still in awe of the bowl.

The soft glow reflecting from the bowl washed the room in serenity and reached to the core of Ashley. Her agitation dissipated.

Lifting her legs onto the table, she leaned her head against the pillow and closed her eyes, relishing in the peace she felt. When the doorbell rang and broke her tranquility, Ashley swore to kill Harry for this disturbance as she made her way to the door.

Thirty-four

~

Because Randy was uncomfortable driving with half his leg still in a cast, he asked Jordan to drive them back to his house. Beyond a brief discussion about the evening, the ride passed in tense silence. Randy wasn't angry with Jordan—or even Ashley for that matter. But Jordan was furious with everybody. With himself for trusting that Ashley had finally grown up; with the Douglases for coddling Ashley and never allowing her to fully mature; with Randy for his coolness toward Ashley; and with Ashley for being the same rash person she'd always been.

When he'd first asked her to prepare dinner, she could have told him that she really didn't know *how* to cook, that it had been . . . whatever . . . the first time. Of course, Zach and Murray had tried to warn him, but he hadn't listened.

Releasing a loud belch, Jordan frowned, ignoring the disgusted look Randy threw his way.

Ashley, on several occasions, had attempted to tell him that she couldn't cook. Jordan ignored all the warning signs. He had thought she was being modest, even overly hard on herself.

She'd only been trying to save him from a trip to the emergency room. How the hell anyone could cook so bad was beyond him. Cooking was a joy. A pleasure! An art form!

Ashley had turned it into a gastronomical nightmare! A horror show in a Julia Child setting. And she served it to them. What would he ever do with her?

Once he had driven Randy back home, Jordan waited an interminable length of time for a taxicab to bring him home.

Jordan was sure the driver wasn't city bred. Even so, a taxi driver should know the streets. It was no more than a ten-minute ride from Randy's house to his own, yet the thieving bastard took nearly forty minutes to find his house, even with Jordan directing him. In the end, Jordan paid the driver what he thought was fair, not the exorbitant price the cabbie insisted he owed him.

Home at last, and vexed almost beyond appeasement, Jordan threw his keys on the console table in the hall, then made his way to the living room. He flipped a light switch, and several lamps lit the room. Inhaling an agitated breath, he stood for a second in the center of the floor, his body humming with the anger and betrayal he felt.

Finally he went to the couch and sat, still unable to relax. He'd put such trust in Ashley. He'd even come to love her—still did. God help him. That knowledge made his anger more acute. Despite all the odds against it, he'd thrown caution to the wind and let himself fall in love with her. Until now, he never realized he'd been seriously contemplating a life with her.

The thought struck him like a mallet in his gut.

Time and again, he'd considered the disadvantages of such a mismatched union. Nothing in his wildest dreams could have prepared him for tonight. Ashley had seemed so careless over the whole shambles. That frenzied story she told about the bowl was absolutely the last straw. How could she think so little of him to tell him such a tale and expect him to fall for it?

Jordan straightened in his seat, another thought striking him. Why had it been so easy to acquire a taxi from Ashley's house? With the journey between their two homes almost timeless? Each and every time.

No! There was no truth to Ashley's story. Magic didn't exist. Especially not a magic bowl. Even the magic carpet was only a fairy tale.

Ashley had humiliated him. Why would she do something so despicable as to ruin what should have been a good meal? It wasn't in her character to be mean.

Trying to make sense of the bewildering situation and thoroughly confused, he made his way to the mahogany serving cart where he kept his liquor. He picked up a bottle of scotch. Noticing the wine Ashley had given him several weeks ago, he set the scotch down. Maybe he didn't need a strong drink after all. That wine poured from the bowl should calm his upset. He laughed derisively. She had said the bowl had magic powers.

Pouring himself a glass of wine, Jordan turned on his stereo, then went back and sat on the couch.

David Sanborn's music interrupted the silence of the room in a very pleasing way. It soothed his raging fury and made the void caused by his parting with Ashley that much more poignant. Since Wednesday he had spent as much time with her as possible and already he was feeling her absence.

Miserably, Jordan sipped his wine, the bouquet tantalizing his senses; the taste was titillating. He'd forgotten how good it was. Scenes from that night flooded his memory. Ashley had been like a feather in his arms, soft and light, willing to yield to him in every way. They hadn't made love. He'd refrained from doing so, mainly because he'd been afraid that Zach's continued disapproval would finally come between them. Ashley valued her brother's opinion, and nothing had broken through Zach's displeasure. Everything had been so up in the air. In his naïveté, Jordan thought he'd feel more guilty if they slept together and their romance ended for some reason.

The guilt he felt now, however, couldn't have been any worse had he made love to her. Maybe he'd pushed her too far. She'd always been a horrific cook, and the beef casserole she'd prepared for him had been delicious, but quite simple to make. This dinner had been so complex. If only she'd confessed that she really couldn't cook, *before* he invited Randy over.

Part of his anger had been nothing but wounded male pride. She'd embarrassed him, after he'd praised her abilities to the highest.

Downing the rest of the wine in one gulp, Jordan poured himself another. Warmth curled within him, and excitement rippled through his veins. He could almost feel Ashley's body wrapped around his own. His manhood grew, and blood roared in his ears.

How could he have gotten so angry with her? She was probably as embarrassed as he was. After all, she worked with Randy as well.

Jordan sighed. He owed Ashley an apology and refused to let the night go by without offering that. No longer angry, he felt mellow—and ashamed of his crass behavior. Ashley hadn't deserved such treatment from him. There was a logical explanation for what happened between the successful dinner and the disastrous one, and she'd eventually tell him about it.

Picking up the phone, he dialed the number for a taxi. Before he'd fully placed the receiver back on its cradle, a horn blasted outside. Stunned, Jordan went to the door and opened it. There, parked at the curb, was the taxi he'd ordered.

Not willing to question the strangeness of the situation, or admit to insanity, he closed his door and went to the waiting cab.

Rushing to the door, Ashley swung it open, ready to give Harry a piece of her tortured mind. "What do you want at this hour, Harry—" Her words caught in her throat, and her mouth dropped open.

"I'm sorry, Ashley," Jordan said sheepishly. "I didn't realize what time it is."

Oh, my God! He's back. Elvis, your magic is miraculous! "Jordan, I-I thought you were someone else—"

"At this hour?" he teased.

Ashley chuckled. "Only *you* are welcome at any hour of the day or night," she said breathlessly. Their glances met and held for long seconds.

"Thanks, Ash," Jordan replied huskily. "May I come in? There's something I need to discuss with you."

Ashley stepped aside. "Please do." A partial view of the kitchen could be had from the living room. She noted Jordan's surprise at how clean it was. Not daring to mention Elvis again, she smiled. "Care for something to drink?"

"No, thanks, Ashley. I've already had some wine. *Your* wine, as a matter of fact."

"My . . . ?" It dawned on her what he meant. She'd forgotten all about the wine that she'd given him—the wine that had been poured into Elvis's cavity. Was the magic still potent in it? "Oh, yes, the wine." She sat on the sofa and patted the spot next to her.

Jordan sat down a little apart from her. "Ashley," he began hesitantly, "I acted like a fool. I'm sorry. I noticed you've tidied up the kitchen. I'm sorry about that, too. I should have been here to help you."

Ashley's heart sang. Jordan was repentant for treating her so badly.

"I know things don't always turn out the way we expect them to," he continued. "Perhaps we can create a winning meal together in the near future. I didn't mean to hurt you."

Having no idea how else to respond to him, Ashley only smiled. To temper thoughts of flinging herself into his arms, she went and placed a CD into the player. She was afraid that if she followed through with her desire, he might reject her, so she didn't dare try. One humiliation with Jordan tonight was enough.

When she returned to the sofa, the music playing in the background, Jordan looked at her intently, then pulled her into his arms. "Don't smile at me like that," he muttered before fastening his mouth to hers.

His tongue twined with hers, sending shivers of need racing through her. Heady sensation stamped out all other thought, and the urgency of his touch persuaded her that she had nothing to fear, that tonight shadows of doubt and mistrust didn't stand between them. The kiss took her breath away, sweet and demanding. Sliding her arms around his neck, she returned the kiss with hunger. Slowly, ever so slowly, the feel of his mouth changed from aching desire to dreamy intimacy.

"Ashley, my sweet Ashley," Jordan murmured as he left her mouth and lowered his head to her breasts, kissing each spot he bared, circling his tongue around her aureoles, then her nipples.

"Oh, Jordan," she whispered. "I need you so."

When he began suckling her breast, she drew in a breath.

"Ash, sweetheart, I want you so badly," Jordan said hoarsely. "I need you."

He was asking her to let him make love to her. She wanted him just as badly, but not here. Not in the living room in front of Elvis. Vaguely she remembered him saying he always suspended his senses to give her her privacy whenever she had company. Perhaps he did, but she wouldn't feel comfortable while she was in the throes of passion.

"J-Jordan," she managed weakly as he tried to reclaim her lips. She pushed him back. "N-not here."

Confusion registered in his features. "Ash?"

"Let's go to my bedroom," she said, caressing his cheek.

Swept abruptly into his arms, she clung to him and buried her face in his chest. Reaching her bedroom, Jordan laid her gently down on the bed. Faint strands of the music reached them, and Ashley moved erotically to the beat, giving him a half-lidded invitation.

Standing over her, he gazed at her through eyes darkened with passion. He waited for her lead. Not having any experience in these matters, Ashley raised herself to her knees, letting her heart and her desire, guide her. She hugged him around his neck and lifted her mouth to his kiss, her body flush against his.

Sliding her nightgown down her shoulders and letting it fall to the bed, Jordan kissed the long column of her neck, the smooth skin of her shoulders and chest. He trailed his tongue along the crevice of her bosom, down to her flat belly and long legs.

Ashley burned with each caress—his fingers brushing her thigh as he removed her gown. His palm slid through her tight curls, then at the point of her ecstasy before he removed her panties.

Featherlight kisses fanned the inside of her thighs, and Ashley moved restlessly, needing more but not knowing what. His lips touched the top of her femininity, and her skin prickled at the heat generated within her body.

Moving slowly up, he teased the indent of her navel and began his slow descent once again, this time finding her center. He slid his tongue down her wet heat in slow, methodical motions. Grasping his thick hair in heated madness, Ashley rocked against him, releasing a loud moan.

Jordan was relentless in his quest to pleasure her. Laving her bud with increased pressure and speed, he expertly brought her to heights she couldn't have dreamed of. She moved her hips faster, in tempo with his lovemaking, until rapture claimed her and she shook with amazing force.

Still fully clothed, Jordan found her lips again and kissed her deeply. His tongue twined with hers, allowing her to taste the muskiness of sex in his kiss.

Mouth to mouth, Ashley roamed her hands over his muscular chest and flat stomach, down to the end of his shirt. She hated to break contact with him, and did so only long enough to pull his shirt over his head.

"Ashley," Jordan groaned his harsh whisper. "Let me help you."

"No!" she said fervently. She wrapped her legs around his back, encouraging him to turn over. She had waited her entire life for this, and now that she had him in her bed, she wanted to touch him and taste him and feel him.

Lingering momentarily at his mouth, she trailed kisses over his strong jaw, his heavy eyebrows, his straight nose, and firm chin. She wanted him to feel her love in each stroke of her fingers, to hear it as she whispered it to him after nibbling his ear.

Undulating against his arousal, Ashley lightly brushed her fingertips across his chest and over his stomach, before finding his belt buckle.

At ease in her role as temptress, she laughed wickedly while unfastening his belt and unzipping his pants. Taking matters out of her hands, Jordan removed his remaining clothes with stunning quickness and threw them to the floor. Afterward, he laid back, not missing her fascination with his hardness.

Ashley tentatively touched his manhood. It was like stroking velvet steel, consumed by fire. Her strokes were gentle, her rhythm slow. Back and forth, she fondled him, tenderly drawing the skin back, then reversing the motion.

"Oh, God, Ashley. Please."

Ashley ignored him. She knew what she wanted to do and wouldn't allow his passionate pleas to deter her. Bowing her head, she pressed her lips to the tip of his phallus. Lovingly she glided her tongue down the length of him before closing her mouth over him.

That's where Jordan's composure ended. "No, Ash," he whispered.

Disengaging her from the pleasurable havoc she wreaked, he flipped her over and lowered his body onto hers. Opening her thighs to him, she relished his kisses. Hot and hard, he pushed into her.

Ignoring the slight discomfort at the moment of penetration, Ashley held on to Jordan as he drove deep inside her. She clung to him with the need her urgency required, moaning senselessly, brazenly. Sweet torture engulfed her, swirling her into another world, infinity wrought with ecstasy.

Jordan pumped into her, the touch of him bringing wave after wave of bliss. She clung to him, trembling from the sensations of their perfect harmony.

When she felt Jordan pull away, Ashley protested. "Don't," she whispered feverishly. "Don't stop now, Jordan."

"I don't ever want to stop making love to you, sweetheart," Jordan said. "I want it to last forever. You're so hot inside. I am about to explode, and I'm not ready for that just now."

"Please, Jordan—"

"Ahh, yes, my love, I can't resist you." Kneeling down, he lifted Ashley's hips, impaling her once again and bringing her closer to the demanding gyrations of his own hips. Resting her ankles on his shoulders, he moved within her with abandon.

His frenzy urging her on, Ashley escalated her own re-

sponse. But she knew Jordan was trying to prolong their
passion, so when he flipped them over and gave Ashley the
lead, she slid down on his erection slowly, her moist heat
welcoming him. The fever of excitement increased to flam-
ing spasms. Her passion peaked as she met his every move,
his hardness reaching to the very core of her. He pushed
up into her, and she glided down on him, their movements
in perfect accord.

Almost overcome with delirium, she tingled. Her heated
body only grew hotter, and she fell against his chest. His
movements became frenzied. Her walls cracked, then crum-
bled. The breath-stealing tempest was almost too much for
flesh and blood to bear. The force of her climax shook her,
the wetness between her thighs overflowing.

Jordan's arms were like steel bands around her, holding
her as she trembled with her ecstasy. His organ quivered
inside her, and she knew he'd found his release.

After a time her body returned to a semblance of normalcy. The sensation of Jordan withdrawing from her
caused her insides to constrict, sending tingles along her
nerve endings. He pulled her into his arms.

"Ashley," he whispered. "I didn't know you were a vir-
gin. Why didn't you tell me?"

Ashley chuckled softly. "I don't know, Jordan. The subject just never came up. It would have been rather awkward
to talk about it at the last moment. The spell would have
been broken."

Jordan tightened his arms around her. "Thank you for
giving me the privilege, sweetheart. You were just so wonderful."

"Jordan?"

"Yes?"

"Why do we keep covering up our feelings for each
other?"

Ashley's question caught Jordan off guard. Was she also

hiding her true feelings for him? He truly loved her, but he couldn't tell her that. She thought of him as a miser, and she'd never be happy as his wife. They would make each other miserable. He loved her too much to ruin her chance at real happiness with someone more compatible.

"Jordan?"

He sighed. "What feelings are we covering up, Ash?" he asked, hating his tortured tone.

Ashley sat up, embarrassment clouding her expression. He hated that, too. Her face was too beautiful to be marred by negative emotions. She should always glow with happiness. But he doubted he could ever put such a glow on her features.

"Well, I-I mean we shouldn't quarrel o-over silly things, Jordan," she stammered. The quiver in her voice told him she fought back tears.

"No, Ash, we shouldn't," he responded softly. "Let's make a pact to always sort things out. I don't ever want to hurt you, Ashley. Remember that." Caressing her cheek, he sat up. "I'd better leave, sweetheart, so you can get your rest. It's awfully late."

Unashamed of her nude state, Ashley stood from the bed. Picking up her robe where it lay across a chair, she unhurriedly put it on. "Yes, it is late," she agreed, watching as Jordan began to dress. Her heart tumbled at the sight of his physique. Whoever thought of the word "hunk" must have had Jordan in mind. He was simply gorgeous.

He grinned crookedly. "I'd better call a cab, Ash."

She cleared her throat and gave him the once-over. When he caught sight of her perusing him, she blushed.

He'd certainly looked at her. Why couldn't she do the same to him? She'd just have to force herself to get past the blushing and gasping stages. A couple of hours ago, a man's naked body was completely new to her. But she'd seen Jordan, and now that was no longer a novelty. The only trouble with that was she couldn't get her fill of him. To be caught devouring him with her gaze really was mortifying, although Jordan appeared to enjoy seeing her admiring his magnificent form. As a man, he would.

"The phone is on the coffee table in the living room, Jordan," she said, walking swiftly to the door with him following close behind her.

He picked up the phone and dialed the number for the taxi service, then placed the phone back on the table. He turned and faced her, gazing deeply into her eyes. Before he could speak, the sound of a horn blasted the silence. He chuckled.

"You must have connections with the dispatcher for this address, Ash," he said. "Or maybe there really is some kind of magic going on over here. I never have to wait for a cab."

The horn sounded again.

Pulling her into his arms, Jordan kissed her. "Good night, sweetheart. I'll be in touch." Opening the door, he gave her one last, longing look before he left.

Thirty-five

Ashley soared through her morning routine the next day with events of the night before flooding her mind. Ruining a good meal in early evening, the heartache of Jordan walking out and the embarrassment of Randy's annoyance.

Then later that night, when all was forgiven and she and Jordan made love. Her body still burned from his touch, and the soreness between her thighs reminded her of all the beautiful sensations he'd evoked within her.

Going about her chores, she wondered if Jordan had acted from feelings of the heart, or if Elvis had given him a little push. Needing to know, she went to her bowl and gently circled the rim with her finger.

The clicking began, and a soft glow emanated through the room.

Good morning, my dear. I trust you slept well.

"Not hardly," Ashley replied. She'd twisted and turned the entire night, her body needing Jordan's once again, her mind plagued with doubts. "I am very concerned about the state of my relationship with Jordan."

In what way?

"Well, we became intimate last night, Elvis," Ashley confessed. "I want to know if that was your doing, or was it Jordan's very own idea?"

I can't believe you haven't figured that out for yourself, Ashley. You are more naive than I imagined.

"Naive?"

Yes, my dear, naive! How could you ask me such a question? My powers are infinite. Yet I had very little influence on Jordan last night—

"Just as I thought," Ashley interrupted miserably. To her, very little meant everything. Elvis *had* influenced Jordan's decision in some way. More than likely, by drinking the wine after he returned earlier, he'd been powerless to resist Ashley. Through her deceit, Jordan's lovemaking had come about.

You've misunderstood, Ashley.

"I don't think so. I know you're an inanimate object, Elvis, but to me you've become a true entity. I care very deeply for you. But I must put you away. Away in the closet on the shelf—" Until she could sort everything out, without influence, magic, or otherwise.

Ashley!

"No!" Ashley responded, just as fiercely. "I won't listen. And you must promise you won't use your powers in any way while you're there. Promise me!"

The clicking this time came much more slowly, almost as if each word were painful to write.

Very well, Ashley. I promise.

The clicking ceased. A bright flash lit the room, then Elvis's glow dimmed, and finally went out completely.

One hand over her mouth, Ashley stared at her beloved bowl. By the darkening of the glow, she knew that Elvis had suspended access to his magical powers. She felt she'd lost a dear friend, but it couldn't be helped. For once, she needed to achieve something on her own.

She wrapped Elvis securely in one of her most plush bath towels, then put him on the shelf in the only closet she had. Gently closing the door, she swiped a tear from her eye.

The rest of the day, she told herself that since she and Jordan were no longer privy to Elvis's magic, whatever happened between them from then on would be of their *own* doing.

The frivolities she'd wrestled with for so long, which had hindered her personal goals, were all but conquered. Did Jordan see the change in her, however? She *had* made strides in that direction, but after the beginning of last night and her explanation about magic, Jordan's belief in her might be tenuous.

She needed to know if the love they'd shared was real or if guilt had made him return after they'd quarreled.

For a solid week after they'd made love, Ashley didn't see Jordan. He even managed to avoid her at the hotel, and her worst fears surfaced. It must have been Elvis who'd sent him to her. Each night she contemplated confronting Elvis and then Jordan. She wanted to see for herself what Elvis had to say about how he got Jordan to feel enough love for her to want to consummate it with her. She wanted to ask Jordan why he had lied about keeping in touch with her.

She really had no reason to see Jordan at work. Since Randy Petersen had returned to work, Jordan reported all pertinent matters to him. Yet, before Randy had had his accident, that hadn't stopped her from seeing Jordan.

Jordan made it a point not to be around whenever she went to the restaurant, however. Either Curtis or Arthur would tell her Jordan had just stepped out or hadn't come in yet. She knew the lame excuses were bald-faced lies encouraged by Jordan. She felt betrayed and violated and almost hated him for it. Almost. But even through her anguish and confusion, she couldn't deny her real feelings for him.

Monday fused into Friday; Friday brought the weekend, carrying in a gloomy, cloudy Saturday. At odds with herself most of the morning, Ashley decided to catch an afternoon movie. Although it was much heralded, she couldn't get into it, but she sat there anyway.

When it finally ended, Ashley left the theater and found the world outside as dark as the inside had been. The sky was black with clouds promising an imminent downpour.

Hurriedly, she left Uptown Square and made her way to Broadway Street and the nearest bus stop. In luck, she noticed a bus about three blocks away. Unfortunately her luck changed at that moment. The heavens opened up, the rain fell so swiftly and so hard that she was immediately drenched.

When the bus finally rolled to a stop in front of her, she was soaked to the skin. She boarded quickly, another passenger bumping into her as he made it to the bus just before it took off again.

The air conditioning was on full blast on the nearly empty bus, and shivers racked Ashley. Finding a seat toward the middle, she sat down, folding her arms around herself to try and keep warm.

"Ashley?"

She looked up. Jordan was coming toward her. She wondered if Elvis had had anything to do with throwing them together again. At least he was being fair if he did. Jordan looked like a drowned rat.

"Jordan, when did you get on?"

"Right behind you," he answered softly. "May I sit down?"

She shrugged her shoulders. "You paid your money. This is a public vehicle."

Jordan sat beside her. "We're a sight."

"Speak for yourself," she responded flippantly. But she had an inkling of how she must look. Her hair felt plastered to her head, and her clothes stuck to her like glue. Still, she was in no mood for Jordan calling her a "sight."

Jordan laughed at her peevish tone. "I stand corrected. You're always beautiful to me."

Her heart fluttered with too many extra beats. Well, she wouldn't have it. Jordan just couldn't say something sweet to her, make her adore him, and then take off for days at a time.

"Ashley, may I accompany you home?"

Ashley looked in surprise at him. "What for?" she asked, her annoyance lacing her tone.

"Because we have to talk, Ash. After you hear me out, you can throw me out if you wish."

She really wanted to hear his story, so she agreed, and two transfers later, they arrived at her apartment dripping wet.

Thirty-six

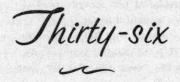

After shedding her wet clothes, Ashley gave Jordan one of her beach blankets to cover himself, while his clothes dried in the tenant Laundromat.

As they settled on each end of the sofa, an awkward moment ensued, each one waiting for the other to speak first. Nervous, Ashley picked up the remote and flicked on the television.

"No, Ashley, turn it off," Jordan said finally as he moved to close the gap between them. He took the remote out of her hand and turned it off himself. Placing it on the coffee table, he began talking immediately. "I'm so sorry I didn't get back to you, my love."

Ashley drew in a breath. She didn't want Jordan's sweet words to affect her, before he gave a full explanation for his behavior. After giving him her innocence, she deserved no less. Silently praying that his next words would be what she wanted to hear, she waited.

"I had a lot of thinking and soul-searching to do, Ashley. I was on my way here when you saw me. I-I want to tell you that I love you and am totally miserable without you."

"Oh, Jordan!" Ashley exclaimed, reaching for him.

When she would have kissed him passionately, he gently held her at bay. "Let me finish, darling. For every reason why we shouldn't be together, a better one surfaces for why we should. They all add up to I love you. I realize my paranoia about money. Because of it, I've found myself in circumstances where I'm always *spending* money in my misguided effort to save. I can see you've made great strides in curbing your fondness for spending. I'm very proud of your efforts."

"What are you trying to tell me, Jordan?"

"Just that if we try hard enough, maybe we can make a go of it."

"Oh, Jordan, yes! Let's try!" Ashley cried, rushing into his arms. "I've loved you for so long I've lost count of the years."

"It won't be that easy loving me, Ash," Jordan warned. "I can be a bastard sometimes."

Ashley already knew the path she'd chosen with Jordan wouldn't be an easy one. She wasn't entirely cured of her passion for buying, either. Although Jordan had loosened his purse strings, it wasn't nearly enough to suit her. But they had jumped the first hurdle and confessed their love for one another. Jordan was right, however.

"You *are* a bastard, darling," she said, giggling when he scowled at her. "But even bastards lose their hearts now and again."

Jordan laughed, just as thunder rumbled overhead. "It sounds like the rain has moved in for the night."

She'd always heard of lovers passing a rainy day lost in the throes of passion. Deep down, she had never believed she'd ever have the opportunity to do that with Jordan. She looked at him dreamily. "Umm, sounds like it."

"Imagine getting soaked twice in one night," Jordan said. "A guy could catch his death."

Knowing what Jordan was hinting at, she smiled. She leaned her head on his shoulder, and he encircled her waist with his arm.

"Ashley?" he whispered.

"Huh?"

"I can't afford to get sick."

"Well, of course not," she replied in a serious tone, hot need coursing through her. "But if you do, Art and Curtis are there to fill in for you."

"Without a doubt," Jordan agreed, sliding his fingers through her hair. "They've become very good friends. I just thought I wouldn't have a chance of getting sick if I didn't have to go out in that nasty weather."

"You could go home in a cab," Ashley suggested with a straight face. "Although, because of the rain, it mightn't come as quickly as you're accustomed to." Or, as quickly as Elvis's magic brought them. Straightening herself, she cupped his sinfully handsome face in her hands. "Would you like me to call one?"

Jordan grinned slyly. "Maybe you'll be kind enough to let me sleep on your kitchen floor."

She stood from the sofa. "Suit yourself, Mr. Machismo. I always thought a bed was infinitely more comfortable than a cold, hard, old kitchen floor." She walked across the room to the small hall that led to her bedroom, then stopped. "But what do I know? I'm just a warm . . . *very* warm, soft woman."

She smiled at him, a mixture of imp and angel, then dropped her robe to the floor. Her exquisitely formed nude body greeted Jordan. Leaving him with that image in his brain, she disappeared into her bedroom.

Getting over his surprise, Jordan chuckled. The little witch wanted to play hardball, huh? Well, two could play her game. He, too, was nude under the blanket she'd given him, but he wouldn't move from the sofa. She had to know the picture she'd presented aroused him.

He desperately wanted to get inside her and feel her warmth, but she had to come to him.

An interminable amount of time passed while Jordan sat on the sofa, his penis erect and hurting. He realized then that he could no longer play her game. She wanted him to *ask* her to spend the night with her. Well, he was fully ready to ask—*beg,* if necessary. He started for the bedroom.

Sitting on the edge of the bed, Ashley waited for Jordan's knock. None came. She thought after he'd seen her naked, he'd want to sleep in her bed. He couldn't have been serious about sleeping on the kitchen floor. Could he?

Aching to have him inside her again, she was sure her body heat had risen ten degrees just thinking about him. Well, she'd go and get him off that damn floor or join him there. Either way, she'd be with him. Bouncing off her bed, she started for the kitchen—and ran smack into Jordan just inside the hallway.

She looked at his erection. "Is that for me?" she asked coyly.

Jordan pulled her against him. "As is the man attached to it," he said before closing his mouth over hers.

With his mouth still locked to hers, he lifted her into his arms and walked the few feet to the bedroom. Once inside, he closed the door.

Thirty-seven

~

Sunday morning brought blue skies, rain-washed air, and a healthy pink glow to Ashley's cheeks. She'd spent a night of sheer bliss in Jordan's arms. Between bouts of making love, she and Jordan discussed their future.

He asked her to invest in the restaurant he intended to buy with Arthur, which she tentatively agreed to do. Now she wondered if that was because he really wanted her in, or if he was testing her to see how and if she'd raise the money.

Not wanting the thought of money to mar her happiness, she hoped this wouldn't be the way things would always be. Would she always take an innocent remark from Jordan and give it deeper meaning about her spending habits? No, she should know better. Jordan always said what he meant.

Forcing the negative thoughts from her mind, she swung her legs over the side of the bed. It was already ten o'clock. Having to be at the hotel today for the new Sunday brunches, Jordan had left over three hours ago.

Holding her arms high above her head, she stretched luxuriously. She was content with the knowledge that Jordan's confession of love for her came from his heart and not from Elvis's magic. He hadn't stayed away because he regretted making love to her, but because he'd wanted to put everything into proper prospective. Now she could put Elvis back in his special spot.

Throwing on her robe, she dashed to her living room closet. Retrieving the bowl from the top shelf, she took it to the sofa table and carefully unwrapped it, then centered it on the table. The notepad and check were still inside it.

"Hello, Elvis," she whispered. Not expecting him to respond, she still prayed that he would. She didn't know if the magic in the bowl was only confined to Elvis or if it could be transferred to something else. Elvis had the power to suspend his magic at will. Did he have the power to return at will? Would he even want to now, after she'd so carelessly hid him from view?

Using the end of the plush towel she'd wrapped her bowl in, she began rubbing its surface. She picked it up and polished the stand and base before placing it back on the table. The bowl's light flashed a blushing red.

Ashley sucked in a sob. "Elvis," she whispered.

When the clicking noise began, it was the most welcome sound she'd ever heard.

Ashley Douglas, you must *stop doing that!* Elvis wrote, his glow receding to pink then white.

"Oh, Elvis, I'm so sorry for the way I treated you." Ashley sniffed. "I promise I'll never hide you away again."

My dear, what are you going on about?

"The week I put you away, Elvis. With only thoughts of myself and not how you must have felt."

Oh, that. Sit down, Ashley.

"Why?"

I'll ask the questions and give the answers. **NOW SIT DOWN!**

The bold letters screamed at her, and she sat down immediately.

A beam of light focused on her, and she felt herself rise from her seat.

"Elvis!" she yelled, suspended in the air. "What are you doing?"

The notepad flew into her hand, and the Teletyping began.

Reminding you of my powers, Ashley. You seem to have forgotten.

"W-what do you mean?" she asked as she floated around the room. "P-please let me down."

Very well. The words flashed across the notepad.

She drifted slowly back to the sofa, landing with a gentle *thud*. "Oh! What are you trying to prove, Elvis? Are you still angry with me?"

Of course not, Ashley, given the fact that I never was angry with you.

The words appeared on the pad she still held in her hand.

I tried to tell you last week that although I have the magic to help Jordan realize his feelings for you, I certainly don't rule them. I had nothing to do with Jordan's decision to tell you how he feels about you.

"I know that now, Elvis. I'm so ashamed for not realizing that before."

Elvis focused his beam on the closet door, and it swung open. Then the bowl soared through the room into the closet, and the door slammed shut. Seconds later, it floated out again and settled back on the sofa table.

"Wha . . . why . . . how did you do that?"

Magic, my dear. To impress upon you that you have nothing to lament. I could have removed myself from the closet anytime I wanted to.

"Oh, Elvis, you're wonderful!"

Thank you, Ashley. I am, aren't I?

Ashley laughed. "You're modest, too. But I don't care. I still think you're wonderful."

Does Jordan?

"No. He doesn't believe in you."

Does that upset you?

"Very much. I think you could be as much a bone of contention between us as our money problem."

Well, then, we'll just have to remedy that, Ashley. Just as beauty is in the eye of the beholder, so is magic in the soul of the believer. Only for some it takes convincing.

"Thanks, Elvis, but I'll do the convincing myself," Ashley said with a chuckle. "By the way, why didn't you tell me I didn't need to keep the notepad inside your cavity?"

You didn't ask.

"Elvis, my love, I missed your sarcasm."

That you've missed anything about me warms my stand, Ashley.

Ashley laughed as the light from the bowl receded. "I'll talk to you later, my friend."

Thirty-eight

Nearly a month after Jordan confessed his love to her, Ashley had yet to try to convince him of Elvis's magic powers. Each day that came and went was to be the day. Each day she'd lose her nerve.

Today, come hell or high water, would be it. At the rate it was raining outside, it would most likely be high water. It was coming down in buckets, and she expected Jordan any minute.

Going to the window that faced the front of her apartment, she peeked out just in time to see Jordan dashing toward the porch. Hurrying to the door, she swung it open.

Jordan let out a loud whistle. "I thought I could make it here before it came down," he said. "But the goddamn buses travel at a snail's pace."

Ashley stifled a laugh. His clothes were plastered to his body. Water dripped from his rain-slicked hair onto his face—as handsome as ever, but marred by a frown. "I take it the rain has you a little put out," she said, grinning.

Absently emptying his pockets into her bowl, Jordan narrowed his eyes at her. "Get my robe, sweetheart. The one

I brought over here last week," he said as he began stepping out of his wet clothes.

His billfold and leather checkfold kept the contents relatively dry, but his keys and coins were swimming in water in his pockets, and he dropped them into the bowl as well.

"Damn," he said, stepping out of his undershorts and reaching for the robe Ashley handed him, then shrugging into it. "Thanks, darling. I think I've created a puddle on the floor. I'll wipe it up—"

A brilliant flash cut off any further words.

"What the hell was that?" he asked in surprise.

"Oh, that was Elvis," Ashley answered nonchalantly.

"Who?"

"My magic bowl, Jordan. His name's Elvis."

Three beams flashed in succession—red, yellow, and white—before the light receded.

Jordan stared in astonishment at the bowl, then he looked at Ashley. "No, this isn't happening. There are no such things as magic bowls. Or magic anything."

He gazed at the bowl again. A puff of smoke emanated from the cavity. When the smoke cleared, the bowl was empty.

"Why . . . it . . . my money's gone!" Jordan said in disbelief.

"I know," Ashley said with a sigh. "I don't think he likes money or checks or anything of a monetary nature. He also took the check Daddy gave me."

"Th-the five-thousand-dollar check your father gave you?" Jordan repeated incredulously.

"Uh-huh," Ashley replied, miserable.

"But how did you buy all those matching pieces of china and crystal?"

"I didn't. Elvis conjured them up," Ashley explained, uncomfortable talking about the bowl with Jordan now that the truth was known. She really hadn't wanted Elvis's help.

But since he'd stolen Jordan's money, it was definitely easier to convince Jordan of the bowl's magic.

Jordan threaded both hands through his thick hair. "Then you were telling the truth about the dinner you prepared for me?"

"Well, I didn't prepare it. He did," Ashley corrected, indicating Elvis with a gesture of her head.

"This is incredible." Awe tinged his voice. "Well, what do you know about that? A real magic bowl," he said, laughing. "Do you communicate with it? I mean with *Elvis*. Elvis? Why Elvis?"

"Because he likes the King," Ashley said, her apprehension evaporating. Jordan seemed to be accepting her magic bowl very well. "And, yes, I do communicate with him."

"How?"

"I don't know. Well, I guess I do. His words appear like magic . . . Well, it is magic . . . on a notepad."

"Fantastic!" Jordan exclaimed. "Simply fantastic. Now, tell him I think magic is fabulous. If this isn't a weird dream, that is. And tell him to bring back my money."

The bowl flashed its brilliance.

"He heard you, Jordan," Ashley explained.

"Well?"

The Teletyping began, and Ashley got the notepad.

What makes you think you deserve your money back, Jordan?

"What?" Jordan boomed.

Puh-leaze, Mr. Bennett. Which word didn't you understand?

"The money is mine," Jordan snarled, all pretense of understanding gone. "I worked my ass off for it. That's why I deserve it."

There's no need to use profanity, Jordan. Most humans do work for their money. But most humans enjoy the fruits of their labor. There are those who deprive themselves of

*simple, everyday pleasures, however, if even a small
amount of money is involved. Do you know anyone like
that, Jordan?*

Ashley took in the disbelief and anger on Jordan's face.
Like herself, there was nothing he could do to get his
money back. At least not until Elvis was ready to give it
back. Which he would do she had no doubt.

She felt, though, that Jordan's anger stemmed more from
Elvis's words than from him taking the money. What Elvis
wrote hit close to home, and Jordan had to know he was
right. After all, he was too stingy to spring for a taxi to her
apartment, even with rain threatening to burst forth any
second.

If Jordan had paid for a taxi, he wouldn't have gotten
wet, thus having to empty his pockets and enabling Elvis
to steal his belongings. He could be sitting high and dry
with his money still in his pockets. Ashley wondered how
long it would take for Jordan to figure that out.

"Oh!" she hollered as Jordan picked up the bowl.

Jordan shook it viciously. "Give me back my goddamn
money!" he yelled.

"Jordan!" Ashley screamed. "Don't!"

Too late. The bowl went hurling across the room, landing
with an incredibly loud clang in the corner near the closet.
Brilliant, deep shades of purple flashed around the room,
so bright that heat emanated throughout the small space.

"My stars!" Ashley cried. "What did you do, Jordan?
Elvis is purple with rage!"

Violet rays intensified the heat in the room. The room
got hotter, and the only color they could see was purple.

"Elvis!" Ashley screamed. "You've been around long
enough to know how anger affects people. Jordan was right.
It was *his* money you took. And as such he could use it as
he saw fit, even if he chooses *not* to use it. You can't
impose your opinions on others, no matter how logical they

may seem." She tipped closer to the bright purple light, shielding her eyes with her hands sweat beading her brow. "Please don't cook us, Elvis. I thought you cared about me. Jordan didn't mean to hurt you if he did. He's a good man, and I love him. He was just angry, that's all. Just the way you are now."

Ashley didn't know she was crying until her errant tears found their way to the corners of her mouth and she tasted them. Strong arms encircled her waist.

"Ashley, what have I done?" Jordan said remorsefully, his face flushed with heat. "I'm so sorry, darling. The thing seems intent on roasting us, and there's no escape. I don't know what came over me. I've never done such a juvenile thing before in my life. As much as I loathe to admit it, Elvis really nailed me. I apologize to you, Ash, and to Elvis for my display."

In an instant the heat receded, and the room once again became comfortably cool. The purple glow turned magenta, then red, then white.

The notepad flew into Ashley's hand, and the clicking began.

Pick me up, Ashley, and put me back in my special place.

Ashley left Jordan's embrace and did as Elvis commanded her. When she'd settled him back in his place, she placed the notepad inside it.

"Elvis," she began, as Jordan joined her at the sofa table. "Why did you try *to kill us?*"

I'm magic, my dear. I never have to try to do anything. I succeed at everything I do.

"But you were burning us," Ashley reminded him gently.

I know. I, too, was angry. I merely tried to frighten you. Especially Jordan. He touched my stand, after all.

"Elvis!" Ashley sputtered.

"What does he mean, Ash?"

She giggled. "You don't really want to know, Jordan.

You're too macho for that. Besides, it's a long story."

Good to hear you laugh, Ashley. I will give you and Jordan back your belongings soon.

"Thank you," Jordan replied sardonically.

"Me, too," Ashley put in.

Elvis's light dimmed, leaving a bright shine on his silver surface.

Ashley turned to Jordan. He seemed satisfied with Elvis's explanation. Seeing that he no longer doubted her story about her magic bowl, she smiled tenderly. The ugly scene from a few minutes ago fell away as Jordan kissed her. "I make delicious popcorn, love. Care to join me in the kitchen?"

"Join you?" Jordan laughed wickedly. "As in joined bodies? You bet." Taking her hand, he led her into the kitchen, his intent more than clear.

Thirty-nine

~

Two weeks later, Zach surprised Ashley with a visit to her apartment. She was expecting Jordan at any minute, and for a moment after she answered the door, she stood frozen in shock as she stared at her brother. Zach had been in the South of France with Fawn, so he didn't know how far things had progressed between her and Jordan.

Not that her parents did either. She'd been careful to keep her regular routine with her family, so she wouldn't arouse their suspicions about her deepening romance with Jordan. She had every intention of telling her family about them, but she wanted to be sure *he* was ready for that.

Tightening her towel around her wet hair, she gaped at Zach a moment longer. He frowned ferociously, his teeth gleaming pearly against his deep tan, his hair lighter from time spent in the sun.

"Zach! When did you get back?"

"Last night," he answered sheepishly. "May I come in?"

Flustered, Ashley stepped aside. "Of course." Leaving the door partially open behind him, she adjusted the belt around her robe, feeling a little self-conscious about her nudity beneath it—considering what she had planned for her and Jordan. "Would you like a Coke or a lemonade?"

Zach looked at her blankly. "No," he said absently. "But I would like to know what's with you."

Going to the sofa and sitting down, Ashley stretched her neck from side to side, her towel weighing her down. "In what way?"

"Don't play stupid, Ashley," Zach snapped, dropping beside her. "You know damned well what I mean."

"No, Zachery, I really don't," Ashley bit out testily. "What I do know is that you've been acting like a raging jerk for weeks now!"

"Are you and Jordan seeing each other?" he asked, blunt and to the point, his look warning her not to lie.

"What?" Ashley asked, dumbfounded. How could he know that? He'd been across the Atlantic. Had he set spies on her? Jordan was supposedly his friend. She hated to think what Zach's reaction would have been had the two men been enemies. She met his unfathomable stare. "What makes you think I'm seeing Jordan?"

"Oh, I don't know, Ash," Zach began with irritated sarcasm. "Maybe it's because before I left, I never saw Jordan anymore. Marie was calling constantly to find out what's going on with him."

Well, that was her cue. The talk she'd wanted to have with Zach was long overdue and couldn't be put off any longer, not if she expected to have any real happiness with Jordan. She couldn't have it said that she'd come between the two best friends. "Zachery, you can't seem to take a hint. I am a grown woman and I see whomever I please."

Not responding to her annoyance, Zach combed his hand through his short hair. "Are you in love with him?" His tone had softened, and he looked at her tenderly.

"Yes," Ashley whispered. A rush of tears welling in her

eyes, she smiled. "Very much, Zach. I never really fell out of love with him."

"I see," he said, sighing in resignation. "Is the feeling mutual?"

"Very much so, my friend," Jordan said, pushing the door fully open and walking in.

"Jordan!" Ashley exclaimed, her heart banging against her chest. She didn't want her brother and her lover to come to blows in front of her eyes. "How long have you been here?"

"Long enough," Jordan responded. He locked gazes with Zach. "I found it unnecessary to let myself in with the key you gave me, since you left the door open. That can be dangerous."

Scowling, Zach stood, his body tense. "You have a key?"

"Uh, Zach," Ashley said, standing as well and wedging between them. "Zach—"

"Yes, Zach, I have a key," Jordan stressed. "I love her, dammit. Why can't you accept that?"

The standoff went on for a tense moment more. Finally Zach gazed at Ashley's worried face. Giving her a crooked smile, he passed his hand over his eyes. "She's my sister, Jordan, and I want her to be happy. She's loved you practically all her life, despite your differences—"

"I know that, Zach," Jordan interrupted. "And I've made great strides to remedy my faults. For her sake as well as my own."

"How?" Zach shouted, throwing his hands up in frustration. "By not buying the car I suggested you buy?"

Jordan laughed, then winked at Ashley. "Are you still ticked over that? Well, pal, I only wanted Ashley with me when I make such an important purchase," he said smoothly.

"Jordan!" Ashley flew into his arms, the towel unraveling and revealing her light blond locks, the wonderful floral essence permeating the room. "Are you serious? Or are you just trying to impress Zach?"

"Ha! He wishes," Jordan retorted. But that old camaraderie was back in his voice. He brushed his lips against Ashley's. "I'm tired of slow-running, overcrowded buses, baby. Most of all, I'm tired of getting caught in downpours."

Ashley hugged him tightly. "Oh, darling, I'm so proud of you!"

"And I'm proud of you, Ashley," Zach added, chuckling. "I don't know how you did it, but you've gotten him, the world's best tightwad, to part with some of that money he's been hoarding."

"When do we get the car? And what kind are we getting?" Ashley asked, leaning her head against Jordan's chest.

"Well, I was thinking about a . . . let's see . . . a Hyundai."

"Oh," Ashley murmured, unable to hide her disappointment. She supposed he had to start somewhere. At least a Hyundai would keep them from the buses. "That's g-good."

"Why? What kind were you thinking of?" Jordan asked, a mischievous twinkle gleaming in his eye.

"I don't think you want to know, pal," Zach said. "It might give you palpitations."

"Shut up, Zachery!" Ashley ordered crossly. She gazed at Jordan, unsure if she should answer that honestly. While she had curbed her habits, she still had her preferences. "Well—"

"Tell me, Ashley," Jordan encouraged.

"Well, honey, I like the BMW Roadster. Candy-Apple Red. I'd look fabulous in one, don't you think . . . ?" Her voice trailed off at Jordan's frown.

"Not today, Ashley." Jordan sighed. "I've already made the appointment with the salesman. We have to be there in an hour." He glanced at Zach. "Care to join us? Afterward you can take off. I don't want you with us while we pick out our engagement ring."

Ashley screamed at Jordan's nonchalant announcement, while Zach clapped him on the back and laughed with joy.

"You old son of a bitch!" Zach boomed, sounding just like their father. "I don't want to come. I'll be too busy spilling the news to the folks." He held out his hand. "Congratulations, Jordie. I have every faith now that you've joined the human race. All you need now is a few credit cards!" He grabbed Ashley and kissed her cheek, then swung her in his arms. "I'm happy for you, baby, and I apologize for acting like such an ass."

"I love you, Zachery the Daiquiri." She hugged him tightly. "Tell Mom and Daddy we'll see them later."

"Okay. In the meantime, let me drop you off at the Hyundai dealership." He looked at Zach. "On Chef Menteur, right?"

"No, dammit," Jordan responded, annoyed. "The place I'm going to is on Veterans Boulevard."

Zach narrowed his eyes at him. "There's no Hyundai dealership there. . . . Where are you going? To Cheapie-Buy-a-Car?"

"Cute," Jordan said with a laugh. "As a matter of fact, smart ass, you *can* drop us off. Ashley, baby, whenever you get ready, we can leave."

"Okay," Ashley said, feeling Jordan wasn't telling the truth when he said he was going to buy a Hyundai. As Zach pointed out, there were no Hyundai dealerships in Metairie, and she doubted Jordan would buy anything less expensive. She started toward her bedroom. When Jordan made to follow, Zach cleared his throat.

"You aren't married yet," he said pointedly. "You'll stay out here with me."

"Yes, Father," Jordan jested.

Ashley laughed and disappeared into the privacy of her room, content now that everything seemed to be falling into place.

When Jordan directed Zach to pull into the Mercedes dealership, Ashley squealed again.

"God, Bennett, I didn't think you had it in you," Zach said as Jordan exited his Land Cruiser.

"I'm sure you didn't, Douglas," Jordan retorted, grabbing Ashley's hand and slamming the door behind them. "We'll see you later on at your parents' house."

After Zach drove off, things passed hurriedly. Jordan and Ashley each test drove the black Mercedes C200 Sedan that Ashley chose after she decided silver was for seniors and Jordan rejected red as being too flashy. Since Jordan was buying the car outright, the transaction was quick and painless.

Driving off the lot, Jordan went straight to the jeweler's, where he bought her a five-carat diamond ring. She felt he was trying to clue her in to his true financial status. They needed to have another talk, because apparently he hadn't told her everything. Unless he wanted to keep some things as a surprise, as he had the car.

"I've been a fool, darling," Jordan said as they drove toward her parents' home. "Even if I denied myself, which I never will again, I could never deny you."

"Jordan, there will be times when we each revert to our old ways, but it will only be momentary relapses."

"I know, but we can depend on Elvis to keep us in line. The console table in the hall on Prytania Street is the perfect spot for him. You have great taste, my love."

"Thank you, but if Elvis doesn't like it, he'll remove himself. He knows how to do that, you know. He showed me one day. Although he has yet to tell me why he insists we stand over him and look into his cavity while he writes.

Especially since he can get his message across anywhere in the room."

"When do you think he'll return our money?"

"I don't know," Ashley said, "but he promised he would."

"Good. I wonder what your folks' reaction will be to all this?" Jordan said with a chuckle. "I bet Zach has opened his big mouth already."

"Yeah. I think now he'll wipe that perpetual frown off his face, and you two won't be going at each other again."

"He knows I love you, Ash, and he and I will always be friends."

Ashley knew how fond her parents and Zach were of Jordan. For that reason, they'd accept him into the family. Of course, it helped that he'd finally discovered how to enjoy the money he had. Only a few blocks away from the mansion, she couldn't wait for their reaction.

Ashley spent the night of their wedding at Jordan's home, both having somehow missed their plane for their honeymoon trip. They'd placed the bowl in the living room and poured wine from it, then sipped from the same glass. Still in their wedding attire, they whirled around the spacious living room.

Elvis's soft pink glow enhanced the atmosphere of romance. As they danced, the clicking began. Looking toward the coffee table where Elvis sat, it shocked Ashley to see Jordan's wallet and checkfolder. They lay next to the bowl, along with her check and his coins and keys. Words appeared on the table itself.

Congratulations, Ashley. I think you both know how to handle money now, so I'm returning your possessions to both of you.

Ashley picked up the check. There it was, just as her father had written it out. Five thousand dollars! "Elvis, you

darling!" She bent down and touched her lips to his rim.
He flushed a bright red.

"What's with him?"

"Oh, he's just blushing, Jordan," she said, and giggled.

Jordan chuckled. "Elvis, you and I are going to have to
talk."

Ha, ha, ha. What for? I'm only a bowl.

"A magic bowl with a lecherous sense of humor," Jordan
said good naturedly. "And by the way, touching your stand
was an accident. I didn't know you held it in such high
regard. But I do understand, however."

Ashley rolled her eyes. "Oh, please," she said, laughing.
"Men. Give me a break! I guess I'm going to be outnum-
bered here."

*Not really, Ash. But Jordan and I can share a beer once
in a while.*

"How can you drink?" Ashley asked, perplexed.

Watch. A slurping noise followed as the wine disappeared from the bowl's cavity. *Consider that my toast to
your nuptials.*

"Thank you, Elvis. And thank you for our money." Ashley handed the check to Jordan. "My investment share of
the new restaurant. The Gourmet Bowl."

Great name.

Laughing, Ashley went into Jordan's arms.

"I love you, Ashley," Jordan said huskily. He lowered
his lips to hers and kissed her with all the passion and love
in him.

"Oh, my love," she said, heat spiraling through her.

"These clothes are a hindrance," Jordan announced.

In a millisecond, they stood nude before each other, their
wedding clothes hanging· over the closet door. Without
questioning their nakedness, Jordan pulled her back into his
arms, kissing her until she was breathless.

Weak with desire and only wanting relief, Ashley vaguely heard the clicking began again.

Mr. and Mrs. Bennett, I will suspend my powers indefinitely. I wish you much happiness. I will come again when there is a reason. Farewell.

Jordan slid his hand down Ashley's back and over her buttocks, before lifting her into his arms. Ashley relaxed against his hard chest as he carried her into the bedroom.

As *she* had, Jordan had finally accepted the promise of love and happiness without conditions—and without reservations.

TIME PASSAGES